THE NEWIRTH MYTHOLOGY · PART ONE · THE INVASION OF HEAVEN

IMMORTALITY IS AN ART

"Must read for the summer! It's part adventure, part fantasy, a bit of mystery, and all fun."

—*Times Weekly*

"It is nice to have an author come up with a new concept when it comes to fiction. And Koep has done just that."

—*Reading Is A Way Of Life BLOG-USA*

"Not only does Koep have a beautiful writing style and a flare for language, the book resurrects the imponderables of youth, bringing them yet again into the forefront of thought. That is a very good thing, indeed."

"Smart and the language is beautiful. 12 out of 10 stars!"

—*Netgalley Reviews*

"The most unique book I've read all year--wholly original."

"Full of tricks, turns and slight of hand. A roller coaster ride right from the beginning."

—*Goodreads Reviews*

"Wow, just WOW! This is the best novel in all the thrillers and paranormal romance novels I have read in a year!"

"I can honestly say that the ending shocked me. I have not seen a twist like the one in this book since the movie The Sixth Sense. That alone makes this a 5 Star book for me."

"I highly recommend this book to lovers of suspended, thrillers, paranormal!"

"This book is totally WOW! A roller-coaster ride right from the beginning!! This is one of the best novels in all the thrillers/ suspense/paranormal genres that I have read in a very long timc."

"It's almost difficult to put into words how strongly this book affected me. It is filled with surprises, turns, twists twists and honestly, the end blew me away."

"Grabs you from page one, couldn't put it down!"

"If you enjoy a touch of the supernatural and art mysteries, then you will enjoy this book. Great Read."

"A remarkably inventive story told in an imaginative way. A story within a story actually. Looking forward to reading more in this series."

"If Steven King's "The Stand" and Dan Brown's "Da Vinci Code" were to have a baby, it would be this book. It was a long tale of a story with the intrigue of religious mythology."

—*Netgalley Reviews*

PART ONE

THE NEWIRTH MYTHOLOGY

THE INVASION OF HEAVEN

MICHAEL B. KOEP

The Newirth Mythology, Part One, The Invasion of Heaven
is a work of fiction. Names, characters, places and incidents are either used fictitiously, are products of the author's imagination, or are brought on by an ancient muse. Any resemblance to actual events, persons, living or dead, gods, immortals or other is entirely coincidental.
~ *Tunow plecom cer* ~

www.WillDreamlyArts.com
www.MichaelBKoep.com

FIRST MASS MARKET PAPERBACK EDITION

Designed by Will Dreamly Arts
Cover art, maps and text illustrations by Michael B. Koep
Back cover portrait by Brady Campbell
The Newirth Mythology, Part One, The Invasion of Heaven
is also available in EBook and audio formats.

For information regarding special discounts for bulk purchases, please contact
sales@willdreamlyarts.com

Library of Congress Registration Number: TXu-1-822-078

ISBN: 978-0-9976234-0-6

For Diana Denise

scale miles
5
10
15
N
UPPER PRIEST LAKE
Loche's Cabin
PRIEST LAKE
the lakes of
North Idaho
Old Town
Sandpoint
Hope
Priest River
Sagle
PEND OREILLE LAKE
SPIRIT LAKE
HAYDEN LAKE
Post Falls
Coeur d'Alene
COEUR D'ALENE LAKE

LAKE COMO
LAKE ISEO
LAKE GARDA
Venice
Milan
Padua
Verona
ADRIATIC SEA
N
scale miles
20
40
60
Northern Italy
Monterosso
La Spezia
LIGURIAN SEA
Pisa
Florence

The Newirth Mythology
part one of three
The Invasion of Heaven

The characters you are about to meet are as real as their stories, and stories are as real as are those of us who tell them and those of us who read or hear them. There is nothing in his story that cannot or has not happened.

MICHAEL HERZOG

The artist needs no religion beyond his work.

ELBERT HUBBARD

Reality is frequently inaccurate.

DOUGLAS ADAMS

There are more things in heaven and earth, Horatio,
Than are dreamt of in your philosophy.

WILLIAM SHAKESPEARE

Prologue

This is really happening, isn't it?

Dr. Loche Newirth, a thirty-seven-year-old psychologist in an olive green wool coat, blue jeans, and leather hiking boots walks with his head down. He is crying. His breath steams in the October chill. Before him the wooded trail blurs as he hikes toward a high cliff above Upper Priest Lake. Through the trees the afternoon is grey and pale. He can hear the wind above the pines and water rushing against the stones below.

He tries to pretend that what has happened is not real. He wishes he had seen it coming. His mentor, friend and fellow psychologist Marcus Rearden told him once, "When a client of yours takes their own life, you'll want to take yours. You'll believe that it was your fault. And I assure you, after that, there's no going back." Loche brushes at the tears and leans into the hill, upping his pace.

"Damn you, Marcus," he says quietly. "Damn you."

His mind replays the sessions with Bethany. Bethany Winship, mid-sixties, fit and healthy, with a husband, Roger, and grown children, convertible BMW, hot tub and a healthy allowance. As a girl she learned to disappear, become invisible, hide. It was a necessary choice after the first time her whiskey-eyed father cracked his belt across her face and thighs. Being unnoticed became habit. And the better she got at it the more she was forgotten—neglected. She shouldered all those memories into adulthood, into her marriage and her children until her strength gave out. Loche sees her pleading eyes, the streaks of black mascara—the remnant of a woman tormented by severe depression, each day falling deeper into darkness. Loche struggles to quiet her voice echoing in his ears, torrents of unmet desires, missed chances and fear. “My life wasn’t supposed to be like this,” she had said. “I wish I could redo it. Have another chance. Rewrite it.” Loche wishes that, too. He wishes he had asked more questions—offered more encouragement—reached further.

But now she’s gone.

There are three fears that every psychologist will face at some point—another of Marcus Rearden’s dictums—what he calls the Three Heavy What Ifs, *What if I can’t help them? What if I can’t handle it? What if I go in with them?* As this thought occurs to Loche he feels his failure with Bethany as complete. The tears blind him and burn lines down his cheeks. *What if I can’t help?* He had done everything within his power to guide Bethany out of the dark. In the end, it was as if he had done nothing. *What if I can’t handle it?* This is suddenly obvious as he sees himself stumbling along the trail, crying uncontrollably, unable to put his emotions into some kind of order. Long hikes had always balanced him—brought clarity. Today it is not working. Each tottering step approaches the edge of a black and swirling maelstrom. He is descending. *He is going in with her.*

Loche stops suddenly—squeezes his eyes shut—he breathes. A distant boat engine drones and fades away toward the thoroughfare. A cluster of birds scatters from the treetops above him. The water laps the shore.

Then the sound of his wife’s voice in his memory, “I don’t know how much more of this I can take,” she had said. Her angry eyes flashed.

“I need a few days,” he told her. “I need some time to work out what has happened.”

“Here’s what will happen, you’ll lose me,” she had said. “I can’t go on like this. With *you*, like *this.* Jesus, Loche—you need time? *I* need time.” Loche’s four-year-old son, Edwin, stood in the open door a few feet away—his hands balled into fists and his brown eyes are sleepy.

“Helen,” Loche said, “one of my clients has died. This is a lot for me to process—and I’ve just received more news," he remembers feeling for the envelope in his coat, "news that will change—"

"I'll tell you what needs to *change*, Loche. It's you. It's always *something* with you," she said turning away. "So where will you go?"

"I don't know, Helen. I'm so sorry, there is so much more to this—I can't tell you right now. It's become much more serious."

"They think you did it? They think you—" she faced him and watched.

Loche felt the air leave his lungs. "Yes. I am a suspect." Helen turned her back.

The conversation was over. He tried to pull her into an embrace. She pushed him away. Loche then knelt and held his son. "I'll see you before you know it," he remembers saying to him. "Before you know it."

Loche starts walking again. Not far ahead the steeper incline leads out of the trees. He reaches into his coat and pulls out the bright red envelope the post had delivered to his house in Sagle, Idaho, two days ago. He stares at it as he walks. He reads the script on the front again, scribbled in Bethany's hand—*Dr. Newirth, open only if something bad happens to me*. He considers pulling the letter out and reading it again, but he shakes his head and pushes it back into his pocket. His jaw is clenched. He could tell no one about the letter. Not yet. Not even Helen. The slope rises steadily into a rocky clearing. He squints, coming under the steel wash of sky. The icy breeze freezes his tears. He crosses the short distance to the cliff edge and stops.

I have one chance, he thinks, looking quickly at his hands, still blotched with oil paint, crimson and black. *One chance to change what has happened. I will lie to reveal the truth.*

He stares out across Upper Priest Lake. It looks small below him, wreathed in ash green, flecks of yellow tamarack like candles in shadow.

I will lie to reveal the truth.

A moment later, the air stills and all hushes to silence. The wind stops, like held breath. There is no longer the sound of water lapping below, no whisper in the trees, no bird call or far away boat engine whining away to the South—only his heart ticking in his ears. The water shines below him like a metal plate. Its surface is motionless—a still membrane of glass reflecting the grey canopy above. So clear it looks as if there is a hole in the Earth. Sky water. The sight nudges the darkness away from Loche's thoughts as he gapes down the sheer fifty foot drop, mesmerized by the heavens he sees below him. His knees weaken. A looming sense of vertigo.

With a jolt, he feels as if he is being watched—as if he's not alone. He twists around and looks behind to the shadow beneath the boughs. He scans the tree line and along the trail that leads down toward the beach. Nothing. No one.

Loche faces downward again, the small lake far below staring back up at the sky. At itself.

Then he sees it.

Something moves in the water.

Round, welling out—a black spot widening. A pooling stain at its center.

But this can't be—

It moves, flitting, searching. Loche steadies himself and rubs his eyes, unsure of what he is seeing. Looking again, the massive dot is ringed with an ice blue iris, its pupil dilating ever wider.

It stares. It sees. It looks at Loche.

This is really happening, isn't it?

Loche Newirth is midair. He thinks several thoughts all at once.

He wonders if he was somehow yanked down over the edge. There is no lake surface below him now—it is an eye—hypnotic iris, gaping black center. It appeared as if a giant from a fairy tale had risen from beneath the world and pressed its eye to a peep hole. Loche and the cold

October sky were mirrored in its glassy lens—and it pulled him down.

Loche then wonders if he had instead thrown himself from the height when his mind managed to discern the anomaly. A massive eye seeing him. Inviting him like the connection that happens when the gazes of two strangers meet—the thrill of recognition in this isolated existence. He wanted to be a part of whatever it was that beheld him, so he jumped.

Then, reason. Perhaps he merely tripped from the shock of such a sight. The impossibility of it. The terror.

Slap.

Needles pierce his skin. A numb, slogging struggle. Then more falling, head over foot, tumbling through a slow-motion, bleary abyss.

Silence.

Flash.

Gone.

The stinging of his hands on gravel rouses him. His limbs are slow, weighted, sluggish. Gasping and clawing he pulls himself up. With great effort he lugs his heavy legs out of the cold water. He has the sense to know that hypothermia will set in soon, and it is a long hike back to the cabin. He totters to his feet and looks back across the water. The eye is gone—if there ever was one.

He crashes through the brush along the lakeshore, searching aimlessly for a landmark, a trail, a direction. He stumbles and falls every few feet. He does not feel the gashes on his knees, but he sees the blood. Sharp slashing branches scratch his face. A few more steps—another crash upon the stones. Before all goes black he mumbles to himself a final, desperate assessment, over and over—

"I am Loche Newirth. This is really happening. This is really happening."

I
The Water's Eye

The black ink spreads open like a pupil in the dark. Loche Newirth presses the tip of his pen down into the last letter of his signature and holds it there—the fibers of the paper pull the pen's life into a widening eye. He stares at it. It stares back.

Loche blinks. He is suddenly aware. Then he wonders, *is that it? Is there more to write?*

He feels a sudden sharp cramp in his hand from scribbling for God knows how many hours, the ache in his neck from leaning over the desk and the tingle of his sleeping right foot. He lifts the pen out of the pooling blot, pries it out of his hand and sets it beside the leather bound journal. Then he closes the cover and stands.

Every joint in his body cracks. The palms of his hands sting with tiny cuts. He glances down at his shoes. They are caked with dried mud. His pants and shirt sleeves are also soiled with earth—blood at the knees. He is not sure why. A sudden ache begins to throb in his ankle.

He turns and scans his surroundings. A table lamp casts a yellow glow across a single room with a kitchen at the far end. There is a dark open doorway next to the sink. Beside him is an unmade bed and a small desk. His coat is crumpled on the floor. Leaning in the corner is a black umbrella. The walls are cedar logs. He then notices the portrait of his family above the cold fireplace—his wife Helen, four-year-old son Edwin and himself. Then a trickle of a memory, he is at his lake cabin, in Priest Lake, Idaho.

Books are scattered on the table, on the bed, stacked on the kitchen counters—most of them mythological texts—Irish, Egyptian, Sumerian, Greek. Many are open with curious notes scrawled in the margins. Pages are ripped out and tacked to the log walls. A huge map of northern Italy is laid out on the kitchen floor with more messy scribbles. There are long rows of yellow Post-it notes stuck on the wall. They stretch around the room from corner to corner, many times over. On them are names, dates, and events—all written in his hand. He tugs one down. It reads,

Lie to reveal. Lie to reveal the truth.

Another.

Basil Fenn. Artist. Keeps his paintings secret. Refuses to show them. The few that have seen his paintings have been hurt. Wounded. Killed. Gods look through them to see us. Gods look through.

Loche shakes his head. The room whirls suddenly, and he pushes his palm to the wall to steady himself. His focus anchors to another note.

What is made up is real. What is real is made up.

He looks out the picture window. The glass is streaked with what looks like thin red paint strokes. A bright red envelope is taped in the center. On it is scribbled, *Dr. Newirth, open only if something bad happens to me.* Outside is a dingy light, a sloping forest and a dark lake beyond—white caps on the grey waves. He catches his reflection in the glass. The cuts on his face and forehead suddenly become painful. Mud is smeared across his cheek and chin. But the face in the reflection is his, carved angles, grey, thoughtful eyes and short, light brown hair.

Is it morning or evening?

Stooping to pick up his coat, he notices a large tear on one of the sleeves, and the thick wool is heavy, wet. He rifles through the pockets for his cell phone. It is not there. He sees it on the kitchen counter. Dead. He locates his charger and plugs it in. The screen winks to life:

4:10 P.M. OCTOBER 29

He scowls and places it back upon the table. His back is sore. Leaning to one side he lowers his arm down to his ankle and stretches the best he can. He then raises both arms above his head and reaches up feeling the muscles in his body strain and pull. He tilts his head back and there, painted upon the cedar in red and black slashes, is a massive, rough-edged eye.

Then with a jolt, he remembers. His legs weaken, and he lowers himself slowly to the floor. A sudden rush of tears burns his vision as he remembers his fall. Three days ago. He was hiking the trails at the upper lake, he had tripped—he fell fifty feet into the water—nearly drowned. Nearly died. There was an eye in the water.

How he survived the incident, he doesn't know. His side smacking against the glassy surface—smeared visions of his blue, trembling hands—thrashing through waves, to a gravel bar, through brush—falling—a trail leading into darkness—lost—hypothermia. Somehow he made it back to the cabin—*but then what?*

That was three days ago.

He has not slept. The cramp in his stomach tells him that he has not eaten. It is cold. His hands are stiff and searing. Then he remembers the book—he looks at the desk and sees it sitting there. The only thing he has done since he made it back here is write, nonstop. No breaks. No food. No heat. No sleep.

The room is churning. He rolls over onto his side and sees long-handle brushes lying on the floor. Spilled cans of paint. He hears himself breathing, gasping. His lungs spasm for air—black spots swarm into his periphery—his sight is darkening. He turns his head toward the fading afternoon light. The bright red envelope is taped to the glass. The painted lines on the window now begin to make sense—they are scratched letters like cut skin—difficult to read but unmistakable. Slowly, they come into focus.

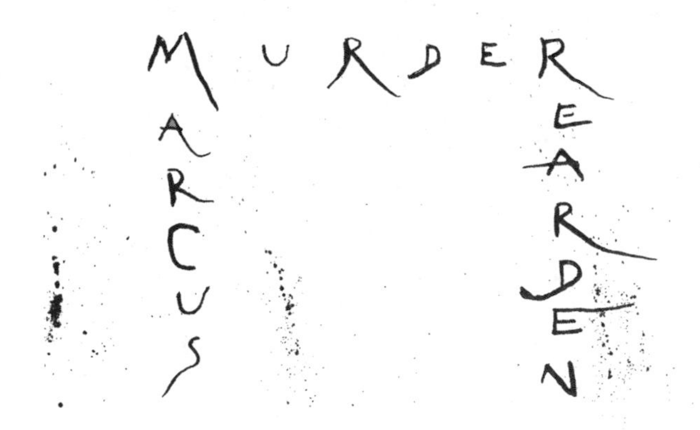

He holds his breath. His heart booms in his ears. There is a message—MURDER MARCUS REARDEN. Loche shivers and he exhales.

His heart slows, and he manages to pull himself over to the opposite wall and lean back. He squints at the massive window and reads the message over and over again.

Loche Newirth cannot remember why it is there.

An hour later he is finishing a glass of cool water. It is his fourth in a row. He has lit a fire. Chicken soup steams in a pot on the stove. He has eaten a fair amount of it. He feels slightly better. Enough to return—return to the world, he guesses. In the bathroom he has drawn a hot bath.

He checks his cell phone—there are fifteen messages. Mostly texts from his wife, Helen. All of the texts seem to end with, *where r u?* He begins listening to the recorded messages. Several are clients. Nothing too serious. Then his wife's voice—her tone is angry, "I won't be here when you come back. I've had it, Loche. I'm done." Loche frowns as if he has forgotten something. He looks over to the book on the desk and considers thumbing through the pages to see if his writing would jar his memory. He recalls telling her that he needed a few days to get his head straight, because of Bethany. He shakes his head and forwards to the next message.

It is his receptionist, Carol. "Hello, Loche. Considering all that's happened, I figured I wouldn't be seeing you for a few days." Loche sees the firelight reflecting in the big window, in the center of the letters—in the center of MURDER. "The police have been here several times looking for you—so has Roger Winship. I am running out of things to tell them. I could use some direction, so call, if you can. I hope you're holding up, and again, I am sorry about Bethany." Loche hits the delete button.

The final message was the one that he had expected. The sonorous voice of Marcus Rearden, "Hello, Loche. Listen, you need to call or come by. There is now a warrant out for your arrest. All of this with your client, Bethany, can be fixed easily—by simply explaining your case. Trust me. But you disappearing doesn't look good—and if I've taught you anything about this profession of ours, abandoning your practice is not an option, and certainly not one of my lessons. Call me so we can meet and talk things over. I can help you with this." Marcus pauses. His tone shifts to impatience, "And what about this painting you left with me?" Loche's eyes snap to the paint brushes on the floor. "What in the hell am I supposed to do with it? Just call me, will you? Damn it. Where the hell are you?" He looks at his hands stained with red and black paint.

Loche sets the phone on the table and raises his face to the big window. Night has climbed into the trees. The sky is black and heavy. MURDER MARCUS REARDEN is still painted upon the glass. The room spins. A wave of nausea forces him to his knees. He bends and presses his forehead on the cool wood floor and waits. Slowly it passes. Hot tears sting the cuts on his cheeks.

He crawls to a nearby pile of newspaper clippings and books. The word *murder* is in nearly every headline and within the articles Dr. Marcus Rearden's name is highlighted in yellow. The details of each story come flooding back to Loche. How Rearden managed to discover yet another insight to the minds of the criminally insane—how he had become sought after as an expert in catching the most dangerous minds—his achievements—photos of him with political leaders, attorneys, judges. Two text books written by Rearden, their covers creased and weathered, sit beside the pile of clippings. Rearden's latest book, an autobiography entitled *Getting Away With Murder,* is there, too. Loche opens it up to the acknowledgement page. Rearden thanks his wife, Elanor, for helping him through the difficult years and dark visions, he mentions many of his close friends in law enforcement and politics, and finally he thanks Loche Newirth as the new hope for the profession of psychology.

"Daddy?"

Loche drops the book and spins around. Standing behind him and rubbing his eyes is Edwin, his son. "Hungry, Daddy." Loche rolls back and away, unsure of what he is seeing. "Daddy?" his son says.

"W-where—where did you come from?" Loche gasps.

The boy points to the back bedroom. He is wearing pajamas. One sock is missing. "Hungry," he says again with a yawn.

Loche grapples with his memory. *Has he been here the whole time?* He feels like crying. There is that feeling that something is missing. He reaches out to his son and pulls him close.

"Pancakes," Edwin says.

Hours before dawn, Loche gathers a few items into a bag, pulls his coat on and picks up the umbrella from the corner of the room. He pulls the bright red envelope down from the window and tucks into his coat pocket. He turns the lights out. The fire in the hearth is low. All around the room are the artifacts he is leaving behind, the sticky notes, the map of Italy, the open myths—the leather bound book upon the desk full of his writing.

Standing in the door he looks down into the pale light of his cell phone. His fingers tap out a quick message.

Marcus, i am at my cabin at priest lake. Come alone. I need your help.

He presses send, locks the door and steps out onto the stoop. The car is idling. Edwin is asleep in his car seat. The air is brittle. He climbs in, closes the door and stares through the driver's side window. There are no stars. The sky is black. The breakers down below rush against the shore. If there is an eye down there, in the water, it is now closed.

Marcus Rearden wakes when he hears his cell phone vibrate on the bedside table. There is a cold space beside him. His wife is not there. He is not surprised. Her trips to the bathroom have become more frequent these days, and she often creeps out of the sheets in the middle of the night for what she calls *little emergencies*. Rearden rolls his grey head toward the bathroom and looks for the slit of light at the bottom of the door. There is no light.

"Elanor?" he calls into the darkness.

No answer.

"Elanor?"

He sits up. His back aches, and the sickly pop of his bones after sleep is a cause to curse quietly. Since he hit seventy-one his use of morning expletives has become more frequent, like Elanor's little emergencies.

He lifts his cell phone up and squints into the bright screen. The text is from Loche Newirth.

Marcus, i am at my cabin at priest lake. Come alone. I need your help.

"Finally," he whispers. "*The cabin.* I should have known." He lifts his robe and slides his phone into the pocket. "Sweetheart?" The quiet of the bedroom stifles his voice. He can see the shape of her clothes draped on the bed. A half glass of wine from last night is atop the dresser. Her purse is hanging on the doorknob. *She's probably down in the kitchen*, he figures, and he swings his legs out of bed and pulls his robe over his shoulders. Standing brings more expletives.

From the top of the stairs he calls again, yawns and waits. He rubs his eyes and tries to focus down the stairway. Below him is a pale glow casting long shadows, and he quickly notes that the light is not emanating from the kitchen. The light is coming from the opposite side of the house, near the garage and the storage room. *The storage room*. Rearden's eyes dart while somewhere in his waking senses he feels that something is wrong.

Adrenaline surges through his limbs, and he lunges down the stairs toward the light—toward fear. As he approaches the half open storage room door he shades his eyes from the vivid and surreal shine, as if the light bulbs above had shattered into glowing shards and were swirling around the room like ice on the wind. But when he throws the door wide, the light appears suddenly normal. Bright and stark. Then horror.

Elanor Rearden is lying on her side, her thin arms twisted like tangled rope, and her eyes gaping into some distant place. Her face is frozen in terror. Clutched tightly in her hand is the corner of a length of black fabric sprawled across the cold cement slab. Leaning against a thin rectangular crate Rearden sees the back of a framed painting.

A roaring pulse swells in Rearden's ears as he drops to his knees. "Jesus, God, no!" He had been warned. Loche Newirth, his friend and protégé had said, "The painting, don't look. The painting, don't look—it is dangerous.*" With hands outstretched he pries the black fabric from her rigid grip. Then riveting his focus to his wife's dead stare and keeping his back to the leaning painting, he hurls the shroud up and covers the frame without pulling his eyes away from his wife.

He lifts Elanor's head into his lap. "No! Ellie no! Not yet! Oh God, not yet!" His eyesight again fills with circling dots of light, and his head feels heavy. He is on the threshold of fainting. He begins a series of deep breaths, struggling to master the pain—come to terms—think it through—do what he knows how to do, reason. Put the loss, the pain into some kind of order. Flashes of memory shoot through his mind—ones that make little sense—such as Elanor's favorite tea cup, her desire to always make the bed in the morning, *to keep things uncluttered*, she would say. Then the memories that define him, the thirty-eight years of marriage. Her glowing tears when he proposed to her. Their fights. Their growing apart. Their hanging on. His bouts with depression. Their disconnection. Her little emergencies. Then the permanence crashes down upon him again. *Where have you gone?* "Oh God," he cries. "Not yet. I haven't told you everything."

The shrouded painting stands tilted slightly back and away, cloaked like some hellish priest. Rearden scans the monolith and lets his gaze freeze upon that yawning black fabric cover—a deep, starless abyss. Behind that protective shroud is something Loche had described as *dangerous*. Rearden refused to fully believe the warning—until now.

With fear and need intermingled, Rearden reaches down and clutches a corner of the fabric and gently pulls. Words hum in his mind, *Whatever it is that lay upon that canvas—whatever it is that took you from me—wherever you've gone, Elanor, I will follow.* The shroud slides slowly, like a tablecloth being dragged down by an infant—the delicate china nearing the edge.

Then a voice inside his head cries out, *Stop, you fool!*

Stop! Rearden's fist splits open and the fabric drops from his spreading fingers. *The painting, don't look.* The thing is still covered and Rearden begins to weep again in thick sobs. He cannot do it, not yet.

"Elanor. Dear Elanor." He looks down at her face. His trembling fingers search for life along the slope of her cheek, along her throat. Her head is heavy. There is a chill in her skin. Rearden wonders if he has been here before, cradling her lifeless body—a kind of déjà vu.

A few minutes later he is sitting in a kitchen chair staring through the open sliding glass door. Icy air claws at his robed body. His phone is in his hand. Lit up on the screen is Loche's text message. Outside it is still dark. Gentle flakes of snow begin their silent descent. Little white lights streaming down from a black sky, like pieces of constellations that shook free. Marcus watches as the world around him slowly erases.

"You come to me. I'll text you the directions. Come alone."

Julia Iris turns her car toward Priest Lake and drives deeper into the mountains. One hand steers, the other grips an antique key that hangs around her neck by a long, delicate chain. She lifts it up. It is tarnished bronze and heavy. Loche Newirth had placed it into her hand a few days ago. It seems like a month—as if it never happened. "This opens my most guarded door," he had said. He then climbed into the car that awaited him, and he was gone. She wonders, *Why didn't I go with him?*

The warm colors of the autumn season had been erased. The usual ochers and greens of the northern Idaho woods are draped with a thick blanket of early snow. A dusting in October is not terribly unusual, but being buried by it this early is something that only a born and raised North Idahoan like Julia could describe with a sardonic "*typical.*" The change had come fast. *Out of nowhere,* Julia thinks.

High drifts have already been formed by the plows along the roadside, and fresh powder is still falling. This is not a day for amateurs. When she started out she hoped for no encounters with newbie *southern* drivers—drivers that are clueless when it comes to *snow meets road*—no idea of how to navigate on a road that will not let one stop when one wants. Julia knows these conditions and is not afraid to up her pace and let the car fishtail around some of the tight curves. Ordinarily she would be a little more conservative, but this afternoon, she feels hurried, and she is glad she has the chops.

Miles ahead *the* Dr. Marcus Rearden is waiting for her to arrive. The man is rather well-known. She knows this due to the quick Google search she had done just after his phone call. Rearden was *the* authority in criminal psychology at one time, and that fact troubles her already worried spirit. Known primarily as an expert for the criminally insane, his career is one long tale of success. A quoted author, a known international figure for the mental health profession and a loving husband. A novelist from the San Francisco area has even based a minor character on Rearden.

Their conversation was brief, Marcus sounded friendly enough, but there was something unsettling in his tone, like he was scared to say too much. "When Loche went missing I was worried—but then I got a text from him this morning saying that he was at his cabin up at Priest Lake. When I arrived, he wasn't here. The fireplace was still warm, and I've found some of his writings," he had told her. "A journal I guess you could call it. It will help us to find him. I've read it. You must read it, too. He writes about *you*, Julia." Julia smiles. *Of course he did,* she thinks.

"You come to me. I will text you the directions. Come alone."

The proud owner of The Floating Hope, a restaurant on the lake in Hope, Idaho, Julia is organized, decisive and professional. In her thirty-three years she has managed to graduate cum laude from Gonzaga University in Spokane, Washington, with a degree in business and philosophy as well as raise the capital to design and build her own restaurant; a restaurant buoyed by 500,000 pounds of concrete encased in Styrofoam floating near the Hope Marina on the north end of scenic Pend Oreille Lake. The Floating Hope has been called a knockout—a must-dine experience for local North Idahoans and tourists alike. The view of the majestic grey-green crags climbing out of the ice blue water was said to knock a patron's experience into orbit, as well as the care that Julia put into the design of the building itself—and the food—and the staff. It is all in the way Julia presents her work and herself. Even friends call Julia a knockout. Sometimes a *dangerous* knockout.

A *knockout* due to the long burnt umber hair, the tall and slender lines, and eyes the color of candlelit brandy—dangerous because if the simple beauty of her smile did not knock you dumb, her wit would.

Julia, however, does not feel dangerous, nor does she see herself as a knockout. Most of her time is spent editing herself and the work that she cares almost too much about. She knows her strengths, both mentally and physically, but she is now all too aware of her weakness—a weakness that she has not experienced before. And as she presses down on the accelerator she quietly whispers the name of the man who has recently changed her life and then disappeared, as if he has been erased like everything else the October snow has hidden.

"Loche Newirth."

Julia discovers her hand is again holding the key around her neck, and wishes that by holding it, Loche can feel her embrace no matter where he is.

"Loche," she whispers, "where are you?"

"A little waker-upper. A little waker-upper," Marcus Rearden puffs. His breath is ice vapor. "Oh shit! A little waker-upper." The snow beneath his bare feet is like razor blades. Wearing nothing but a huge grin (of either joy or complete insanity), the old man is nude, running down a snow-covered trail in the sheer violet light of early afternoon. The words come in crystalline huffs, "Oh shit, oh shit, oh shit—"

Freaking peculiar are the words that he hears in his head. *But what hasn't been freaking peculiar today*? His wife is dead. The pain, profound. His career is over. *Everything has changed*, he thinks as his seventy-year-old lungs suck in the icy air. *Everything.*

When he had dropped his robe beside the cabin door and stepped out onto the icy trail, his feet immediately felt the sting. The sting turned to burning, until now—now his feet are numb stumps at the ends of his legs. "Oh shit, oh shit, oh shit!"

"Why are you doing this?" He says aloud. *Don't ask. Don't ask,* comes an answer from inside his head. "You've not lost it completely, have you?" *Don't ask. Don't ask.* He is certain, however, that he has not lost it—or at least, mildly certain. "My mind is clearer than ever," he tells himself—but the supposed clarity is not due to the loss of Elanor, rather it is because he has just had an epiphany. The discovery of Loche Newirth's writings that he read this morning have added extreme emphasis to the circumstance of *freaking peculiar*. Inside the volume he has found comfort, answers and a hope that *everything* might work out, after all. And a sad thankfulness that he had indeed heeded the chant in his head—it saved his life—the warning, *the painting, don't look, the painting, don't look*. But his wife—his dear wife.

Marcus was once quite tall, but age has given him a slight hunch. His pasty skin rivals the whiteness of the surrounding snow. But his body is spry despite his years. There is still a trace of muscle, joints that work well (some not so well), and in his face is the ghost of a boy. Many of his colleagues have remarked through the years that he doesn't seem to age. Women would say that he has aged gracefully. He is still attractive. But he feels the years. Especially now, for he has not moved like this for a long, long while, and it takes very little time for him to recognize the pain of that fact.

Crazy, sure, to be out in this weather, he thinks, *but what liberation, freedom, hope.*

The early morning hours after his wife had looked into that damned painting are a blur. He had moved the painting to his car. The paramedics arrived along with some of his friends in local law enforcement. They determined that Elanor died of a heart attack. It took every bit of his strength to stay in control while they moved his wife to the ambulance. They tried to console him, but Rearden would have nothing to do with their pity. He smiled instead and asked for some time alone—somehow his demeanor was convincing enough for them to allow his wish, and they left. A half hour later, Rearden was on his way to Loche's cabin. There he found the leather bound book. The power of Loche's writing has nudged the anguish of his wife's passing to the side. He has a new perspective. A new set of eyes. And a plan.

He dashes along the snow-powdered path and plots the short incline ahead. On the other side is an empty space, cold and white. He noticed it when he drove in. He hurries up one side, looses his balance slightly, then dives head first into the soft flakes with a wail of painful delight. Once swallowed by the icy pillow he quickly emerges with a howl ending with a, "Good God in Heaven!" He struggles to his feet and circles back. Flakes of ice cake his beard and begin to melt as his body reels toward the warmth of the cabin—his stride a bit quicker than before.

Oh shit.

A woman is standing beside the cabin door. She is watching him approach. Marcus Rearden slides to a stop. His grin slides to a stop, too. The numb stumps of his feet flounder him behind a nearby tree, and peeking around he stammers, "Uh, hello?"

"Hello?" Julia replies, her tone midway between alarm and humor.

"Uh, Julia?"

"That's right."

Oh shit.

Rearden's head disappears behind the tree.

"Uh," he says. "Terribly awkward I'm sure—my apologies. Uh, pleased to meet you, I'm Marcus Rearden."

"I was guessing it was you," she says.

"You're a tad bit early aren't you?"

"It's only a little over an hour from Sandpoint. I left just as we hung up," she says. "What, if you don't mind my asking, are you doing?"

"Uh, tough question. I'm—I'm—" *A little waker-upper*. "I'm just waking myself up a bit. And well, I think I'd like to answer that question inside. Little chilly out here." He clears his throat. "And oh, please don't be afraid, I know this looks a little—"

"Odd?" Julia says.

"Right." His head pops out from around the tree trunk, "Would you mind, well, not looking—"

"Way ahead of you," she says, perhaps a little too emphatically. Julia turns away as Marcus enters the cabin. After a few moments Rearden opens the door, a robe and blanket wrapped around him. "Come in, won't you?"

Closing the door behind her Julia glances around the cabin. Rearden had already started the shower in the tiny bathroom. "Make yourself comfortable, Julia," he says, "I'll be out as soon as I can warm these old bones. There's coffee if you'd like some."

"Thank you," she says. "Take your time."

A thick leather bound book catches her attention first —at the end of the single room upon a large, antique desk. Beside it is an unmade queen-sized bed. A large window above the desk provides a glorious winter view of the sloping forest down to the lake shore, not twenty yards away. Julia notes a strange smearing of red pushed into the corners of the window frame. The kitchen counters are filled with maybe a hundred neatly stacked books. Piles of yellow sticky notes, a folded map and a half eaten bowl of soup crowd the small table in the dining area. A bright fire is crackling.

Julia moves to the wooden desk and the book. She glances back at the bathroom door and then back to the book. Opening the cover she reads the cursive inscription.

To my husband, Loche—for your words.
I love you,
Helen

Julia's heart feels a sharp sting. It is not easy knowing that he is married, and she has struggled to imagine it as only a dream—a bad dream—but seeing the feminine, cursive hand makes it undeniably real. She wishes that she could erase the words.

How little she knows about him, after all. She shakes her head and flips the page. Loche's hand had scratched the date and place.

October 26th, Priest Lake.

Four days ago. She steps back, pulls her coat off and sits down at the desk. "Loche," she whispers. "Where are you?"

Julia fixes her gaze on the hand scrawled manuscript. The world around her fades away. She reads. Greedily.

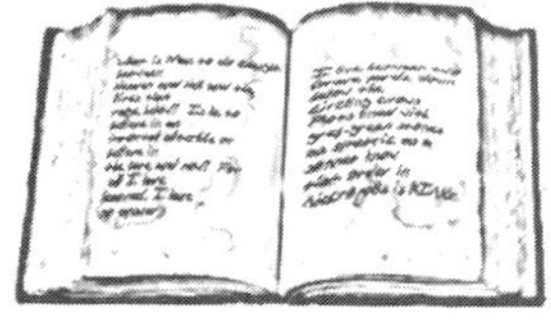

October 26th, Priest Lake.

What is real and what is make believe? Have I become what I have longed to cure? Have I finally gone crazy? I stood at death's door this morning—I cannot stop the flooding memories—I cannot push aside the visions in my head.

Marcus, this chronicle is for you—for you are the best in our field. You know the darkest places in man's mind. You are the only one that can help me—and in doing so, Marcus, you will help yourself. But beware of what you read here, beware of this story, for I cannot tell if what I am writing is memory or delusion. But then, what is true and what is real, after all?

Marcus, what is a man to do caught amidst Heaven, Earth and the fires that rage below? Is he to believe in a creator or in himself? Should we believe in the stories of an everlasting afterlife, or embrace the drama and passion of the here and now? Should we continue to accept delusion as our comfort and salvation, or will we finally discover the truth in that simple word equation we hear so often? It is what it is.

As a therapist, albeit, an idealistic and hopeful one, as you are fully aware, I allowed myself to imagine that there could *be an answer. A cure—a cure for those that suffer the disorders of the mind. There was a time when I thought I had an idea of how life was to be lived. A notion of how to proceed through the short years we have to breathe. I've struggled to understand the human psyche. I've learned ways to help clients cope. Organizing chaos was my mission—but, with all I've learned, all I've studied and all I've endeavored to master, I have not found an answer, until now.*

Something remarkable has happened, Marcus. Something I cannot explain. At sunrise I hiked to the upper lake north of my cabin. I stepped out onto a trail that led to a high cliff above the water. Gaining the summit I nearly tumbled over the edge at the sight, the water's eye was sky, and the dawn's light was reflecting itself over and over so that I, gazing across the lens, could see into eternity. I was forced to steady myself to keep from falling into the heavens. Sky water. It was, in every way, a magical sight. An eye had opened upon the water.

But there was more. Something pulling me. As I forced myself to turn away, my right ankle tangled in an unearthed root. I tripped. Trying to regain my balance I tumbled forward and down. I did not feel my body hit the water. There was no sound of splashing, no icy depth, no crushing chill. It was as if the eye took me in, and I fell through its center.

I have returned, Marcus. I will now share with you the events of the past two weeks of my life, the terrors that I've experienced, and the horrifying the realities that once existed only in my imagination. Some of these memories will be familiar to you because you will remember our exchanges, but most of what you will read, you do not know.

The pages recount my recent experiences with Bethany Winship, my wife and others, but most importantly, my short relationship with painter, Basil Pirrip Fenn of Sandpoint, Idaho. You have one of his pieces in your possession. My warning remains, do not look at it. His work, Marcus—his paintings are by far the most powerful pieces of art mankind will ever encounter, that is, if mankind ever sees his work. There is still a possibility of that happening. But for now, this chronicle must serve to tell of his grave importance and our shared connection. I will tell his story, and my own.

Forgive my attempts at crafting this tale. If only my skill with words could be as strong as my love for them. Maybe one day. But until then, believe in me. I will deliver you.

Read on, Marcus. Read on.

The last time I saw Basil Fenn was five days ago, on October 23rd, in Florence, Italy.

The sky was grey and ragged. As the sun settled on the mountains in the West, it shot its rays of gold below the cloud cover. It was the kind of sky that was too dramatic to be believable, gory and light. I shook my head at it through the passenger window.

Our limousine driver cursed at the Italian traffic. We were brought to a halt with no way out and a long wait ahead. I noticed that we were just three city blocks from our destination so I motioned to the chauffeur that Helen and me would walk the rest of the way. We stepped out into a sunlit mist of rain, but I kept my umbrella closed.

Approaching the Uffizi we saw the elegant, cut marble sign hanging above a newly constructed Roman-styled arch. It read, *Basil Pirrip Fenn, A Collection of Answers*. I chuckled softly, darkly, thinking of the night he told me the title to his latest collection of paintings. That chuckle quickly fell away as I remembered what sort of *answer* Basil was to share that evening.

Prior to moving through the arch we were forced to navigate a sea of photographers, journalists and paparazzi. Their designated area was a city block from the gallery, surrounded by a very efficient security force. We joined a line to the entrance, and I reached into my jacket for our invitations—but there was no need. A security guard spotted our approach and, recognizing us, quickly maneuvered us through the first security gate. We were ushered through the metal detectors and then allowed to proceed.

Within the Uffizi courtyard a smug host of the world's artistic aristocracy had gathered. Along with them were leaders of the free world, including cabinet members of the United States Presidency, other politicians, celebrities and corporate executives. They glided across white canvas covered floors in their black gowns and black suits, tipping their champagne glasses as the scent of money, politics and the power of art rose into the chilled air. I suddenly felt an aversion to the pomp and circumstance. Many of these people didn't seem to be here for the show itself, but rather for the fashion of it all. However, this event would prove to be the real thing, the real artistic experience—well beyond what any gallery enthusiast, art connoisseur or chatty socialite could conceive.

I paused on the threshold. Helen's smile, her gown and her movement—she was glowing. I squeezed her hand as if trying to extinguish a flame.

One of Basil's works stood just fifteen feet away. The painting and stone easel was covered with a thick ebony shroud. The sight of it filled me with dread. Helen pointed and smiled at the thing.

After showing our formal invitations and being searched a second time, we maneuvered our way into the crowd. All of Basil's works were covered in a similar fashion. Each shroud attached to the white silk ceiling by thin black cables. All above was a complex matrix of cabling and pulleys drooping like a wet spider's web. The white of the ceiling and floors contrasting with the black vertical cables resembled naked winter tree limbs towering over a white December landscape. The dark shapes swarmed the forest floor like a dreary funeral scene. A replica of Michelangelo's David stood looking over the gallery. His weathered face tarnished by years of rain and wind was strangely comforting. I knew the expression the sculpture wore. *Soon*, I thought, *everyone in the gallery would know it, too*. Beyond the treelike cables, against the river arch stood a small stage, a podium and an enormous red velvet curtain just behind it.

"I've been wanting to know *the answer* my whole life," a voice mocked, standing in the center of four or five gallery dwellers. The two ladies in the huddle laughed at the remark. One added, "Oh, Philip, the *answer* is right there underneath the black cloth. And look, there's another *answer*." The group gave a collective giggle and continued to discuss what could possibly lay beneath Basil's mysterious pall.

"*Basil Pirrip Fenn*," another voice commented, "Who in the hell is *Basil Pirrip Fenn*? And at the *Uffizi*? *No one* has seen *any* of his pieces? That is unbelievable." Helen snapped her head to respond to this person at my right, but I gripped her hand again, stopping her. "Yes, it is unbelievable," a bejeweled woman made the reply, "he must be in *powerful hands*." *Powerful hands*, I thought. Yes, Basil was indeed in powerful hands.

We moved through the forest of blanketed easels, listening to the rising pitch of the crowd's questions, a hopeless murmur of queries and tones of impatience.

I scanned the large rectangular courtyard. Basil was not in sight, but his adopted father sat at the far end of the gallery. Howard Fenn, in his wheelchair, was backed against a stone pillar. Standing beside him was Corey, a recent acquaintance. Howard gazed thoughtfully at those that had come to see his son's work. It was easy to see that he was uncomfortable amid these people. Looking our direction he nodded.

The knelling of the Duomo bell brought the gallery to silence. The pavilion lights dimmed as the carefully placed directional lights shot down onto each black shroud in the gallery. The thick bell struck seven times and stopped. A spotlight filled the stage and two men that looked to be in their mid-fifties climbed the stairs and approached the podium. Helen and I moved near the center of the crowd as it funneled toward the stage like a wave of nighttime surf. I could sense Helen's excitement pulling me closer to the stage.

"Good evening, ladies and gentlemen," the man began, adjusting his tie. The other man stood a few feet to his left and with a microphone he translated in Italian. "Welcome to the Uffizi, my name is Albion Ravistelle. Thank you all for joining us here in Florence. This will be a night to remember—a night when we will see an entirely new form of artistic craft and expression. On this night we will enter into the universe of Basil Pirrip Fenn." An excited round of applause began as the Italian voice began translation. There was another wave of clapping.

"To be here in Florence, within these timeless walls of the Uffizi, is indeed a magical occasion. Basil Fenn's work is now held firmly in the embrace of Michelangelo, Botticelli, Credi, Francesca, Weyden—whose muses have touched and changed our souls and made possible the rendering of our delicate, beautiful, human condition. Tonight we shall all experience a passion that is *beyond* their hands. The gods themselves will be peering in to see tonight's unveiling. These works will bring us all into the new millennium with open eyes and a new, powerful understanding of the essence of art. I'm proud to announce that after tonight's exhibition, Basil's work shall forever remain here. A new room has been constructed behind the Belvedere Terrace that will house fourteen of Basil's first forty-two works." The statement caught the gathering by surprise, and awestruck they slowly began to applaud. I, too, stood wide-eyed and shook my head in disbelief. *Basil, immortalized at the Uffizi, and his work has never been seen.* I glanced over at Howard who was still in thought, studying the gathered onlookers. He didn't appear to hear, nor did he acknowledge anyone speaking. His hands gripped the wheels of his chair as if he was hanging from the crumbling edge of a high cliff. I suddenly became aware of my own hands. One tightened into stone, the other clutched my umbrella handle.

Ravistelle seemed pleased with the applause. "Before unveiling these *Answers*, I would like to turn the stage over to this evening's honored guest, a young man that I have learned much from and shall endeavor to serve as he continues to make the art that will ever transform, reveal and deliver us. Please welcome Mr. Basil Pirrip Fenn. Basil?"

The gathering cheered and moved to get a clearer view of this mysterious new artist. Basil limped up the stairs and shook hands with Albion Ravistelle. The two leaned into some quick, unheard words and smiled at each other. My eyes smiled sadly—Basil's walk, a result of a childhood leg injury that had haunted him all his life—the unsteady, but strangely purposeful confidence in his broken stride had charmed me since our first meeting, just weeks ago. He wore a black tie and jacket and his face was grave. He paused and a barely perceptible hint of joy rose in his face. It passed as he approached the microphone. All fell silent.

I will never forget his eyes in that moment, knowing and silent—eyes that see but have no need of sight. No echoing questions in them. All the eyes pointed up to Basil were filled with loud questions, needs, wants and desires. Mine, too, I thought. One characteristic we all share as human beings is the constant question mark in our vision—in our hearts. Basil looked out and smiled his nervous smile.

"I'm not much for speeches," he quaked, "so I-I-I hope I can speak to you well. And I won't take too much of your time." He paused nervously and looked out at his covered works as the interpreter echoed. "No one has ever seen my w-w-work in this way. I was told when I was a b-b-boy that my paintings were for the eyes on the inside," he held a fist to his heart, "and that it was d-d-dangerous to look at them with these eyes," he pointed to his wide, dark brown eyes. Basil paused again and began to fidget with his hands. "Because these eyes can lie. These eyes are unsure. You might believe that what they see is the truth, but it is only a belief. Nothing but. The eyes on the inside always tell the t-t-truth." His eyes stared out, and he sighed. I sensed abject frustration. I knew his thought, *what's the point in talking to these people?*

He turned his back to the audience and pulled a long

cord attached to the thick red curtain behind the stage. As the cloth split across the back of the gallery it revealed a blank, snow white canvas, as high as the pavilion ceiling. Returning to the microphone he continued, "I can't make you understand what you are about to see. Each of you will see something different. If you can see with your inside eyes you will understand better. And please, p-p-p-please be careful."

Basil scanned the crowd. His pause was long this time, and I could feel an unsettled air rise from the assembly. His eyes stopped on me, and he smiled warmly. "I hope that you will go away from here tonight and tell of what you saw. *Write it down.* I've been told that art is something that lasts forever. Whatever that means. Forever is impossible to understand. Those who have made art have become immortal to all of us. Their names w-w-won't be forgotten. From what little I know about immortality, I don't think I would like it. What is a man to do caught amidst Heaven, Earth and the fires that rage below? Is he to believe in a creator or himself? Should we believe in the stories of an everlasting afterlife or embrace the drama and passion of the here and now because that is all that there will ever be? The answer isn't what you are about to see, but the answer lies in what I am about to do. I am protecting the q-q-questions. The questions are worth living. Goodbye."

Basil took one quick step back from the microphone. He lifted a small revolver that he had concealed in his suit jacket. Piercing screams came from those near to the stage and the assembly reeled backward. Helen's voice in whispered terror, "Oh my God, no." Basil pressed the barrel firmly below his chin and angled it back toward the canvas behind. His eyes fixed to mine. He smiled calmly, almost playfully and pulled the trigger.

Screams. Chaos. Basil had dropped to the floor but my eyes were drawn to the canvas behind the podium that was now *filled.* A thick splatter of blood blotted the center. Its white surface was misted with speckles of red—hair, bone and brain.

What others saw, I know not, for what I perceived was the color of a spirit, the hue of innocence, the mirror of nature and a door to the answer.

I'm fighting myself writing these lines. I should have the ability to make sense of the event. I've listened to my clients tell me about their trauma and their pain. Some have told me of near death experiences. All of their stories contain one thing in common—their past sweeps into their present like an ocean squall. *Is this really happening?*

The piercing screams, the metallic pulse of bells, the cries of a bewildered crowd and the sound of distant sirens all swirled together into one gnashing white noise.

Was I swooning? About to faint?

No. That wasn't it. My vision was clear. Clearer than it had ever been. I blinked. My eyelids ached and my peripheral vision faded into a blank, devouring mist. All that I could see was Basil's last canvas. His final work. I tried to move a step in his direction, but my feet were suddenly heavy and impossible to move. Basil was gone, and I could not tear my gaze from the grisly sight before me.

It had already begun. Thin threads of light, bright as sunlit silver, slowly snaked out from a tiny point in the canvas center. One line of light for each person that stood before Basil's final work. I have recently learned that those ropes of light, those tethers are called *The Silk*. When the slender sensual line touched my eyes I could not look away. It pulled at my thoughts like hands searching for something lost in the dark. And as it discovered me it pulled from my mind my recent past—and it played like a film—as if projected upon the canvas. Everything and everyone around me faded away, and I felt suspended and cradled. Upon the canvas I saw Basil standing on the beach, the grey waves of Priest Lake, Idaho, slapping at the shore. Was I there? Yes. Yes I was there.

Silence.

Flash.

Gone.

I had seen him there before. It was early in October—the day we had met for the very first time. He was standing on the beach outside of my lake cabin.

I stepped out onto the deck and closed the door behind me. The October chill sliced easily through my wool coat and I shivered. My breath puffed white and hung in the air. I turned to see Helen and Edwin watching from the window. Both of them were still in their pajamas. His little hand waved. I waved back. Helen was focused down the wooded trail to the beach. She was straining to see the stranger that stood there. I pulled my hat down over my ears. "Be right back," I said.

The world was edged in crystal. Frost had sharpened the cedar boughs and they shined in the early light. Coming out of the trees onto the beach the cold sky glittered. A spray of stars in the purple dawn.

I could feel the lake jeering at me. Since I was a child I've feared large bodies of water. Purchasing a lake cabin was a part of my own self-imposed therapy. And it had helped, but not completely. Every time I came near to water I could feel a dread deep within me. A dread that I've learned to accept.

The man stood before the outstretched arms of the lake. He turned toward me as I approached—a slight smile on his lips.

"G-good morning," he said. He wore a brown corduroy jacket with a long pointed collar, blue jeans, worn hiking boots, and a green stocking hat. His hair was dark and shoulder length. He looked to be in his early thirties.

"Hello." I stopped a few paces from him. In a stern, but friendly tone, I said, "I've noticed you standing here on our beach a few times over the last couple of weeks—and that you've been looking up at our cabin. Can I help you?"

"Yeah," he said keeping his hands in his coat pockets. He stared at me. After a few moments he said, seemingly to himself, "The big deep heavy."

"Excuse me?" I said.

"Sorry," he said, "sorry if I've freaked you out—not my intention." He looked up at the sky and traced the surrounding mountains. "Beautiful up here. And cold."

"That it is," I said. "But you haven't answered my question."

"I know. Sorry. It's strange. You're a psychologist, right?"

"That's right."

"Yeah. Okay." His tone was skittish. "Your name is Loche Newirth, yeah?" I made no response. "That's your cabin up there?"

I turned and glanced up the path to where he pointed. "Yes," I said, "it is my cabin. What is this all about? How do you know my name?"

"Right. Listen, I've never done anything like this before. I mean, I've never followed anyone around like this. But there's some strange circumstances that I need to tell you about. Very strange. And I don't know any other way to do this—and, yeah, I have been up here before—a couple of times. The first time I lost my nerve to talk to you. Then the next week I saw that you had your family up with you. Or at least, I think that's your family. I couldn't tell really—I was down here and it looked like you had a woman and a kid up there."

I felt my body tighten, and I took a step backward. "Yes that was my family—and they are up there right now. What is this all about?"

"Whoa," he said with a sudden sigh and raised his hands. "Hey, please don't think I'm dangerous or anything—like I said I know this seems weird—look, I have some questions—and some information for you."

"Well, what is it?"

He glanced up over my shoulder. He opened his mouth as if he was about to speak. Instead he issued a long exhale of white steam into the cold. Surprise was on his face.

"Basil? Basil Fenn, is that you?" Helen's voice rang out behind me. I turned to see her and Edwin walking glove in glove down the path toward us. They were both bundled up in coats, hats and scarves. "What in the world are you doing here, Basil?"

Looking back to Basil, I studied him. His lips were still parted and his eyes were wide. "Uh, hello, Helen. *Crazy*."

Helen rushed forward and pulled him into an embrace. Basil kept his hands in his pockets while Helen voiced a flurry of amazement. "I haven't seen you since—I don't know when. How have you been? You look great. It's been so long."

Basil didn't respond immediately. He seemed to be struggling with an unexpected shock. Finally he pulled his hands out of his pockets and managed a courteous hug. He looked at me while he did this. "And this is your husband? And your son there?" he said.

"Yes, this is Edwin." Edwin tucked himself behind my leg. Then Helen said, turning to me, "This is my husband, Loche Newirth. Honey, this is Basil Fenn."

Basil extended his hand, and I shook it. "Pleased to meet you," I said.

"So," Helen said, her voice quavering slightly, "So, Basil and I dated in high school. Pretty much all through high school."

"That's right," Basil agreed, still with an expression of wonder. "I can't believe that you are—I mean, I can't believe it. This is so strange."

Helen stared at him for a moment and then looked at me. She was grinning. "Yes, *it is* strange. So what are you doing up here?"

"What am I doing up here?" he repeated. "Well, I, I was just passing by. I stopped here on this beach because of the view through those hills there." He turned awkwardly and pointed. I could sense that Helen's presence had changed his intentions.

There was something about his tone I liked, though at the time I couldn't quite tell what it was. His nervous tick. His quirky mannerisms. Whatever it was, there was a genuine charm.

He carried on nervously, "I was having some breakfast at Elkins Resort just south of here and thought I'd walk the hash browns off. What a coincidence," he looked at me. Basil saw that I was observing him. He looked at his boots in the frozen sand. He shuffled a second. "Well, I should get moving—"

"Are you still painting portraits that you won't let anyone see?" Helen looked carefully at Basil and her tone seemed to contain a hint of caution.

Basil's face lit up. "Yes."

Helen said to me, "Basil never lets anyone see his paintings. The hardest worker—prolific, disciplined and driven. And has *never* shown his art. For the whole time we went out, I never saw a single piece."

"Perhaps, Helen," I said, "he's got the right to do whatever he wants with his work. After all, it is his."

She shook her head, "Then what's the use of creating art if no one sees it?"

Basil began to laugh. "Helen, I can see that you haven't changed either."

"I suppose that's true. At least where *that* is concerned."

"Well, if it makes any difference to you, there is some interest in my work. Professionally, I mean."

"Really?" Helen said with extreme interest. "So you've finally shown it?"

"Well, no, I'm not q-q-quite ready for that."

Helen ignored his quiet stutter. "How on Earth could anyone be interested in your work if they haven't seen it?"

"Art isn't confined to the Earth, Helen," Basil said.

Helen stared at him and slowly shook her head. Her response held some old resentment, "Oh dear. The artist.

Esoteric as ever. So what's the interest?"

"Do you remember our friend John Whitely? Or I should say, *Father* Whitely?"

Helen laughed, "So he went to seminary and finished after all? That's a miracle in itself."

"Yes," Basil agreed. "He wants some divinity paintings for the Catholic church, or something. I don't know the whole story yet. Just talk so far."

"Well, that's no way to think—you should stay positive," Helen said.

I changed the subject, "Would you like to come in for some coffee?" I asked.

"No, but thank you," he replied. "Uh, maybe next time?"

"So you're still living in Sandpoint?" Helen said. "Working?"

"I still live in my studio. And I'm washing dishes at The Floating Hope. I was the dish-pig down south at the Rustler's Roost, but the commute got to be a bitch."

"Oh," Helen said, a little embarrassed for asking, but Basil's tone was firm and certain. He didn't seem to notice Helen's judgmental air. "I've never heard of the The Floating Hope. Where is it?"

"On the lake in Hope, Idaho. It's both an amazing meal and a breathtaking view."

"Well, that's great, Basil. We would love to have you for dinner sometime," Helen said with a weird enthusiasm. "We've just built our house out in the boonies —right in the middle of a beautiful glade in Sagle. You've *got* to see it."

"I'd be honored. So you don't live here?" He pointed up toward the cabin.

"No," Helen answered, "this is just our little hideaway. We come up as often as we can. Mostly in the summertime."

"I see," he said. "Well, I really should be going. Starting to get cold. Nice talking with you both." He looked down to Edwin and gave him a wink.

"Nice meeting you," I said.

"Yeah. Hope to see you again soon." He said making sure to meet my eyes. He turned and started down the beach. There was a limp in his stride.

After a few moments Helen said quietly, "That was weird."

"You've never mentioned him before."

"No," Helen said, "I haven't thought of him in years."

"Before you came down here he said that he had something to share with me. Me specifically. When you showed up he changed the subject."

"Weird," Helen said. We watched Basil limp down the beach until he disappeared around the point.

Rearden's voice startles her. She quickly slams the cover shut and spins around. "When I found the book, I was elated," he says.

How much time has passed, she wonders.

"Loche has been out of contact for too long, especially considering his recent issues with his client, Bethany Winship."

Rearden is a few feet behind her dressed in what he has recently named his traveling clothes, grey polyester slacks, black high-top hiking boots and a thick, black turtleneck sweater.

"Sorry about that. Didn't mean to scare you. I'm glad you've begun reading it." He sees tears streaming from her eyes. "Are you all right, my dear?"

"Is this true? Is Basil dead? Oh my God. What is all of this?"

Rearden lays his hand on her shoulder. He says gently, "I know. I know. But Julia, there is so much more. So much more."

She brushes at her tears. "Is Loche alive?"

"I have reason to believe he is. He was here very early this morning. But as far as his mental state, I am unsure." Julia notes a *professional* tone in Rearden's voice—confident. A tone that she immediately connects with his achievements in psychotherapy.

"What are we going to do?"

"Well," Rearden says rising to his feet, "we need to get the hell out of here for starters."

"Where are we going?" Julia asks.

"We are going to try to find him."

"Where?"

"South. Let's go."

III

Three Travelers

The mountain road follows the river down from the north end of Priest Lake. The incoming storm conditions make the going dangerous, though Julia drives fast, or at least, as fast as she can—faster than Marcus is comfortable with. His hand grips the door handle.

"Who are *they*?" Julia asks.

"*They* are dangerous men," Rearden says. "You'll learn a little more about them as you read, Julia. But I can tell you, they want to find Loche just as much, if not more than we do. And I'm afraid they've learned that I am his psychologist."

"*You* are Loche's psychologist?"

"Why yes. We shrinks must keep an ear to each other. It's all a part of the job."

"Does any of this have to do with the painting that Loche left with you?"

Rearden does not answer immediately. A burst of that surreal light stuns him, the horror stricken face of his wife rattles his senses—and the painting he refused to look upon. "Yes," he says, "in a way. I *know* what is in that crate."

"You didn't open it, did you?"

The death-pale face of Elanor blinks into his memory and he flinches. Then the echoing chant, *the painting, don't look, the painting, don't look*. "No," he said, "no, I didn't open it. But I know what's inside. Loche told me."

Julia nods and breathes a little easier.

Rearden, however, holds his breath.

They had both loaded that crate from his car to Julia's before leaving the cabin. And strangely, he could feel it back there, like a body in the trunk.

He thinks of the danger that may lie ahead. "We must risk it," he says gloomily.

"Risk what?"

"Julia," he asks, "you know what's in the crate, right?"

"I was told that it was one of Basil's important paintings. I've never seen it—or any of his work for that matter, but Loche told me that it was *dangerous* to open it. I didn't ask why.

"Julia, you must prepare yourself." Rearden pats the leather cover in his lap. "There are things that you may not want to know in this book—things that will change your life. *Yours* in particular."

"I need to know the truth. What happened to Loche?" She asks.

The doctor watches the fields of snow pass in a blur. Shaking his head he turns to her. "Remember Julia, it will change your life. I don't know how, but it won't be easy for you to comprehend."

Julia turns her eyes from the road onto Rearden, "My life has already changed. It feels like it has just begun."

"Is this decision for me to make?" Rearden asks himself aloud. "I don't know. I don't know. I don't think —I don't think it's my—"

"Yes," Julia interrupts, "you can make this decision."

Rearden does not seem to hear her. He is talking to himself. "She was meant to know—to know everything. Yes or no, Marcus. One or the other? It is time to choose. Oh my, there's always two. Always two."

"Two what?"

Rearden is decided and he gives a determined nod. He will bring her in to it all. After all, that is why he called her up here in the first place. She is his only hope.

Okay," he says. "Let's talk about Loche Newirth.

"Loche Newirth is by far the most inquisitive, curious and thoughtful fellow I've ever met. *Doctor* Loche Newirth. A psychologist like myself, but Loche is a *young* man, unlike myself. He's thirty-eight, if I remember right."

"Thirty-seven," Julia says.

"Yes, that's right, thirty-seven. He began practicing four or five years ago. Quite a remarkable young man. I am *his* psychologist, and he has shared his life with me, his frustrations and his *anger* toward mental illness. He wants nothing more than to figure out how to *heal* the mind, restore the hope and answer the questions that plague human nature. Obsessed is nearer the mark."

"For as long as I've known him, he has always been extremely conservative, reserved and dedicated to his profession. He's always kept a close eye on the time, has a pressed stack of shirts in the bottom drawer of his desk, and is never without a rational explanation for every client. A student of the mind.

"He and his wife, Helen, live very comfortably. Loche's profession has afforded them a freedom that most folks in northern Idaho only dream of. They built their *castle*, as Loche likes to call it, out in the woods of Sagle, Idaho. And it is, indeed, a castle. It's small, but a castle nonetheless. High stone walls, medieval architecture—there are even battlements. Loche is very proud of the work he and his wife have done there."

Julia studies the frozen oncoming road and tilts her head slightly. Yet another sting—another sting from not knowing enough about the man that has turned her life upside-down. A montage of Loche's home life drifts across her imagination, his wife *Helen* planting spring flowers in their garden *(what,* she wonders, *does she look like?*), Loche returning home from a long day at the office, a warm embrace, coffee in the kitchen, family portraits lining the hall to the bedroom—Julia can feel the tugging of some far away discipline that she has honed all her life—the part of her that is steadfast in her career—focused on doing the right thing. She wonders how she got into this position after all of her preparations and the focused effort toward her ideals. As the cold, colorless path ahead lengthens and curves like a question mark, her awareness returns to Marcus' voice. She is here, now. And it is not her way to second-guess her choices. The book is the key to understanding. Maybe the key to understanding herself.

"The type of man who would proofread his signature," Rearden continues. "When I found the book in his cabin, needless to say, I was stunned that he would leave it behind for someone to discover." He pauses and stares at the cover, considering his next words.

"I was also quite surprised to find his hand had scribbled out lines of *poetry*. Writing prose is one thing, but poetry? Can you believe that? Ha! Loche a poet. Never once in all our years has he mentioned an interest in poetry."

"A poet?" Julia asks.

"This surprises you? Hmm, how curious. A writer. Yes, writing is Loche's other love—journaling, short stories, novellas—perhaps even novels. Something that he discusses within these pages," Rearden pats the book in his lap. "I had no idea that Loche had such a love for the written word. He speaks of having volumes of writings at his home—and apparently he hasn't shared his work with anyone. He says that he hasn't yet fully developed his *gift* yet. Though I am quite taken with the story, he's no writer. Not yet anyway. One day perhaps, if he keeps at it. But that aside, he says that there is something to come, something terrifying lurking within him that will one day emerge. Something in his writing, in his craft—" Rearden sighs and scowls. It is obvious to Julia that he is having a difficult time trying to organize his thoughts.

"Julia, have you ever wondered why you exist?"

She flips a look at the old man that says, *what in the hell are you talking about?*

Undeterred, Marcus carries on, "Have you ever wondered why you can never be satisfied with your life, no matter how terrible or pleasurable it is?" Julia does not respond. "Yes, you know, the coffee table conversations. The deep, late night, nicotine, alcohol, pot-induced interrogation of the universe and all its gods and human beliefs. The self-help message of positive thinking, manifestation and all of that. Yes, your mocking smile seems appropriate—is there a God? Does my life matter? Is there a heaven? A hell? An afterlife? What is eternity? By your bemused grin I can see that you believe that those questions won't be answered for us. So what is the use of asking them? Right? Right! That is just how I felt, though, being a psychologist, asking such questions is quite useful in treating a client. It opens the shrink and client relationship, if you understand me.

"Well, Loche Newirth believes that those lofty questions have answers. *Real answers*. He believes that if he can gather those answers around him he can heal and restore his clients. And mankind. He wants to ease the pain in the world. Now, I don't know the depth at which you've considered such concepts. Perhaps you don't trouble yourself."

"I *don't* trouble myself," Julia says.

"Ha! That's it, young lady. That's the smarter way to go. Either way, mankind, as a collective, has struggled to come to terms with these disconcerting mysteries since the beginning of time, and all we've got to show for it is a cream cheese bagel, as one of my clients is fond of saying—that is, by the way, zero, zilch, nada—nothing. Nothing but more questions, more gods, more self-help witchery, more classes studying Plato, Catholicism, eastern philosophy, Oprah and motorcycle repair.

"I believe that all thought has its place. All opinions matter—every man that believes, truly believes what his heart or intuition tells him, matters. Whether or not it matters to anyone else is the bitch.

"I believe in the eternal chess game." Rearden nods simply. "I'm certain that a delicately carved, decorative set has graced many a coffee table, over which you and your friends and acquaintances have discussed the meaning of life."

"I don't play chess," Julia says.

"Humph," Rearden snorts. "Either way, a lovely game. It is all about strategy, patience and forethought. What fascinates me about the game is the class of pieces—pawns, knights, bishops, royalty—the whole caste system. Ha! I can think of many times when I was referred to as a pawn. You too?" Julia gives him a sidelong glance. "Yes. There are some among us that we call kings and queens. Some of us are knights. Some of us are as stout and strong as castles. But most of us are pawns. Just pawns. We start the game and seldom survive long enough to become kings. I believe *we* are the pieces, if you will, to a long, long, *long* chess game. We are being moved around a cosmic playing board in complex strategies. Every so often, a pawn is presented with a chance at greatness. And when that chance comes, one must take it. For good or ill."

The doctor cracks his window. "Ah, cold air." He then looks at his listener. "I apologize for the long speech. I think I like to hear myself talk." Marcus lifts the book. "Julia, just remember there has to be two players for a good chess game. After all, there's always two. This book is about all of these things. It's as much about Loche, as it is about Basil Pirrip Fenn. And in some strange way, it is about you, too." The mention of Basil does not move Julia to respond as the old doctor had expected. "You knew him."

"Yes," she replies painfully. Loche's description of Basil with a gun below his chin flashes before her eyes. She scowls, shakes it off and grips the steering wheel. "Yes."

He opens the cover to the journal and sighs. "I'll read to you while you drive."

"Don't leave anything out," Julia says.

"I wouldn't think of it. Where did you leave off?"

"Just after Loche and Basil had met."

"Very good. Now you understand that he is writing of one single second, right?

"What?"

"You see, after Basil's death, Loche saw upon that final canvas his short history with Basil, as crazy as that might sound—he lived it all over again—in the flash of an instant, as he says. So really, he's writing about what happened at the Uffizi. He then returned to the States and went to his cabin to write it all down. Get it?"

"Just read," Julia says.

"You do understand, don't you?" Rearden asks.

"Just read."

Marcus clears his throat and begins.

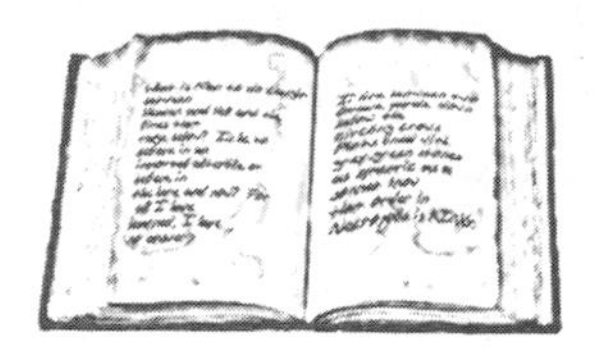

Upon Basil's last canvas there appeared the door to my office—it was the following morning.

"Dr. Newirth, William Greenhame is in your office, and he is quite out of sorts."

"Yes, I know. He called me at five thirty this morning." I said as I handed Carol my coat.

"He was outside the doors when I arrived, pacing and talking to himself." Carol lifted a clipboard and a file folder from her desk. "I let him in and he went straight to your office. I told him to wait in the lobby, but he insisted —"

"It's okay, Carol. He's probably reading by now."

"I don't think he likes me very much," she said carefully. She turned her back and hung up my coat. "How was the lake visit?"

"Very fine," I answered.

There was a crash, the crackle of broken glass, then a voice echoed down the hall. "Heu, heu, heu! mihi misero! Vitae meae finem disidero!" Carol shook her head.

"Latin today?" I asked, pouring myself a cup of coffee.

"Is that what that is? I can never understand that man, Doctor. What was he speaking last week?"

"Middle English, he told me, and some bursts of

French, then he ended the session with word scrambles."

"Does he always speak in different languages?"

"No, only when he's having an episode. When he's calmed down a bit he speaks words I can understand, though, I use the word *understand* loosely." I smiled at Carol as I turned the corner and walked the ten paces down the hall to my office.

The door was ajar. I pushed it open. William Greenhame stood on my desk posed like a ballet dancer frozen in time. His long arms were raised above his head, twisted into a spiral. One foot kept his balance while the other hung in the air, stretched straight out at forty-five degrees. I marveled at his ability to hold such a difficult pose. His treelike limbs and slender frame remained effortlessly still as his gaze, earnest and yearning, peered out to some distant place beyond my office ceiling.

Trembling, I studied the room, with my fists clenched at my side.

He wore a tailored English tweed jacket of deep olive green with thin sienna stripes that crossed in a wide graph pattern. Underneath was a muted yellow-gold waistcoat with carved wooden buttons, and a comfortably tied clay-red cravat that covered an ivory collared shirt. His pants were earthen-toned, and well-worn leather boots finished off the ensemble. A finely crafted umbrella with a curved ebony handle dangled down from his right wrist. *Antique shopper* was the first thing that came to my mind upon our first meeting, and every meeting since, for this was his consistent manner of dress.

Several of the items from my desk were strewn about the floor. The framed picture of my wife and Edwin lay broken in a pile of paperwork. I stepped carefully into the room and took a moment to assess the damage. I steadied myself with a deep breath. I then looked up at the man.

I finally addressed him. "William," I said calmly, "nice pose." Greenhame didn't respond, but kept his eyes strained into that distant place where all sculptures seem to gaze. I continued, "I especially like the coiled arms. Very graceful." I sipped, walked around my desk and put my briefcase down. I felt the irrepressible desire to tidy up, but I attempted to appear unaffected, for his sake. "Do you want some coffee?"

"Yes, with cream and sugar."

"Carol," I said into the intercom, "please bring William some coffee."

"With cream and sugar," Greenhame reiterated.

"With cream and sugar," I echoed.

I walked around to the front of my desk and began to pick up my things. Greenhame spoke again, "Anxiatus est in me spiritus. Cur moratur meus interitus?"

"What was that?" I asked. "My Latin is a bit rusty."

"Luctus, dolor et desperatio."

Carol arrived at the door. Seeing the mess, her eyes moved up Greenhame's posed frame. "H-here's your c-coffee, Mr. Greenhame."

"Oh, thank you, dear Carol," he said, leaping down to the floor and taking the cup from her. He took a sip. "Perfect. Perfect." He smacked his lips and added, "That is, if you didn't poison it."

Carol looked at me and raised her eyebrows, "Can I bring you anything else, Doctor?"

"Not now, Carol. Thanks for bringing the right medicine."

"I do what I can," she said eyeing William cautiously as she walked out.

"Now Greenhame, I've heard those Latin words before. Let me see if I can get this right, you are filled with *sorrow, grief* and *despair*—and you are *miserable*." He nodded and sat down, holding his coffee cup as if it were a rock climber's last hand hold. "That's all I could gather. Was there more?"

"Ithic veli agtig?" he whispered.

I shook my head.

"Ithic veli agtig?"

"I don't know what you're saying." Nor did I know the language. I'd not heard anything like it before. Yet strangely, the sound of the words seemed to form a sentiment in my mind, and a simple question. I somehow knew what he was about to translate for me. But perhaps that was due to the many times he'd said the same thing in English.

"Why does my death delay?" he translated.

I looked at him a moment and processed the question. William Greenhame was forty-four-years-old. He looked thirty. The expression he wore most often was contemplative, but on the verge of some joke that was just about to be pitched. Below his right eye and tracing across his cheek was a thin scar—an injury from childhood, he told me. There was a light and strength in his face, and it was good-natured, especially when he smiled. Long, dark hair draped over his shoulders, and his bright hazel eyes looked to me for answers. We had been acquainted for some time. After our first three sessions I had diagnosed him with Schizotypal Personality Disorder along with obvious Narcissistic Defenses. His panic, manic and bipolar episodes were difficult to track.

However, his odd beliefs and his unusual perceptual experiences were quite interesting to observe. Having lived some years in England myself, his English accent made me comfortable. It reminded me of my youth. William was not born in England, nor had he ever visited.

There was also something familiar about his eyes. I supposed that the familiarity was due to our shared search for peace of mind. William's education was worn outwardly, and his firm conviction to his beliefs was captivating. He claimed to hold degrees in both history and literature. But the most interesting thing about his condition was his *imagined* state. William had taken a theme—a fantasy—and had weaved it into his thought process, much like a method actor or a historical reenactor. Greenhame *believed* that he was born in 1332, outside of London. He *believed* that he was immortal.

"So," I asked, "what happened this morning? Your scheduled appointment wasn't until eleven-thirty."

"Living the life, living the dream," he said, "and that is extremely overwhelming, you see—for when you've been alive as long as I have you tend to think of too many things all at once."

"I can imagine," I said as comfortingly as I could, "there must be a lot of memories to sift through."

"No," he fixed me with a quick, stabbing glare, "you *can't* imagine—and yes indeed! Memories, memories, memories!" he exclaimed. "So many memories."

"Did something happen that lead to your call this morning?"

"Have you ever really looked at a statue?"

"What statue?" I asked.

"It doesn't matter what statue, my lad. Just a statue?"

"Well, yes," I replied, "I've seen many statues."

"I saw a statue in my dreams last night. Then I became the statue." He slowly shook his head and closed his eyes. "I couldn't move. I felt frozen and all I could see was what was directly in front of me."

"What did you see?"

"The horizon. It would fade into view. Light came from behind. Then I could see the sun drop down and set on the Earth, fall in, and dim. Then black for awhile. Over and over, the same thing. I saw the sky change colors, days into nights and back again. Sometimes there were grey skies, sometimes blue, sometimes snow." He stood suddenly, raised his arms and his right foot into the air, and took the exact shape I had discovered him in when I entered. His eyes gazed into the distance. "A host of pigeons, perched on my nose, on my finger tips, on my leg. Shitting all over me," he said. He remained still for nearly a minute then sat down. "If you were over six hundred years old *and* felt like a statue *and* watched each day pass without moving *and* you've got centuries of pigeon shit all over you, how would you feel?"

I thought for a moment. *How would I feel?* "If I were that old, William, I think I would have figured out how to cope with a host of issues. I think I would be a very patient and ordered individual. After all, there would be plenty of time to come to terms with the many frustrations of living."

He smiled. "That's very good, but you do not understand," he said with gravity, "you cannot yet understand."

I leaned forward. "William," I said, "you were born in 1971, in Athol, Idaho. Your parents own a cattle ranch, and you are the night watchman at the Coeur d'Alene Resort. Let's not forget these things." I spoke gently as he bowed his head. "Sometimes dreams *seem* real. But they are only shadows of our cognitive beliefs. What you *believe* isn't always real."

He looked up at me. "What is *real*, you wouldn't believe."

I sighed. "William, the statue dream didn't lead to your episode did it? Was there some other event that took place that you haven't told me about?"

"I haven't even begun. I am a moving, living, breathing statue. I cannot die. All I can do is wait for the next event. There must be an end to all of this."

I was perplexed. He was certain that he had lived for centuries. No matter how many times I showed him his records to remind him of his true age, it made no difference. He would glance at the facts and brush them aside as if they were absurdities that he had created to disguise his real identity. It seemed that the only way to get to the bottom of his illness was to humor his delusion —or more accurately, I would use what's called *the mirroring of interpretation of narcissistic vulnerability,* which simply means, empathize and listen. He seemed to speak freely if he thought I believed his stories. And I listened, and tried to pinpoint areas that mirrored his reality. From there, I would try to coax him to health by providing anchors for defense and resistance. But ultimately, it was about identifying his pain and finding a way in which he could organize it.

"Well," I said, looking at my watch, "It's almost eight o'clock and I have a session at eight thirty. You can begin now and we can finish up at your eleven thirty appointment."

"When I called this morning, the world was too much

with me. I had given my heart up to be sacrificed by a past I cannot change, a present I cannot hold and a future that promises nothing but the same emptiness that I've known since my coming of age. Childhood was my only heaven, for it was then I knew naught of this bane of ever-last." William then said in friendly tones, "Talking with you has restored my discipline. You have a way of doing that for me, even for one so young." I started to respond but he stopped me, "I know, I know, you didn't say much. You don't have to. That is why I come to see you each week.

"And you are like a statue, too, Dr. Newirth. But you have a strength that you haven't yet realized. Believe me when I tell you that. I've met a great many characters in my long, long lifetime. You will weather the storms that shall come, and you'll stand steadfast and confident like a Roman sculpture, even after Rome falls. But when it falls, you will come to life. And if I am not mistaken, the fall will come soon."

"Sooner than last week's prediction?" I asked with a grin.

"Don't mistake me," William said, "an unexpected turn has set events in motion."

"Mysterious." I stood. "And I am sure there is so much more to learn."

He smiled, "Ah yes, there is indeed."

I opened the door. "Will I see you at eleven-thirty?"

"No. I feel better."

"Now William, try to keep your focus on your job, your family and friends, but most of all—*yourself*. You are the key to getting well."

"I'm not sick, Doctor, I just need a disciplined, normal man to talk to," said William.

"Yes, I know. Just focus on what's tangible, solid and real. We'll discuss the big deep heavy next week."

Greenhame spun around in the doorway and met my eyes. "Why do you call it, *the big deep heavy?* Why did you say that?"

I shrugged and raised my brow, "Just a saying." He

continued to stare at me intensely. "Is there a problem?" I asked.

"No. Not at all. Just a curious phrase. Let me see now, how shall we say it?" He laid a finger across his chin and mouthed out the sounds, "*Thivy bag hedepee.*"

"Another language?"

"Not exactly, Doctor. Rearrange the letters. *Thivy bag hedepee.*"

"Ah, another scramble," I humored him. I repeated the sounds and tried to move the letters around in my head. William's expression then turned sympathetic. He nodded.

"You see, when you've had time to think like me, such things are very easy, *thivy bag hedepee—the big deep heavy*. Farewell."

After one of his curious nods he sauntered down the corridor and began to hum a strangely familiar melody.

Turning, I looked into my office. The floor was still cluttered. Stooping and moving the mess onto a chair I began the organization process. My hands shook as I did this. My nature has always been plagued with a need for order before I begin the day. I separated the billing forms from my patient documents, the to-do lists from the itemized spending sheet for my family's newly built home and found my glasses missing. I dropped down to look beneath my desk and found more remnants of Greenhame's episode, but no glasses. They were tucked down in the cushion of my chair when I rounded my desk to sit. Placing them on my nose and studying the organized piles of my life, I put everything back in place, sighed and felt at ease again.

I looked around for any final arrangement before my first appointment. There was nothing to be done but wait. Sipping my coffee I stared at the grey-green plaid wallpaper of my office, straight lines, woven columns and uniform colors. I thought back to the day, two years ago, when I ordered the wallpaper. My wife hated my choice.

"It's awfully formal, isn't it, Loche?" I remember her saying. "But then again, it's very you. I wish you would lighten up a bit. Or show some passion. I'd love that. How about burgundy or red. Something with some life."

"Shades of crimson wouldn't calm my patients," I told her, "green is the perfect middling hue."

Her response, "They look like prison bars. And the color looks like the inside of some institution for the mentally ill."

I remember replying, "Well. . . what do think I do for a living?"

"I wish you would write."

Over the intercom came Carol's voice, "Dr. Newirth, Beth Winship is here to see you."

"Send her back," I said rising to my feet.

Bethany Leona Winship opened the door with great care and peeked her head in. She wore a red blouse.

"Hello, Doctor," she whispered.

"Come in, Beth," I said, "come and sit down."

She was both crying and laughing. "Oh my word," she said, her eyes glinting and wet, "I know that I get up and I get down, but this is ridiculous."

"How so?" I asked.

"Sure, I'm manic depressive—but I've got to tell you, the highs are amazing sometimes," she said, wiping her nose and cheeks with a tissue. "There are times that I believe I can do anything." She sat down quickly, her face shining and grinning. I noted her energetic movement and focused posture, shoulders taut and back straight. Bethany was sixty-five and behaved and dressed sometimes as if she was a college student. Her body was long and fit and the only signs of age one might notice were the wrinkles that haunted her eyes. She was having what she called *a good day*. A day when the illness was seemingly one long release of serotonin.

I smiled at her. "Tell me," I said.

"You know, I wish that I *could* tell you. I wish I could so badly. But I'm afraid that this spot of joy must be kept to myself." She then shook her head so that her long hair danced around her shoulders, and she laughed. "It just means so much to be needed. When someone tells you that you belong to them," she raised her fingers and formed quotation marks in the air, *"saving angel.* There's nothing quite like being told that you are the only thing in the world that can heal someone of their pain."

"Someone has made you feel special?" I asked.

"Special? What a terrible word. How about, *needed, wanted*. How about *antidote*, or *saving grace*, or *medicine*, or *soul mate*. I can't begin to tell you how *good* I feel right now."

I nodded, "This friend must be important to you."

Bethany's smile faded. "Yes," she said. "But I can't tell you anything more. It's really not a good idea."

"You don't have to tell me anything more, Bethany. I am just delighted that you're feeling well today."

"I feel good."

"Good then. But let's keep in mind, that the other side will come. You're having a good day so let's learn what we can from it so that when a bad one comes we're able to—"

"Not now," she said. "I think I just want to roll around in this for awhile and not worry about the roller coaster drop, okay?"

I studied her face and slowly nodded. "Very well," I said.

"So how have you been?" she asked, smiling. "How is that little boy of yours? Any new pictures of the little guy?"

That afternoon I arrived at my appointment with Dr. Marcus Rearden. He sat behind me and his voice was calm and filled with thoughtful question marks. "Anymore dreams?"

I laid on the couch staring up at the tiled ceiling. Each line was perfectly straight, parallel and green. I've spent nearly every Wednesday afternoon since I began my practice talking to Dr. Rearden from his grey couch. He knows more about me than my wife does.

"A few," I replied.

"Still dark?" He asked.

I didn't answer. My first cases were heavy trauma, abused children, and since those days my sleep has suffered. My dreams were often haunted with their stories —with what their eyes had seen—and the simple words they would use to describe their terrors—words like *mommy and daddy* combined in broken phrases with *burned me, hit me, touched me*—cases of violence and neglect—it took much for me to keep the painful reality of it locked into some kind of order—so I could help in some way. Marcus often brought up the Three Heavy What Ifs. The three things that therapists fear when faced with extreme cases. *What if I can't help? What if I can't handle it? And what if I go in with them? Going in with them* meant becoming like them—becoming the very thing we long to cure. And every therapist I know that has worked with kids has faced at least one of those *what ifs*, if not failed at all three. But we keep our courage and we practice what we've learned. We organize the pain.

I still see a couple of traumatized children in my current practice, but nothing like those in my early training. Most of my clients now suffer from what Marcus and I call the *dim light parade*. The average person suffering everything from depression and obsessive compulsive disorder to body dysmorphia and ADD. Certainly these are maladies not to be taken lightly, but because the majority of these clients are adults and are able to conceptualize and reason, unlike young children, we feel that we can shine a light upon the parade of their distress, albeit dim. At least we can reach them (most of the time). Child cases are pushed down into deeper water.

But my dreams of late have not been so dark. Maybe that is because I have become much better at keeping difficult memories placed into their proper compartments. But I think I've been spared of nightmares more often because of my obsession with the implausible goal of *curing* mental illness. Something that my tolerant mentor, Marcus Rearden, might see as a symbolic distraction that keeps me centered. But I see the cure as a lighthouse, and I am way out to sea, floating on my back in a dream.

"I am still very frustrated though, Marc," I said finally.

"With your profession, or my last move?"

I gave a little laugh. "Both," I said.

We both turned in the direction of the chessboard near the door. The game had been in progress for over a month. It was my turn to make a move, after my appointment, of course. Rearden was an incredible chess player, and after each of our many games, I tried to learn his strategies. *One day*, I'd often tell him, *I'll figure out how you do that.*

"Ah," he replied. "Don't be frustrated. Chess is a game I've played for many, many years. You'll get the hang of it. So, too, will you get used to the profession—ours is not an easy job. There are no cures for our clients. Cures don't exist for us."

I nodded. "All that I've studied, and all that I know, and they keep coming back."

"That's a good thing," he said. I could hear his humorous tone, "If they got completely well, who'd pay our bills? We are in the profession of helping them to cope. We can't eliminate their pain, but we can make it easier to steer around it."

I pictured the old man Rearden in my mind's eye. Dr. Marcus Rearden, pale, gaunt, professional, and frighteningly intelligent. He'd spent his life sitting behind some of the world's most dangerous criminals, listening. At our first introduction at a conference in Los Angeles he pointed his spectacles at me with a curious jab and said to those gathered near, "So, this is the future of the mind? Well, I'm very pleased to meet you, Dr. Loche Newirth. I hope we can stumble upon some new thoughts together." Of course, Rearden continued practicing in LA until he had finally had enough. "Too much darkness," he told me when he moved up to Sandpoint, Idaho, ten years ago.

Since then he had tried to focus on what his wife would call *a safer life,* and she was glad for it. "It's time to begin thinking about lighter things and try to ease away from the dark side of man." *What if I can't help, can't handle it, or I go in with them*—Rearden claimed that he began to fail each one. His clients now were similar to mine, everyday people learning to cope. The *dim light parade*.

As my education continued, Dr. Rearden listened meditatively from a chair behind my back. I don't think I could bear to see how many times he has winced listening to my idealistic ramblings. Rearden knew me. Sometimes more than I'd like to admit. I wish I could say that I knew him just as well, but he is a professional. He kept a screen between us. A slightly transparent one, but a barrier nonetheless—it kept our relationship from developing into true friendship.

"I won't give up," I said. "I want the ability to *cure*, not ease. I want the knowledge to heal and repair. I know that everyone suffers. Whether it's a disease, a mental disorder or just the plain problems of being human. Each and everyone of us wonders about why we exist and why there's no clear answer. I hear that question so often, Marc. *Why?* I want the answer." And there it was. The reverie. Me floating on the dream—the lighthouse blinking from the oncoming reef. I could feel him wince.

"I hear that question, too. And I often ask it."

"Don't you wish you had that answer?"

"No," he sighed.

"No?" I said incredulously. "Come now. If you had such answers, think of all the help you could provide."

"Loche, we aren't philosophers, we are psychologists."

"I'm not talking about philosophy, Marc. I am merely pointing out that we, as psychologists, should pursue an answer, not an excuse. I want to steer right through the problems instead of going around them. I sometimes wish that I could manifest it—in writing, if you like. You know, a sort of mission statement, or a story, to create the cure."

Marc drew a heavy sigh. "I used to think like you do. I

used to be frustrated with my clients, because they wouldn't get well. For some of them, the drastic cases, there is no hope at all. When all those pills came in I felt certain that we'd bridged the gap between the mental and the physical. We found that the chemical reactions in the brain were lacking this or that particular chemical, so we were able to prescribe it. Then, we found out that some of the medication was addictive. Much like the addictive question that we began with." He let out another heavy sigh, "And now the whole world is addicted to being *unwell*. Television commercials pound viewers with each and every little malady and boast a fix. This pill will make you smile if you find smiling tough, this pill will fix this or that, this pill will make you smaller—ha, and this one will make you *harder*. Goodness. We've not bridged a gap. It isn't a gap. It is a canyon that society is digging. A wide, deep hole, and we can't see the bottom. And that hole, Loche, is too big to bridge. Our society must change in order to find some kind of hope. And if history has taught us anything, society doesn't seem to be heading toward health. So we must steer around the holes we make—and pull people out of them. That is our job."

"I don't think an answer is beyond our reach, Marc. I want to know. I will know." My eyes closed. I could see the pale white dot of the lighthouse flickering from the shoreline. "I will know."

Rearden's chair creaked. I then felt him sit down on the edge of the couch. "What would you do if you had the *answer* as you call it?"

I opened my eyes and caught a new expression from the old man, his head bowed down in sorrow. "Where do you want me to start?" I asked.

"The beginning," he said, with his eyes still pointed down.

"I watched my mother battle depression, Marc. She was tortured her entire adult life. She died depressed. I grew up not knowing why she would suddenly break down in tears, why all she would want to do was sleep—why a woman that could at one moment seem overwhelmed with joy, and in the next be threatening suicide. And all the so-called professionals gave her nothing but advice, and pills. They experimented on her with every new coping drug, and offered nothing more than, 'Maybe this time the drugs will work.' But it's not only because of my mother that I'm *reaching beyond my grasp*, as some might say. The children in my early training—that was almost too much for me to continue—and there's more. There are people that could be brought to health. Health, Marc. To provide for each person the ability to live their lives through compassion, empathy and kindness. True well-being. The health of the human mind would bring with it a new consciousness. The elimination of these things that we've identified as mental disorders would change the world. There is a cure to our condition. There is an answer."

"You seem to think that the answer would be favorable. A hopeful one."

"The truth is always the best answer."

He looked at me. His eyes were aged and tired, "Is it? The truth is always *an* answer, but not always hopeful."

"You say that like you've discovered something." I studied his expression. It was tinged with sadness. Something was wrong. In the last few weeks I had noticed a change in him—a manner that didn't seem to fit.

"No," he said as he rose and walked to his desk. "I've learned quite a few things through the years. Some things, I hope you'll never have to confront. I've learned only recently that a man must experience his true nature to truly know himself. He must *be*—and not simply imagine being. Face the fear is the dictum of our world these days. We celebrate youth. A carefree youth was something I never really had. You couldn't describe me as a risk taker—never *passionate,* if that's the right word." Rearden looked gloomily out the window, "I've been endeavoring as of late to *be* passionate—and it *is* dangerous. One can risk his very life for it. But, truth, answers, questions are all a part of our natures. They define our lives. Without them, life would be quite plain and unadorned. When I solve a frustrating riddle, I often look for another to pass the time. I love the riddle of man's mind. I've endeavored to solve it, as you have, but I've learned that some riddles aren't meant to be answered."

I noted the tone in his voice. A tone that told me he was reliving some nightmarish session with a murderer.

"Some riddles are there forever."

I looked at him. The lines in his face were deeper than I had ever noticed. His slender limbs seemed to creak like his chair when he moved.

"How could I possibly benefit if there were answers to this life? I'm nearly through it," he said. "What if the answer is, *Over and out? Winked out of existence. Nothing beyond. Have a nice day.* Would I feel better about the approaching shadow of death?" He looked at me, "Or would I pine for the pain and passion of living? Like young love. Oh yes, young love." His smile was sad. "Instead of *answers* Loche, you just may need a few days up at your cabin."

I looked across the room and thought. "We'll see," I said quietly. "How is Elanor?"

He shifted slightly. "The wife is fine," he said. "We're getting along as we always have."

Nodding to the chessboard I said, "Knight to queen six."

He rose and crossed the room pushing his spectacles up to the bridge of his nose. He moved the pieces. "Ah, dreaming again are you, Loche? Nice try, though," He said, smiling as he slid his bishop across the board to take my queen.

I saw the road to my home, rushing by in a blur. The October sun was setting behind me, and I could smell hearth smoke in the chilled air—the fall. My car sped through the deep green woods. Frustrated, I thought of William Greenhame, Beth Winship and the five other clients that came to visit me that day. Why couldn't I bring these people to health? Restore their hope? I thought about Marcus Rearden and our usual exchange—is there an answer, or not? But these inadequate feelings were quite natural to me—the rational answer lay in my clients' respective environments and their biological and genetic configurations. Their minds were injured, and I was the trusted counselor to figure out how to treat the injuries. Help them to organize. Cope.

To do that, a psychologist must confront the particular illness as if it were as intelligent, as knowing and as conscious as the subject that hosts it. I recalled listening to a speech by Dr. Marcus Rearden before we had met, "I'm talking about an exorcism, ladies and gentlemen. Not anything supernatural, mind you, but rather the removal of the behavioral patterns that the disease creates within the brain. It *is not* like a cut on the arm, but *it is exactly like* a cut on the arm. The only difference is that this kind of cut can think. This kind of wound can learn to cut again. This kind of cut can talk itself into never healing. It has hands, eyes, experiences and a wealth of understanding of its host. But it also understands you. The medical doctor uses sutures and bandages. We psychologists use *words*. You must outthink it to stop the bleeding, and try to pull the knife from its hand. I wish I could offer you something more than mere words. If I knew how to stop the pain, the bleeding, the hopelessness, I would most certainly share it. I'd share it with the world."

My grip on the steering wheel was tight. When I released it the tension quickly moved to the muscles of my face. I drew a deep breath and focused my attention to the road ahead of me. That road was the one thing I could count on to soothe my frustrations—whether a wooded path on foot or a twenty-five minute drive through bull pines, white firs and old growth cedars—I used the motion, the time and the sights to purge the stress of the day—the life. But I couldn't forget. I couldn't leave my profession or my responsibilities behind completely. Too many people relied on my help and my counsel. But for my wife and child, I tried.

I arrived at home as the late afternoon light was failing. The windows were dark save a single lamp shining out from the living room. I entered quietly, hung my coat, set my briefcase near the spiral stair that led to my office above, and inhaled deeply—the aroma of apples, warm bread, candles and my small family—home.

The two were asleep on the couch. Edwin was wrapped in his mother's arms, mouth wide open and breathing softly. Helen, with a similar expression, stirred as I leaned down to kiss her.

"I've been thinking," Helen whispered without opening her eyes turning slightly toward me, "I think we should go away for awhile."

I kissed Edwin and knelt. "Go away? We just got back from the lake—"

"I know—I want some alone time with you. Just you," she said.

"We can surely visit up there next weekend if you'd like—"

"No. I want to go somewhere we've never been before. Something new. Just to get away. We can leave Edwin with Carol. I already called her."

"That sounds wonderful," I whispered. "But it will have to wait. Things are a little nuts at work."

She sighed. "I knew you were going to say that." Her tone was suddenly sharp.

"Helen, we can schedule something after the holidays perhaps. But right now I am too busy—"

Helen rolled out from under Edwin's sleeping body, draped a blanket over him and started toward the kitchen.

Calmly I asked, "Darling, would you like to talk?" I followed her.

"Don't you *fucking* do that," she said, "don't you fucking do that to me—like I'm one of your goddamn patients."

"Do what?" I said rounding the corner.

The sharp features of her face were pulled tight with tension. She rested a hand on the kitchen sink and faced the window. "I didn't ask for a doctor. I asked for my husband."

"I *am* your husband," I said, calmly.

"*I am your husband*," she echoed in my calm tone. "Jesus! Will you, for just one-second, listen to yourself? You sound like *Mr. Rogers*. I'm not ten-years-old, though you like to think I am." She began digging in her purse. "I'm not a patient of yours."

I sighed and put my head in my hands pulling my forefingers across my eyes in an attempt, to rub out the fatigue. "I'm sorry, Helen." She didn't answer but instead pulled out a cigarette. Lighting it, she stared thoughtfully at the glowing red tip and shook her head.

"So who's there? *Mr. Fix-it*? Dr. Loche? Mr. Newirth?"

"Your husband," I replied.

Who was she speaking to?

For as long as I've known Helen, that question had troubled me. In college, Helen battled depression and struggled to erase the black memories of her difficult upbringing, an alcoholic father, an abusive and neglectful mother and the loneliness of being an only child. When we met, she would often tell me about her dark past and the pains of coping. My desire for her love and her hand in marriage had mixed with my youthful desire to become her cure. After all, I was studying to become proficient in matters of mental disorder, why shouldn't I help her with what I'd learned? But, as time passed, I began to notice the disparity between husband and doctor—lover and caregiver. And so did she. I tried not to give advice. I tried to be empathetic, though, in the end, I knew that wasn't what she wanted.

Helen took a long pull from her cigarette, folded her arms and then unfolded them. Agitated, she smashed the cigarette into the ashtray on the counter and began to cry. Then, like a wind will sweep clouds aside, her eyes lit up slightly. With a sad smile through sparkling tears she said, "I'm sorry." Her voice was quavering.

I moved to her and pulled her into my arms. "I'm sorry," she said again, "I just don't feel well today, and I just want to be near you." The smell of her hair, her skin—my wife—I could feel her cling to me, her body deflating, her pain rising away. "You are my everything," she cried. "I'm sorry. I love you."

"And I love you," I said. I held her tighter and stared at the black window above the sink, wishing that I could see a light out there. Some kind of hope for her. Some kind of cure.

There was a knock on our front door.

"Oh," Helen said stepping back from me. "We have company tonight." She reached for a box of tissue.

"Who?"

"Basil Fenn. I bumped into him in Sandpoint today, and I invited him over for dinner. I hope you don't mind. I didn't mean to nap for so long. I lost track of time. The food is in the oven. Let me get cleaned up." She walked up the hall toward the bathroom.

He sat on the couch—his right leg stretched out straight on the ottoman. He received a gin and tonic with a gracious sigh. "The fall is here," he said.

"Beautiful isn't it?" I agreed. "How was the drive?"

"Glorious."

Helen had now returned. There was no trace of her tears. With drink in hand she perched herself on the arm of my chair like a cat and swayed gently to the Led Zeppelin record that she had put on. Basil noticed the ashtray on the coffee table, "May I smoke?"

"Please do," Helen said as she reached into her own pocket for her cigarettes. Basil offered one to me.

"No, thanks," I said.

We talked for a long while about our new home. Basil took great interest in how we designed it and had it built.

"Every nook and cranny," Helen proudly stated.

"It's very cool," he said. "I love the way it feels just as you enter. The high ceilings and the big feel. The windows, too. The way you can see the grounds all around the house. With the trees it makes it difficult to see in. Nice. I love the whole castle thing."

"Thank you," I said. "It's a kind of hobby for me. I sometimes think that I was born to live in another time." Basil stared at me with an expression that was difficult to pinpoint. It seemed familiar for reasons that I couldn't explain. "Old things, old stories, mythologies."

"Swords and sorcery?" he asked with a laugh.

"No," I said, "not exactly."

"What about ghost stories? Most castles are haunted, right? How about this one?"

Helen interjected, "That's so crazy! We sometimes think this place is haunted."

"Really?" Basil said.

"Well," I added, "we joke about it. Sometimes we think we hear a strange thump coming from the basement. Or a weird clicking sound, very far away and distant. All it is, really, is the furnace turning on."

"Yes, but it's still strange," Helen said looking around. "Sometimes it feels like there's a presence—like someone, or some *thing* is in the room with you."

I shook my head and looked at Basil. "But no, our castle isn't haunted."

"Well, I know that feeling. Like you're not alone. Have you ever been in a real castle?" he asked me.

"Yes, actually, quite a few. In Germany, when I was young." I said.

"I haven't had the chance, well, until now I guess." he said. "Feels well protected in here. It would be fun to visit overseas someday—but who's got the cash for that kind of thing?"

Helen laughed. "If you'd start doing something with your art you just might be able to buy *yourself* a castle."

Basil suddenly changed the subject and turned to me, "You got an office? A man cave?"

I felt my eyes widen. A tone of reluctance entered my voice. "Yes. At the top of the tower."

Basil nodded and looked down at his hands.

"You should see his office," Helen remarked. "His *real* home."

"I'd love to," Basil said, but before he could read my unwilling expression he added, "but I'll wait to be invited."

Helen pressed me with her eyes as if asking me to jump to my feet and escort Basil up the spiral staircase to my only refuge from the world. "Maybe next time, Basil," I said, "the room is a bit disheveled."

"Believe me, I know what you mean," he agreed. "My studio is completely trashed right now. But you know what they say, a messy space is proof of work getting done."

Helen was quick to interject, "Then Loche mustn't have completed much up there. He keeps it incredibly tidy. Why is it disheveled now, Loche? Are you changing some things around?"

"No," I replied uneasily, "I've left some work out on my desk that I'd rather not have anyone see."

"What sort of work?" Basil asked.

"Loche *writes*," Helen answered. "He's a writer, though it is very doubtful that he'll share it with you or anyone."

Basil turned to Helen with interest, "Have you read his work, Helen?"

"Of course," Helen beamed. "Not all, but most of it. He's wonderfully talented. Loche will at least share his work with his wife."

Basil's eyes seemed puzzled. He was about to ask a question when Helen changed the subject.

"How's Howard?" she asked. Her face shadowed.

Basil's gaze fell to the floor. His tone was unconvincing. "He's getting along great. He's still able to make the trip to Olympia to teach in the summer. His right leg is able to run the pedals on his van."

Helen interrupted, "Basil's adopted father has been in

a wheelchair for close to fifteen years."

"Yeah," Basil nodded, "An accident. He's getting along fine now."

"I couldn't help but notice *your* leg, Basil. What happened?" I asked.

"Oh," he said with a smile. He reached down to his outstretched leg and assisted bending it up to a normal position, "I was in a car accident when I was a baby. My leg never healed properly. But, at least I can walk." He took a last sip of his drink.

Helen quickly rose and took his glass, "Another?"

"Sure, I'm not afraid," he said.

"Loche?" she asked, "another?"

"No thanks, dear. I have an early appointment in the morning."

"Well, I'd love to have one more," Helen stated, looking at Basil. "I'll go check on Edwin and be back. Dinner should be ready in a few minutes." As she left the room she called for Edwin.

Basil lit another cigarette and looked out the window. He seemed to see something out in the dark.

"What's wrong?" I asked.

"Nothing," he replied. "I just, well . . . this is strange to say, Loche," he turned his gaze back to me. His expression was suddenly somber, "I need to talk to you."

I leaned toward him. "What?"

"Do you ever feel like you're being followed? Watched?" he whispered.

"What do you mean?"

"Well," he looked back to the window and then toward the kitchen. "Again, I'm sorry if I freaked you out the other morning. Seeing Helen freaked *me* out a little. And even bumping into her today was weird—although it felt right to accept her invitation for dinner." He paused and added, "Maybe this isn't the best time to—well, you know, to talk."

"Talk about what, Basil?"

"This isn't the right time. I think it would be best if we were alone." He glanced out the window again.

I turned to see if Helen was in the kitchen. I then heard her upstairs. “Is there a problem?”

Basil leaned toward me. “I feel like I’m being followed,” he whispered.

“Followed? By whom?”

“I’m not sure. Every so often I see, or I think I see, someone outside my studio. Or when I’m walking down the street.” He shook his head with a smile, “I must sound like a paranoid freak.”

“No,” I replied, “not at all. I suppose I need to know more before we come to such conclusions. Have you notified the police?”

He scratched his head, obviously uncomfortable. “No. I’ve considered it, but no. I’m totally sure it’s really happening. You see, I have some things to share that might seem—well, unbelievable—and—”

“Why don’t you come down to my office and we’ll discuss it there?” I could sense that he was genuinely concerned about one of two things, either he was truly being watched, or he was teetering on the edge of delusion.

“No,” he said shaking his head, “I don’t think I can do that. I was hoping to talk to you in a place that isn’t so *office*-like. Besides, it’s not like that. I don’t need therapy.”

“Well, that’s where I’m most comfortable,” I said. “I do a lot of listening there. You’d feel—”

“I’d rather both of us just talk.”

“Tell you what, I have a meeting tomorrow out near The Floating Hope and if you’d like we could have some lunch?”

“That would be great,” he said.

“But I would rather wait to discuss anything that might require my professional opinion—save that for my office.”

“Done,” he said.

“Am I invited?” Helen asked as she placed a fresh gin and tonic on the table before Basil. She had come in quietly.

He looked up at her, “Thanks, Helen. But—but I can’t stay for dinner. I’m so sorry. Can I get a raincheck?”

Helen’s eyes widened in surprise, “Well, of course, Basil. Are you okay?”

“Oh yeah. It’s just that I remembered I need to take some things over to Howard’s—and I should do it before it gets too late.” He stood up and limped around the couch. I followed him to the door and handed him his coat. “It smells tasty, Helen—sorry I’m going to miss it.”

Helen shrugged. “Don’t worry about it. Next time. Please tell Howard hello from me, will you?”

“I will,” he said. “And I’ll see you tomorrow, Loche.”

“Tomorrow,” I said.

❦

The sky was one even wash of grey. Below, Pend Oreille Lake matched perfectly except for the cresting tips of white caps from the shore to the mountains. Floating fifty yards out, attached to the shore by a wide boardwalk was The Floating Hope. High pilings poking up out of the water surrounded and held it in place like thin wooden fingers. I stood in the parking lot and studied the route as if it were a tight rope from the shore to the front doors. The old dread of large bodies of water started my hands quaking. I took a deep breath and remembered myself and my strides toward mastering the phobia. I stepped onto the boardwalk and traversed the distance with my right hand clenching the rail with every step.

Opening the front door I turned and looked back. I was terrified, but I had made it.

Inside I was met with the warm smells of bacon and coffee, and the low chatting voices and tinkling china of the lunch crowd. There was a long counter with high stools and ten or so single place settings. As I sat, a woman turned with a coffee pot in hand. Her long reddish brown hair was woven into a thick braid, and her smile—warm and genuine. “Coffee?”

“A cup of tea would be wonderful,” I said, a bit taken

with the brightness of her eyes.

"Right away," she replied and turned.

"Has Basil been in yet today?" I asked.

She placed the teapot and teas before me. "Not yet. You must be Loche."

"Yes, that's right."

"My name is Julia Iris."

Again, her eyes—amber brown, lit and glowing. I lowered my gaze to the delicate angle of her nose and down to her full, smiling lips. Framing her face were soft ringlets that had loosened from the braid.

"Pleased to meet you, Julia."

"Last night he said he'd be in for lunch. Noon was it? That means twelve thirty or so. He's always a half hour late. That's just Basil."

"I see," I said. "Always late?"

"Yes," she replied, "I even went to the trouble of changing his work schedule, starting his shifts earlier to see if we could shake him from the habit. Didn't work. But, I must say, he's never been more than a half hour late nor has he *ever* missed a shift."

"You manage the crew here?"

"No," she said flatly, "I own the boat."

"That's fantastic. The place is beautiful. Quite a view," I said, nodding to the window—shuddering at the grey waves. "My wife and I will have to come back for dinner. We haven't been here before."

She smiled. "I would have remembered if you'd been in before. I have a good memory for faces."

A couple at a table near the counter had placed their menus down.

"Excuse me," Julia said, "Basil will be along soon." She then went to take the order.

The braid dangled like a rope of dark woven silk. She was dressed simply, in a long, cream colored tunic. A faded red and green scarf tied loosely about her throat.

"Hey, man," came a voice. A grinning Basil plopped down beside me. "Careful, Loche. Looking at her too long can cause serious damage to one's marital relationship."

He wore a Beatles T-shirt and headphones hung around his neck. He grinned at me. His eyes looked as if he hadn't slept, red and lazy.

"Now I know that it's like totally inappropriate to meet with a psychologist while thoroughly hell-baked, but I thought I might be able to speak a bit more freely." He was stoned, and his heavy lids and twisted smile irritated me. My disapproving expression was obvious to him, and he leaned a bit closer and whispered, "Now, Loche, don't be angry. Prozac, weed, what's the difference? I choose to self-medicate, and I happen to like the pot."

"There's a big difference between the two."

"Yeah, yeah. Let's not make a big deal about it, okay?"

"Basil," my voice was blunt, "I would rather talk with you when your head is clear."

"Ha!" he blurted. "I'm afraid this is as clear as I get. Now then, I've set us up outside for some chow. You still in? Even though I'm happier in spirit than you?"

I frowned.

"Come on. There are heaters out there, and we'll be alone."

Julia approached the table, "Basil? Is that table on the dock set up for you two?"

"Yes, ma'am," he replied.

She handed me a menu, "Enjoy your lunch."

"Thank you, Julia," I said.

"Not a problem." She leaned down and whispered some words into Basil's ear.

Basil grinned. "I know," he said. "I don't work until five. I'll be fine by then."

"Paranoia is a condition of drug abuse."

"Do I look paranoid to you?" Both Basil and his T-shirt stared back at me. *The White Album* quartet seemed to ask the same question. "Come on, man," he said. "Turn off your mind, relax and float downstream."

The noon air held a sharp chill, but the overhead

heaters allowed guests to sit comfortably. Basil seated us at the last table, furthest from the restaurant out on the tip of the dock. We were surrounded by the cold Pend Oreille waters. This was the last place I wanted to be. I held my feet firmly against the wood planks and held on to the edge of the table.

I didn't know Basil well enough to care about his drug use, but his nonchalance bothered me. And when he fixed me with those glazed eyes I felt a sudden urge to flee.

Basil shook his head. "Whoa, Loche, lighten up will you?" He lifted his coffee mug to his lips. "Oh, coffee. God bless coffee." Setting it down he leaned into the table. His voice softened, "Okay, so here goes. My name is Basil Fenn. I'm an orphan. I was raised by Elizabeth and Howard Fenn. Elizabeth passed away three years ago, and Howard still lives here in Sandpoint.

"Now, what I'm about to say is fuckin' out there—you can choose to believe me or not, but here goes. I had a series of dreams, alright? Dreams. And you were in those dreams. Right? They were so vivid and memorable that it was hard to know what was real and what wasn't—if you follow me."

I nodded. My diagnostic mind began its process.

"These dreams were real enough to put me on a beach in front of your cabin. I dreamt of that exact location—I must have walked every inch of the Priest Lake beachfront until I finally found the exact spot—the spot from my dream. And there *you* were. The dreams gave me your name, your vocation, that you had a family, and—" He stopped. He must have discerned my disbelief.

"Look, I know it sounds fucking mad, but I'm telling you the truth—but the weirdness doesn't end there, Loche. Not by a long fucking shot." He paused again and squinted as if looking for a different way to start. "I'm an artist. I'm thirty-four-years-old, and I live in a studio off of Pine Street. I paint there. Only one person has ever seen my artwork—by accident—my adopted father, Howard. Not a good thing, but I'll get to that. My real parents died when I was a baby. We were in a car accident, and I survived. I have no memory of them, so when I refer to my mother and father, I mean Elizabeth and Howard.

"I started painting at seven, and haven't stopped since. I've done over four-thousand paintings, ranging from monumental to postcard size. Each of them are beyond comprehension. What do I mean by that? Well, just that. My paintings are, well, different, and they're my life, and my life is my work, if you follow me. *The paintings*, the paintings must be kept secret. They're not for any living person's eyes, save mine. This is the *most* important thing. Now then—"

He talked fast and my mind filled with questions.

"Hold it a second," I said.

Basil stopped and waited patiently.

"Why must they be kept secret?" I asked.

He stared at me. "Loche, before we get to that question, I need to tell you more, okay?"

"Very well."

"I told you that I felt I was being watched. Well, I was serious about that. On two separate occasions I've seen two different men casing my studio."

"Casing?"

"Yes. One comes at night and another takes his place in the morning. They've been watching my place for the last few days and follow me wherever I go. In fact, I'm certain they're watching me right now."

"Basil," came my calm reply, though, under the table I could feel my hand begin to tremble, "We should save this conversation for my office. It sounds to me like there's much to discuss. There's much more going on here than a chat over lunch can solve."

He shook his head. "What's the difference? Here or your office?"

"Well, for one," I said impatiently, "we are in the middle of the lake, having lunch in a public place. This is not the right environment for—" Basil began to laugh. I grew a bit angry, "What's the laugh for?"

"You'd rather me come to an environment that *you* are

comfortable in?"

"Yes."

"What if *I* were uncomfortable there?"

"That's not the point."

"Ah," he said as he lifted his water glass, "what is the point?"

"Basil," I said calmly, "this is not the way I work. Matters that require my professional opinion take place —"

"In your *office*?"

"Yes. In my office. If you'd like you can make an—"

"*Doctor*," he said with a grave look, "matters that require your *professional opinion* happen everywhere, not just your office. Fuck your office. Right now, this moment, this place, is where you should begin to think differently. If you'll just let me explain what I've been experiencing right now I'll—"

"It will have to wait. You told me that you had some questions about psychotherapy and that you've been troubled. Right now you are stoned, and this isn't the time to—"

He held out a hand to stop me and said, "Dr. Newirth, they are watching *you,* too."

I closed my eyes and sighed. When I opened them Basil's color had changed. He believed what he was saying. "They are watching *you,* too," he repeated.

"And I suppose that was in your dream, as well?"

"You think I'm crazy, right?" Basil said. I gave no response. "Well, if I were in your shoes, sure, I'd be ready for the check and I'd be out the door. But listen, Loche, I'm not out to lunch. Wait, yes I am," he said with a laugh, "But I'm very serious about what I'm telling you."

"And so am I, Basil. We need to spend some time talking."

"I've got a pretty good idea why this is happening."

"And I have my own suspicions."

"You do?" he asked enthusiastically. "Do tell."

"Basil does any of this have to do with my wife, Helen? The two of you have a past. Is there something I should know?"

He shook his head emphatically. "God no. No, no, no. My seeking you out has nothing to do with her. Although, I must say it's blowing my mind that she's your wife. I dreamt you had a wife, but for it to be Helen is, well, fucking insane. Loche, all of this has to do with my art, my paintings," he said throwing his napkin on his plate, "not some unrequited romance. My paintings, man."

"The paintings that *no one* has ever seen."

"Yes."

I stood up. "Call and make an appointment to see me in my office. Sober, mind you. We'll talk then."

He looked up at me, surprised, "Loche—I've insulted you. I'm sorry, man. Please don't think I disrespect you." He stood up, "I am what I am, Loche. I know this is real. I'm not after your wife. I'm telling you the truth—at least, as far as I understand what the truth is. But I'll come in to see you if you'll feel more comfortable."

"Fine. Next week."

He gave a sort of nod, "Actually, I made an appointment for later today, this afternoon. I wanted to make *sure* I'd see you. There's more to tell you Loche—so much more."

As I turned and began to walk away, I caught a glimpse of Julia through the windows, setting a table. She smiled. "Keep your eyes open, Doc," said Basil from behind, "if you see anyone paying close attention to you, think about what I've said. See you in a couple of hours."

Julia does not notice that Marcus has stopped reading. The drone of the wheels on the ice rises and brings her back.

"The day we met. . ." she says quietly. "I won't ever forget it."

"You love him," Rearden says.

"Yes."

Rearden wrings his hands.

Julia notices. "What's the matter?"

"Nothing," he says. "I've long missed that feeling."

Julia glances at the old man. "What do you mean? You must love your wife."

She doesn't know, yet. Of course, how could she? No one knows that Elanor is gone. It's best that she doesn't know, for now. It was that painting Loche left with me—the painting in the trunk—it would be too much for her to understand right now. Marcus shakes the voice out of his head. "I do—yes, I do love my wife, but we've been married for over forty years, you know. Believe me when I tell you, that spark of passion can, and *does* disappear.

"I would do anything for Elanor, *anything* to keep her safe—safe and happy. Yet, some beautiful things have faded away from us—passion, desire—once they're gone, believe me, you miss them. You never stop wanting those things, you know, you just get good at pretending you don't need them, and it is maddening when you can't seem to rekindle them. It makes you do crazy things."

These feelings were not completely alien to Marcus, but he had never given them this much credence. His entire life had been built around easing morbid thoughts and negative thinking, and with that came perspective—rational awareness—stalwart organization. With the terrors he had explored in the minds of killers, protecting what he had was paramount. At least, what he had left. And he was a psychologist after all, he could not allow himself to feel too much. For the duration of his long career he had kept his passions, his real wants, even his real needs, at arms length, knowing that if he gave in, he just might somehow become like those he was treating, weak, disturbed, unhinged, mad. But lately, his arms do not seem to have the length they once did. Much had happened over the last year—and he notes a manic behavior in himself. He has done things he never thought he would do. And now, his wife has passed away—it is only natural to feel depressed. It amazes him, however, how well he can mask those feelings, in the same ways that many of his dangerous clients did. But as he lifts Loche's book up to his eyes and begins to read, he shivers at the coming paragraphs. He knows what is to come and understands Beth Winship's disorders. Perhaps too well.

To his left Priest Lake is a blurred slate beyond the passing ash-green pines. The frozen beach claws out from the shore—jagged panels of ice reaching to smother the sky's reflection. Northern winters are unforgiving, and when the cold comes, it will do everything in its power to cover up and put to sleep the delicate things that commune with the sun. If the winter could kill the sun itself, it would.

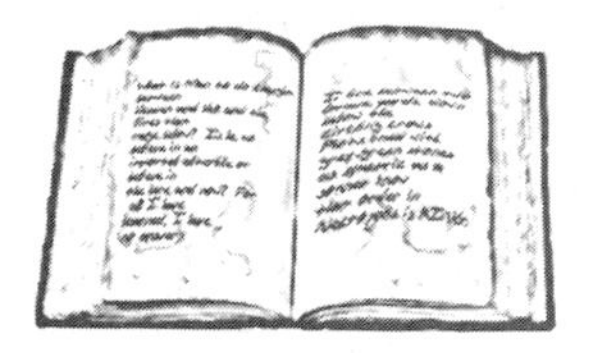

As the glass doors of The Floating Hope closed behind me, a mirror appeared. The one way mirror in my office.

Few get the opportunity to observe a person from the other side of a mirror. I've stood face to face with several unknowing clients, with a sheet of glass in between us. I've studied them as they studied themselves—as they witnessed their vanity, as they wondered at their reflection, at how their eyes had deepened and dimmed with all they had seen. I have often felt shameful, almost guilty when using the mirror to study behaviors, for its power has a godlike quality. But who am I? A god? Just as the supposed divinities might look in upon our lives and make their judgments, I can do the same. The mirror is looked upon as an invaluable tool. A way in which a psychologist may gain a clearer insight into the client's natural method of solitude. What they do, how they move, what they say, and how they spend time when no one is around, is our concern. And again, that strange twinge of guilt visits the pit of my stomach as I enter the "Spy Room," as Carol calls it.

I now watched Beth Winship. Through the mirror I could see her anxious and shaky manner. Her left foot jittered with agitation as a news channel bounded through their daily human suffering broadcast. I watched the muscles of her face twist out dreadful expressions. She raised her hand to her cheek and began to cry. Each second that passed brought stronger waves of anguish until she finally stood and began to search frantically for the remote control. She moved to the television and searched for the power button. Finding it, she stopped the pain.

Beth then began to pace slowly, wiping tears from her face and struggling to gain control of her emotions. When she looked into the mirror and attempted to repair the damage that the outburst had left upon her face, her eyes looked directly into mine.

I shrunk back, but I held her gaze. She stared not into my eyes, but into her own, sky blue eyes clouded by a raging tempest. Her cheeks streaked with mascara like distant blurring rain storms touching down on a bleak horizon. Then her fingers angrily flew up to erase the downpour with quick self-conscious strokes. She grinned at herself. An artificial grin. A mask. The smile seemed to say, "Nothing wrong here. I'm just fine. See? I'm smiling." I couldn't bring myself to smile back.

Beneath the painfully applied make-up remained traces of natural beauty. A faint glimmer of youth. At our first meeting, Beth had brought with her a photograph of her at age thirty-nine with the summer lake stretching out behind her. Her radiant smile was genuine, her lovely frame was fit and strong; she told me that when the photograph was taken, she was a volunteer lifeguard at the city beach. But now, after six years of working together, her snow-white pallor, the wrinkles that lay heaped around her eyes like black sticks on a frozen lake, beneath the ice, I could see her drownin.

She sat on the couch twisting a tissue in her fingers.

"Beth, I'm sorry you aren't feeling well," I said sitting down across from her.

"I'm so sorry to have come in without an appointment, but Carol said it was-"

"It's fine, Beth," I said. "That's what I'm here for. I'm just glad that I could accommodate you."

Beth didn't reply. Her eyes were clamped shut and she heaved silent, mournful sobs. I watched her with great difficulty. When she finally spoke I noticed that my gaze had dropped to the floor.

"I fucking hate this. . ." Her eyes were still tightly closed when I brought myself to look at her again. "HATE!" she cried.

"I know, Beth. I know."

"How can *you* know what this is like?" She asked with a sudden sharp glance. "You don't know! You don't know!" She began to cry again.

I sighed heavily, "You're right. I don't. Perhaps we should talk awhile Beth. Perhaps we can—"

"It never goes away, Doctor," she cried, "talking doesn't help!"

"Beth," I said patiently, "I know it's not been easy, but

we're making progress. There is still more that we must break through in order to get at the center. We've a lot of digging yet to do. Talking will help, Beth."

Beth knuckled her swollen eyes and then quickly folded her arms over her chest. Her anger modulated into fear again.

"I miss my husband," she said wearily, "and my children."

I raised my brows. "What do you mean?"

"Just what I said."

"What do you mean you miss them? You make it sound as if they've gone away."

"They may as well be gone. So should I, for that matter." Beth wiped her nose and said, "I miss the way they used to treat me. I sometimes don't recognize them. They aren't the family I've lived with all these years. I hate the way they look at me."

"How do they look at you?"

"Like I'm sick. Like I'm stupid. As if I'm some stranger, but their mother just the same. They don't respect me. My eighteen-year-old, Sheryl, never comes around the house anymore. My son, Nate, has no patience for me, always telling me to cheer up. Telling me to, *just think positive*. I overheard him telling his wife two days ago that he thinks I've changed. He's uncomfortable around me! Oh God!" Beth began to sob again, "My boy is uncomfortable around his own mother!"

"How is your husband?" Beth didn't answer. Instead, she cast a dark expression toward the lines in the ceiling. "Beth? Have things gotten any better?"

"I think he's seeing someone." Tears froze beneath her eyes. "I think—" her voice trailed into a distant whimper, "I think—"

"Why do you think that?" Beth was silent. Her tears now began to trickle down her cheeks. "Beth?"

"Maybe because *I've* been seeing someone."

I willed myself to hold back the expression of surprise. *Let her talk it out*, I thought.

"I've been unfaithful, too," she sobbed.

"Is this the person that has been making you feel needed? Wanted?"

"Yes," she said. "But it is over now, or it *will be* today."

"What do you mean?" I asked.

"I can't go on like this. He's an important man and we can't be together—he's married, too."

"How long have you been having this affair?" I asked gently.

"Five years," she said looking down at her hands. "It began with romance and excitement—but as time has gone by, he's become controlling." She snapped her gaze up to me, "And frightening. It's like he wants to keep me depressed—sick—dependent upon him—even though he tells me that he loves me—tells me things that sound good and true, but somehow—" her voice trailed off and she looked away into nothing. "I can't explain how he does it, but he keeps me coming back. He seems to know how I think, what my fears are, how to keep me sick. I wish I could tell you more."

"You can tell me anything, Beth," I comforted.

With blinking eyes, she studied me as if considering. Then she shook her head, "No, no. I can't—I can't tell you. I need to stop. I've already said too much, and that scares me. He scares me." She bowed her head, "Maybe I should just stop thinking altogether—*stop* everything. Stop." I paused before speaking again. The red of her clothing caught my eye. I considered her emphasis on the word "stop." Stop what? I thought. "Sometimes I think there is only one way out of this. . ."

"What do you mean?" I asked.

She bowed her head again and remained silent. Then slowly, "I am going to end it today—I am going to tell him that we are through. I want to be free."

"Beth," I said, "are you in danger?"

She raised her head and stared at me. "No," she said finally. Her gaze was again far away.

"Does Roger know?" I asked quietly.

"No. No. And he *won't* know." Beth began to cry

again. I watched her struggle to push the tears back. As she had before, in the waiting room, she gained control and forced a smile with a shake of her head. She appeared eager to change the subject.

"Let's shift gears, Beth. Would you like to try something?"

She didn't respond.

"I have something I want you to do."

"What is that?"

"Do you still swim?"

"Not in years."

"I think," I said with some positive energy, "that you should go down to a health club and swim, three times a week. Do you think you can do that?"

Beth looked back at the ceiling, "I used to love swimming in the lake."

"Well, perhaps in the summer, but for now, the club downtown has a large pool. It seldom gets used."

"What is this supposed to do for me?"

Noting that her time was up, "I'm hoping that you can tell me, next week. It is something you loved to do. I'm giving you some homework here. Swim at least three times, between now and our next appointment, and I want you to recall all of the reasons you love to swim. I especially want you to consider these things when you are in the water. I want to talk about those things with you. Can you do that?"

Beth Winship sat up without looking at me. "I can try." She opened her purse and produced a stack of envelopes gathered tightly by a rubber band. She stared at them thoughtfully. "I will see you again soon, right?"

"Of course," I said. "next week, usual time. But I would very much like a phone call from you tomorrow—just to check-in. You have a difficult few days coming up with your decision to end this affair—and I'm here for you. I'd like to know that you're okay."

Beth nodded. "Have you and your wife been out to your cabin this fall?" She pulled from her purse a sealed, bright red envelope and a pen.

I wondered at her question. "I've been up a few times this season. The trees are bursting with color and it's been awfully cold. Why do you ask?"

"No reason," she replied absently. "My life wasn't supposed to be like this," she said after a pause. "I wish I could redo it. Have another chance. Rewrite it."

I stared at her.

"Goodbye, Doctor."

After Beth had gone I began recording our session in my notebook. I felt confident that our next meeting would yield some positive results if she followed through with swimming again. I skimmed through my notes and read the line, her words, "Maybe I should stop everything. Stop." *Was she considering suicide?* Then, in my periphery, I noticed the stack of envelopes that Beth had pulled out of her purse, sitting on the floor opposite my desk.

❧

I rose to pick up the envelopes, but just as I got to my feet there came a quiet tapping on the door, then a loud, passionate call, "William Hubert Greenhame to see you, my lord."

When I did not answer right away he called again, "William of Leaves calls." Greenhame burst into the room with a grin. "Doctor," he said bowing his head. He was, as usual, impeccably dressed. When he raised his head his eyes were pointed and sharp. His grin faded. "In the name of *action*, dear Doctor, I cannot feign madness any longer. The time has come for us to understand one another. My truth has been too long delayed." There were no signs of his illness, though his words echoed our past sessions.

"William, now is not your scheduled time, I—"

"You have met someone, one that *we* have been watching over, one we knew you would eventually meet. And now the time has come for introductions." I stared at him, my patience was growing thin.

"I have no idea what you are talking about—"

"Why sir, you do indeed. You have met the painter, Basil Fenn."

I took a step backward and studied his eyes. "How did you?"

His raised hand stopped my surprise. "Doctor, do you know who the man is? Do you know his importance? Do you realize that he is not who you think he is?"

"Greenhame, how do you know who I acquaint myself with? My personal life is no business of yours." My temples began to pound.

"Ah," Greenhame said, a smile returning to his face, "but it is. You will know anon why this is true. But first, Basil is coming to see you this day, is he not?"

I felt blood rush to my cheeks, "Mr. Greenhame—"

His raised hand stopped my words again, "Is he to see you this day?" I made no response save a pointed glare. "By your silence I can see that this is true. Good. This is well." William whisked to the chair across from me, sat down and crossed his long legs. "I know what he is coming to tell you. I merely want to assure you that everything he will tell you is true. Doubt him not. For you will, Doctor, you will. I say to you again, doubt him not. His tale will leave you clutching for reason. Your statue-like life will crack and all beneath will melt into motion."

I'd become accustomed to hearing this reference to statues from Greenhame, and I quickly seized the opportunity to bring him to some sense. I posed two even and direct questions, "Are you still feeling like a statue, William? Have you had any more episodes?"

His lips slowly curved into a wide humoring smile. "Oh yes. Every never-ending day. But I think you may have missed something terribly important in our dialogue —you are the statue, my friend," he said pointing his long, thin finger at my chest. "Perfect symmetry. Perfectly still and ordered. White as marble. Not a stain.

"Oh, dear Doctor, you believe me mad." He nodded to himself, "Yes, and why shouldn't you? I am accounted a good actor by those of my kind. You cannot see beyond my play. You are not yet wise enough to see the truth. Even now, as you sit with your brows raised in question, your finger gently touching your temple as if it were some trigger to activate your mental alchemy, to treat me, to help me. I am flattered that my skill at *seeming* has fooled such a captive and respectable audience." Greenhame stood and, with the grace of a stage actor, took a royal bow. "Thank you," he said, now melodramatic and eccentric, "oh, thank you." He then stood straight with his arms at his sides and looked at my desk and the framed picture of my family, "Now the play is over—but the action has not yet ceased."

He sat down again, crossed his legs and observed my expression. "Curiously enough, dear Doctor, I've never lied to you. I've merely played upon your compassion and your desires. No, nothing I've said has been false. I am who I am. William Hubert Greenhame, a humble guard, and you are Loche Newirth, *the Poet*. The Wordsmith." The vertical stripes of the wallpaper behind William blurred and I felt a wave of confusion crash through my mind. The blood that colored my cheeks dropped into my limbs. I could tell by Greenhame's wide, satisfied eyes that my face faded into alabaster.

My reply was weak and torn, "Poet?"

Greenhame nodded emphatically, "Yes, dear sir—*Poet*."

"How did you know that I—"

Standing, Greenhame raised one arm and began reciting a piece of poetry I had begun a year earlier.

> "I live between two graveyards, down below
> The circling crows. Plots dotted with grey green
> Stones, symmetric as a sonnet know
> That order in Necropolis is king. . ."

He lowered his arm slowly like a ballet dancer and looked into my horrified eyes. "That is one of my favorites, though I don't think you've quite finished it, yet. Have you?" I made no answer. "Ah, perhaps not. I look forward to seeing it complete. *Necropolis* is a place that interests me indeed. It will be a sonnet, yes?"

I stepped back and away as my desk chair toppled over with a crash. Greenhame took a step closer with outstretched arms signaling me to be calm. "Please, Loche, *ag shivcy, ag shivcy*, do not fear."

"Our relationship is over, William," I stammered. "You have crossed a very dangerous line."

"Doctor—please."

"Greenhame, please leave!"

William bowed his head again and whispered, "*Ni avu ustu ~ plecom uta veli ustu.*" I shook my head angrily and began to nervously arrange some items on my desk, but the words, whether he'd said them before or I had heard them elsewhere, I seemed to know the meaning. When he spoke again he lifted his head and latched his eyes to mine, and he confirmed my thought, "*At once your eyes will be opened; everything to come will be revealed to you. I will take my leave. Gallina.*"

Greenhame whirled around, opened the door and paused with his back to me. "Believe what you hear today, of all days, Doctor. Basil—doubt him not." He then disappeared into the hallway singing that same familiar melody.

My private thoughts had been seen, my writings. They have been read, without my permission, without my knowledge, without my consent. My writings were meant for no one's eyes but my own. How could this be? All of my private journals and writings were kept in my tower office at home, locked safely away.

I sat down and drew a long calming breath. Was my home broken into? If so, when? How? The battlements I had built to keep the world out had been breached. My thoughts raced to the iron latches and door locks of my house. Helen and I keep a secure home. We guard our privacy. How then could my words have been seen? And Helen, even Helen has no knowledge of how to unlock the words in my office.

Grabbing the telephone, I dialed the number to my home. Helen answered.

"Hello?"

"Helen. . ." my voice faltered. What could I say? "Helen, is everything alright at the house?"

"What do you mean?"

"I mean," I stood up and began to pace, "I mean, have there been any visitors at the house today?"

"No," she said, and in the next breath spoke to Edwin, "what have you done to your shirt, little boy?"

"Helen?" I cried.

Helen went on, "It looks like our son has been rolling in the mud outside. You go and take off those shoes before coming in here, young man. You'll track mud all over the floor."

"Helen?"

"Loche, what is it?"

"No one has been out to the house today?"

"No. Were you expecting someone?" she asked.

"Are the doors locked?"

"What is wrong with you? What's going on?"

"I—I don't know." *How could I explain*? I gathered my wits. "Nothing. Nothing is wrong. I just, I just thought that a friend of mine would call today. No one has been by the house?"

"No. Who are you expecting?"

"Oh," I squinted, struggling to deflate my anxiety, "just a client. It's nothing. If you see anyone on the property, give me a call, will you?"

"You sound strange, Loche, are you sure you're alright?"

"Yes, dear. I—I've got someone waiting and a lot on my mind. A client, I think, got wrong directions to the office and may have been sent to our house. If you see anyone, you'll call me, right?"

"Yes, but Loche—"

"Bye." I hung up the phone. Then there was a quiet tapping upon my door.

"Loche?" came a voice. "Loche, are you in there?

There was no one at the reception desk." It was Basil Fenn.

I looked at the door and longed to wedge a chair against it.

The metal disk in the center of the doorknob caught a gleam of light from the slanting fall sun. It would have taken but a moment to reach the door and turn that center locking gear. I could have been silent. I could have dashed to the window, raised the glass, escape into the chilly air and flown to my home. It would have taken just seconds. . . Lock the door, I thought. Lock the door.

"Yo, Loche," came Basil's muffled voice from outside, "can I come in?"

My hesitation was short-lived. I lifted my chair from the floor, placed it back on its legs, covered my face with my hands and took a deep, deep breath. I then rested my hand upon the stack of letters that Bethany left behind. "It's open, Basil. Come—"

The door opened with a creak that I'd not noticed before, and Basil, carrying a large rectangular package under his arm entered with a smile. "Nice pad. Wow. Very green in here."

I nodded. "Y—yes. It's supposed to be calming." I clenched my teeth attempting to gain my composure, "It works. *Sometimes*."

"Hmm," he continued without looking at me. "I like." He set the package down, leaned it against my desk and lifted the portrait of my family. "Edwin is looking tough."

I nodded again. When his eyes finally fell on me his expression changed. He set the photo down. "You alright?"

Clearing my throat I rose to shake his hand with a fake grin, "Y-yes. Fine. . . Just a busy day. A lot on my mind."

His nod said that he understood—understood everything. This frustrated me, and I turned toward the window.

"You need to see this."

"Basil, what is going on?"

"Huh?"

"A man that came to see me today warned me about you."

"*Warned*? Really? Who was that?"

"Why don't *you* tell me?" I asked.

Basil shook his head. "I don't know who you're talking about."

"Basil, you told me when we were having lunch that you—that *we* were being watched."

"Yeah, I told you that."

"Who were you speaking of?"

He looked out the window as if he were expecting to see someone. "I don't know who *they* are. I don't know."

"Well, I've got a good idea." I circled around my desk. "Listen to me, I don't know what is going on here, but I had a person come to me today who claimed that he has been watching you. He mentioned your name and said that you have something to tell me."

"Who told you that?"

"I can't share any names with you, Basil."

"Why not? If there is someone watching us don't you think you should share—"

"No," I said shaking my head, "that is confidential information."

"Well, what this person told you is true," he said, "I do have something to tell you."

"What is it?"

Basil stared at me. I thought briefly how familiar his eyes were. A vague, intangible feeling, like childhood growing pains, tingled through my thoughts. A gleam of golden sunlight angled its way into Basil's face. "Well, for starters, you're my older brother," he said. Then he shrugged.

I took a step back. "Excuse me?" I gasped. "Basil—"

"Loche, you're my brother."

"What is this?" I cried, "some kind of joke?"

"Listen," he said quietly, "crazy right? I know that this

is a lot to take—"

"A lot to take?"

"You must believe me. You and I have the same blood. We share the same parents."

"Oh, please!"

"It's true," he said firmly.

I turned away from him and retreated to the safety of my desk chair. Pausing beside the window, I noticed two men standing at the entrance of the office parking lot. Both were faced in the direction of my window, though they were too far away to see clearly.

"What is it, Loche?" Basil asked.

"There are two men—"

Before I could finish, Basil moved to my side and peered over my shoulder out the window. "I've seen them before," he muttered. "Who are they?"

"Well, why don't we find out," I said. I threw the sheer curtain to the side, flipped the latch and opened the window. A biting chill swept into the room.

"No!" Basil cried. "Stop!"

"Why? Why shouldn't I confront these men? I think it's time for some answers. The only way to get them is to ask."

"Now is not the time, Loche. Let's talk first. Is that okay?" He moved toward the package he had brought with him, "Check this out. This will answer some things for you."

Basil lifted the package and began to unwrap it. Beneath the brown paper was, what looked like, a large picture frame shrouded in black cloth. He set the veiled object down on the couch, propped it up with a pillow and then turned toward me.

"I am about to show you something that will change your life, Loche."

His words came in stuttering clicks. "I-I-I am a little, a-a-a little, a-a-afraid." He smiled a grim smile. "But, th-th-this is the right thing to do. It feels r-r-right. You and I are brothers. You'll be okay."

He noted my obvious confusion and he held his palms

up to me. "I-I-I'm alright, Loche. This happens s-s-sometimes when I'm nervous. My mouth w-w-w-won't let my voice work. I don't know w-w-w-why that is. It's just the way it is." He smiled again, still with a strange hint of sorrow. "Would you like to see?"

"Are you sure you would like me to see?" I asked with some caution.

"Yes. I-I-I am sure," he stated with an emphatic nod. "And w-w-what's more, this will prove some things to you."

"Such as?" I asked.

"You will understand that we are brothers."

"Your painting will prove that we are brothers?"

"Y-yes."

"Well then," I said moving across from the frame, "by all means."

Basil's face became calm. "The big deep heavy," he whispered. As he moved to uncover the work, a loud knock came upon the door.

"Dr. Newirth! Dr. Newirth! Are you here?"

"Yes, Carol, what is it?" I called.

The metal disc at the center of the door twisted and that strange groan came from the hinges again. As the door widened I could see Carol, and beside her two police officers. Carol's eyes were filled with tears. "Doctor," she cried. "Oh, Doctor. I didn't think you were back from lunch yet—"

I stepped out of the office and closed the door behind me.

"Carol," I gasped moving to meet these new visitors, "what's the matter?"

"She's dead," Carol whispered. "She's dead."

"Who's dead?" I exclaimed.

"Dr. Loche Newirth?" One of the officers said stepping forward.

"Yes. . ."

"Doctor, Bethany Leona Winship was found on the lake shore about a half hour ago. She's drowned."

My mouth opened, but no words came. The

policeman went on, "We are very sorry to have to inform you of this. Would you like to sit down?" I looked at Carol. Her eyes glistened with tears. She avoided my gaze. I looked to the officers. Their expressions were patient and sympathetic. One of them reached out and placed his large hand on my shoulder. "Would you like to sit down?"

I took two delicate steps away from the policeman's touch. "No," I replied. "What? What has happened?"

"Beth Winship," said the shorter officer, "we have reason to believe that she has committed suicide—but we've begun an investigation."

I looked away and let my eyes follow the long lines of the hallway into the lobby.

"Her husband told us that she had come in to see you this morning. Was she here today?" I nodded an affirmation. "Have you been here all day?" I again nodded, still too stunned to speak. "Doctor, would you like to sit down?"

"No," I said, "I—I am with a client currently. If you will excuse me I'll end our session." I turned, opened the door and stepped into my office. The policemen followed close behind. I noticed the chill in the room. The sheer curtain was swaying gently beside the open window. Basil Fenn was gone.

"What do you want to know?" Helen asked.

"Everything," I answered.

"Everything?" She looked nervous.

"Yes, everything."

"Let me put Edwin to bed. I'll be right back." The little boy pulled his hand out of my wife's grasp, ran over to me and leapt heavily onto my lap. He kissed my cheek and returned to his mother. "Good night, Edwin," I smiled.

"What has he told you?" Helen asked descending the stairs.

"Nothing," I said.

"Then, what's the big deal about Basil? We had our relationship, we broke up. What else do you want to know?"

"How did you meet?" I asked taking a seat at our dining room table.

Helen gave a sigh. She put one hand on my shoulder and began to gently rub. "Are you alright? Your call today freaked me out."

"A lot has happened today, Helen." I bowed my head. "I'll share everything with you after you tell me some things."

"So, what are those things?"

"How did you meet?"

Helen took a long pull from her cigarette and placed it in the ashtray in front of me. Placing her other hand on my shoulder she pressed down, rubbing into my fatigue.

"I shouldn't have invited him over the other night,"

she said. "Loche, you're not jealous, are you?"

The incredulity of my reply was thick, "Helen. . .no. That's not it."

"When I bumped into him I found myself in an awkward position. We agreed to get together. Remember?"

"Helen," I said with patience, "just tell me about him. That's all."

"Why? What's the big deal?" she pleaded. Helen was obviously reluctant to answer my questions.

"He came to see me today, Helen, and I'd like to know a little more about his background."

I could feel Helen's eyes on the back of my head. The long pause told me that she was considering a reply. She reached over my shoulder and took another drag of her cigarette and then placed it back into the ashtray.

"We met in high school," she said with an exhale of smoke. "Basil was, for the most part, a geek. He didn't have many friends. We had a biology class together, and he sat right behind me. Always wearing black, always looking as if he had just gotten out of bed, and he always had those damn headphones wrapped around his head.

"One day—spring time, just before we got out for the summer, he leaned up behind me and asked me if I liked art. When I turned around I saw something in his eyes I couldn't describe." Helen reached around me and lifted her cigarette to her lips. I could feel her look away to some distant place. "I still can't describe it. I told him yes. Then I asked him, what kind of art?" She dug her left hand into my tight shoulder, "Any kind of art, he said in that *Basil* sort of way. You know, sort of flippant. I said, sure. He leaned back in his chair and smiled at me, nodding. I turned back around and pretended to look busy when I felt his breath in my hair. Then he told me that I would marry an artist someday.

"I remember turning shades of red right there. When our teacher excused us, I turned around to try and catch a glimpse of those brown eyes of his, but he was already gone. From that day on I had a crush on what they call the artsy type."

"Then what?" I asked, turning to watch her speak.

Her expression quickly changed from a thoughtful gaze to a fake smile. "He finally asked me out that August. He told me that he spent the first part of the summer with his folks in Olympia, Washington. He said that he thought of me the whole time he was gone, and I was the first one he called when he got back."

"What about that John Whitely friend of his?" I reminded.

"Oh yes, John. He was around during that time, too. We did our share of partying. Though, I guess John is now a priest."

"You said Basil's parents lived in Olympia? Did you ever meet them."

"Once."

"What were they like?"

"They were nice people. His adopted father, Howard, he was in an accident that put him in a wheelchair."

"Where did you meet them?"

"Here in Sandpoint. Basil took me to their house."

"They had two homes?" I asked. "Did they have a lot of money?"

"Not that I know of. I never really thought about it. Basil didn't like us spending time with his family. He said they wouldn't understand."

"Understand what?"

"You know, that was one of our big problems. He used to tell me his parents didn't want him to get involved with anyone at such a young age. It seemed to me that they knew how weird he could be, so they were either afraid that I would hurt him, or that I might get hurt."

"How did they receive you?"

"Like I said, they were very nice and polite to me, but sad. I can't explain it. Those were strange times." She pushed her cigarette into the ashtray. "His dad is a college professor—teaches English at North Idaho College and he taught some courses at Evergreen State College in the summertime."

"I see."

"I recall something about his father, Howard," Helen circled around me and sat down. "His father was close to his family. Still is, I would guess. Basil told me that his father thought that the highest, most noble thing a person could do is stay close to, and care for family."

"What about his mother?" I asked.

"Don't know much about her," came her flat response. "Dead now," she said, as she crushed her cigarette. I watched her hand kill each ember in the tray. "As far as I know, anyway." When I looked up she studied my face.

I shook my head and replied lightly, "Dead you say? Do you know how?"

"What is this all about Loche? I've answered you, now you answer me."

I stood up and crossed the room. With my back to her I replied, "Basil stopped in to see me today."

"That's what you said. What did he want?"

"He came by to show me one of his paintings."

I heard Helen rise from the table, pick up the ashtray and walk briskly into the kitchen. When I turned around I could see her standing at the sink staring into the drain. She set the ashtray into the basin and stood motionless. "He wanted to show you one of his paintings?" she echoed.

"Yes," I said as I walked into the kitchen and stood behind her, leaning my back against the far wall.

"And what did you think?" she asked quietly.

I dropped my gaze down to her heels. "What's the matter, Helen?"

"Nothing is the matter," she cried, whirling around. "What did you think?"

Surprised by her sudden movement I stood up straight. "I didn't have the chance to see his painting. Something came up."

"You mean he opened up to you—offered a glimpse at his work, and you didn't take it?" Disbelief filled her expression.

"No, Helen. Something very serious happened today that prevented—"

"Like what?" she cooly interrupted.

"A client of mine drowned today." My tone was sober. I said it as if I had never known Bethany.

Helen raised her hands to her mouth. "Oh God. . . Oh God. . . Loche. . . A woman was reported drowned today. Was she your client?"

The lines in the tiled floor began to waver. My eyes felt heavy. I slid down the wall and heaped myself onto the floor.

"Loche, I'm sorry."

"Drowned," I mumbled. "Gone. We had come so far. She did what I told her to do. I tried to help her."

"Loche," Helen said, "what happens now?"

"What do you mean?"

"Have you spoken to her family?"

I shook my head.

Helen continued to look at me in silence. My vague explanation of the day's events was perplexing her, it was easy to sense, and I could tell that she found it difficult to voice her confusion. "Loche," she appealed, "what's going on? Why didn't you tell me about this at first? What's going on with Basil? I don't understand."

I rolled my eyes up to her, paused and held my breath. "I don't understand either." Sitting up, I pressed my fingers into my stinging eyes. The image of the tightly gathered envelopes that Beth had left behind flashed into my memory. They were in my briefcase beside the stairs to my office. "Right now, Helen, I need to think awhile. I need to consider what is to be done. Beth was unwell, and my advice to her may be seen by those close to her as dangerous. There will be an inquiry. The Mental Health Board will want some answers. So will the police. I have the feeling this terrible tragedy may be. . ."

"May be what, Loche?" Helen pursued.

"The end."

"The end? What do you mean? How could you be responsible? They can't blame you, can they? Was it an accident?"

"No. Or, at least it appears that it wasn't an accident. It looked like a suicide. She left a note on the shore. A very short note—it said, *It is time for all of this to stop.*

"That isn't your fault. They can't blame you—"

I let out a heavy sigh, "Yes, dear, they can blame me. But that's only part of the issue here. My care, my words, my ideas lead to her death." I stood up, crossed the kitchen and looked out the window. "It matters little to me what they will do. The question is, what will I do? My counsel was wrong. I missed something very important about Beth—it was my job to help her, to keep her from doing harm, not. . .not to lead her to the water." I paused. "This is really happening, isn't it?"

Helen nodded and looked at the floor.

When Helen and I designed the house I had one request, albeit, a lofty one, castle-like. Since my childhood and my visits to many European castles I had been obsessed with building my own stone fortress. Of course, building a castle in all of its manifestations would be well beyond our budget, but we managed to build a structure that was at least a nod to the best parts of that old architectural style. After all, castles by definition were not places of comfort and warmth—they were for protection and security. The cold of the stone made them nearly impossible to heat. What light that made it into the interior was quite dim due to the windows that were mere slits in the walls. But given the advent of electricity, running water and some major breakthroughs in design and architecture over the centuries, plus my own processing as to how one might overcome the past's unsavory characteristics, our castle would have both the aesthetic as well as comfort and warmth.

The foundation was heaped on a ten-acre plot in the woods of Sagle, Idaho. A realtor might describe the home starting from the basics—a four bedroom, two bath with a huge recreation room, living room, two car garage and an upstairs study. But then that description would shift into things like, a wide, deep green lawn, and up and out of its center jut age-worn grey stones that form the two story facade of the building. Three proud, high-peaked roofs crown its top. Below the raised center peak inlaid in the stone, is a Roman arched entrance with a round-topped wooden door with brass fittings. The exterior shines with huge windows. Rising up from the right side of the structure is the turret, a tall stone cylinder with a winding stair that leads to the circular study above. And above are the battlements that provide a view just over the surrounding treetops.

Inside, the home had three fireplaces, soft pillows, hardwood floors and open spaces—all the modern conveniences, but the look of a stronghold from the ancient past.

My study was to me the most coveted space for there I could escape my vocation. The one place I could write.

As I pushed the heavy, planked door open, I paused in the center of the room and stared at my oak desk. My mind cycled through what lay within each drawer. How did William Greenhame find his way to my work? I turned and looked at the windows. None of them had been forced. Everything was just as I had left it.

I let my eyes trace the parallel lines of shelves that lined the walls from floor to ceiling. On the shelves were the books that my wife and I had collected over our time together. She had a knack for finding extremely beautiful hardbound classics. They all looked undisturbed and ordered. Sitting down behind my desk I scanned the surface for any anomaly. Seeing nothing of note, I reached into my pocket and produced the key to the third drawer down. I slid the key into the lock and twisted. The click of that lock was a familiar sound. From the drawer I drew out another key that allowed access to the dark oak standing cabinet across the room. I moved to it. With my hand on the cabinets's iron handle I paused and thought, *What will I do if my written work—my papers—my life—*

is missing? Unable to imagine such a thing, I flung the door open and threw my hands inside, groping. They were there, and I began to breathe again.

I ran my index finger across the bindings until I came across the volume I sought and tilted it out into the light. Laying the book down on my desk I flipped through the pages, keeping a tight focus on each fold, crease and sound the book made. The poem titled *The Grid*, the piece that Greenhame had recited to me was near the center of the book. I followed my hand-scrawled lines and knelt down in front of my desk reciting, as if in prayer, ". . . order in Necropolis is King." I lowered my head down atop the book's spine. I could hear my heart's dull thud and the sound of my breathing.

"What do you write?" came a familiar voice near the door, from the shadows. I sprang to my feet and spun around. "Don't be alarmed, though I'm sure I've quite startled you." William Greenhame was crouched down beneath a window, inside the room. His shape was hidden in shadow.

I backed away reaching for something heavy. Identifying my distress he stood up and held his hands out. "Loche, I'm sorry I startled you. But it was necessary. You don't know how careless you are. Ha, and I thought my clamor would have raised the dead."

My fingertips found a pen and I held it out like a knife. "H-how long have you been there," I demanded with horror. "W-what in the hell are you doing?"

Greenhame lowered his hands and smiled. "I'm watching out for you." He leapt to the center of the room and seated himself on the floor. "I love this room, Loche. You've got exquisite taste. I also like your choice of weapon. But you won't need a weapon. Not yet anyway." With his long hand, he patted a spot on the floor in front of him.

"Greenhame," I exclaimed, "you get the hell out of here—"

My words were stifled by his shaking head and his calm patting of the floor. "Come, please. All is well. Let me explain."

I lowered my pen and glared at the man. "I'll stand. Say what you have to say."

"So be it," he said lightly, "this is, after all, your home, you should do what you like." He looked up at the high ceiling and smiled broadly. "So, how does it feel to have a brother? A brother you didn't know you had?" He wrinkled his nose at my fierce expression. "Loche, please don't glare at me, it's not polite. I assure you, you have nothing to fear from me."

"And whom *should* I fear?" I retorted.

"Why, the Enemy of course," he answered simply. "Ah, but you don't know whom, or rather, what the Enemy is, do you? Listen, Loche, you need to relax and sit down. I need to talk with you about your brother. He is in danger. Eyes are watching him."

"Yes, I know, he told me that much. *You* have been watching him."

"Did he say that?" William said, surprised. "I didn't think he knew it was me. I shall have to be more careful." He scratched his chin and looked back up at the ceiling. "Yes, I admit, I have been watching him. Or I should say *we*. Or rather, I should say, we have been watching *over* him. But we are not the only ones that have an interest in your brother. There are shadows watching him. We've driven them back, but they still come, and they won't stop until they've made contact. And when they do," he looked at me with anguished eyes, and broke off.

"The truth is, Loche," he continued, "You and your brother are, how do I say this, *important*."

The sight of Greenhame filled me with rage. Every session that we'd had together raced through my mind, and all of his eccentricities, ill-formed perceptions and dramatic characteristics forced my body to suddenly lurch toward the phone—to call for help. I sprung for it, and as I lifted the receiver Greenhame was suddenly at my side. I thrust my arm out to push him away, but he was too quick. Catlike quick. He lifted my body from the floor and hurled me over the desk. I heard my bones crack as I hit the floor. When I raised my head, the phone dangled over my head. Greenhame was no longer there. He was behind me. Close behind me. One of his hands grabbed the back of my neck and the other dug into my spine. I struggled to move but I found that my body didn't respond. I opened my mouth to call for help, but no voice came from my throat. William began to speak, though I didn't hear words, but rather echoes, repeating chants in my ears, in my heart—I was unsure of which. He spoke poetry. Or was he singing? A melody that I recognized? The same melody that he used to sing after every one of our sessions, but now there were words in that melody. My words. Every tender sentiment that I'd scribbled down, I was hearing, echoing—"That bit about the Lily," he sang, or said, I'm still unsure, "the flower that couldn't reach the light through the sidewalk boards. . . The aged couple, on the porch at twilight. . . Seasons ending. . . The stopwatch in the pocket of man. . . Yes, I feel your words." He did. He felt them. Not understood, but felt. The emotions I'd poured into my verse were communicated to another, not as mere words on a page, not the poetic devices or imagery, but the passion of the sentiment. As I felt them. . . As I felt them. . .

The music of that dream state seemed to cross-fade with William's voice, but he was again speaking in a language that was foreign to me. He trailed on in round, lyrical tones and then began to repeat a phrase I'd heard him say once before.

"*Ag shivcy. Ag shivcy. . .*"

"Don't fear?" I said.

"Ah," he said gently, "yes, but in this case I mean, *don't panic.* Don't panic, my dear fellow. Relax," Greenhame said gently. "I know, this is difficult to grasp. You aren't ready to know everything, yet. Please, Loche, understand that I am not here to hurt you, but to protect you—and to teach you. Calling the police will just make things easier for the Enemy. Ridding me from your life would be catastrophic."

William's hand was still on my spine, but gently now.

"Let go," I said quietly.

"That's my line," he said. "But you are not ready for that, yet."

"Let *me* go," I repeated, "I will listen to you."

The pressure of his finely pointed fingers disappeared. He leapt up and landed in front of me on his belly. We both lay stretched on the floor face to face. I noticed the light scar below his right eye. "How's that?" he asked.

"Better," I admitted, "I can feel my limbs again."

"It's amazing what one little pressure point can do to the rest of the body—what say you?"

I nodded but kept silent.

"Your importance is something that is too monumental for you to conceive at this time. Even if I were to share with you what I know, you couldn't, or wouldn't believe it."

Greenhame could read my troubled eyes and he nodded. He knew that I was now well beyond controlling my own world and struggling for a wall to hide behind. "Patience," he continued, "be at ease, if you can, but now listen to my tale."

"Do you believe in God?" Greenhame asked simply.

I fixed him with my most rational expression, "I believe that *god* is what we've made it to be, an ideal to strive for, a compass for our morality and a hope that lies out there to counterbalance our fear of the unknown."

"Good, good, my boy, now then, answer the question, do you believe in a god?" he asked again.

"I just told you what I believe," I answered.

"Yes," William said patiently, "but you haven't answered the question, yet."

"Do I believe in a *god*?" I repeated. Greenhame nodded enthusiastically with a huge smile. "You mean, do I believe in God the way most people believe in God?"

"How do *most people* believe in God?" William asked with an eager expression.

"Their belief is that God is the divine designer, the creator of everything."

"Yes." Greenhame nodded again, "Do you believe God exists."

"No."

"Ah," he sighed with an air of understanding, "just stories then, eh? Just mankind's way of justifying his existence?"

"That is what I've already said," I replied.

"Well then," William said rising to his feet, "your answer tells me much about you." He lifted himself up from the floor, moved behind the desk, placed the telephone back into the receiver and sat down in my chair. I stood and watched him stare into that statue-like distance. His palms were pressed together and his index fingers crossed his lips. He hummed that strangely familiar song again. At length he said, "What would you think, if I were to tell you that God is a real entity? That gods exist. With or without faith? Better still, a fact."

I moved to the chair opposite him and replied, "I would have to say that you share the same feelings that most believers do."

"And that is all?" he asked, "that I am just like my fellow believers?" I didn't answer. "Loche, do you want proof?"

"Proof that God exists?" A smile came from a hidden space in my being. That smile I will always remember, for given the day's events, no smile could possibly seem genuine. "Yes, if you can provide such a thing—if it wouldn't be *too* much trouble."

"Do you want the Jesus loves you bit, or the scientific facts, or what?"

I didn't answer.

Greenhame glanced across the room, up to the ceiling, and then back to me. "Very well, I will provide you your proof. But first, let me tell you a story.

"Your brother, Basil, was born three years after you. And your birth mother entrusted both you and Basil to Rebecca Pirrip, and her husband, Jules. Your birth mother was Rebecca's sister. Her twin sister. But Rebecca and Jules would not live to see either of you come of age. Basil was thought to be the only survivor of a tragic car accident that claimed the life of his new caregivers, and you, one chilly evening in November. Forgive the newspaper style of delivery, but I've read it over and over for several years.

"Jules, Rebecca and you were all declared dead on arrival. Basil's right leg had been broken in three places. His family was gone. However, undetected by the medical staff, you were barely clinging to life. You were set beside Jules and Rebecca in an anteroom while the small medical staff attended to Basil's injuries. When the nurse returned to the anteroom she discovered only the bodies of the parents remained." Greenhame paused and eyed me carefully, "*You* were pronounced dead on arrival at Moses Lake Memorial Hospital, then secretly resuscitated in that anteroom, and along with your little brother, quietly whisked away without a trace."

"The accident at Moses Lake was an assassination attempt. The car accident was planned by those I was once associated with." He paused. Color faded from his face. "But we must not speak of that just yet. It was an order from on high. You see, Loche, Basil was created for a purpose. And, so were you. The two of you were supposed to die that night. You shouldn't be alive. Yet, you are.

"Basil was taken to live with Rebecca's oldest friend Elizabeth Fenn and her husband Howard.

"Now, Rebecca's twin sister, her name, my dear Loche, you know quite well— Diana."

I wasn't looking at him any longer but instead my eyes traced the curve of the moon that drooped across my window. I scanned its gentle glowing arc over and over. I quickly flipped through a series of memories— boarding school in Canterbury, my first love, my friends, my desire to attend college in the United States. Then my return to England years later to attend my mother Diana's funeral.

Greenhame continued, "Diana was forced to flee the

United States to Europe just weeks after she gave birth to Basil. You were so young, and Diana and Rebecca were identical twins, the switch was seamless and you were completely unaware. You forgot all about the accident and your younger brother and the man that you thought was your father. You and your real mother were brought together again in England.

"And the surprises just keep on coming, your mother's recent death? Just awhile back?" he said with a curious eye. "Tragic, I know. The news must have been very difficult for you. But as they say, news is only news. Your mother, Diana, lives."

I made no response, but just stared at the man.

"She is alive—in Italy. She has been made aware of the recent events and is looking very forward to seeing you again." Greenhame's head tilted in bewilderment. "I thought this news would please you."

"This is impossible, Greenhame. Why are you doing this?" I cried in disbelief. "I spread her ashes."

The man smiled. "Ah, ash to ash, dust to dust. Silly rituals—" William seemed to suddenly recognize my frustration. "Oh dear," he sighed, "I forget how little your kind can handle. I have known all there is to know and I often act and play as if those around me have the same knowledge. It's a habit I'm afraid. In acting we find so much more truth than we do in real life. My dear Loche, it is indeed a pity that I must talk down to someone like yourself. But, you are quite unaware of your potential, just as most great artists are. You believe that you are in control of all you create and that the natural world has its laws, and science is its god. The paints that Basil uses to color his canvases are made up of this chemical and dust from that particular metal or soil or egg, but when splashed about and manipulated into some form, the laws that you so desire to obey suddenly disappear when passion takes over. The composition of paint is never considered when a rendering moves us.

"I am doing nothing to you, dear Loche. I am just showing you the pictures of your life. You would perhaps be quite pleased if you found that human psychology is an exact science. At least, that is what you pine for. An explanation for why we are the way we are. Is this not so? You would have your life's riddle solved and all would be well? There is an answer to all of your wanderings despite the fact that you rarely understand yourself, much less others. By all accounts, you think me mad by my wild, unbelievable utterances. It is time you forgot the concept of belief and turn to the idea of knowing. Know this, your mother lives.

"And your writing. . ." Greenhame said as he lifted my notebook from the desk, "is a very important—"

I reached out and grabbed the book out of his hands. "The writing is mine!" I growled, "and not for yours or anyone's eyes!"

William Greenhame rose from behind my desk and flung an open hand through the air. The crack of his palm across my cheek silenced me. His form seemed to change. He was no longer the long limbed, thin man suffering from mental illness, but instead a man like a great mountain with the wisdom of the wind in his voice. "Listen to me!" he roared. "Listen to me. Don't think for a moment that the things I'm telling you are lies. You've been living too long behind these battlements. Your words will be the proof of God. The proof that mankind has been searching for. You hold the answers in your grip, at the end of a pen. Know what I say, my son!

"Think. Why does mankind *believe—think* God exists? Is it, do you fancy, that we've all met the fellow at one time or another? Did he stop by for tea? Pop in and tell you that you were a fine person, and then give you a piece of candy saying, 'Good lad, keep up the good fight?' No." He must have noticed that my eyes were wide with terror. With an exhale his demeanor returned to the man I was accustomed to, and his eyes were again kindly.

"Who are you?" I demanded. "How do you know all of this?"

"We know of the Divine because of two important, simple things, words and pictures. Nothing more and nothing less. Oh, there are some who have claimed that they have experienced God first hand—and how did we find out about that? Was it written down? Why yes—yes it was. Did we see an artist's rendering of the account? Why yes—yes we did. Does it prove anything? I'm afraid not. As you've said—now what was it? 'I believe that God is what we've made it to be, an ideal to strive for, a compass for our morality and a hope that lies out there to counter balance our fear of the unknown.' Well, said indeed. Thus far, that is all anyone truly knows, isn't it? Yet, no matter how devout a believer might be, no matter what they say, they still wonder. Wonder why they are alive—why they've been put here in existence to worship a Divine host of kings and queens—to believe that they are real entities. A king they cannot touch or see, much less, understand without a world full of error. Imaginings! Fictions! Their faith is based on what man has given them, poetry and paintings—art.

"You want proof that God exists?" A grin filled his face with joy, "I've been waiting for this opportunity for longer than I can tell you, Loche. I've rehearsed what I'm about to say a million times. And I do mean, *a million*." He took a step back and struck his dramatic pose. "Are you ready?"

Too astonished to reply, he gleaned that my answer was *yes*.

"You," pause. "Will," pause. "Soon," pause. "Find out." He grinned at me with complete satisfaction. I remained silent. "That is the proof. Let me explain. Your age is, what, thirty-seven?"

I nodded.

"And you have roughly fifty or more years to breathe in this inexplicable thing called, merely, Life? *Alya*? Inevitably you will pass away, to the *Orathom*, to the Dream. And then you will know. Not so long. Be patient. Yet, I am confident that you will find the answers you seek much sooner than you think. When I say you will soon find out, I mean that very soon you will see the world very differently. Very soon."

"But why now? If you have known all this time, and as you say, *the Enemy* has known, why didn't they intervene long ago?"

"Tricky question, but simple. There's been a war going on for quite some time. And you have been at the center, but you would have never known it. Why now? First, because of your meeting with Basil. The two of you together will move the foundations of all, and second, because Basil is reaching a peak in his craft. It is his work that has brought the winds of war with it. The Enemy has long known your location. They know much more about you than perhaps you know yourself. And they have been watching Basil, too."

His eyes then moved from me to the moon-filled window and began to recite verse—his own, I suspected.

"*There are only two,*
And they have always been.
The Alya.
And the Orathom.
The Life, and The Dream.

"You are the Poet and he is the Painter of the *Alya,* the Life."

The moon now filled the corners of the window. Its pale face blurred with ecliptic flares, and my vision was pulled toward the glow from the dark side of the room.

"*The Alya? The Orathom?* I don't understand." I asked, without tone.

Greenhame leaned toward me with his hair dangling in his eyes and his sculptured features completely relaxed, he replied, "The Life." Then he smiled with a wrinkle of his nose. His hazel eyes focused on mine. I struggled to return the gaze. He then turned away and looked back over his shoulder. I leaned to my right and saw my little son Edwin standing in the doorway. I rose to my feet moving toward him.

"Hey there, what are you doing up here? It's past your —"

"Who are you talking to, Dad?" he asked as his head raised up with my approach.

I lifted him into my arms and said, "Just a—just a visitor." Edwin didn't look at me, but instead looked up and focused on the ceiling. I looked up to see what had captured his attention and found nothing there. Lowering my eyes I found Greenhame gone. I took a startled step back and scanned the room. He had vanished. I thought I heard a gentle patter of footsteps on the roof above.

"A friend?" Edwin asked. His eyebrows wrinkled together in question.

I held my son a bit tighter and looked up to the ceiling. I couldn't answer him.

"Why are you stopping? Keep going." Julia says.

Marcus stares out the window. He struggles to track the speeding landscape.

"Doctor?"

Marcus finally turns. His eyes are cast downward and narrowed as if in the process of making a difficult decision. There is little he can do at this point, he thinks. He places a white fabric bookmark in the book and closes the cover while muttering to himself, "There's always two."

"Are you alright?"

The old man studies Julia's face—a face that seems to glow in spite of the dreadful weather outside. Her hair is pulled away from her face and it coils down over her shoulder. "Julia, how much do you love him?" he asks.

She holds her response until she has taken a very deep breath. "I've already told you. And I suppose the answer to that question you should know already." She gestures toward the book.

The doctor nods and sighs. "Can you tell me about the

last time you saw Loche? He mentions your last meeting in the book, but I would like to hear your side of the story." She squints her eyes. "Were the two of you intimate?"

Julia nods toward the journal, "Is that book censored?"

"No," Marcus says.

"Then you can believe what you've read," Julia says.

Marcus' smile broadens, but with a slight shadow, "Do you believe what you've heard already?"

Julia reaches for the key hanging at her breast. "If Loche wrote it," she says, "I believe it."

"Good." The old psychologist shifts in his seat and flips the journal open again. "Because if she doesn't believe there is no sense in going on is there?" Marcus mutters to himself. "If she didn't love him, she wouldn't be here, would she? Oh Marcus, what shall we do now?"

Julia snaps her eyes toward the doctor. "Do you always talk to yourself?"

Marcus does not appear to hear her. He says, "There are things that will change—"

Julia interrupts. "My life has already changed. It feels like my life began when I met him. I don't know of any other way to explain it."

"Julia, when I called you to help me find Loche it was because you seem to be the only one other than myself that he could trust. This journal told me that, but I'm afraid Loche wouldn't approve of my involving you in all of this." Rearden shakes his head, "But I couldn't do it alone. I'm too old for this sort of thing. There are a great many people looking for Loche right now, and I'm afraid we may be the only ones that are friendly."

"I've gathered that much," Julia says impatiently. "You seem to know why I want to find Loche—why do you want to find him?"

Rearden does not answer.

Julia's reply to his silence is both a question and a statement, "The existence of God?" she says. Rearden bows his head.

"No," he says. "I know the answer to that."

"What then?" Julia asks with eyes wide.

Rearden forces his weary voice to say, "I want to know if love is truly tragedy." The old man does not give Julia a chance to respond. Instead, he begins reading aloud again with slow, hoarse precision.

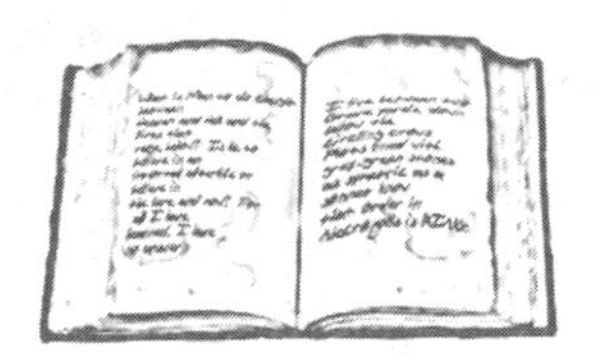

The next morning I watched Julia Iris lock her car and throw her heavy bag over her shoulder. It was a quarter to six, the air was brittle and the night had left an icy frost on the pavement. I thought of running to her and demanding the address of Basil, my *so called* brother—demanding that she give me his telephone number, at least. But then, I noticed something about Julia. Her purposeful stride and her elegant movement forced the immediacy of my chaotic circumstances into my periphery. I leaned closer to the windshield and watched her unlock the front door to The Floating Hope and step inside. Once the glass door closed behind her, she paused and stood motionless. She turned around. I could feel that she sensed a presence nearby. Julia spotted my car parked across the street. My stomach leapt into my throat. I turned the engine off, opened the door and called out, "Good morning," as casually as I could muster.

"Loche?" she said, as she opened the door. "I thought that was you. You gave me quite a chill."

"I'm sorry," I said, "I should have said hello when you drove in, but I—I'm waiting for Basil. Does he work this morning?"

"Yes," she said with a bright smile, "he'll be in at six." She gave a bit of a laugh and then corrected herself,

"Six thirty, I mean. Would you like to wait for him? I'll buy you a cup of coffee."

I nodded and followed her inside.

She sat me down at the counter—the very place we had met for the first time. I could smell the frying bacon and hash browns from the back kitchen. Julia immediately started a pot of coffee for me as two waitresses arrived at the front door. They took little notice of me as they began their preparation for the breakfast crowd.

"Loche," Julia said, "I'll be right back to join you for that cup of coffee. I have to drop some things off in my office."

I sat with my head bowed and traced the lines in the counter top tile with my index finger. After Greenhame had disappeared the night before, I took Edwin downstairs and tucked him into bed. Between waves of paranoia, the distraction of Basil, and Greenhame's invasion of my home, I spent the rest of the evening trying to understand just why Bethany left the stack of envelopes behind. Within each was a typed letter, some two and three pages long. They were love letters to her, but not a single one was signed. In fact, in a few of the letters, the author wrote that leaving a signature would be dangerous to both himself and to Bethany. I wondered just what he meant by *dangerous*. There was a lovely tone to the letters, compassionate, kind and genuine, but there was also a brooding obsession. A controlling passion. Something sinister just below the surface. I remembered the red envelope that Bethany had pulled out of her purse just as she was leaving. I wondered why she didn't leave that behind.

Helen found me before dawn with my hands flat against the window and my eyes wide with horror. The touch of her hand brought me back. When I turned to her she must have reflected my expression for her face suddenly turned from concern to terror and then amazement. "Loche," she said, "don't worry so much about Bethany Winship. It wasn't your fault." She reached to touch my cheeks and pull my face into the safety of her embrace, but I recoiled.

"Leave me be," I cried. "I need to be alone right now." My words were like icicles and I could see them stinging her. Her arms dropped to her side and her hands clenched into fists. "You'll never be alone," she stated. "Not as long as I live. Talk to me." Again, Helen's features twisted into something that I cannot describe. Her words were not pleading, nor were they sympathetic, they were orders.

I drew in a deep breath. "Helen, you know I can't discuss any of this with you. It is against the law."

"Law?" she cried. "I'm your wife! If something is tearing you apart no law will stop me from helping you."

"Don't," I yelled. "I can't. . ." The words of Greenhame and Basil combined with the tragedy of Beth Winship's suicide were colliding. My voice halted.

Helen relaxed and her face softened. "Talk to me," she said gently, "tell me about it." I fixed her with defiant eyes and remained silent.

"I'll find out sooner or later," she said.

"Leave me be, Helen," I commanded.

"I can't go on much longer with you like this." My wife turned and walked up the stairs. As I watched her ascend I felt an irrepressible desire to flee.

"Are you okay?" came Julia's voice from right beside me. "You look like something heavy is weighing on you."

The flash of my gold wedding band immediately filled my sight. I lazily looked up to see Julia standing before me. The mirror across from the counter told me that she was quite right. "Yes," I replied, "I'm fine."

"You don't sound so certain," she said. Her tone was comforting.

When I brought myself to look at her—her almond eyes and the fair slope of her cheek—I couldn't respond. I stared at her. I stared at her and forgot everything—Basil, William Greenhame, Beth, and Helen. There was something in her face that silenced all the voices in my head.

"I know we don't know each other at all, but I'm a good listener if you need one." The invitation was gentle and quiet. If there was ever a time that my loyalties strayed from my wife, it was that moment. As I think back on that early morning with Julia, just a few days ago, I knew that some line had been crossed—a crossing that I will never understand. Of all the recent chaos, her nearness was an anchor. A house of light on a rocky shore. I suddenly became aware that several seconds had passed. She still fixed me with a caring expression.

"N-no," I stammered looking down, "I appreciate you asking, Julia. I'm afraid that I can't."

She nodded sympathetically.

I forced my eyes to remain fixed on the steam of my coffee.

"Basil's not in trouble is he?"

I shook my head, "No."

"It would be much more dramatic if you said I *was* in trouble," came Basil's voice. He lurched into the seat beside Julia, and nodded to one of the waitresses for a cup of coffee. "Good morning," Basil said politely to Julia. "Hey, bro," he nodded to me. "I had a feeling you might be here. You had quite the day yesterday." He pulled the coffee mug to his lips, took a loud sip and sighed, "Ah, yes, coffee."

"Well, Loche tells me that the two of you need to talk," Julia reported.

"That we do. But I will be at my post at six thirty," he assured his boss, "Can you pretend you didn't see me until then?"

Julia stood and smiled, "I can turn the other way, Basil." Julia then placed her hand on my shoulder, "I hope that you'll stop by again, Loche. I'm sorry that you're having tough times."

"Thank you, Julia," I said without raising my eyes.

"Julia," Basil called as she walked away, "did you find a safe place for that package I brought over?"

"I did," she replied disappearing through the kitchen

doors. "Don't worry. It's safe."

Basil and I sat with a stool dividing us. Neither of us spoke. Basil reached into his pocket and producing a cigarette he flipped a Zippo lighter open to ignite it. He clicked it shut and placed it back into his jacket—a brown corduroy jacket from the 1970s. His shoulder length hair looked as if it hadn't been washed in a few days. He smelled of patchouli. I looked at him through the mirror on the other side of the counter. He glanced up into the mirror and smiled at me.

"This is really happening, isn't it?" I said.

"If you say so. You don't look so good," he said.

"A man named William Greenhame broke into my home last night," I said without hesitation. "He claims to have been watching us for quite some time. Do you know who he is?"

"I don't know him," Basil said. "Did he threaten you?"

"Not exactly."

Basil nodded taking another drag from his smoke. "Well," he said at length, "you know what this means, don't you?"

"What?" I asked.

"It looks like we are going to have to go."

"Go?" I exclaimed, "Go where? What are you talking about?"

"Listen, if this Green-*ham* or whatever his name is, is watching us, I expect it's because of what we possess, and he wants a piece. I can't allow that. What's more, I don't like being a pawn where my art is concerned." He stabbed his cigarette butt into the ashtray and turned toward me. "And if the son of a bitch is breaking into your house—Jesus, Loche!" He broke off and continued to stare at me. "Do you think the man will just go away?"

"What exactly do we possess?"

"You haven't discovered anything about your *gift* yet?" he asked incredulously.

I began to laugh. A laugh laced with madness.

Basil gave a sort of nod and furrowed his brow. "You've not noticed a Center?"

"A Center?" I asked.

"A pinhole, a window? Like an eye."

"Basil," I cried, "I have no idea what you are—"

"Yeah, yeah. I know." His face became serious and his eyes shadowed. "It's difficult to explain, and to be honest, I'm not completely sure what our gifts are all about. My dad, he knows more about it than I do. Or at least he has put some frame around it. Prepare yourself for a new world." He paused and looked around. "My dad is convinced that you and I have been given the ability to render the magic of the human condition, whatever that means. Not for anyone's eyes but for, well, for the gods. For the deathless souls that can no longer intervene in our lives. For the gods, Loche, for the gods. The big—deep—*heavy*."

My coffee was the most comforting sight so I dropped my eyes into its steam. "For the gods, you say? Oh, fine. What in the hell are you talking about Basil? This is too fantastic. This is the most ridiculous thing I've ever—"

"Yeah, It doesn't seem natural, does it? I care very little about who or what my talents are for. I paint for myself, and no one else. But, I guess there is something that we've been given that's not of this Earth. As I've said, my dad has his theories."

"And how did he come by this knowledge?"

Basil replied quietly, "He's seen one of my works."

"Oh," I said sarcastically, "*that explains it.*"

"Loche, you don't understand. But you will. You'll understand soon. Listen, we are brothers. If my father is right, we've been chosen to provide a very dangerous service. We've been commissioned to show *them* the passion of being human."

"Are you saying that these gods, as you call them, don't understand our plight as mortals?"

"I don't know. How could anyone know that? My dad thinks they can't feel like we do, emotionally I mean. They can't feel mortality. They're deities. Why do you think every mention of God or gods in our written language has something to do with them messing with us?"

I sighed, "So we could understand ourselves. We created them to make sense of the universe, and ourselves —"

"Yeah, yeah, right. Just stories to help us in the dark. I once thought that. But once you see one of my works your rational point of view won't mean shit—and you'll be forced to look again at these so called fairytales."

"Basil, you can't expect me to believe—"

He interrupted, "We think they want what we have. Take Greek mythology. Every story is filled with how this god or that god came down and did this or that—they couldn't stay away in those days. We have something they can never have—a limited time to live. And it is this limit that fascinates them—and what we do with the time. Nothing is more powerful than what we feel in our lifetimes. Eternity, infinity, immortality, everlasting life, all nothing compared to the beauty of our tragedies and the stuff we love. We're figuring that they want to *feel* like they're human without having to *be* human—wanting nothing more than to live within the ultimate creation—*within our lives*. We think they can do that through you and me. Through my paintings and your words—*our art*."

"Basil, deities were created by man in order to make sense of existence. Do you really believe all of this?" I asked.

"What does it matter what I believe? I'm an artist. I am my own artist. I create for the sake of creating. Whatever theories my dad and I come up with are really secondary to my craft. I don't care much about his ramblings. I do care about my work, though. That's all I really care about." Basil stood and repeated, as if trying to convince himself. "*All* I care about."

I looked up at him and was enveloped in his serious sentiment. "Let's hook up at my studio later and we can talk more. It should be slow here, so I'll be there around eleven-thirty-ish," he said. After a gentle touch on my shoulder he turned and walked into the back kitchen. He paused halfway through the door and turned his head to me, “And bring some of your writing.”

VI
A Collection of Answers

Upon entering Dr. Marcus Rearden's office I could sense that I was expected. It was nine o'clock in the morning. His secretary's usual, "Good morning, Dr. Newirth," didn't ring with its usual cheer. Over her shoulder I could see Rearden, bent over a table of file folders with one hand searching and the other balancing a cup of coffee. He turned when he heard my name. His face was grim.

"Loche," he said, "come with me."

I obeyed.

Marcus opened the door to his office and let me pass through first. "Sit," he said. I, again, obeyed. He didn't take his usual place behind the couch. Instead he placed a chair directly across from me and sat down. He looked tired.

"How long have you been treating Beth Winship?" His voice quaked. "Tell me what went wrong, Loche. How did this happen?"

My face told him that I was at a loss.

"Did you record all of your conversations?" he asked, and then leaned in, "did she ever mention suicide?"

"Not in so many words, but there was a tone that—"

He nodded his head, let out a freeing sigh and looked away. "Did you file a Suicide Assessment Report?"

"No, I didn't."

Rearden's eyes snapped back to me.

"I didn't think it was necessary," I explained. "There was no suicidal ideation prior to our last session, and her —"

"You should have filled out a form," interrupted Rearden. "You should have told someone!" I'd never seen

Rearden react in this way, angry and sad at the same time. "You should have shared this with me."

I squinted. "You, Marcus? Why?"

He waved his hand as if trying to erase his emotion. "I just," he stammered, "I mean—I wish I would have known. I hate seeing you go through this."

I let it go and agreed. "Yes, I should have filled out the forms, but she voiced it in a way that I didn't deem to be serious. My gut told me she would never cross that line." I paused and thought. "We discussed suicide once before—very early in our relationship."

"How did she respond?" Rearden asked gravely.

"She told me that she loved her family too much to follow through with such an act—but she had thought of suicide, yes. I sensed she didn't have it in her—her disposition didn't alarm me. I felt that her thoughts on the subject were normal. Several of my clients answer similarly to that question."

"You recorded all of this I suppose."

I nodded, "I record everything, Marcus. You know that."

Rearden wanted more information, but we both knew that legally I could only share so much.

"And did you implement a precautionary list?"

I shook my head. "I didn't."

"You did alert the family, at least?" Rearden's eyes pleaded.

"As I've said, Marcus, we spoke of suicide once before. There was no time to—"

The confused expression on Marcus' face stopped my voice. The old man shook his head in disbelief. "You? Neglecting the steps for this client's safety? She was calling for help. You know that! Loche, what were you thinking?"

Beth's voice suddenly echoed through my mind, "*Maybe I should stop thinking altogether—stop everything. Stop.*" I remembered thinking, *Stop what? Stop*. That word, that single word, didn't seem to be enough for me to take action. But I should have.

"No time?" Rearden continued, "A phone call to the family for a meeting takes but a few minutes. It could have saved her." Rearden drew his fingertips across his forehead and added darkly, "And you, too."

I knew what Rearden feared. When a client makes any reference to suicidal behavior it is the therapist's duty to take every necessary precaution. Failure to do so could lead to a malpractice suit, a revoked license and in the worst case, manslaughter charges.

"I was looking to heal her, Marcus," I said quietly. "I never felt as if her reference to suicide was a threat."

"That sort of response doesn't mean a goddamn thing right now, Loche."

"I know," I admitted. "I'm not defending myself, I'm just telling you the truth. I missed something along the way."

"I understand she had a scheduled appointment with you today," he ventured.

"Why, yes," I said. "But how did you know that?"

"Well, the paper for one. And your receptionist, Carol, as well. As soon as I read the paper I called and she shared with me how she learned the news and when she informed you. She's quite upset."

Marcus leaned toward his desk and pulled the *Daily Bee* newspaper out. "Have you seen this?" he asked, offering it to me.

I shook my head, eagerly unfolded the paper and held it up like a wall between Rearden and myself. The headline sent a tremor down my spine. *Family Mourns Drowned Mother.*

I quickly skimmed the article.

Bethany Leona Winship was found dead on the shore of Lake Pend Oreille late yesterday afternoon.
Suspected suicide. Still under investigation.
Husband Roger Winship blames tragedy on maltreatment.
Lawsuit pending.
Therapist, Dr. Loche Newirth.

"The family is making a hell of a lot of noise over this, Loche," Rearden grumbled. "They want it all, and it seems that they are going to use every possible weapon. Believe me, I know how this game works. Back in the day, during the height of my career—all of those terrible murders—there were ten people at least looking for someone to pay for each death. And the media will stir the pot and they'll get the general public whipped into a frenzy. I can't tell you how many major interviews I've given to attempt to repair the damage they can do to a community."

I couldn't wrench my eyes from the article. I read my name over and over. Rearden's finger hooked over the top of the paper and pulled gently down.

"So, Beth didn't mention anything about suicide when she saw you yesterday?" He asked quietly.

I shook my head. *Stop. Stop. Stop thinking altogether* —

He held my gaze. He finally came to some agreement within himself and he nodded. "Fine. We'll do what we can to figure this out. Is there anything else you can tell me?"

"She left behind a stack of letters. Fifteen letters."

"What?" Rearden hissed.

"I don't know if it was by accident or not."

Rearden stood suddenly, "What did they say? Who were they from?"

"They were unsigned, but they were clearly letters from someone she was having an affair with."

Rearden's face twisted with lurid disbelief. But as quickly as the look came, it faded. "So have you read them?"

I answered, "Yes, but I've said all that I should, Marc."

He nodded and glanced down at the newspaper article in my hand. "Have you spoken with your lawyer yet?"

"I have."

"Good," he said quietly.

I folded the paper slowly without looking at the doctor and rose from the couch. I crossed the room, stopping in front of his chessboard. Our game had been going on for quite some time. Pawns were scattered over the board and his royalty were preparing to surround my king.

Rearden sat staring out the window with eyes that aged by the second.

Five beautifully ornate frames displayed Rearden's academic and professional achievements, his Harvard diploma, along with his masters and doctorate. I caught my vague reflection in the glass and turned away.

"There is no going back after this," Rearden said.

"I could have prevented it," I replied.

He looked down at his hands and in a monotone, distant voice he mumbled, "It was *her* choice," He then turned toward me. "There's always two. A client told me once that he couldn't live without his wife, and it wasn't until his wife divorced him that he truly began to live. Strange business, fate. All of these what ifs." He lifted the framed portrait of his wife and held it up for me to see. He sighed. "Elanor. Isn't she lovely?" He turned the picture toward himself and stared at it. "Her greatest fear is dying before I do. She told me—now when was it? Just last night? Yes, it was last night. She said, 'Marcus Rearden, who is going to listen to you talk when I'm gone?'" He shook his head, "Can you imagine that?" he asked me. "Afraid that I won't have anyone to talk to. Then she said, in that cute way she says almost everything, 'You'll go crazy when I'm gone, sweetheart. You know it's me that keeps you sane.'" Marcus placed her picture back on the desk and angled it just so. "Crazy old bird," he said with sad, smiling eyes, "she doesn't know that I'm crazy already." Rearden looked back to me and said, "I guess what I'm getting at is this. We can't be responsible for another's thoughts." He turned back toward the window, his eyes darkened and he added, "Or another's deeds."

❧

Pine trees lined the path to Basil's front door. At the crest of the hill there was a view of sprawling subdivisions that cluttered the valley.

Basil had converted what was once a large storage shed into a passable living space, and it stood relatively secluded despite the large mansion below. The property owners were a wealthy California couple. Basil was the groundskeeper.

I paused at the door and inhaled the brisk noon air. My hand shook.

Before I could knock, the door latch rattled. "Wait a sec—" came Basil's voice from inside. "Just a second." The peephole in the center of the door darkened. I knew he was looking at me. Then, I heard rustling sounds and quick footsteps. The lock rattled again and the door opened. Basil stood in the doorway. He wore what I would later find to be called a thobe, a middle eastern garment that resembled a western dress-shirt, only instead of ending at the waistline the length stretched to the floor. The thobe was a deep grey, and the breast pocket held several wet paintbrushes. On his head sat a tilted, white felt top hat splattered and smeared with many bright and subtle colors. He looked down at my side and saw that I carried my brown leather document case. As he lifted his eyes back to mine the weight of the case in my grip seemed to double, as if it held gallons of water.

He didn't speak, but instead nodded for me to enter. Relaxing music played at a low volume. The smoke of incense and the fume of oil paint was in the air. A space heater cheerfully glowed beside the door. A window at the opposite end of the room had been cracked open to allow a faint breeze of cool air to drift in. He pointed to a vintage wooden dining chair to the right of the door and said, "Sit for a second, Loche." As he closed the door I saw two feet, low to the ground, jutting out from a small kitchen nook. The feet were framed inside of a wheelchair. "This is my father, Howard," Basil said. "Pop, this is Loche. I'll be right back."

Basil turned and grabbed hold of a ladder that led to a loft above the door. In a moment he had disappeared from view.

Howard rolled out from around the corner. He wore a blanket across his knees and a green and red flannel shirt buttoned tightly at the collar. I nodded politely, and he nodded back. His complexion was frail and weathered, and the lines along his cheeks and crows feet framing his eyes told me that he had spent a good deal of his life laughing.

"Good morning," I said. Howard nodded again, but remained silent. The old man held a newspaper opened to the article that Rearden had just shown me. Uncomfortable, I moved to the chair Basil had pointed to, sat down and placed my case between my feet. I could feel the old man's gaze follow my movement. Ignoring his stare I looked around the room.

Five wood easels stood near the center of the room in a circle. The paintings faced inward, but they were all covered in black fabric. There was another shrouded easel backed into the far corner. Three rolling tables crowded with paints, brushes and other painting supplies were beside the works in progress. A substantial collection of records and compact discs, a stereo, three work tables, two freestanding shelves packed with books, microwave oven, a mini refrigerator, a few articles of clothing, five bright floor lamps, a couple of rickety chairs, his frame pack, and all of his painting supplies were packed within the space. Beneath one of his long tables was a pillow and a few Earth colored wool blankets. The studio was certainly being used for everywhere I looked was clutter.

I could still hear Basil rummaging above. It sounded as if he was searching for something.

"Do you like music?" Basil called.

"Yes," I replied.

"Why don't you choose something," he suggested. "Feel free."

I looked at the stereo. "No, thanks," I said politely.

"Come on, Loche," he insisted, "let's switch it up. We

need something bigger than *Yes* right now."

I stood up and reluctantly approached the stereo. The volume was low. I lifted the needle off of the vinyl and slid the record back into its jacket. I then scanned the impressive collection. Very few of the names were familiar.

"Well, if you're not going to play anything, I'll choose for you," Basil said, still hidden from view. "How about some *Wagner*?"

"Richard Wagner?" I asked. "Where will I find that?"

"Under *W*," he said.

I scanned the collection again. All the CDs and albums were in alphabetical order, like my own music collection and books at home. I smiled and thought, *Well, we have* that *in common*. When I found Richard Wagner I noticed there were several records. "Which one?" I called.

"No need to yell," Basil said, standing beside me.

He pulled the LP *Das Rheingold* from the shelf and placed it upon the turntable. "I love this record," he said looking at me. "And its probably the best soundtrack to what you're about to see. Either this or Red Fang's *Prehistoric Dog.*"

Basil twisted the volume knob to a moderate level. The needle crackled on the vinyl, then there was a low drone of bass. Haunting. Slowly, soft horns began to weave the texture of a chord. He then looked at me and said, "Come and check this out."

He took me by the arm and turned me around. Upon the easel in the corner of the flat a shrouded rectangular form had been set up. Placed before the monolithic shroud was a folding chair.

"Please," he said, "sit right there."

I picked up my leather bag and moved to the seat.

He pulled another chair beside mine and we both stared at the shroud. Wagner's prelude was still lilting and rising. Howard wheeled his chair across the cluttered room and stopped to the right of the easel. He rotated himself into a position where he could face Basil and me, making a conscious effort to keep his back to the black shroud. A smile drifted slowly to his lips.

"Hello, Loche," Howard said quietly.

The sound of his voice startled me and I looked at Basil. Basil faced his father with a quiet understanding.

"Look at me, my boy," the old man said. He grinned at me. A pleasant smile that reminded me of Dickens' old Ebenezer Scrooge on Christmas Day. I suddenly felt at ease. "You are awfully quiet for a wordsmith," he said. "Have you anything to say concerning what you are about to see?"

I opened my mouth to answer, but no words came.

"You still have no idea, do you?" Howard clapped his hands on his dead knees and laughed. "Of course not!" he cried. He threw his hands in the air and spoke as if I wasn't present. "A perfect life, married, has a child, beautiful home, lucrative profession all bound by a chain of orderly conduct. A man who has studied his entire life to help the mentally troubled and yet has no inkling of what real trouble is. By the book—that defines Dr. Loche Newirth. Even with all the current anomalies, newly found brother, mysterious eyes watching him—the death of a client—" He broke off and looked down at the newspaper folded over his legs. "You seem to be controlling this chaos quite well," he muttered to himself. "You are living a life of fear. Afraid to really live—you —"

When I interrupted, the old man's eyes grew very wide. My voice was raised, "I didn't come here to be lectured. Yes, you are correct, I have much to consider. Many things have happened all at once and I'm having some difficulty assessing the situation, but I'll get to the bottom of all of this. I came here to see a painting—a painting that is *purported* to prove that we are brothers. I have searched through what few records I have of my childhood, and I found nothing that points to having a brother. All I've heard are wild claims, dreams and theories, but I am here to find out if proof exists." I suddenly noticed that my voice was raised, and I felt Basil's hand on my shoulder. When I turned to him his face said, *Easy, Loche, take it easy*. I sighed heavily and apologized. "I'm sorry," I said, "I'm very tired."

"I see that you're beginning to crack, after all," Howard said.

His arms rolled his chair a few feet out into the middle of the room and he spun slowly back toward me and stopped. "Some years ago I met with a terrible accident. Coming home from work early one day I entered Basil's bedroom looking for a pair of pliers that had disappeared from my workbench. After glancing about the room I noticed a black cloth covering my young son's desk. Looking at it my curiosity got the better of me. Without considering what might lay beneath the black shroud I lifted a corner only to discover that Basil had been painting. Removing the shroud completely, I beheld the entire piece." Howard frowned. His face held the expression as his voice fell to an earnest whisper. "It flashed upon my naked eye. In an instant, I was unconscious and lying like a crushed, twitching insect on the floor—the entire universe, the infinite speed of time, the sight of eternity charged through my brain. My life changed forever." He glared at his motionless legs. His hands knuckled the blanket.

"Basil found me lying on his bedroom floor that afternoon. He screamed for me to answer. I only moaned, a terrible and wretched bellow of pain. The shroud had been removed from his table and Basil suddenly knew that his instinctual precautions were now foiled. He had always hidden his work. He was never sure why. Certainly, the power of his art he could feel, but not to such a degree—not in the way I felt it. He feared that his art was dangerous to others—his fears had now come to a bitter reality. I was proof. I had looked into his work and witnessed that which only a god could discern and feel. My body was employed in the whole, the center, the godhead, for a fraction of an instant." The old man loosed his grip on the blanket and brought his hands together gently in his lap.

"Doctors guessed. They diagnosed psycho-trauma, a

stroke, diabetic seizure, schizophrenia, manic depression —bullshit, and yet, all of them matched my state. I spent my first few nights at the hospital in a coma. During that time, I lost the use of my legs.

"Several months were spent in *the bin*—a psych ward, that is—after I woke. The coma had left its wretched hands strangling my voice and my reason. Basil scarcely left my side, anguished at what he still to this day claims is his fault." Howard looked at Basil and reached out to touch his face. "But we've been through all that," he smiled.

"Then, one evening in May, Basil made a connection with me. He brought a painting when he came to see me at the hospital. He asked for permission to visit me alone."

"No," Basil interrupted, "I brought John Whitely with me."

"Yes, yes," Howard agreed, "But I don't remember him being there. Basil propped up on the bed a painting he'd been toiling over for the last month and called to me. 'Pop. Pop. Look up here.' Basil pointed. It was a portrait of me. My pupils immediately dilated, and I swooned sleepily."

Howard fell silent as Basil picked up the story, "It was like a thread—or a spider's silk—a thin line of light shot out of the Center of the painting. It went directly for his right eye. It was fast. If you blinked you would have missed it. There was a bright flash and this weird sense of fear—like you were being watched or observed. Then the light quickly funneled back through the *Center*. Howard looked at his legs and then at me, blinking his eyes. John stood behind the painting and witnessed the whole thing. He nearly fainted."

"I slowly made progress from that day," Howard said, "by July I had the strength to return home. But I will never regain the use of my legs. I still suffer from the experience—nightmares and bouts with a horrible fear. I often say of myself, *I'm nutty as a shit-house rat*," he chuckled darkly. "But I have been laughing more and more these days."

"Like the old days," Basil agreed.

As I listened and observed the two, I noted a genuine and close bond. Their connection was familiar in some way, and I found that my wonted diagnostic mind was not fully present. I was captured by their chemistry and harmony. Their caring. But the story was too vague to grasp—too many holes. I wasn't believing it.

Howard went on to tell me how he tried to console his son, and went to great lengths to take the blame of the accident away from him. After all, it was Basil that had saved him. Even so, Basil's anguish had never faded. Guilt coursed through his heart every time he put one foot before the other. He wished to give legs back to his father, and if he had the power to trade his legs for his father's wheelchair, he would have accepted it as a blessing. Howard wouldn't have it, and as the years passed he struggled to turn Basil's guilt toward something much more important: Basil's meaning and the reason for his paintings.

Howard couldn't describe his experience within the Center to anyone save Basil, he told me. But even when attempting to communicate it to Basil, he fell short, and often his words trailed off to a distant, horrified stare. He had come to terms with a very important issue, however. Basil had a power not of this Earth, and Howard did all he could to assist Basil with its grave repercussions. He called it a gift, occasionally a curse. The two spent many evenings in Howard's study trying to gather answers. There had to be some reason for Basil's existence. A reason that could only be stabbed at in a vast, pitch-black universe.

Basil had a purpose. Howard was sure of that. "Some metaphysical purpose. He is the icon for a new spiritual phenomenon. I have spent endless hours researching the connection of mortality and eternal life. Infinity. Mathematics. The delicate line between science and spirituality. Between magic and technology. Myth and fact." *Nutty as a shit-house rat*, I thought, and he has the research to prove it.

"So now you are to see all of this for yourself," Howard said to me.

I suddenly felt a chill crawl through my body. "What makes you so sure that I won't have an experience like yours?" I asked Howard. He could read the impatience in my voice.

He shook his head and replied as a confident father, "You won't. I have no doubt. You are Basil's brother."

"Why are you so sure that I am his brother?"

"For a couple of reasons," Howard said. "First, I recall, long ago, your real mother had spoken of you. Well, not your name, but she said that Basil had a brother. After some investigation, you are the one. Most importantly, I think, is Basil's dream."

"A dream?" I gasped. "A dream is evidence that we are truly brothers?"

Howard's expression was empathetic. "Yes, seems illogical, right? Though, I've come to trust in dreams more and more these days. Especially Basil's dreams."

"You have the same talent, the same blood," Basil answered. "You will understand."

"You keep saying. . ." I said.

Howard reached to Basil's hand and squeezed it. Basil grasped the edge of the fabric.

"I-I-I think you're ready," he stammered. "Other than to help p-p-pop, you're the f-f-first to see m-m-m-my painting. T-t-tell me what you th-th-th-think." Basil's hand tore the shroud away from the frame and I nonchalantly looked into the work.

It was a rendering of me. A portrait in oil. The expression I'd seen on my face many times in mirrors—calm, thoughtful and careful. There was some tragedy in the eyes. The background was a wash of muted orange and grey. The image was loose, painterly, composed of simple, accurate strokes. I shook my head, amazed. Then, I blinked.

A small flicker of light caught my eye. First it looked as if a flake of glitter was pressed into the portrait's painted right pupil. I thought to check the other eye for symmetry, but I couldn't move my gaze from the spark that had already captured me. The glitter then multiplied and seemed to spiral outward. Gold and silver-blue streams of light gathered and pulsed, forming the rim of some deep abyss. I felt my hands clamp down on my knees as I gazed into a framed, pupil black chasm. All balance, all reason, all meaning—forgotten. The light spread beyond the borders of the frame. Then eclipsed, it became an enormous pitch black circle, that was unimaginably deep, from the rim fired lines of color, stretching out in all directions, until my periphery filled with the unfathomable gulf.

I could still feel the heat in the room. I could smell the incense and the fumes of wet paint. A hair thin line of silky light —*The Silk*—shot from the Center to meet my gaze. The music was now reaching its climax. A mesmerizing drone of sound reaching toward a higher, loftier dynamic. Then the Center captured me.

Silence.

Flash.

Gone.

I could no longer feel my body. The abyss pulled my sight in or down, I wasn't sure which. A wide grey blur was growing below. The larger it became the more I could detect features that were familiar. It was water. A wide, flat body of grey and black water, raging. A light mist laced over the waves. The horror, I thought. I will drown.

Just as I thought my vision would plunge into the dark liquid, I stopped, suspended above and hovering up and down over each crest, nearly eye level to the raging waves. Silence.

A hand shot out of the froth. A young hand. It grasped for some hold in the air that didn't exist. Then, the face of a young boy appeared with his mouth agape, struggling for breath, drowning. I forced my sight to find my body.

There was nothing but the foam and spray of violent water.

Then, sound. Water thrashing.

The face surfaced again, struggled, coughed and gurgled, then disappeared below. I watched helplessly. When he emerged again his eyes were wide and filled with terror. His skin gleamed a sickly pale blue. He let out a hoarse, fractured scream. A scream that echoed across the silent void.

Then, he saw me.

His hand reached out, and his eyes were pleading. I could do nothing. The helplessness was maddening. With a final desperate cry, the face and the pleading reach sunk below the bleak surface. Silence.

My sight flitted across the rolling water, searching. I was now closer to the water than before. I must have the ability to move, I thought, I must go in for him. I forced my view down. The water was so close that all before me was both a dark wall of moving black and a glazed view of what lay beneath. I saw, like blinks from a dream, the sinking youth. My courage failed. I could not enter the water. Instead, howling words came to my mind. The words came but without voice. Silence.

I should have been seeing tears blur my vision. There were none, though my entire being cried out an anguish immeasurable. I could do nothing to aid the boy. A few moments passed.

A voice came, soundlessly.

—I could swim, but something froze my limbs. I could not move. Why did you not come in for me?

I whirled around to see the boy hovering above the water. A young boy of nine or ten. His naked skin was a blur of pale moonlit blue. His face was calm and his voice like song.

I struggled to answer, but I could make no sound.

—I couldn't move, my mind cried

—Is that true? the boy asked.

It wasn't true, I thought.

—You are afraid, the boy said.

—I am. The water—I couldn't reach you to help, I thought.

The boy smiled peacefully.

–You will find that you cannot help here, nor can you help outside the Center. It is forbidden. Some must *drown. Some must suffer, but the trying is the passion, he said.*

The glistening body swiftly slipped down into the waves. The water calmed. The dark surface shimmered and then stilled. A black mirror.

Suddenly, I could feel my body. My feet felt wet and chilled. I looked down to see myself standing on the water. I turned around to see a chair beside me. Taking an uneasy step toward it I found that the liquid surface held my weight. I moved to the chair and lowered myself onto it.

The boy's head appeared in the water below me.

—What are you doing here? he asked.

—I don't know, I replied.

The boy fixed me with eyes that swirled like glitter in a jar, and then he drifted behind me.

—You've come in through the Center, and yet, you are still able to see. . . and stay. The boy hovered close to the side of my face.

—You are the subject of the Center, are you not? You are the Poet.

—I don't know what I am, I replied.

—Speak to me. Make me feel your words, Poet.

—I don't know what you mean, I confessed.

His eyes flashed as if in understanding.

—You haven't the talent, yet. You will. You will make life. You will write the doors, open them, close them, for all of us. Within your story, so it shall be without. You will create within the Creation. But not yet. The day will come. The Eye will find you, and you will see how it sees, what it sees.

—Who are you? I asked.

The boy circled around behind me and appeared to my right.

—I am a Watcher. One of the many Watchers. I come

here to feel the Creation.

—Whose Creation?

The boy's answer was a smile.

—Learn your world for us, he whispered. Learn your talent and, we will ever arrive to witness, for the love of man. So we can feel what we cannot become. But now you must go. Go, Poet. Go back.

I blinked.

Not a moment had passed. The black fabric that Basil had pulled from the frame fluttered, still in motion. I could see it waving like an underwater hand in the corner of my eye. As quickly as he had pulled the shroud from the painting, he replaced it. I raised my hands to my face and lowered my head.

Howard touched my shoulder. The old man gently called my name, "Loche? Are you alright, Loche?" I drew a deep breath and let it out slowly. I uncovered my face. I was still seated on a chair in the sweet smelling smoke of the flat. I looked up to see Basil. He stood beside the shrouded portrait with a stare of concern.

When I found my voice, I was only able to say one word, "Brother."

Basil's eyes smiled.

Howard and Basil hung on every syllable that slowly spilled from my lips. “It is truly beyond words. Beyond words. How could I possibly describe the emotion of—of knowing?” I told them of the young boy and the black void of water. Bits and pieces of the experience were too amazing and far beyond the ability of language to articulate. What had happened? Why had all of my beliefs been based on what I could conceive as rational? Suddenly, I could feel the universe and the hope of my very soul swirling together through a wondrous, gleaming *answer*. There is a life beyond this life, and I was there, if only for a second.

What now would I do? What now could detain me from using this knowledge to help my clients—my fellow man? How wonderful and terrifying my existence had become. There is more than this. . .more than life and death. “You sure you’re okay?” Basil asked.

I looked at him. “I don’t know if *okay* is the right word. This is really happening, isn’t it? I mean, every fiber in my rational mind wants to discount—not believe—that I was just in the presence of—of a god. This is really happening.”

Howard said, “For me it was like looking directly into the summer sun. It was overwhelming. The second painting, the one that brought me back, I saw nothing but myself healing, restoring. It was as if Basil managed to place a kind of filter over the Center to keep my mind from exploding.”

“I suppose that’s what I did,” Basil said. “It’s hard for

me to tell." He turned to me, "I think I know what you're talking about, Loche. I sense a kind of ominous audience behind the paintings, but I don't see them. Much less have conversations with them."

"The boy, or whatever it was, told me that they come to look in on man—to feel what it is like to be human. Somehow you're making windows for them to see through." I turned to Howard, "Are you telling me that I have the same sort of power that Basil possesses?"

The two smiled as they looked down to the leather case between my feet. "Yes," Howard agreed. "With words."

"My work is in no way comparable to Basil's. Absolutely not," I stated.

"You wouldn't know," Basil said. "You wouldn't be able to feel anything other than the desire to write and the desire to keep it away from others. As I've said, I can't feel the power of my work the same way you did. All I know is that I created a portrait of my brother, Loche, and paid an incredible amount of attention to the Center."

"The right pupil?" I asked.

Basil's hands flew up to his face, and he covered his eyes. When he removed them tears moistened his cheeks and they made his smile shine. "Yes, the right pupil." He then began to shake his head and wipe the tears away. "Sorry. It's just that I don't get the opportunity to talk with anyone about my paintings other than Howard. All my life I've kept them hidden. All of my life—I couldn't share what makes my life worth living. The accident with Howard had me convinced that I could never share my work. And here you are, seeing it. You must understand that this is hard for me to explain."

"I think, like Basil, you wouldn't be able to detect your own work's super-nature," Howard ventured. "Your writing to you is merely your writing. Nothing more than your life's work, sure, but it will become something magnificent." He asked carefully, "Has anyone ever read your work?"

"My wife has read some, but not all—and," a chill

plinked down my spine, "William Greenhame. A client of mine. He broke into my office, and I would guess that he's read everything."

"Who is William Greenhame?" Howard asked.

"I believe he's the one that has been watching Basil and me," I answered.

"Is he dangerous?"

"Well, I—"

"One thing at a time," Howard interrupted. "First tell us about your wife. You say that she's read your work."

"Yes," I said. "But not all of—"

"And nothing strange or out of the ordinary has happened?" Howard shrugged.

"No. Nothing."

Howard looked at Basil. "That is curious. And you say that this William Greenhame has—"

"Yes," I said.

"He is a client of yours? Is he mad?"

"I have diagnosed him with several disorders. But what plagues me is all that he knows about Basil and myself. He knows too much. If he's broken into my home, I can only expect that he's been here, as well." I could feel my throbbing head. All that had happened in the last fifteen minutes would take a considerable time to digest.

"Well, I doubt he's seen my paintings." Basil growled, suddenly angry. "If he had, I think I would have discovered him on the floor, twitching and crying out—or dead, maybe. Besides, I make sure my stuff is always locked up and covered—"

"You have no idea," I said. "None whatsoever concerning my precautions. My work is securely hidden away, and only I can access it. It seems to me, Basil, that a person could enter your studio when you are away and lift one of your shrouds with ease." Basil glanced around at the studio. "William Greenhame has foiled *my* precautions," I said.

"I'd know if someone broke in," Basil pursued, "and there is no evidence of—"

"No," I stopped him. "I detected no forced entry,

nothing. It was as if he just materialized in the room."

Howard raised his hand and silenced us. "I see you have brought some of your work, Loche."

Inodded.

"Will you allow Basil to see some of it?"

"Yes," I said, still with a slight tinge of hesitancy. "Yes. Of course."

I lifted the case onto my knees and pulled from it a single sheet of paper. It felt strangely heavy in my hand. Lines of branch-like letters sliced across the page. Basil took hold of the paper and lifted it close to his face. He turned the paper upside down, scanning it from top to bottom, turned it again and gave it a puzzled expression.

"Aren't you going to read it?" I asked.

His eyes rolled up to me from behind the paper then dropped back down still studying. "Nope," he answered.

Howard watched Basil closely. "What do you see?"

"A poem on a piece of paper," Basil answered.

Basil's eyes scanned across the page. Howard and I watched for any out of the ordinary expression to cross his face.

"Read it," Howard said.

"What the hell?" Julia cries, her eyes frozen to the rearview mirror. "Where did *you* come from?"

Rearden closes the book and looks over his shoulder. A grey sedan is following close.

"Not good," the old man mutters. But as he turns forward the windshield fills with another car, parked in the roadway, blocking their route.

"Julia!"

Julia's eyes snap from the mirror to the car ahead and she reacts. She is going too fast. With her hands clasping the wheel and horror-wide eyes she tries to maneuver. The car, now freely sliding, begins to spin to the right. Rearden drops the journal and braces his feet against the floor. The deafening crunch of impacting metal bangs through the vehicle.

Rearden opens his eyes and feels his limbs tingling. The vehicles are mashed together like two aluminum cans. He looks to Julia. Her body is slumped against the driver's side window.

"Are you okay?" She is unconscious. "Julia," Rearden yells, "are you okay?"

He leans his body across the front seat and reaches for her. No movement—a smear of red is streaked across the driver's window.

"Jesus!" Rearden feels for signs of life. He feels the dull throb of her heartbeat in her wrist. He scans the scene. Idling a few feet behind is the grey sedan. The driver's door opens, one man steps out and moves steadily toward the crash. Is there only one*?*

Rearden steadies himself and rolls his window down. The man approaches and stoops. In the rearview mirror there is a blur of another man positioning himself just slightly out of Rearden's sight. They are both dressed in dark overcoats.

"Are you the police?" Rearden asks, his voice shaky.

The man blinks and a hidden smile crosses his face. "Yes. Detectives," he says. "Are you Dr. Marcus Rearden?"

"No," Marcus says, "never heard of him."

"May I see some identification?"

Rearden replies quickly, "My friend is injured, help me—"

"Some identification, please," the man repeats reaching into his coat, letting his hand rest there.

A flash of anger lights in Rearden's eyes. *Detectives, my ass.* "How about you show me some identification first, young man," he growls.

Their well-dressed and sharpened features are strangely out of place, Rearden thinks. They carry a kind of European posture, too stylish to be detectives from Sandpoint, Idaho. The man's lips pinch into a smile. A mocking smile. "Very well," he says. He stands up straight and exchanges a dubious look with his partner—a look that to Rearden says, *Harmless, scared old man. Let's get on with this.* From his coat comes a gleam of black metal, and he lowers the weapon to his side.

With a sigh he leans back down and starts, "Dr. Rearden will you please step out of the—" but he is met with a snub-nosed revolver pointed directly between his eyes.

"Fuck off," Rearden spits, firing a shot, slapping the man's head back in a pink mist—he quickly turns and aims over the back seat. Another shot pops from Rearden's gun crashing through the rear window and into the chest of the other man behind the car.

Rearden calmly opens his door, crouches down as best he can and moves to the back of the vehicle, listening intently. Sprawled in the snow and moaning for air, the second man struggles to crawl away, clawing with one hand. "Any more of your pals sneaking around out here, *detective?*" Rearden asks him. The moaning stops as Rearden fires twice into the man's head. The report echoes against the hills.

"Don't be too troubled, gentlemen," the old man says, "I'm sure this is just a delay for you both." Taking a final look around, and satisfied that there is no further threat, he points his focus upon his victims, studying the grisly wounds he has inflicted. The gore of it all is of no circumstance to him. He feels justified in what he has done. "It's us or them," he mutters, "and we won't be taken."

The fatal head wound is gruesome to behold, and Rearden thinks he sees a film of white foam forming around the hole. Looking closer he realizes the anomaly is merely blood gushing away from the white jagged fragments of skull.

There is a shuffling behind him. He spins his body around with the gun outstretched.

Julia's eyes are two wide pools of still dread, devouring the macabre picture. The two men lying in the blood-speckled ice—Rearden pawing at them—the gun still in his hand. Rearden reads a profound terror in her face, as if she did not recognize him. He suddenly sees himself through her eyes, and he wonders briefly if he would recognize himself. Julia collapses across the seats.

Julia begins to stir, mouthing eerie sobs as the nightmare lets go. When her eyes flip open Rearden reaches out and squeezes her shoulder. He becomes aware of the rush of white noise, and the chilly breeze, and he tells her, "The back window of the car is out, so I've been cranking up the heater. It's not too bad once you get used to it. Are you alright?"

She keeps her eyes on the road ahead. Rearden thinks she is considering the injuries she might sustain if she were to jump from the moving car.

"You had a tiny cut above your eyebrow. It isn't serious. It's stopped bleeding," he chats on. "Head wounds bleed like crazy. A lot of blood for such a tiny cut. Typical."

Rearden can sense her terror, but there is little he can do. Certainly, the journal has begun acclimatizing her to Loche's world and circumstance, but she is obviously unprepared for the full reality of it. Rearden is also terrified, but calm, and at present relieved that he had the good fortune of beating those men to the punch. *Us or them*, he repeats in his head.

And further, Rearden has experience with such things, not that he has ever shot anyone, but his younger eyes had seen terrible realities, and they are a daily meditation. It did not occur to him immediately that his hand was steady when he pulled the trigger, or that he felt nothing in particular about his actions. It was made up in his mind by his usual dictum, *there are always two, us or them*.

"I'm sorry you had to see that, but we had no choice.

Those men would have left us there and the journal—the painting—would be gone. And hope would be gone."

Rearden sees her fighting back tears. He imagines the snapshots that must be firing through her memory. Loche's cabin, the book, Basil dead. Art. Poetry. The Center. *Murder*. And to cap it all off, him staring up at her as he crouched over a dead body. She wants to run, he thinks, but knows her heart is screaming—screaming for Loche. If turning back means losing him, she will continue. Rearden sighs, confident that he, the crated painting in the trunk, and the journal are her only links to the man she loves. She is not going anywhere.

The smothering blanket of fear is now falling away from her. Hope is underneath it. Years of experience with watching clients have taught Rearden to see such things. He smiles at the next words from her lips. Words he thinks she never thought she would say and truly mean, "We've got to get off the road and get rid of the car," she says.

"Yes. I think we can make it to Coeur d'Alene—maybe an hour—the roads are pretty slick."

"I've got friends there," Julia says. "They'll put us up for the night."

Rearden shakes his head, "We're going to St. Thomas Church and Father John Whitely. I think a conversation with him might prove worthwhile," Rearden says.

The two fall silent. Wafts of warm air mingle with the bitter chill coming from the shattered back window. Julia stares down the oncoming white road, pulls her coat a little tighter and then grips the key around her neck. Rearden mutters softly to himself.

Slowly, Julia opens the journal to the place where Marcus had left off. She takes a deep breath. "Marcus," she says. "I'm scared."

"No, Julia, you're not scared. Not yet."

"Read it," Howard said.

Basil's eyes blinked. He scowled and focused harder. Nothing. Finally he said, "I like it," and looked to Howard.

"Nothing, son?"

"No."

I took the page from him. "What does this mean?"

"I'm not sure," was his reply.

Howard reached his hand out for the poem, but pulled back quickly seeing my reluctant expression. "No?" he said. "I thought that I'd give it a try. No? I'll wait." He rolled his wheelchair back a few feet and let out a heavy sigh. "It seems to me, Loche, that you've not yet mastered your talent."

"Apparently so," I said.

"I think you need to familiarize yourself with exactly what your importance is and who you are to be."

"Ah. That sounds simple," I huffed.

"Well, let me share some of my thoughts on the matter." From a countertop he pulled down a thick folder of documents. Flipping it open he rummaged through the pages. "Though my humble intimations on your importance might seem like egregious patchwork, I should admit that I have merely touched the tip of the proverbial iceberg. Since my accident I have developed an obsession for all those unanswerable questions, and because of my personal experience, I should say, *harrowing experience* with Basil's work, I find little else that interests me these days. I suppose all of those belief systems that I had once considered to be purely mythical and metaphorical, even contemptible to me at times (for I've never been a religious man), have suddenly become filled with a new reality. A super-reality, if you like—a delightful and long-reaching game of connect the dots. Though some of my theories might sound like grotesque pseudo-intellectual blather, I hope you won't repudiate the connections. There is a good chance that some of my notions might be propitious to my own want for clarity, and for that I apologize. But of the many caveats, there is one that should stand out before all the others, especially knowing what your arts have demonstrated. And that is *it can all be true."*

"What can all be true?" I asked.

Howard's smile was comforting somehow. "Think of every myth, every god, every deity you've ever heard of —Greek mythology, Norse, Egyptian, Sumerian and on and on, Christ, Cupid and Calliope. Think of their stories and how they continually meddle in the affairs of us mortals. Our beginnings, our reasons why, our hopes, all resting on the shoulders of gods. The stories that man has made to define our history, our existence. Stories that men have fought and died for—for faith—for ideology. And, I should add, there is not a shred of scientific proof that any of the stories are true. Not one shred."

He then shook his head and said with some incredulity, "Like most people, I am wonder-filled by the back and forth religious dialogue between what believers take literally versus what should be accepted as simple moral teaching. So often these days, leaders of the church, when challenged, will rightly rebuke the sadist and evil characteristics in their tomes and belief systems, but simultaneously purport that those characteristics are only seen as evil because they are taken out of context. In other words, some passages in these divinized compositions are to be taken metaphorically, not literally. Sometimes it's the other way around depending upon if the church is winning or losing the debate. It's all really a matter of convenience. Monstrous, really. But to challenge the church leaders further, I ask that we actually lean more and more into literal interpretation and see what comes of it. Hopefully, we can steer clear of as much evil as possible.

"So, for example, there is a whole lot of *supernatural* in religious writings. The Christian bible is no exception. Since you've some familiarity with the Christian version (which is really a retelling of older myths), we'll use it. For now it's the easiest route.

"Christian writings tell of the one God, of course, but they also speak of others. There *were*, or I should say there *are* other gods, but no longer on Earth (as far as we know). If you want the Old Testament's account there's that tired mention of *the Sons of God and the Daughters of men*—the *Nefilm*, in chapter six, during the days before the great flood. These Genesis passages have been overused by nearly every pseudo-scholar that has tried to prove the existence of everything from Atlantis to UFOs to God himself. However, given our circumstances, the *Nefilm* may now have a more concrete meaning. The word *Nefilm* is used throughout the writing and it can be translated as *giants* or as *men of renown.* But the surrounding passages are also wrapped in some rather saucy and interesting events that inevitably led to the smothering of all the inhabitants of the Earth by a great flood. Because of the Sons of God, the world was a rather dirty place, so it was washed clean of them."

I stared without expression at Howard, but I was listening.

"It can all be true. The same sorts of records can be found in nearly every faith-based religious text. Even the Ancient Greeks had accounts that play a part here. There has even been scientific evidence of a great deluge.

"The terms *god, men of renown, giants,* connote some interesting imagery for us these days. What or who exactly determines what a god is and then defines a being as such? Yet another one of those *mind mangling* questions. The Sumerians and the Egyptians depicted these gods as flesh and blood beings that were subject to third dimensional laws, but possessed *superhuman* powers with technology beyond comprehension. Can it be assumed that ancient civilizations were ruled by these beings? It's not difficult to imagine how men of ancient times could call these beings *gods,* or *Sons of God.* I suppose a flashlight could have been pretty mind boggling for those folks.

"So, in short, these were flesh and blood gods, setting up kingdoms on Earth and rising to god status—living and experiencing life alongside human beings. The ancient writings that we've interpreted as morality tales—well, let's entertain the notion that those tales were that, and more. In fact, let's say that there is truth in those fairy tales. How much of it is bullshit and how much of it is used to keep mankind under the yoke is still in question here. So why? What's the motivation? And, I guess, we should ask the biggie, w*hy are we here*?"

"Always a show stopper," I added.

"Ironic that you should say that," Howard joined.

"What do you mean?"

"We are the show. There's your *why.*" He said flatly. "All ancient texts stem from the Sumerian legends dating back some six thousand years. These myths tell of an administration of twelve gods that the Sumerians named Anunnaki, which translates as*, those who fell from the sky*. The ruler of these gods, Enlil, was credited with the Great Deluge. Another god named Ea was responsible for preserving mankind, and saving a select few by *strongly* suggesting that they build an ark."

"What does Noah's Ark have to do with Basil and me?" I asked, with as much patience as I could muster.

"We believe that the event had everything to do with you. Loche, truly, it is quite simple. You were born to give the gods access to the Earth again—through your art. Through your work they can again *feel* the passion of the human condition. Since the beginning of time these entities have been meddling with us until The One forbid them to come here."

I shook my head. "They are gods—why can't they do whatever it is they—"

"The flood," he said raising his hands. "Washing the Earth clean of the gods was The One's primary purpose.

No more interaction—no more mucking about in human affairs. Or, it is also possible that the darker powers, Satan, if you will, had no more takers for coming here. After all, how could they survive against The One's strength? After that, The One forbid these gods with interfering with the Creation."

"Satan?" I asked in disbelief.

He fixed me with a troubled and intense stare. "It can all be true. Iblis, Set, Mara. Pluto. Yes. There are many names. And, given the super-reality of what we are discussing here, I think you would do well to be wary as the days and months ahead unfold. One consistent theme in religious dogma that hasn't been overly wrapped in metaphor is the notion of this dark figure. The devout believe that it exists. You are stepping into the abode of the gods, and they have an enemy. And so do we. But the show must go on. And the show is real. It can all be true. All those stories, all those myths. What is real can be made up. What is made up can be real."

The ring of my cell phone startled me.

"Dr. Newirth here."

"Doctor! Thank goodness you answered," came Carol's voice. "Roger Winship is here to see you. He's very upset."

"I see." I looked at both Howard and Basil. "How long has he been there?"

"He's just arrived."

"I'll be there in a half hour," I said without emotion and hung up.

"Your office?" Basil asked.

"Yes."

Howard leaned forward, "Sorry to hear about your client, Mrs. Winship. It's been in the news."

I nodded and rose to leave.

"Difficult few days," he added.

Basil followed me to the door and I extended my hand. He took it and gave it a firm grip. "There's something strange about that client of yours, Beth," he said.

"What do you mean?"

He let go of my hand and dropped his gaze to the floor. "Something about it, I don't know—since I left you with those police officers at your office. I heard the conversation through the door. Anyway, I came back here and started a painting."

"Can the two of you come to my home this evening?" I asked.

Basil looked at his father, "I can, but the old guy here needs his rest. What time?"

"How does eight thirty sound?"

Basil nodded. "Sure."

"Loche," Howard called, rolling slowly from around the corner. "Do you understand what we've discussed today?"

My eyes searched his face and then Basil's. *No*, I thought, *not in a million years could I understand this*. "Everything ever written about religious deities is fact and not myth, an all powerful God put a fence around the Earth to keep these Sons of God, gods and whatever else from entering into our little day to day dramas—and Basil and I were born to write and paint for them so they have an outlet for their *stressful*, god-lives—so they can feel what it is like to be human. Is that about on target?"

Howard smiled. "Dead center."

Carol met me at the front doors. "He seems angry."

"Don't worry, Carol, it'll be fine."

Carol didn't seem to share my confidence.

I let my mind calm as I walked down the hall to my door.

He turned as I stepped in.

Roger's eyes glared. I couldn't muster a response nor could I hold his gaze. For a fraction of an instant I thought I saw the symmetry of the grid-like wallpaper behind him bend like tree limbs in the wind.

"It has been over twenty-four hours since her death, Dr. Newirth, and I wonder why I haven't heard a word from you?" He asked. His expression trembling on the verge of fury.

"Roger," I said, my voice even and steady. "I am sorry for your loss."

"My loss? My *loss*?" he yelled. "I want an explanation! You had to have seen this coming." The word *stop* plinked through my memory. *Maybe I should thinking altogether—stop everything. Stop*, she had said.

"Why haven't I heard a word from you? God damn it."

"Please," I said, "please calm down."

A voice from behind gave the answer, "He's had much to deal with, Mr. Winship, and I would assume that his attorney asked him to refrain from comment. I believe the best thing we can do right now, Roger, is mourn." Marcus Rearden entered, removing his coat. His voice was gentle, like a light through a shadow.

"And you are?" Roger asked sharply, stepping toward Rearden.

"I am Dr. Marcus Rearden." Marcus placed his hand upon Roger's shoulder and held it there. The cadence of his condolence was slow and gentle. "I am sorry about your wife."

A skilled listener seldom responds. Rearden was the best—especially over a drink. We sat across from each other at a pub just blocks from my office. Once we finished with Roger Winship, Rearden suggested we talk things over. "You look like you could use a drink," he had said.

I felt as if someone was watching me. Any one of those surrounding us in the pub could be watching us—listening in— and I felt it would be best to keep quiet the fantastic revelations of the last couple of days. I desperately wished that I could speak with Rearden about all of it in the same way I had communicated with the boy god—in a telepathic, nonverbal manner.

As I began the labor of telling the story since my return from the cabin at Priest Lake, I felt a sudden wave of hesitation. *He's not going to believe me*, I thought. I began with meeting Basil, and how he and Helen had once dated, and slowly progressed toward us as being brothers.

"My God," Rearden blurted, briefly drawn out of the pressing issue of Beth Winship. "You learned this just *yesterday*?"

I nodded solemnly.

"Did he have proof?" he asked plainly. "How do you know he's telling the truth?"

"I know," I said with resolve. The memory of my portrait staring back at me—a window into oblivion. "I have no official records, yet. But there are things that are undeniable—things that are beyond mere paperwork."

But how to explain Basil's art was not going to be easy without sounding completely mad. Especially to Rearden's ears. I explained that Basil was a portrait painter and that no one had ever seen his art.

"Why is that?" Rearden asked curiously.

Uncertain how to explain it, I lamely shook my head. "His work is dangerous."

"I see," Rearden nodded. I sensed a faint tone of condescension. "Dangerous how?"

The eyes of my mentor were studying me as I would study a client. It's no wonder that he practices his psychotherapy from behind, where a client can't see the concern on his face.

"This all seems like a dream," I said. "So much has happened." Rearden's expression was still observant. *Start with William Greenhame* an inner voice suggested. As I elaborated on Greenhame's claims to immortality, his breaking into my home and his ranting about my writing, the old doctor's nodding and squinting seemed to tell me that he was following the story with his usual feigned sympathy. At the mention of my writing Rearden tilted his head. He was not aware of my interest in stories and poetry. However, the further I went, the less he nodded. He lifted his gin and tonic to his lips more often as I labored on in the telling. It wasn't until I arrived at Basil's portrait that he stopped me with, "Wait a moment."

I paused, wanting to carry on the story. He held up one hand and said again, "Wait a moment."

I shook my head, "Marcus, I know this sounds—"

"Stressful?" he added.

"No, not stressful, I—"

"Loche," his smile was laced with mock sincerity, "You've been under a lot of stress since you returned from the lake. This tragic situation with Mrs. Winship is not easy to bear." He chose his next words carefully. "Maybe you should take some time off."

It hit me as if my body was thrown down a deep well into cutting dark waters. His voice trailed off and mingled with the countless conversations that surrounded us in the busy pub. Watching him speak I could only catch phrases, *suicide, relax, take some time to think things through, it will pass. . .* Dr. Marcus Rearden didn't believe me. *Nutty as a shit-house rat.*

He motioned to the barman for another drink and suddenly asked, "How long has Mrs. Winship been in your care?" It was asked with authority.

I shook my head with a puzzled expression. The gesture said, *You know we can't discuss that.*

Acknowledging me with a nod he added, "Come now, Loche. It's *me* you're talking to. I can help you." His tone rose slightly, as did the speed of his speech, "I'm not saying that these things that you're telling me aren't true, though we must consider another way—"

"Marc," I said looking at my watch and rising to my feet, "I've got to go."

Rearden stopped speaking and glanced up at me.

"Thanks for the drink," I said as genuinely as I could, "I sure needed it today. I'll be in touch."

The old man nodded, but kept silent, holding my eyes in his. I turned and walked away feeling angered and betrayed. Still, I was strangely relieved that I didn't elaborate upon the aspect of gods and their frighteningly real relationship with Basil and me. At the door I looked back to see my friend Marcus dialing a number on his cell phone. Worry had darkened his eyes.

Rearden leans over and takes a quick look at the page. "Yes," he says turning back to the road, "all of those things he writes there about Basil and William Greenhame, none of that happened. He was certainly acting strange that afternoon, and I was concerned about him. However, those things didn't come up. Everything else is accurate. But his recently found brother, and this *Greenhame*, supposed immortal client—no."

"I don't understand," Julia says.

"I don't either. I have my theories. After I read the book this morning, I figured that his written additions to our conversation were things that he had wanted to tell me, but somehow couldn't. A kind of subconscious plea. If Loche was having a mental break, such a withholding seems plausible. Writing what he was really thinking—for me to find later—is some token of hope that he knows he is in need of help, and that he trusts me. That's a comfort." Rearden broods and then says, "Or he's just making up stories to suit his delusion."

"Every exchange that he's written about between us is accurate," Julia states. "I remember every word, every second we've shared together."

Rearden weighs Julia's words carefully. "And Basil," he asks, "did you know they were brothers?"

"Basil told me."

Rearden turns to Julia and grins. "Good," he says. In his voice is a tone of relief.

"Do you think he kept quiet because he was being

watched?"

"Possibly. Though what I find curious and frighteningly intuitive is the way he wrote about how I would react. In fact, as I read it the first time, I found myself almost mouthing the responses that he wrote for me. Thinking the words before I read them. He knows me well. And he knows that I wouldn't likely accept his stories during such a traumatic time. Stranger still, it takes a lot of concentration for me to remember that conversation rightly. I drift from what really happened to what he wrote, and I have some difficulty remembering the truth from his fiction. Certainly, the matter of Bethany Winship has unhinged him," he says. "He's a possible suspect in this case—you know that, right?"

"I've been keeping up with the news, yes. But I don't believe it."

A shadow angles across Rearden's face. "You don't?" He feels his pulse quicken. He could see Beth Winship at the water's edge. A nightmarish sky above the frigid waters. *Beth had just left Loche's office. She went to swim. He told her to swim.* "Well, Julia, you are a comfort in all of this. Your company and association brings me a clearer focus. Because of you, Loche's writing convinces me of things beyond my wildest dreams. And you are, in the end, the key to my part in all of this."

Julia studies his gaunt face. There's something haunting there. He has spent his life studying horrifying crimes. *Rearden must suspect Loche of some wrong doing*, she thinks. How could he not? She shivers and draws her focus back to the book in her lap.

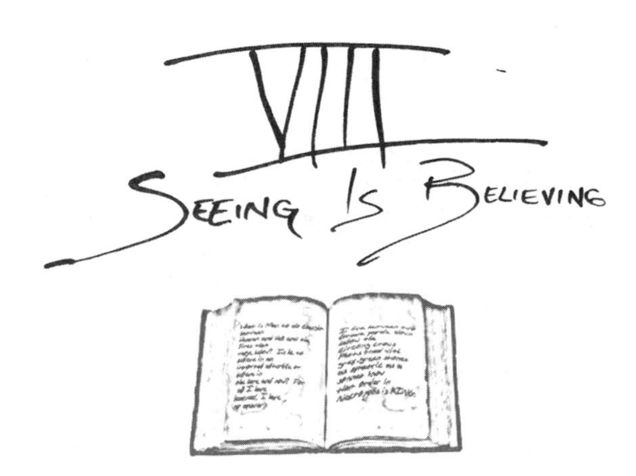

Daylight was fading and cold air was rushing up the valley. The drive home seemed shorter than it ever had. At each turn I saw the Center, the drowning god, Beth's tears, Basil's eyes, Rearden's disbelief—repeating over and over like waves slapping the shore. Arriving at my driveway these thoughts disappeared.

The front door to my home was wide open. I sprang toward the house and called out, "Helen! Edwin! Helen! Answer me."

Inside all was dark save one small desk light down our long hallway to the stairs. Clicking the light switch next to the door I found a horrifying sight. Chaos. Furniture was overturned, drawers were open and their contents littered across the living room floor. Lamps were toppled and broken. Hurrying down the hall toward the desk my eyes scanned the disorder.

Upon the desk was one of our home computers. The screen was a glowing, deep red, and in the center there were small blinking words, *Loche, click here.*

I glanced around the room and cried out again, "Helen, Edwin! Where are you?" Silence and a cold breeze from the open door was the only reply. I shivered.

The letters still flashed, *Loche, click here.*

Grabbing the mouse I moved the cursor over the link and clicked. The screen's window changed to black, then fading in was a blue sky. The scene descended slowly and peaks of buildings came into view. As the picture panned back I could see that the setting was Venice, Italy. Two long gondolas were slowly paddling toward the camera. Then a face moved into the frame from the left. A young man, probably in his twenties. He acknowledged me with a nod, looked to his right gesturing an affirmation, and then disappeared from the screen.

Then another face appeared. His eyes stared directly into mine, and he was smiling. Mid-fifties, I thought. Light brown and grey hair, thinning and combed back. He wore a brown coat and tie. An elegant looking gentleman. The smile on his lips slowly faded. He continued to stare into the lens, and into my face.

"Dr. Loche Newirth, greetings," he spoke finally in a thick Italian accent. "My name is Albion Ravistelle." His face turned away, and he gestured to the beautiful city behind him, "I am speaking to you from Venice, Italy, and as you can see, today is lovely." His gaze returned to the camera. "I am afraid your day may not be as beautiful, and for that we take some of the blame. My most sincere apologies for the manner in which you are receiving this message, but I assure you, it is for the best and for your safety." He paused as the camera pulled back. He seated himself on an iron bench beside the canal.

"I would first ask, Doctor, that you sit down in the seat that has been provided for you." He waited. Behind me was a chair. I lowered myself slowly onto it. He continued, "It is paramount that you listen very carefully and follow my instructions without fail. I am trusting that your years as a psychologist will prove useful in what I am about to tell you. Attempt to stay calm."

I opened my mouth to speak, but he raised his hand to halt me. "I'm afraid, Doctor, that we have disabled your microphone. We have done this to insure that you will indeed listen. You and I will speak together soon enough.

"Your wife and child are safe, and by safe I mean they are in our care." I felt a scream inside my head, but no sound from my lips. Panic crashed through my thoughts as my hands gripped the table before me. Tears stung my eyes. "Stay calm," Ravistelle reminded. The words kept me from flipping the table over and smashing the computerized face to shards.

"Again, Doctor, it is of the utmost importance that you focus and control your fear. If you do as I say, all will be well." My shaking hands wiped the tears away and I could hear a pained and enraged moan rise from out of my gut. *Control*, my mind demanded.

"You see, Dr. Newirth, in the last few days you have been introduced to a very important young man—a man that has come to mean a great deal to you, I'm sure." Albion looked up and over the lens and mused, "I wonder what that must be like—to discover that one has found a brother that he didn't know he had." He looked again at Loche, "Moreover, a brotherhood of unimaginable gifts. You must have had much to think about in the last forty-eight hours. Yes, indeed.

"But now, to the purpose. Your involvement with Mr. Basil Fenn is of great interest to us. We are, you might say, guardians of the greatest of human artistic endeavor. I represent a group of curators and a highly affluent aristocracy of art collectors that have been waiting for the right time to procure Basil's work. And yours as well, Dr. Newirth. It seems, however, that your talents have not yet reached their full potential, though, I might add," he gave a bit of a chuckle, "I do appreciate your attempts at verse, so far. But it is not quite *divine*. How do we know, you ask? Many of us have perused your poetry and I'm afraid we find it to be, how shall I say, not yet fully developed. Bland. Not all is lost, there are some lovely themes and thoughts, but it lacks the *silk* of your Brother's work.

"You'll find it missing from your office. We have taken your work away along with your family.

"Your brother's work, on the other hand, is something beyond our wildest dreams, to say the very least. It is his work that we are most interested in possessing. Unfortunately, Mr. Fenn keeps his work very well protected. No, not in the conventional sense by lock and key, but rather, it is protected by militant group of fellows that are terribly difficult to remove. You have met one of these men, Mr. William Greenhame. Doctor, I must warn you to take precautions against this man and his colleagues. We have attempted to communicate with Mr. Greenhame, but he has made it obvious to us that he is unwilling to cooperate. Thus, we have been forced to use *other* methods. Now, don't mistake me, Doctor, we are *not* kidnappers. I like to think of our involvement in this endeavor as a necessity to the rounding out of the collective human spirit. We have only the best intentions for the human condition—and, unfortunately, this can sometimes *seem* ugly. But always, things work out for the best. Always for the best."

"Why is this happening?" I yelled at the face in the monitor.

Albion paused and watched me. He appeared to revel in my hopelessness. I dropped my forehead down upon the desk.

"I am sorry, Loche. But do pay attention. William Greenhame and his *cohorts* were involved in the first assassination attempt in Moses Lake when you were quite young. The car accident was no *accident*. They felt that the gifts that you and Basil possess were too powerful to be a part of this Earth. They wanted you dead. Where they failed, we have succeeded. Not only by saving both of your lives, but also by protecting you so that your talents would bear fruit. We seek only to help you, but with Greenhame and his people involved yet again, the situation has become dire, and the world risks losing the both of you. Their intention is to seize and manipulate the work of your gifted brotherhood and use it to set up their own power structure and control us all. They wait only for you to find your muse. In short, Doctor, we have arranged for you to escape from the watchful eye of Greenhame and his schemes.

"A car awaits you at your office that will transport you and your brother Basil to a private plane. Basil's father, Howard, is currently en route to Venice, along with Helen and Edwin." Ravistelle paused and laced his fingers together. "I have been informed that Basil's paintings will be in our possession within the hour. The pilots will wait, and they will see to it that you arrive here safely, but you must hurry…" His face filled the screen. "The authorities, Loche, should not be contacted," he droned slowly, "they only confuse matters. Please keep this in mind for the sake of keeping those you love safe.

"I wish for you to comply. Here in Venice you will discover your worth—you will finally come home. We have built an entire world around you and your brother. Come home, Loche. Until we meet, I wish you safe travels." The screen went black.

"Loche!"

I spun around to see Basil, and someone I didn't recognize standing in the doorway. Their eyes reflected the confusion of the disheveled room. "What the fuck is this?" Basil cried.

"Who's with you?" I said standing up.

Basil stepped into the room and took in the view, "My friend, Father John Whitely." The man gestured a hello while scanning the chaos. He was dressed all in black. A clerical collar around his neck.

I turned back to the computer and grabbed the mouse attempting to replay Ravistelle's invitation. But the machine would not respond. Panic struck.

"What is it?" Basil demanded as he navigated his way toward me.

"Helen and Edwin are gone."

"What do you mean, gone?"

I didn't answer. Lifting my horror stricken eyes away from the monitor I saw a framed picture of my family shattered on the floor. "We've got to go."

Seconds later we were tearing across the dark

countryside back to the city. A cold rain was falling. Basil sat in the passenger seat of my car and Father Whitely sat behind him. The priest's eyes were wide with shock. Basil kept shaking his head in fear and disbelief as I shared the recent events. As I told him of Ravistelle's plot to take Howard, he locked his eyes on the road ahead and said nothing. Pain was in his face.

"When did you last see him?"

"I dropped him off at his house an hour ago."

Anger pulsed through my vision. "He's gone," I whispered.

"Why didn't they just come for us?" Basil asked. "I don't understand."

"Nor do I."

John Whitely sat in the back seat. "We should go to Basil's studio," he said.

"They want us to go to my office," I replied. "Ravistelle said there's a car waiting there to take us to a private plane."

Raindrops were glittering in the headlights like a meteor shower. "No," Basil said. "John's right. We've got to get to my studio, now! It's the paintings they really want—and if they get them, we might as well forget saving anyone."

I leaned harder on the accelerator.

We parked the car two blocks from the main house. As the three of us walked to the private gate sloping up to Basil's door we could see several shoe prints ahead of us in mud. Each set trailed off in different directions—over the yard, down the dripping fence line and through the gate. "Looks as if someone has been here," came John's hushed voice. I looked up the dark hill to see a single lamp shine through the studio windows and out into the gloom of the trees. No movement. Silence.

As I reached for the gate latch Basil nudged my arm, "Wait," he hissed. "This way." He limped off, hurrying as best he could down a trail along the fence line to the south of the property. A minute later Basil stopped and whispered, "Watch your step," and slowly staggered into the brush. He bent down, ducking underneath a gap in the broken fence. Once we were through he looked down searching for tracks. None.

We started up the hill on a narrow trail that was barely visible. We were twenty yards from the studio when a voice I knew well came from the left. "Do not move another step." The outlined shadow of a man stood leaning against a tree. He held a pistol. "Come, come, William Greenhame at your service," he said softly, prompting us to leave the trail and join him. "We wouldn't want the artists getting hurt, would we?"

Cautiously, we stepped behind the tree next to him. He held the gun pointed at us. Its black barrel was fixed with a silencer. "Not a good time to be creeping home, Mr. Basil Fenn."

Basil didn't answer, but looked at me. Before I could say a word William pointed to the studio, "Watch this."

More shadowy figures began to scramble through the tree line, each armed with what looked to be automatic weapons. They took siege positions around the flat.

William moved his hand to his throat and touched a small transmitter, "Samuel," he sighed. "Oh, Samuel. I see five poorly dressed robbers." A moment later he laughed, "Yes, I'm sure they are not salesmen." He looked amused as his eyes returned to us. "The *artists* have just joined me, plus one priest. May have to sit this one out." He listened and nodded, "Will do, out. It seems that a number of art fanatics are looking to pick through your collection, Mr. Fenn. Not to worry. They won't make it beyond the-"

A shrill whistle slashed the air and cracked splinters from the tree beside William's head. It came from behind. "Get down!" William hissed, quickly grasping both Basil and me, and shoving us down into the mud. As fast as the first shot, there came another. It cracked and splintered again, only this time it met its target, William. He slumped against the tree with his eyes wide open, blood rushing from a small piercing in his left cheek.

Above us, all hell broke loose. The five robbers began to scatter and fire in all directions. More figures appeared, dropping from the trees, vaulting down, flames spitting from their weapons. I saw one of the five men fall when Basil grabbed hold of me and pulled, "Let's get the fuck out of here!" he yelled. I felt a grasp on my ankle as I began to crawl away. It was Greenhame's hand. Reaching back I pried his death grip away while staring at his pale, dead eyes. *Why does my death delay*, I remembered him saying not a day ago. Then I heard myself whisper the phrase he had used, "*Ithic veli agtig*," as if I had known the language from childhood. "*Ithic veli agtig*, William," I said again as I turned to flee.

The three of us got to our feet and scrambled back down the trail. As we lurched through the broken fence, Basil lost his balance and cried out as he clasped his weak leg. John and I reached down to help him up when I felt something hard and cold jab into my ribs.

"Dr. Newirth. Don't you have a plane to catch?"

Revolvers were aimed at our backs as our captors marched us toward a white van, parked a block away. Basil's arm was around my shoulders. I aided his awkward stride. "A little faster, gentlemen." Basil caught my eyes and looked over at John Whitely. *How much does John know*, I wondered. Was he merely along for the ride only to be swept up by our dark unfolding fate? Was he interested in Basil's work? In divinity paintings? Was that it? Basil let out a sigh of pain and looked up to me again. *Let's get him out of here*, his eyes said.

Ravistelle needed *us* alive, that much I knew. These men wouldn't execute us, but John. . .

I let go and our two captors stopped. I positioned myself between the gunmen's pistols and John. With my back pressed against him I forced him to slowly step away, backward.

"Dr. Newirth," A steely barrel raised up. It gleamed in

the florescent street light. "Not recommended. Please stop."

"Or what?" I said, still pushing John back. "You'll shoot me? I don't think so." I noted a fearful tremor in the resolve of my words. To mask the shaky tone I added, "You've come too far for that."

"No," the other snarled, "I'll shoot him," and he placed his gun against Basil's temple.

John stopped me, "Wait," he cried.

"No, they won't," I told him. "They won't shoot us," and resumed pushing John away. There was another parked car along the street and some thick trees beyond that would allow John some cover. "Go! Now!" He turned and ducked behind the car and disappeared into the deeper shadows.

The first gunman started after him when the other called out, "Wait. Let him go. He's not what we came for." Once John was away I returned to Basil, still hunched down on the street. "Dig your confidence," he sighed as I lifted him back to his feet. "Glad you were right. Gun barrel and my skull—not a good combo."

"Yes," the second gunman scoffed, "we can't kill you. But there are other ways to make you behave." The side of his pistol crashed into the back of my head.

Later I would remember the cold, wet pavement against my cheek.

As I came to, a dream was ending. Vestiges of the dreamscape hung like a heavy fog in my mind. There was a rumble in my ears, gaining intensity like the rising wind and the raging sea together. Basil was there. He held a steel pick-axe and was chipping away at the back foundation of my home. My hands were tied and Helen was pacing to and fro in front of me saying, "Are you alright?" over and over again. I struggled to move and my eyes snapped open. I felt a sharp pain at the back of my head, and the left side of my face felt as if it was scorched.

"Are you alright?" Basil asked. He was seated next to me. His was in handcuffs. Struggling to sit up I could feel cold steel cuffs around my own wrists. Dizziness, nausea and fear intermingled.

"Where are we?"

"No idea." The drone of jet engines explained the roaring in my ears.

"What—what?" I struggled.

"What happened? Well, you've been out for close to two hours, and I've been sitting here in these plush leather seats waiting patiently for a drink. The dudes back there behind us need to brush up on their flight attendant etiquette." I glanced over my shoulder. One was sleeping, and the other casually read a newspaper. He noted that I was awake and nodded. I quickly turned and faced forward. Blood surged through my temples as I raised my bound hands and held my head.

"You alright?" Basil asked again.

"That's a good question," I said incredulously, "am I?"

"Well, from where I sit it looks like we are both fucked."

"This is really happening, isn't it?"

Basil gave me a weak smile, "That was a brave thing you did for my friend, John. I didn't think you had it in you—I mean, for you to risk your life for someone you've just met. You don't seem the hero-type."

I replayed the scene, felt again the surge of adrenaline and the disbelief that I actually did it, and I nodded. "Did he get away?"

"I think so."

Inhaling deeply I tried to make some sense of what had just happened. Despite the throbbing pain in my head I felt strangely awake and alert. The nausea was beginning to subside and was replaced with bursts of much needed serotonin. How my view of reality was shifting. The terrible violence at Basil's studio had changed my perspective on everything. Now Helen and Edwin have been kidnapped, two of my clients are dead, one suicide—one killed right before my eyes. I've been shot at, my personal belongings plundered, my work stolen. . . I clamped my eyes shut. How can this be happening?

"Isn't it strange? It doesn't seem real."

"What doesn't seem real?" I asked. "I assure you, Basil, this is real."

"Is it?" he asked. "I wonder. I can become so completely immersed in my work, in my thoughts, that I sometimes lose track of what's real, whatever the fuck that means. Since I've met you, I see the world totally different—a lot different. I truly have a reason to be. Maybe you've done that for me. You've got to understand, Loche, that I can create things that would make these men," he gestured to our captors, "cry for mercy in the first two seconds. Shit themselves, to be clearer. Things that would blow their minds, literally."

Watching him speak I thought of my portrait, and the pale blue god with swirling eyes, drowning.

"Problem is," he said with gravity, "not only would my work scramble their brains, it would scramble the brains of the entire world. The big deep heavy. I guess that having some sense of the big deep heavy makes everything else seem not so real, or at least, not so important."

For a brief moment, I saw Basil's silhouette against the dawn sky at Priest Lake. "The big deep heavy," I repeated. That phrase was now embedded in my memory.

"You had mentioned to Helen and me, the morning that we first met at the lake, something about John Whitely being interested in your art."

Basil nodded. "Yeah, John wanted me to meet with a Catholic Bishop, Father Alin. Remember, John was there when I took the painting to my father's hospital room. He watched the whole thing. He witnessed my father go from a coma to suddenly being able to speak. He's never seen my work himself, of course."

"Did you meet with Bishop Alin?" I asked.

"Yes, but only to win an argument with John. Ever

since John saw the my painting helped pop, he was freaked out about how it fits into his faith as a God-fearing Christian."

"Did Alin see your work?"

"Are you kidding? No! I wouldn't want to scramble that guy any more than he already is. No, we just discussed it. John did his best to describe what he had seen, I told him about what I do and the rest of the time was spent answering questions. The old guy was interested, that much was clear."

"So he believed you?"

Basil shrugged. "I suppose so. Like I said, I didn't pay too much attention. John and I have had many arguments about religion—which is the reason I had him come with me to show the painting to my father, in the first place—to give him some sense. After that, it seemed important to him to have an *authority* pass judgment. Enter, Bishop Alin."

"Authority?" I said.

"Well, you know—those Christians seem to think they have a main line when it comes to spiritual matters. Alin is apparently a powerful bishop—lives in Rome for several months out of the year. If there's something that doesn't match up with the Good Book, those dudes want to be the first to know it."

"So what did John have a problem with?" I asked.

"Doesn't your head *already* hurt?"

That it did.

He continued, "John's problem is really about why his *almighty* God would allow deity intervention—especially after Christ's crucifixion and resurrection. My work certainly doesn't fit into his Christian model so, is it the work of Satan? That's the biggie for him. It's got him all wound up."

Hamlet's words to his dear friend drifted through my mind, *There are more things in heaven and earth, Horatio, than are dreamt of in your philosophy.*

"Father John bases everything on biblical interpretation. Everything. And he couldn't wrap his head around what he had seen. Finding a *reason* for my work is hard for him. Some say seeing is believing. Christians have a bit of a different view, believing is seeing. At any rate, he continues to be faithful to his religion, but he's bothered by my work and what it represents. It's changed him. At the end of our meeting with Bishop Alin, John was on *my* side."

"What side is that?" I asked.

Basil shrugged again, "The big deep heavy side."

I turned my gaze to the window. The horizon was pale with morning, and our flight was tearing toward it, the controls set to the heart of the sun. Something inside of me desired to write all of this down—to keep track of it all. The urge came on as if nothing else mattered. Tilting my head back and closing my eyes I began to see words stringing together. Colors, sounds and perspectives all under a single theme, whirling like diamonds in an endless sky of possibility.

"I want to write." I said unconsciously.

"I'm sure you do."

Raising my head I asked, "Why don't I have that—for lack of a better word, *power*, yet? The power you have?"

He held his hands up and demonstrated the effectiveness of handcuffs. "You aren't free, yet."

The cold steel was cutting into my wrists.

"Why do you write, Loche? What is it that makes you want to put pen to paper?"

He could see that the question was disturbing. "What is it," he continued, "fame? Power? A need to let everyone around you know that you have an opinion—or a view? Is it money? Do you think that because you are writing people will take your word and nothing else? Entertainment maybe? What is it?" His tone was laced with condescension.

"My interest has always been centered on stories. When I was very young I remember wanting to write stories, and I did. Composing in a way that brings a reader in and takes them on a journey. Poetry is something that has always intrigued me because of the different ways the work can affect a reader, with few words – to provide an experience."

"Sure," Basil said, "that's all well and good, but you don't have any *readers* now, do you?"

I frowned at him, "And what sort of audience do *you* have?"

His reply was a face tinged with sadness, and silence.

"I'm sorry," I said finally.

What more is there for an artist than to have recognition for the work? To know that a creation has aided in the development of another's life journey, or at least mirrored it in some way?

"*Giving it back* has always been the best way for me to define the *whys* of my ambition." I said to Basil. I explained that I wanted to give it back to the desire that inspired it. The Greeks called that desire the Muse, and by addressing the soul an artist could invoke inspiration from those lofty seats on snow-covered Olympus. Throughout history artists have credited these Muses as the true inspiration of art. A Muse's gift of enthusiasm and ecstasy to a mere mortal that pines to put his own spin on the imitation of nature allows for godlike traits on Earth. But so, too, could the Muses take away what they have given leaving the artist as barren as orchards in drought. Thus, Ovid's prayer, *Salve vocem! Salve linguam nobilem!* God save my voice! God save my noble poetry! And thus, his poetry was given back to the Muse through placation, as well as shared with an audience, his fellow man.

My fascination with writing has also been dominated by the way stories can influence people to act. They are vehicles of inspiration. Certainly, my interest in writing and my desire to help troubled minds to cope has been integral in my ability to provide treatment. Stories that reveal our nature, reveal a path to healing. Rearden would often say, *a good story can change the game—feed them what they need to get them to change.* Sharing stories, fictional or no, has allowed my clients to form new perspectives, attempt to swim deeper waters—to try harder. Stories are what we are. We are what we share, and what we have experienced. But most importantly, we become what we manifest. The stories we envision, become us. This is the real gift. The real gift to give back.

But my writings had never been seen or shared. It was clear that whatever divine quality they were supposed to possess was absent. But still, I hoped that if one were to read my work, they would be moved to believe. To read on and on, until they allowed the fiction to become something more than mere words on a page. Perhaps my stories could deliver someone—suspend their view of reality, and make them accept a different course.

"You're doomed."

"What do you mean?" I asked.

"Look, you aren't doing anything but writing for others, period. Besides, you don't have a clue as to your potential, yet. *Giving it back*? What kind of bullshit is that? The way I see it, you aren't required to give back anything to your fellow man or to that *other* audience. The sooner you understand that you, and you alone, are able to create the works that are solely yours—the better. No one can make you write, especially the kind of writing that carries that godlike quality, just like no one can make me paint. I paint because I must. Sure, every artist would like to have an adoring audience, but the day your work hurts someone close to you, you'll see things very differently. Once you see yourself, and forget all else, is when your work will mean something.

"And once you reach your full potential, the only thing that will matter is *your* creation. It will live on its own. The characters you create will become real and mean something to you. Don't let this heavenly audience control you. You control them—without you they've got nothing." He craned around and motioned to the two men behind us, "And these douche bags—they've got no clue as to what they're dealing with."

I nodded along, almost frightened by his rebellious tone. "You aren't any *ordinary* artist, Loche," he kept on, "you are what every artist wants to be—*extraordinary*, and more. But you'll have to learn how to forget what you *think* art is, stop trying to control it, and for your own sake, let it *give* to you!"

His passion continued to surprise me. Since I'd met Basil I had become accustomed to his taciturn speech and uncommitted nature. Suddenly, I was aware that he was far more cognizant of our situation than I had wanted to believe, and his seemingly detached manner was merely the product of living his true art and accepting it as his self-determined identity. *He is who he is*, I thought. My mind raced back to my walled-in home and my reserved day-to-day world that I had so intricately constructed to protect Helen, Edwin, and ultimately, myself. Too often had I dealt with clients whose eccentricities slowly led them toward mental illness. It seemed to me that the only way to keep myself from such a fate was to keep a vigilant eye on passion, and not let it get out of control.

And now, my family has been kidnapped, I've seen men killed, and in the blink of a few hours everything I knew to be true had been shattered and taken away. And far below my awareness, in a dark place that I'd not yet delved, a distant voice called out, *Take it back*.

"Ah, food," Basil said. "And drinks—killer! Nice faire for *prisoners*." One of our expressionless captors brought us both trays of perfectly prepared lobster, fresh bread and wine. I couldn't remember the last time I had eaten, and as the food and alcohol eased into my limbs and my mind, I could feel a heavy sleep hanging on me. After the meal, Basil lit a cigarette and grinned at the *no smoking* sign. "What are they going to do?" he mocked.

The white noise of the Learjet's engines lulled me into an unnatural dream. Basil lowered his cigarette, leaned his head back and said sleepily, "There's a lot for us to catch up on, Loche."

"Yes, there is," I muttered. My vision began to blur. Every muscle began tingling. It wasn't until I rolled my head to the side and saw Basil asleep with the cigarette still between his fingers that I thought, *what was in those drinks?* With heavy eyes I sensed someone approaching from the rear of the plane. A voice from over my shoulder was my last memory of the flight, "Time to sleep, Dr. Newirth." My eyes fell shut.

Another dream.

Beth Winship's arms groped from the churning water. My desk was on the beach and I watched her struggling against the throes of hypothermia. With a final, desperate cry, the face and the pleading reach sunk below the bleak surface. Silence. I stood up from behind my desk and called out, "Beth! Beth!"

"She's gone," a voice said. It was Rearden, holding a stack of paperwork and flinging single pages into the surf. Basil stood just behind Rearden with his brush aimed into a painting. I rushed to the water and dove deep, reaching for Beth's body. Murky darkness and blurred shapes on the lake floor drove my thoughts into madness. *She's gone.* The sharp chill of the water stung my skin. My limbs seized, my strength was failing, and I began to rise like a log to the surface.

What began as a blur of pale yellow light slowly sharpened into sheer curtains glowing with bright sunshine. A terrific headache was crashing against my temples, and my body was sluggish. Blood ticked in my ears. For a brief time, the anxiousness of my waking nightmare faded, Basil, armed men, my family's abduction—only a dream, only a dream. I raised my head from the soft pillow while trying to adjust my eyes, and the moment of relief dissolved into confusion. Fear returned. This was not *my* room.

Something beside me moved.

There, nuzzled against my shoulder was the tiny sleeping face of my son, Edwin. The scent of his breathing filled my heart with hope, and with great effort I was able to lift my left hand and gently touch his cheek. Tears welled in my eyes.

"Good morning," I whispered.

The little boy stirred and his brow wrinkled—an expression I had seen every morning of his short life. With all my strength I pulled him to me, squeezing him to my chest. His arms wrapped around my neck.

"Hi, Dad," he said, still half asleep.

"Where's mom?"

Just as I had asked the question, a door at the other end of the room swung open and Helen came rushing to the bed. She flung her arms around us and wept, "Loche. Oh God, Loche. They told us you were in an accident—to get us into the car," Helen told me. "Next thing I remember we were on a plane."

"Are you hurt? Are you okay?"

Throbbing waves of nausea surged through my abdomen. Helen was obviously aware of my discomfort and sent Edwin to the next room. Rolling to my side I heaved in spasms over the edge of the bed. My wife's hand was gently stroking the back of my neck. As quickly as the cramps had come, they dissipated, and I turned over onto my back. "Jesus," I cried. "Where are we?"

Helen wiped my face with the bed sheet, "Venice."

"What have they told you?"

"Loche," she whispered, "why didn't you tell me that Basil is your brother?"

I shook my head and told her the truth. What time was there? It had happened so quickly. At first I didn't believe him. *What more could I say?* "Where is he?" I asked.

"I don't know. Edwin and I arrived here at five this morning. They told us that you'd been asleep for over twenty-four hours."

Every muscle in my body ached, and the lump on the back of my head throbbed. Pushing down on the bed I struggled to sit upright. The dizziness came without mercy, but I forced myself to bear it. After a few moments it was gone. I glanced at the clock. It read 6:30 a.m.

"Are you okay?" Helen asked.

"I think so," I lied, though I could feel the effects of the drug beginning to fade. "Tell me *everything*."

Helen's eyes motioned toward the entrance to the

room. Standing in the doorway was a vaguely familiar face and in his arms was my son. It was the face from the computer—Albion Ravistelle.

"*Everything*, Dr. Newirth? I shall do my best," he said.

"Put him down," I demanded. I attempted to spring from the bed and take him. Helen held me back.

Ravistelle's expression was confusion mixed with humor. "Very well, Doctor," he said simply as he set Edwin on his feet. The little boy rubbed his eyes and stumbled over to Helen and me, still lost in his sleepy dreams. I held him close and stabbed the man with my eyes. "What do you want with us?"

Ravistelle looked at Helen, then back to me. A strange sensation crept through my mind. Helen and Albion seemed to have a rapport.

"Doctor, I know that our measures may appear extreme, but I assure you they were necessary for the safety of your brother, your family and yourself. You are no longer in peril. Please try to calm your thoughts. I'm afraid I should have let you rest a while longer before visiting, but I admit, I couldn't restrain myself. Meeting you has been my life's mission." He raised his hands in a gesture of retreat, "I will leave you to your family for the time being. We have arranged for a delightful breakfast on the terrace at nine. Basil and Howard will be joining us. I hope that you will join us, as well."

"Is there a choice?" I scowled.

His smile surprised me. It was too genuine. "There is always a choice, Doctor. We will not force you to do anything more against your will. You are here now, and we only ask that you allow us to plead our case. After you've heard us you may then do as you will."

Helen caressed my shoulder. I had no words.

"Loche Newirth," he said as he backed away, with a slight bow, "it is an honor to meet you." He turned and walked out.

Helen rose from the bedside, crossed the room and closed the door. With her back to me she said, "They told me everything. About you, Basil and what you are to become. They told me that your art will change the world." She turned with tears in her eyes. "I don't know how to make sense of any of this, Loche. Help me to understand."

I kissed Edwin on the forehead and laid him down on the bed. "So much has happened in the last few days that it's nearly impossible to describe."

"Try," she said.

I recounted the past day's events, the drowning of Beth Winship, my discussions with Basil and Howard, the viewing of Basil's art, the gunfight at Basil's studio, and William Greenhame. At the mention of William, Helen stopped me. "Was he a client of yours?"

"For the last six years."

"They told me that he was dangerous."

"I suppose he was," I remarked, "but not anymore. He was killed right in front of me." Helen's eyes grew wide. "Like I said, there is no way to describe it. Are you okay?" I asked.

"I don't know what I am," she muttered.

I reached for her hand. "I know how you feel."

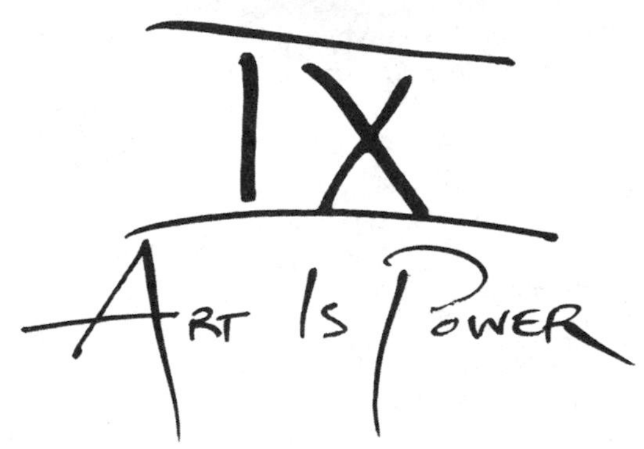

Basil was seated on the veranda, smoking a cigarette and gazing out over Venice's Grand Canal at the Chiesa della Salute. The red table umbrellas and elegant white cushioned chairs of the Bauer Hotel were arranged along a wide dining platform beside the water. Opposite the water was our gothic hotel looming up like an ancient ghost in the morning sun. Beside Basil was Howard Fenn. He looked sleepy.

After exchanging awkward greetings, Helen, Edwin and I joined them. There were no other guests on the terrace that bright October morning. A single waiter stood beside a serving cart three tables away polishing silverware and eyeing us with great interest. I noticed two empty seats at our table.

Basil mashed his cigarette into the ashtray. "So Loche, you and I always seem to meet near the water. Remember the last time we ate together?" From what hidden place my slight smile came from I'll never know, but I did recall our last lunch date on the docks of The Floating Hope in Idaho.

I nodded, "Yes, I didn't believe a word you were saying."

"*Matters that concern my professional opinion take place in my office*," he mocked in his best impression of me.

I glanced at Howard. "Everything okay?" I asked.

Howard smiled. "As good as can be expected. Strange

couple of days. You?"

"Well, the cocktails on the plane took a bit to recover from, but I'm feeling much better now," I said.

Howard looked at Basil, "He had a tough time of it, as well, but he was up and on the terrace early, drinking coffee."

"Yeah," Basil added, "after blowing chunks."

Albion Ravistelle appeared at the terrace entrance dressed in a grey business suit and tie. He approached with long, confident strides. Accompanying him was another man, also wearing formal business attire. His face reminded me of a ten-years-younger Marcus Rearden, thoughtful and excruciatingly insightful. His tiny, wire rimmed glasses rested down near the tip of his nose, and as he advanced toward us the grey-green eyes behind those glasses smiled with disbelief.

"Buon giorno," Albion Ravistelle greeted charmingly, "and welcome to Venice. May I introduce to you Dr. Angelo Catena, psychologist and art curator of Venezia?"

"Good morning," Angelo said in English dripping with an Italian accent. "It is indeed an honor to meet you." He removed his glasses, like one might remove a hat out of respect.

"Appropriate title," Basil said, "*psychologist and art curator.*"

Angelo seemed uncomfortable, but his response was perfectly rehearsed, "I've much to learn about both of my vices, art and the human mind, but yes, in this situation I can say that all of us gathered here have something in common."

"May we join you?" Albion asked, smiling. His well-mannered tone was flawless.

"It's your date," Basil quipped.

The two men took their seats as three white-coated waiters appeared out of nowhere and approached the table with trays of champagne. Albion must have noticed my skeptical expression and said, "The drink is not tainted, Dr. Newirth. I assure you that you won't experience any ill effects. We felt that sedating you aboard the plane was necessary for a number of reasons. First of which was that we didn't want the two of you to become rebellious, and second, you'll find that your jet lag will be lessened." He smiled, "And finally, we thought it important for you both to become more acquainted here in Venice rather than over the Atlantic ocean. I do apologize for the ill effects that you experienced upon waking. I'm afraid your overzealous escorts may have given you a bit too much." He paused, and with a troubled expression added, "I also understand that you were assaulted by one of our associates. That individual has been punished for the incident. I'm very sorry that you were struck. Completely unacceptable."

My scowl at Ravistelle quickly faded as the aroma of food rose before me. I was surprised at my sudden hunger. Warm breads, fresh fruit, jam, scrambled eggs and waffles were brought to the table.

Albion scanned the faces around the table with an expression brimming with sincerity. "I must also apologize again, to the entire group this time, for the drastic measures that brought you to this country, and simply, things are not always as they appear. We will not harm you, though it may have seemed as such. I hope that by now you understand the serious danger that you were facing. The danger has not disappeared, but I assure you that you are now dining at the safest place on Earth. What may seem like a luxurious hotel is truly a fortress sustained for one purpose, or rather, for *two* purposes, Basil and Loche. But so, too, will it protect the ones you love," he nodded to Howard, Helen and Edwin. "Inside these walls are men and women dedicated to preserving and protecting the greatest of human artistic endeavor, and it was not until all of you arrived safely that we have rested easy." He nodded upward toward the building's windowed face and I could see several figures peering down at our small gathering. "You see?" Ravistelle said. "You are quite well-known here. The excitement is difficult for our associates to repress." I looked at Basil. He was glaring at our host.

"The men under William Greenhame's charge, the *Orathom Wis*, will never stop in their mission to end both of your lives, and it is by our persistent watch that we've managed to keep that from happening." His next statement was tinged with sorrow. "Many men and women have freely given their lives for your protection, and for the work you produce."

"But why?" came Helen's voice.

Albion fixed her with his eyes and smiled slightly. "They hold *the answer*, dear Helen—the answer that there *is* life after death—the answer to human suffering—the answer to our inhumane, warring religious ideologies. An answer to the questions Helen, that this little one here," he gestured to Edwin, "will never be troubled with. The arts that these two possess can rid the world, once and for all, of sorrow, pain and illness."

"And how do you propose their art can do that?" Howard cried as he tapped the wheels of his wheelchair. His voice was shaking. "I know firsthand just who and what their art is for, and I assure you, it isn't for mankind."

Dr. Angelo Catena held up his hand with gentle patience, "Mr. Fenn," he consoled, "what happened to you was a tragedy. It was a terrible accident. You were not meant to see Basil's work, and the effect of it has stayed with you. The physician that treated you in Olympia, Washington, is still a colleague of mine, and I might add, while you were unconscious I visited you many times. But what you must realize is that you were brought back. You were brought back."

Howard blinked and shook his head. "You see," Angelo continued, "Basil had the foresight and the ability to create a work that was conceived as a *treatment*. It was he that healed you. Without his craft you would still be suffering from the many diagnosed mental disorders you sustained by looking into his work."

"So what you are saying," Basil interrupted, "is that you want me and Loche to work for you? Is that it?"

Dr. Catena looked at Albion and then back to Basil. "I

suppose you could say that."

"But there is much to learn," Ravistelle added, "much to train for and discuss before we jump to such hasty conclusions."

"What *are* you saying?" I asked. The sound of my voice startled me. My tone was both angry, and surprisingly interested.

"Dr. Newirth," Angelo said, "you and your brother have the ability to heal. Or I should say, *will* have the ability to heal others by transcending the barrier between this life and the next, through art. You can learn to manipulate your work to heal the human condition. The answers are within reach."

I shook my head in disbelief and echoes of conversations past with Marcus Rearden replayed in my mind. *I am merely pointing out, Marc, that we, as psychologists should pursue an answer, not an excuse. I want to steer right through the problems instead of going around them. I want the ability to cure, not ease. I want the knowledge to heal and repair. Not merely help one to organize their darkness. I know that everyone suffers. Whether it be a disease, a mental disorder or just the plain problems of being human. Each and every one of us wonders about why we exist and why there's no clear answer. I hear that question so often, Marc. Why? I want the answer.*

A sharp chill scuttled across my shoulders, and for a split second my thoughts raced, *my art will be the antidote to my nemesis, mental illness.*

"Gentlemen," I interjected, my voice chilled by cold restraint, "I am fully aware of the power that Basil possesses, and I am told that I, too, carry a similar *gift*, if you want to call it that. I've been made aware of the threat of William Greenhame and his *so called cohorts*—I've witnessed how dangerous he can be—and for the protection you have given us we are truly thankful. However, you must realize that the gravity of this situation has left all of us out of sorts." Both Albion and Angelo nodded sympathetically. "Your tactics, despite the dangers and this show of courtesy, are deplorable. Trust is a virtue that is earned. And, you are correct, there is a great deal more that we need to learn about you and your intentions."

Albion nodded with certainty. "My sentiments exactly, Doctor. Remember, things are not always what they seem. I will have delivered to your room a box of documentation that I believe will interest you greatly. Your distant and most recent past is outlined in great detail. I believe you'll find your official birth certificate from Moses Lake, Washington, secondary school and college transcripts, as well as your marriage license to Helen here. Furthermore, you will find literature that will educate you as to who your enemies are, the reasons why the two of you have been gifted and the scriptures that prophecy your coming—our involvement, our intentions and what our combined futures hold—it's all there." I looked at Helen, wide-eyed. "Doctor, I implore you to take some time and allow your new and world changing life to introduce itself to you. Prepare yourself to change humanity."

"Well, you can count me out," Basil said suddenly. "Albion, Angelo, you guys are clueless. This is some bad craziness to be sure and I think the best thing you can do is stay out of the *healing the world* business. I'm learning that the audience for my work is not of this Earth, and I can't imagine that *they* would take too kindly to a change of style. And no one dictates my work, but me."

"Mr. Fenn," Angelo responded in delicate tones, "I think we should—"

"Look, there are some questions that make art worthy, and knowing what you call *the answers* destroys what I do," Basil said flatly. "So what's next? When does our plane leave?"

There was a long pause. Albion Ravistelle's gracious style intercepted the complicated silence. "We can have a flight prepared for you," he began, "but I think it would benefit you to learn just a bit more about our intentions."

"It sounds to me like you want to *control* us," Basil

growled as he lit up a smoke. He shook his head slowly. "Not gonna happen."

"Our intention is not to control you," Angelo broke in, "but to *teach* you—"

Ravistelle held up his hand, wordlessly stopping Dr. Catena's voice. A barely detectible loss of patience crossed Albion's face. "Please, Mr. Fenn, as I've said, there is more to know. If you would only take a few days to look over the materials we've provided and spend some time communicating with us and our colleagues, you will begin to gain a clear picture that—"

"What part of *no* don't you understand?" Basil sneered. I turned and saw in his face a wall, guarded and barb wired. "I'll take my chances with this *Greenhame* and his *pals*. Don't fuck with my work. Believe me, it won't go the way you want it to."

Albion sighed deeply, keeping direct eye contact with my brother. And Basil held his gaze.

"Mr. Fenn," Ravistelle said, "doctor Catena is treating a woman here in Italy that suffers from schizophrenia and manic depressive disorders. She is kept in a psych ward outside of Venezia. I cannot begin to describe the suffering that this once vibrant and outgoing woman has endured over the last three years as these maladies crashed down upon her with vicious speed. Dr. Catena has struggled to develop several new treatments, including cutting-edge medication and other types of therapy, but with no results. As we speak she has been placed in a padded room due to two unsuccessful suicide attempts."

"That's sad," Basil consoled with sincerity, "but I can't do anything about it."

"We believe you can," Angelo joined.

Basil again shook his head, "She is not my responsibility."

Angelo looked to his colleague. Ravistelle's focus was pointed, "The woman is your birth mother, Diana."

Basil was unmoved. "Our birth mother is dead."

"Not everything is as it seems," Ravistelle answered.

A white cardboard box was on the table in our recently cleaned hotel room. Beside it was an envelope with my name printed in graceful, friendly pen strokes: *Dr. Loche Newirth.*

The letter was from Angelo Catena and it explained that the attorneys for the Winship family had been contacted by my lawyer in the United States, Alan Chatfield. It explained further that Chatfield was the official representative for my practice as well as managing the affairs of my estate. There were also words of encouragement and condolence to Bethany's and my misfortune as therapist and client. He ended the letter with, *Please set your mind at ease concerning the litigation in this matter. You are in good company, and Mr. Chatfield will take care of your affairs with diligence and integrity. Though I know that my support is but a scratch on the surface of this sorrowful circumstance. I hope that it can in some way allay your loss. Yours, most sincerely, Angelo Catena.*

The envelope also contained a formal letter from Alan Chatfield himself. In short, he outlined the process that I faced, the responsibilities that he would supervise, and strangely, he called it his *honor* to do so. He invited me to contact him at any time with questions, but for the time being, the investigation was still being conducted and my absence had been officially authorized as temporary professional leave. Chatfield had made contact with Carol, and with her assistance he was certain that my case was open and shut—nothing to worry about.

Turning to hand the pages to Helen, I saw her sitting on the edge of the bed staring into the closet. "What's the matter?" I asked.

"They've filled our closets with clothes."

I gave her the letter. Glancing at it she said, "I've already seen it. And I went though most of what's in that box during my flight over here. They provided me with my own *FYI* portfolio." I turned and went for the box that supposedly contained my life history.

It was all there. Perhaps the only thing missing that detailed my existence was a recording of my first words as a toddler. There was even reference to Marcus Rearden being my psychologist with a short summary of his publications and successes in criminal psychology.

Thumbing through several file folders I found the name Diana Goddell. Lifting it out of the box I felt a chill. Ravistelle had told us her story in brief, but insisted that we discover for ourselves, with the provided documentation, her importance. It was William Greenhame who first told me of the car accident that separated Basil and me. As I read I found Greenhame's tale was confirmed, but the details eluded me. I must've muttered, "I don't get it."

Helen was standing beside me, scanning the page over my shoulder. "What did Greenhame tell you?" She used his name in a way that startled me. It was almost too familiar.

"He told me that Diana was my mother, but we were taken to live with Jules and Rebecca Pirrip in hiding," I said.

Our parents were Diana Goddell and Bill Hagenemer originally from Canterbury, England. Shortly after Diana gave birth to Basil, she was forced to flee the United States, and we were left in the care of Jules and Rebecca Pirrip, who were to be our surrogate parents. When we were discovered, some three months in the States, the first assassination attempt was implemented by the *Orathom Wis*. I pointed to the word and Helen nodded. "The *Guardians of the Dream, or Dream Guard*," she said simply. My expression must have said, *how the hell did you know that?* She nodded again, "It's an *Elliqui* word, their own language, Albion told me about it."

I continued to scan. In short, the attempt was unsuccessful and both boys had escaped, but Jules and Rebecca were not so lucky. After the disappearance of the two children, the bodies of the parents were stored in the basement morgue. The next day they, too, were discovered missing. They were eventually found. Their bodies were chopped to pieces and spread out over a field of grass two miles north of the hospital. The cartilage-colored photographs are still etched in my memory. The macabre description pointed out that some parts, specifically, the back halves of their skulls, were never found. How Basil and I escaped was left unclear, though there were several theories. The adopted scenario was that word of the assassination attempt was leaked to friends of our mother, Diana, and help arrived just in time to intercept and get us to safety. Everyone involved, doctors, nurses and even the ambulance driver, was suspected in our disappearance.

The account picked back up a decade later with Diana living in England, and suspicions that the young boy living with her was indeed, me. Basil was adopted by Howard and the late Elizabeth Fenn of Idaho and had been rediscovered by the *Orathom Wis*. It was supposed that the boys had been separated to throw off pursuit.

My father Bill Hagenemer's whereabouts were still unknown. I shook my head at the cold words, *whereabouts still unknown*. "Perfect," I muttered. Colder words followed—*presumed dead*.

Many of the facts outlining Diana's life were known to me. Her education, her upbringing and her daily routine were frighteningly accurate. The disturbing notion that we had been observed for so many years had not yet sunk in. When the words began to outline the last few days of her life I narrowed my focus on the page, moving it closer to my face. Every detail was correct. From her rare blood disease, to her final words, her last will and testament, to those who attended the funeral—again, precise.

The dark days of six years ago shuddered through my spirit. When I received the news I immediately booked a flight to London to find that she had already been cremated, and most of the funeral preparations were underway by friends. There was little to do but sign papers, box up the few items that she had left behind, and greet faces I'd not seen since I had left for the States to attend college. Helen, busy with her job, was unable to make the trip with me, which, at the time, was preferable. Helen had never met my mother. A day before my return home I faced a steel-grey sky at Tintagel, Cornwall, and gave my mother's ashes to the sea. It was the only time I had cried for her.

The next page was labeled *confidential* in bold red letters. It's contents filled me with dread. The *Orathom Wis* had finally breached Diana's anonymity and were planning her abduction in an attempt to gain the location of her sons. Albion Ravistelle made contact with my mother and offered protection, and with his aid, her death was faked.

"As simple as that," Helen said, still over my shoulder.

I couldn't respond. The details continued but I could no longer see the page. This was real. I believed what I was reading to be true. My eyes were blurred. Helen turned me to her and pulled my body close. "Loche, she's alive. Your mother is alive."

And so she was. From behind a two-way mirror, Basil and I looked at our mother. Ravistelle and Dr. Catena stood just behind us.

"How did this happen?" I asked watching Diana rock back and forth with her eyes staring out much farther than the padded, brightly lit room would allow.

"Soon after she came into our protection she was showing signs of psychosis," Angelo offered. "The symptoms progressed rapidly in the last three months. It wasn't until her suicidal tendencies intensified that we took more aggressive measures." He placed a warm hand on my shoulder, "I'm sorry that you must see her this way."

I closed my eyes and searched for a way to come to grips with the situation. Nothing I had learned as a psychologist seemed to make a bit of sense. The only thought that kept me from sinking below the waterline was a phrase that I must have said aloud. "I need to talk to her."

"Indeed, Doctor. Right this way." Ravistelle immediately turned toward the door behind us and reached to open it.

"But not here," I stopped him. "Basil and I should be alone with her for our first meeting. With all due respect, no supervision."

Ravistelle paused, and with a sidelong look to Dr. Catena he said, "Very well. We'll make the arrangements."

"No," Basil interjected. "Give us a car and we'll take her to lunch." A grin spread across Basil's face.

"Take her to lunch?" Angelo gasped. "Mr. Fenn you must realize that her condition is serious and—"

"And it's lunchtime," I joined.

Basil continued, "We'll have a proper mother son reunion. Not in a rubber room. This is a perfect opportunity to earn our trust. Trust us and we *might* trust you."

I knew the idea was potentially dangerous, but it was the only way we could truly be alone with her. "She'll be fine," I said. "You have my word. Give us two hours."

Ravistelle's eyes weighed the request. "Very well," he said finally. "There is a restaurant a short distance from here. You may take a car, but *we* will transport Mrs. Goddell."

"Fine," I said.

The table was set with gold and crimson napkins fringed with lace, short but elegant wineglasses and a bouquet of fresh daisies. The restaurant was quiet save one whispering couple seated a few tables away. Basil had already ordered a glass of wine. He stretched his legs out beneath the table and leaned back in his chair. I stared at him, unable to understand his ability to cope effortlessly with the chaos that surrounded us.

"What?" he asked noting my incredulity.

"How do you do it?" I asked.

"Do what?"

"Remain calm. You seem like this is just another day of the routine."

The waitress placed Basil's wine down before him. "No, nothing routine about this," he smiled. "The wine is better here."

I shook my head at him and tried to release the tension in my face.

"Maybe you should have a glass of wine, Loche. It might ease your nerves." I thought a moment, but resolved to pass. Basil added with a grin, "*Mom* won't mind."

Then Diana Goddell entered the dining room. She wore a long pink dress, and her coat was folded and draped over her arm. Her uncertain steps and slightly bowed head told Basil and me to rise at once and escort her to our table. As we approached, her gaze remained rooted to the floor beneath her feet. Our presence seemed nothing more to her than another couple of white-coated residents helping her to her chair. We lowered her down and stood by her side. Basil and I locked eyes not knowing what to do next.

"What lovely flowers, boys," came her melodic voice. The voice of a bird, I thought. She reached to the center of the table and lifted one of the daisies from the vase. "How pretty," she said, "how beautiful. Quite out of season, but lovely just the same. And against these red napkins—oh, you two shouldn't have."

Basil and I moved quickly to our seats and stared at our mother, wide-eyed. All of her attention was on the daisy. She turned it over and inspected it closely. "Daisies can be full of bugs sometimes, you know?" At that she met my eyes. "Bugs that eat away at the stem."

I looked to Basil. He nodded. Whether it was some shared instinctual knowing that her suggestion made us believe that we were being monitored, or the influence of popular spy movies was difficult to determine, but we gathered that her words were loaded with more than just daisy bugs. *But now what,* I thought. *How are we to talk? Is our mother truly suffering from schizophrenia?* I suddenly found myself studying her for symptoms. Observing her prior to this meeting she was clearly exhibiting signs of social isolation, a lack of care for personal hygiene, as well as excited motor activity. Dr. Catena had also recorded her speaking to voices and other beings, including her late husband and my father, Bill Hagenemer.

"Have you two seen your father?" she yelled. The waitress at the other end of the room turned, startled.

"Easy there," Basil said.

"He'll be very angry you came here!" Her voice slightly lower now.

"Mom," I started, and then paused. The word *mom* brought tears to my eyes. I had never thought I would hear my voice call to her again. "Do you know me?"

Diana's eyes slowly lolled in my direction. Her sharp gaze was clearly present. She did not answer, but there was the feeling that she was saying, *Yes, son. Sorry that we had to meet like this. Can't talk now,* they *are listening.* She then began hammering the table with her fist. Basil reached out and gently placed his hand over hers. At his touch she let out a cry of obvious frustration. She looked at Basil and quickly turned away. "I can't. I-I-I can't. . . Billy! Billy! Tell my kids that I miss them! Billy! Where are you?"

The couple having lunch nearby didn't respond to her ravings. Basil noticed that I was looking in their direction and he turned.

"Excuse me," he said finally. "After you leave, which should be right about now, please let Albion know that we are doing fine." The two didn't move. "You two," Basil pursued, "out the fuck you go." The man turned in Basil's direction with a blank expression and rose. The woman stood, as well, and they walked out the front entrance.

As soon as the door closed behind the couple our

mother began raving again, only this time it was more violent. She began by crying out for her lost *Billy*, and with one hand she pounded the table while the other tore at the buttons of her blouse. Before we could restrain her we noticed a wire taped just below her neckline. She carried on with her rant, scanning the room as if searching for her next move. Basil decided to play along and raised his voice, "Diana. . . Mom, its okay. It's okay."

She stopped. "Ready?" She said, weighing our demeanor. With terrific force she yanked the wire from her breast, seized the tiny microphone at its tip, and tore it off.

Then with rehearsed precision she whispered, "How I've missed you, sweet Loche. Dearest Basil, I've so much to say—but not now. I can't let them know that I recognize you. They will use me if I do. You are both in danger. Ravistelle is not who he seems. Beware of his plan. Don't believe him. I must continue to feign illness in order to keep a great many secrets. Play along and when your father arrives, we'll make up for lost time. . . Trust no one!"

The front door of the restaurant swung open and rushing in came five dark-suited men followed by Albion Ravistelle. My mother's timing could not have been better for just as the first man stepped into the room she began crooning at the top of her lungs, "Billy, Billy! One, two, three, four. Can I have a little more? Five, six, seven, eight, nine, ten. I love you!"

Albion's expected grace seemed unabated in spite of his brisk approach. "Dr. Catena feared this might happen," he said, without heeding the wire in my hand. The five men accompanying Albion surrounded Diana, and with gentle force, moved her swiftly out of the restaurant. "Since she's been in our care she has had episodes of violent behavior." He reached for the wire in my hand. "I hope that you can understand that we felt it necessary to keep an ear on the situation. And it was best that we did so, it seems. Seeing her two sons was too much for her."

Basil stood up and was about to respond when I interrupted him. "No," I replied with calmly, "I'm afraid she doesn't know who we are. I was a little concerned, as well. Of course, professionally I knew it could have gone this way, but we had to try. Thank you for indulging our emotions on this one, Mr. Ravistelle. You can't imagine the feelings the two of us are experiencing."

Albion nodded sympathetically, "No, I'm afraid I cannot. I'm sorry that the reunion didn't unfold as you would have liked. But there is still time."

"I would like to see her again tomorrow, as well as look over her records."

"I'm sure Dr. Cantena would be most willing." Albion motioned toward the door, "Shall we return to the hotel?"

"Yes, indeed," I said, "we'll see you there." As Basil followed me back to our car I could feel his eyes boring a hole in the back of my head.

The drive back to the hotel was silent.

Once the car was parked and we began the short walk to our rooms, Basil's voice sliced the chilly October air. "What the fuck?" I turned. His eyes were angry. "What the fuck?" he said again.

"What is it?" I asked.

"What was all that bullshit with *Al baby?* What? It's suddenly okay to listen to us when we don't know about it?"

"Basil, we've got to play along with all of this. Of course it's not right—especially considering what she told us. Playing along will get us more information."

"I don't know about you, Loche," Basil's nostrils flared, "but I want the fuck out of here. The only thing that was keeping me here was the possibility of helping Diana out of the freakishness—but she's not sick."

"Oh," came my sarcastic reply, "and so her faking a malady means that she's safe and happy?"

"Look, dude, first chance I get, I'm out."

"What about Howard, or me for that matter?"

"You don't get it do you? This is all about something

much bigger than any of us. If I let anyone meddle with my work. . ." he trailed off shaking his head. "Holy shit, man, you've got to think this through." He caught my eyes, "Yes, I'm concerned about you and everyone else, but, Loche, my gut tells me that the widening of the Center is dangerous. The Center and my *gift* is of *their* making," he gestured to the sky with his hand and a rolling of his eyes. "Gods use it—to see us—to be us. Hell, I don't know. It's wrong for us to use it."

"Wrong?" I asked. "What do you mean, wrong?"

"I don't know," he cried. "Wrong, as in, *not right*! Look, I used it once and got away with it. Somehow I managed to paint something that revealed only a small part of the Center. Howard was able to speak and reason after he saw it. That's the most I could ask for, but one fuck up, one wrong paint stroke and I could have killed him. My guess is that I got lucky. I got lucky. Maybe it isn't my ability at all. Maybe it has more to do with the person looking at it. I don't know, their particular mental state?"

"You mean that someone who is suffering from a disorder might be—" My voice quavered, "Cured?"

"Whatever that means," Basil said, "but yes. Maybe for those that are doing just fine in this life, living normal, happy lives—maybe seeing one of my works is a mind scramble. Potential killer. But for someone who is mentally ill—I suppose there's a chance that it could pull that stuff away. The Center might pull it in somehow. Again, this is all in my gut, but either way, using it for anything other than their intentions is scary to me."

I considered his words in silence. Could it be that Basil's work was indeed the cure for the terrors that can haunt the human mind. Can a man in the throes of some maddening disorder be purged by looking into the face of a god?

Basil's voice startled me, "And damn, not to mention, whatever else happens to be on the other side looking in —I still don't know if I've done something wrong on the other side."

"How do you mean?"

"Look, there's always two sides, okay? We know that seeing my work is dangerous. We've got Howard's experience, my gut fears, and your surreal drowning boy to support that, along with Albion and an armed compound of nut-job believers here in Venice dedicated to my work and the work that you've not yet mastered, right?"

"So it seems," I agreed.

"Well, when you looked into one of my paintings, you weren't injured at all. It just wised you up to your own potential. I think that's because you have something powerful within you—the same sort of gift. But what happens to an average person or a sick person in this world must mean that something happens on the other side, as well."

"You mean that a simple human being that sees a painting of yours can affect the world of the Divine?"

"In so many words. Shit, Loche, I don't know much about quantum divination, supernatural weirdness—I'm an artist. But the last thing I want is to do something that will hurt my audience. I feel that if something changes here, something changes there."

"How could *you* hurt your audience?" I asked. "You are a human being. They are gods, points of light, streams of spirit."

"You're right. It won't be me that hurts them—it will be mankind."

"How is your mother?" Helen asked as I entered.

I paused scanning the room, certain that we were being monitored. "Not well."

"Did she know you?"

"Let's take a walk," I said, "let's go visit the canals and have a glass of wine together." Helen smiled and quickly rose from the couch. "We can leave Edwin with Basil and Howard. They're going to look at the boats."

"What about Albion? I mean, will he let us go out?"

I nodded. "Yes, I just spoke with him. In fact, he insisted that we visit the city. He has also suggested a couple of places to eat."

"He'll let us go alone?"

"Well, not exactly, but he said that our escort won't bother us and that we won't even know he is there."

She crossed her arms over her chest. "And for a second I thought we might have a *romantic* evening."

"Albion just wants us to be safe—I'm sure that our watcher won't interfere with us."

"Okay," she said, "I'll get my coat."

The late afternoon sun gleamed on the high spires along the Venice skyline. Albion stood on the dock holding hands with a teenage girl. "My daughter, Crystal," he said. "If ever you need a sitter here in Venice, Crystal would love the opportunity. I know they would take to each other like brother and sister." Both Helen and I greeted the young lady with smiles, and Albion motioned me toward the waiting gondola. "You should experience the entry way to the city, at least," he told me. "From there you can take boats to wherever you wish. There's so much to see." He handed me a billfold of money and a map. "The Basilica di San Marco will be crowded with tourists, but that shouldn't deter you. It is quite lovely. I've circled several other places on the map that are equally divine, less crowded places the average tourist won't likely visit."

"Thank you, Albion," I said.

"Have a delightful time. And tomorrow, Loche, let us continue to discuss our path. Until then, buon pomeriggio."

"Helen?" I called. She was still speaking to Crystal. She hugged the young lady and hurried over to join us.

"She's lovely," Helen said to Albion.

"Yes," he agreed, "almost fifteen and just like her mother."

"Where is her mother?" Helen asked.

"Away on business. But she should be returning soon."
"We would very much like to meet her," I said.
Albion nodded, "You will."
He stepped back and the gondolier oared us out into the canal. The two stood on the dock watching us float out and away.

Speechless, Helen and I watched the Venetian architecture pass by as if in a dream, and I marveled at the beauty of the city's elegant decay. Water-worn brick and stone feathered into paled earth tones—the walls and foundations of men, made to age with immeasurable grace, lined the maze of canals, all snaking away to secret nooks and memories. Every direction sparked the feeling of romance, old books and candlelight. I heard myself sigh.
"Kind of reminds me of *our* castle," came Helen's voice suddenly. She was looking at me with an expression I'd not seen in years—excitement, desire, love.
"Yes," I said taking her hand in mine, "built to last."
I glanced back at the gondolier. Removing the billfold that Albion had given me from my coat pocket I pulled out the lira and set it on my knee. A plain black wallet, I thought. I thumbed through its compartments carefully.
"What are you doing?" Helen asked.
"Just checking to see if Albion sent a microphone along with us." It was empty. I placed the money into my pocket and laid the wallet on the seat to be left behind. The gondolier took no notice.
We eventually stopped at a small wine nook near the Basilica of San Marco. I drank deeply and knew that it was time to discuss with Helen the reunion with my mother—a woman that my wife had never met.
"Strange," I began. "I wish we were here under different circumstances."
She leaned in and kissed my cheek. "At least we are here. And you're about to bring hope and healing to the world."
"Strange," I said again. The wine was slowly

performing its medicinal duty on my nerves. I stood up and studied our surroundings. There didn't seem to be anyone watching and there was no one near enough to hear our conversation.

"Loche. . ."

"I'm just making sure that we can talk."

"You are acting paranoid," she mocked.

"My mother isn't ill, Helen," I said, sitting down.

Her face flushed. "What?"

"Albion is not telling us everything."

"Wait," Helen stopped me. "Wait a minute. Your mother is *fine*?"

"She's doing a hell of a job fooling everyone."

"How do you know this?"

I explained to her the incident and watched her eyes widen with awe. When I shared my mother's warnings her hands gripped the table.

"I can't say that I'm surprised by anything," I said. "Especially with all that's happened. Of course, it's too early to trust Ravistelle and his intentions, but my Mother is terrified of something—and it seems she's doing all she can to survive right now."

"Why would she fake being sick?"

I shook my head, "I'm not sure. My guess is that she knows something."

"Like what?" Helen asked.

I shrugged. "She told us that Ravistelle can't be trusted."

Helen turned her head toward the canal. A breeze brought a faint sour stench from the waterway. "We should get back," she said coldly.

"Don't you have an opinion on all of this?"

She looked at me. Whatever magic was in her eyes a few minutes earlier was gone. I sensed that thoughts of Edwin in danger were now triggering her mood. "Are you okay?" I asked.

At those words her eyes softened. "Yes. . .well, no. I don't understand any of this." She looked back out over the water, "Why would she lie?" Her tone was frustrated, as if she were talking to herself.

"I don't know. But no matter what happens, we can't share this information with anyone."

"What did Basil say?"

"He wants out. And he wants out now." I lifted my wineglass and took a sip. "He believes that his gift is for a divine audience, beyond this world, and us manipulating his work, using it for our own ends would be catastrophic. Not only to the world, but for the other side, as well."

Helen's eyes squinted. "He told you that?"

"Yes."

"What is he going to do?"

"I don't know," I said. "But he's adamant about not letting his paintings be seen by anyone."

"How can he stop that now? Albion has all of his work."

I shook my head. "I think we need to let Albion think that we're playing along until we know what to do next."

"What about you?" she demanded. "What do you want to have happen here?"

I let my eyes trace the grid of red and white stripes on the tablecloth and took a deep breath. "Loche," she pursued, "What about you?"

"Basil may be right, and he may be wrong. I think if he can heal the human condition—and I will one day have the same ability—then it is without question our duty to examine it—regardless of anyone involved, my mother, you. . . even Edwin. If we have the power to heal, it *should* be used."

Her hand squeezed my wrist. "I'm glad that's what you want."

5:30 a.m. I could see a dark grey and foggy morning through the window. Sitting up I saw that Helen was not there. I stood, put on a robe and entered into the living room.

"Good morning, Doctor." Sitting on a chair was

Albion Ravistelle. In his hands was an open book. His greeting startled me, and I recoiled.

"Do not fear," he said closing the book and placing it on the coffee table.

"Where is Helen?" I snapped.

"Loche, I'm afraid it is time we become better acquainted. Please—" he motioned to the sofa.

"I'll stand. Where's Helen?" I demanded.

"Dr. Newirth, we need to discuss your brother's reluctance to our shared endeavor. It is paramount that he understands the gravity of our intentions as opposed to resting on his own selfish integrity."

"Helen?" I snapped again.

Albion's always graceful expression was now gone. He glared at me. "It is good that you care so much about her. That, my friend, is the key to your fulfillment." His face lightened. "Helen is fine. I've asked her to allow you and I some time to speak together."

I remained silent, uncertain what to say.

"I need you to convince Basil that his part in this is more important than his pride."

"Basil's craft is his own, and he won't be told what to do," I stated. "Forcing him to do anything to the contrary could be disastrous."

"So he says, does he?" Albion stood, "Ah, dear Basil." He turned his back to me and lowered his head, letting out a deep sigh. "Throughout history, mankind has developed powers to further our evolution. Medicines, weapons, technologies—and with each good that comes, so does evil knock upon our doors. Today, for example, we're mapping the genome, and thus rages the argument of stem-cell research, and the resistance to such godlike science. Science is the path to building the perfect human. We can reverse our physical imperfections—create longer life, disease-free, potential immortality. And the soothsayers whine with fear of immoral uses—for after all, there are always two, and if the findings can produce greatness, there will always be someone to use it for just the opposite—our demise." He turned and faced me.

"But you and I are standing on the fringe of a greater power. The ability to eliminate pain. Not only mental illness. I'm speaking of the possibility of human psychic harmony. A single path toward godliness and goodness—the destination that is desired by all. By achieving a quantified common good, there will be no need to fear progress. The true destiny of our race is to eliminate man's desire for power, for control and for domination." He reached out and gently touched my arm. "And it is you and your brother that can share this gift with us all. Don't you see, Loche, that you and Basil are the keys to the *door*? Can you not see that it all begins with the two of you?"

"The elimination of power, control and domination?" I asked. "You're telling me that Basil's work can achieve such things? That I will achieve such things?"

"Yes. With the right training. But not without commitment, time and desire."

"But as you say, and history shows, something could go wrong. We are human, and we can't have good without its counterpart. There are always two. We are fallible."

"So true," he breathed. He laced his fingers together before his face. "But I believe that we have one other part to this good and evil equation. A part that the shortsighted animal of man has never conceived possible."

"What is that?" I asked.

He paused with unmoving eyes pointed sharply into mine. "Omniscience," he answered. I shook my head and struggled to fully comprehend his meaning. "What are you willing to do to achieve this?" Ravistelle asked simply.

Omniscience, I recall thinking with disbelief. Omniscience, the knowledge of all things, good and evil. What would it mean to know all? Could it be possible? The questions ripped through my thoughts like a raging torrent of ocean wind. *A hurricane is coming*, I thought.

What would it mean to not only the billions who suffer from mental illness, but to those regular people, like Dr. Marcus Rearden? Or to my close friends whose daily lives are ruled by dreary routines and deadlines, for the sake of earning money to survive? What if we managed to evolve? Tunneling through each of our souls, digging inward through our grey matter is this worm, shaped like a question mark, whispering, *Why am I here? Is there a reason?*

What would it mean to have such questions answered? I closed my eyes and imagined myself lying on Rearden's couch, sharing with him my crazy dreams of a cure—a cure for those that suffer. And out there, through the closing distance, through the fog and rain, I could see the breaking shoreline, and the lighthouse looming—its thick beam of light tearing out through the dark storm. *Only a short distance now*, I thought.

"It can be done," Ravistelle's voice interrupted my thought. "Everything is up to you, Basil, and us. We have the chance. Let us take it. Let us go and heal ourselves. Let us share it with the world."

It can all be true. And then Rearden's voice again, *what if I can't help, can't handle it or I go in with them?* It seemed to me suddenly that the only way I could help manage the pain of their suffering was to indeed, go there with them. To Ravistelle, I must have appeared fragile and overwhelmed for my hands began to tremble, but I felt a smile curve across my thought.

"I know," he said gently. "It is difficult to take. I can only imagine what it must have been like for the martyrs —men told that they were in some way a part of a divine plan, men *fated* to suffer for mankind."

"Fate?" I cried, turning away. "I do not believe in fate. We can change our lives through our actions."

"True," Albion smiled and pointed to a glass placed on the table. "You see the glass of water there? I am fated to pick it up, right now." As he began to reach for the glass I jerked my hand down to seize it, thinking that I could alter what he thought was *fated*. The move was awkward and my fingertips slipped, tipping it over. The glass shattered.

"Of course," he smiled, pushing my hand out of the

way and brushing the broken glass nimbly off of the table and onto the cover of a book. "And so it is." Albion held the broken shards up for me to see. "You see, as I thought. Like you, I believe that a man can change his fate, only if he *chooses* to do so. But fate, it seems, tends to play tricks on us. Sometimes it has its own plan. Mingled like the moon that changes and the sun that is constant, our futures are both choice and destiny, controlled by omniscience. The invisible hand. The One. We call it, *Thi.*" He lifted one of the pointed shards of glass and raised it to his right eye, gazing at me through it. "Your choice will be your fate. What fate will that be?"

"What if-"

He interrupted, "What if? What if you had chosen *not* to get in the way of my fate with this glass?" His eye grew wider in the glass. "A bit less of a mess, I would think. And *what if* is not a question to be taken lightly, or to be carried into the twilight of our lives. Unless, of course," he smiled darkly, "that is *your* fate. One longing regret to haunt you. We've the chance now, Loche, to share with the world the remedy of our suffering condition. What *is* your fate?"

Raising my arm I pointed my trembling fingers toward the broken pieces of glass atop Albion's book. They were jagged and sharp, but clear as ice in spring. I lifted one from the pile and placed it firmly into the meat of my hand and squeezed. The hot sting of it cutting my flesh brought the words of old Rearden echoing through my memory. *Mental illness is not like a cut on the arm, but it is exactly like a cut on the arm. The only difference is that this kind of cut can think. This kind of wound can learn to cut again. This kind of cut can talk itself into never healing. It has hands, eyes, experiences and a wealth of understanding of its host. But it also understands you. The medical doctor uses sutures and bandages. We psychologists use words. You must outthink it to stop the bleeding and try to pull the knife from its hand. I wish I could offer you something more than mere words, for if I knew how to stop the pain, the bleeding, the hopelessness,*

I would most certainly share it. I'd share it with the world.

Blood dripped from my fist as I lowered it to my side. Albion Ravistelle still peered at me through the sharp slice of glass.

"I don't trust you, Albion," I said. "And I am not convinced that we have any answers, yet. But I know that Basil's work is something beyond our understanding, and that it is powerful. It has been used to heal, once. I have dedicated my life to helping those that suffer. We must try. If what you're proposing is true, I'm in. Let's share it."

Albion lowered his jagged eyepiece with an air of joy mingled with sober gravity. "This fate that you choose—it will be more than you imagine. You are prepared to face this?"

I nodded slowly. Laying his palm open and setting his eyes firmly into mine he sliced the sharp edge across his skin. He then reached for my hand and pressed his cut grip to mine.

"Here's to the big deep heavy," I said.

Albion smiled. "Come with me." He turned toward the door.

It was as Basil had told me the previous evening. Our craft was larger than any of us. If we had the chance and the ability to heal the woes of humanity, it must be explored, and my intention was to do just that, with or without him.

Albion led me to a lift at the far end of the east wing of the hotel. Jutting from the wall beside the door was a small black box and from its center shot a faint, glowing beam of laser light that crossed the pathway to the lift entrance. Albion angled his left eye into the ray.

A computer-generated female voice droned from some hidden speaker, "Identita cresima—Albion Ravistelle." The metal lift doors opened, and we entered. Instead of a control panel with a number of lit buttons there was only one. Printed on the plastic casing of the control panel was a symbol that, at the time, I couldn't place, but I was certain I'd seen it before. It depicted a simple ladder capped by a crescent moon opening downward. Conjuring its meaning was far from my attention, and as vague as the distant life I had led in North Idaho. I let the thought pass as Albion pressed the button three times and the lift descended.

White light shot into the compartment as the doors opened. Albion and I stepped out into an enormous pillared cavern. It was so large that I had a difficult time seeing the opposite walls. Bright lights bathed the room with perfect illumination, and each surface was brilliantly white. The further in I ventured I noticed that the room was round. Along the perimeter were numbers, barely detectible, embossed in the white marble floor.

"Welcome to the Sun Room," Albion said smiling. "I've long waited to show you this place." He motioned to the walls, "This is our test facility. You see the shrouds?" He pointed to the fabric draped walls. "If you would, please stand on a number on the floor, any number."

Nearest to me was the Roman numeral one. I stepped onto it and waited for further instructions. "Please face the curtain, Dr. Newirth." I obeyed. "Behind that curtain will soon be one of Basil's paintings. In fact, his entire catalogue will soon correspond with each floor number in this room."

I gasped, staring at the closed curtain, "That's well over two thousand paintings."

Behind me, Albion sounded as if he were grinning, "Two thousand seven hundred and ten to be exact."

"All in this circle?" I marveled. "Big room."

"Yes. But larger still. We have space for four thousand of his works. Works that we are hoping he will complete here in Venice."

I nodded hearing Basil's defiance in my ears. "Where is his work now?"

"I'm glad you asked," Albion replied. "It has only just arrived—last night."

There was a slight fissure in the curtain before me.

"So how does this work?"

Ravistelle moved beside me. "Each painting will be placed behind each respective curtain." Reaching into his suit pocket Albion produced a small device no larger than a cell phone. He held it up to his mouth and said, "Open number one." Like a theater curtain, the fabric parted revealing a wall as black as night. There was no painting, yet.

"I see," I nodded. "But how will you manage to hang the work to implement your experiment? I can tell you now that you will have, for lack of a better word, *casualties,* if your associates attempt this. I would fear an accidental viewing."

"Ah, very good," he answered. "We have a crew specially trained. A very special crew indeed."

"And what of the content of the paintings?" I rambled on, "How will you match painting to patient? We don't know enough about that, yet."

"My dear Loche," Albion said, "I believe this will be your first task. Your talents as a psychologist, as well as your ability to survive viewing Basil's work, will help us determine treatment. But first, before we get to that, let us meet our volunteer patients. Shall we?" I followed my guide to the lift again and we descended further into my fated, unknown world.

A smiling Dr. Angelo Catena, with his wire-rimmed glasses still angled down on the tip of his nose, was waiting for us a floor below. He wore a white medical coat buttoned at the chest over a suit and tie. The enthusiasm in his eyes was unmistakable. Beside him was another man wearing similar dress. Angelo reached out to me for a handshake. "Dr. Newirth. Again, I cannot begin to express my excitement and the honor it is to finally be working with you." As we shook hands, he squeezed. I quickly reeled back wincing. I had forgotten about the fresh cut I had given myself. Angelo immediately noticed the blood on his hand, "Goodness, Doctor, you're hurt. Are you quite all right?"

I apologized, "I broke a glass in my room this morning, and I had all but forgotten—"

Angelo said to his assistant, "Corey, will you rush to the infirmary and bring a bandage?"

"I'm afraid Mr. Ravistelle also cut himself on the same glass," I told Angelo.

"I'm quite alright," Ravistelle said raising his hand. It was wrapped in a white silk handkerchief. "A tiny cut. Here," he said to me as he produced another handkerchief, "use this. He's fine, Catena. We don't have time for this—let us meet our patients."

Angelo's assistant, Corey, nodded and took the white silk and kindly tied it around my hand. I noted that Corey's eyes shifted from my bandage to Albion's.

"There you are," Angelo said to me as he patted the top of my hand gently, "bene. Corey?"

Corey, as if shaken from a dream pulled his eyes away from Albion's hand, "Si?"

"Would you get me a sanitary cloth?"

"Si." He dashed away.

"Now then, gentlemen, this way."

Angelo led us down a long hallway that opened up into a massive ward. Fifty people, both men and women, were spread out, some seated at tables, some watching television or wandering aimlessly. Each wore a robe of light green.

"Here are the *Saved*," Angelo beamed. "The most difficult and unfortunate cases in Europe." He turned to me and raised his head so that his grey-green eyes filled the lenses of his spectacles. "These are the lucky ones, Dr. Newirth—at least they are now. Two years ago they were the worst off. You see, each of these men and women have been institutionalized for their respective mental conditions—which are wide ranging. Schizophrenia, Alzheimer's, acute psychoses, manic depression, post traumatic stress disorder, et cetera. They also share the unfortunate reality of having no family. Most of them have no official records, and as far as the European Mental Health League is more than insistent to point out, no money."

I took in the sight. I saw hopeless cases of perhaps every mental illness known. Visiting rooms like this in the past for me had always been an exercise in futility. *Here are the Saved*, Angelo had said. I felt a rush of adrenaline surge behind my eyes.

The man in the corner who was quietly muttering to himself while he stared away to that place I've longed to destroy, was soon to be healed, healthy and aware. The woman seated at the table to my right, crying and wringing her hands will soon learn to smile. I shook my head. *Soon. Just hold on. We are coming.*

I felt the touch of Albion's hand on my shoulder at the moment I saw my mother, curled up like a cat in the corner of the room with two resident staff members standing nearby. "Your mother, of course, is a special case," he said softly. "We will make certain that our tests are effective before her treatment."

"Yes," I replied, keeping my professional and objective tone intact.

"But, most importantly," Catena said, "we have been given consent by the European Mental Health League to care for the rest of them, and to provide our new treatment. The EMHL is most hopeful."

"Do they know our methods?" I asked.

Angelo glanced at Albion, and then to me. "The EMHL is fully aware."

"Believe me," Albion interjected, "as the *Director* of the EMHL, we are honored to begin this new, enlightening treatment."

Albion couldn't help but notice my wide-eyed expression. "At your service, Dr. Newirth. But come, we've one more stop to make before we embark on the journey to bring these people home."

Through a one-way mirror behind the coffee counter, I watched my brother. Again I felt that twinge of guilt—that godlike viewing position. I saw the thin, yarn-like wisp of smoke coiling from the cigarette Basil's fingers. "Si," he said to the waitress. She nearly missed his coffee cup while she poured. She was obviously fascinated by the American artist—his dangling hair and his dark eyes that were far away. "Grazie," Basil said quietly and smiled. She smiled back with her eyes, perhaps wanting to say more. And I imagined that she considered it. I imagined her thinking, *I could tell him exactly what I felt, what I wanted and he wouldn't understand a lick of it.* Safely experiencing what it would be like to say what she would never say to a stranger. A stranger that was as mysterious as the feeling of her own self-restraint.

The face of Julia Iris filled my mind suddenly—the morning she served me coffee at The Floating Hope in Idaho. I wondered briefly if my eyes had made similar suggestions. Would I have dared to say aloud the flood of imagery that she created for me in those few precious moments on our first meeting? I shook off the memory.

Albion, Angelo, Corey and I watched Basil and the waitress from behind the mirror. "He knows he's being watched. He has a talent for that, you know," I offered.

None of my new companions answered. We watched my brother in silence. As the waitress turned, Basil pulled a pen from his breast pocket and began to draw on a napkin. The waitress leaned over to get a look at what he was sketching. Noticing her, he abruptly yanked the napkin from the counter. "No, no," he said to her gently. Startled by his quick movement the waitress drew back.

"Escuse," she said, embarrassed, and retreated toward the back kitchen. Basil watched her go. The look in his eyes was both stern and disappointed. My brother's bane —never share your work.

He turned his attention back to the napkin. A few moments later he placed his pen back in his breast pocket and took a long sip from his steaming coffee cup. Setting the cup down he raised his head and looked into the mirror behind the counter. He grinned.

"Albion, Angelo, Corey," I said, "please turn away."

"What, why?" Angelo asked.

"Just do it," I warned.

"What do you fear?" Albion asked.

Basil stood and began to limp around the counter moving steadily closer to the mirror.

"I'm not sure," I said, "but he can render the Center. And if he puts *that* in your way, you can join the people a few floors down. So, please—"

Albion and Angelo immediately turned away from the mirror. Corey remained still, staring at Basil.

"Corey! Do as I say," I warned.

Angelo added angrily, "Corey, turn away."

A subtle smile hinted upon Corey's lips as Basil now stood staring directly into the mirror. His face was expressionless. He raised the napkin and slapped it up against the glass. "Corey!" I yelled.

Corey's eyes narrowed slightly, and his smile faded.

Pressed against the mirror, on the thin porous paper was written, "I'M IN."

"A lot of mirrors in this place, *Al baby*," Basil quipped. "Not a whole bundle of trust?" Basil now stood with us in the surveillance room behind the coffee shop's mirror.

Albion shifted uneasily in his stance. I could see that Basil's irreverence bothered the Director of the EMHL—a man who had pledged his life to the betterment of others through patient academia was now forced to place his trust in a cheeky, self assured, pot-smoking American. *An artist*. I wondered if Albion thought of the word *artist* as a rude expletive.

"Only for your protection, Basil," Albion replied.

Basil tapped the mirror, looking through at his still steaming cup. "Even in the coffee shop?"

"Yes, dear Basil. We will forever pride ourselves on your safety. While you are in our care, no one will harm you."

Basil nodded in long, barely suppressed sarcastic ups and downs. "Nice," he said finally. "Good to know. Good to know."

I decided to interrupt. "Basil, what prompted you to change your mind?"

He didn't respond. Instead he moved to the opposite end of the room and said, "So, how do we get started? What do you need me to do?"

Angelo eagerly stepped forward. "Miss Rentana. We would like you and Dr. Newirth to meet her. Dr. Newirth will provide for you a prognosis. Hopefully from there you will be able to find the right imagery to bring her to health."

"That simple, eh?"

Angelo nodded, with lights in his eyes, "We hope so."

"Very good. I'll need a studio."

"A studio has long been prepared for you, Basil," Albion said. "I think you'll be quite at home."

"I'm gonna need some weed," Basil said.

"Not an issue," Albion replied.

"And a kick-ass stereo."

"Already done."

"With a turntable. No digital shit."

"We can make that happen." Albion said, "It might take a few days--"

"And the entire *Rush* discography on vinyl, to start."

"Very well."

Basil's eyes squinted and he took an awkward step toward Albion. "And no cameras, mirrors, microphones, or any of that shit in my studio. Nothing. Believe me, when I'm working, I'll know. I'll know. Nothing in there, got it?"

Albion paused, looking at the artist. "It will be done. No surveillance."

My brother took out a cigarette, raised it to his mouth and grabbed it with his teeth. "Okay, then." He sparked his lighter and lit it. Angelo was gazing at Basil in wonder. Basil looked at him thoughtfully and said, "So, you got any *Floyd*?"

I had spent nearly an hour educating Basil on Rentana and her illness later that afternoon, at least what I was able to determine from her records. Despite his aloof demeanor I lectured carefully, mindful that Basil's knowledge of mental illness was limited. I took care to choose words that he would understand and often ended particularly important diagnostic statements with, "Is that clear?" *Sure,* he'd say from time to time as he hobbled around his new studio, inspecting every inch. Dejected, I finally challenged him.

"What's the problem? Does anything that I'm telling you matter?"

"Yes, and no," he said, thumbing through the delicate, long-handled brushes that were laid out like surgeon's instruments.

There was no need for me to respond. He could see my body language saying, *What do you mean, goddamn it?*

He sighed with impatience. "Yes, in that Rentana is wacked-out. No, in that all that crap that you are throwing out doesn't mean shit to me—nor will it to her. If we're lucky, she'll be walking and talking and having a grand old time by this evening. She'll even remember who she is—or better, *why* she is, and she'll be what Albion Ravistelle might call, *the perfect human.* You just need to watch, take notes, and pay attention. I'm making this shit up as I go. And besides, once you learn how to use your gift, I am out. Get it?"

"Basil, don't you understand what it's going to mean to the world—what you are about to do for the sick—what you are about to share?"

He paused, staring, into some distant place. "Not exactly. And let's just hope we get lucky."

"Why did you change your mind—to do this?"

"Three reasons," he said reaching across and picking up a handheld device. "No turntable yet—instead there's this—*an iPod*," he said with disdain. "Four thousand songs in this little thing. Makes me feel cheap using it." He looked at me with one brow raised, "Listening to music should involve some responsibility, shouldn't it? Like pulling out a record, caring for it, reading the lyrics, being dazzled by the artwork, something, right?" He circled his thumb on the white plastic dial, "Ah, who gives a shit these days anyway? People are fucked."

"What reasons?" I asked.

"*OK Computer*." The room vibrated with distorted electric guitar as if a chainsaw was tearing through the wall. Basil smiled broadly. Moving around the table he stood close at my side and spoke into my ear as the studio speakers raged.

"No matter what assurances Albion gives that I'm not being monitored, I'm not taking any chances." He turned the volume knob a click louder. "They want to manipulate me. I'm not entirely sure how, but I won't let it happen. It is *my* art. No matter what happens. And yes, something tells me that I can help these people. But I'm not entirely sure how. But that isn't the biggest problem. I just don't know what it will mean for my work. What it will do to the other side." He paused and stared down at the marble tiled floor. "I don't trust Albion Ravistelle and his minions. There is something more happening here. I'm afraid he'll hurt you, Diana, Howard. . .all of us. Something tells me that if I don't cooperate—" he broke off.

"He'll what?"

Basil shook his head. "Funny," he spoke into my ear. "I just found you. I never thought I'd be as glad as I am to have real family. *Reason one.*"

I pulled my ear away from him and studied his expression. It was the first time I'd seen Basil show soft sincerity. The cut on my palm stung like fire. I squeezed my fist tight and closed my eyes, struggling to come to terms with my covenant. Albion's words, Basil's words, my own words echoed,—*more important than any of us*. The speakers groaned and Radiohead's vocalist, Thom

Yorke, completed our refrain—*I am born again.*

Basil limped to the other side of the table and lowered the volume to a tolerable level. "Well, nice sounding system," he said loudly.

"I don't trust him either, Basil," I said, "but how can we not take the chance—"

"Either way," he said, "you do what you've got to do, and I'll do what I've got to do." He smiled at me, and said, "*Reason two*, I'm feeling like helping out some sorry, screwed up bastards. And *three,* I *have* to paint. I have no choice."

I held his eyes. He nodded, "Don't worry, Loche. I'm done with fear. Let's do this thing. Get Miss Rentana in here."

As I moved toward the door Basil added, "And have Angelo send up some za."

"Za?" I said confused.

"Dude," he sighed. "Za. *Pizza*, you know?"

Due to Rentana's extreme disorders we were forced to use the glass room at the end of Basil's studio. The enclosure was engineered to protect Basil and myself from our terribly disturbed, *Saved* patients. It was also the only way Basil could work without having resident supervision in the studio.

Rentana mashed her cheek against the glass. Her hand fluttered up and down as if mocking Basil's busy brush, smearing saliva across the pane. Basil's quick glances at her were pained and uncomfortable.

Rentana crooned with Basil's cranked up music and occasionally slapped the glass with the flat of her wet hand. She looked to be in her mid to late forties. Dr. Catena's record of her background was torn and gap-filled, but there were threads that told a bit of her story. She was liberated from a Serbian concentration camp just outside of Banja Luka by American Peace Keepers in 1995. The war in Bosnia during the early nineties—the war that was somehow overlooked by the international community—bred its share of psychological casualties. Serbian militants rose to yet another ethnic cleansing frenzy. Albion had provided literature prior to my meeting Rentana, and it outlined the horror that descended upon Banja Luka—a city of nearly 100,000 Muslims, Croats and those of mixed parentage. The city was subject to terror attacks by armed Serbian soldiers at all times of the day—rape, torture, mass murder, fear and suffering. Where was the world? The so-called leaders of freedom? What kind of God could allow such pain?

The psychological damage that Rentana had sustained had left her without voice, reason or hope.

It was uncertain that *Rentana* was indeed her real name. UN Peacekeepers had supposedly learned her name from another prisoner from the camp. She was brought to the EMHL in Italy and had been living out her days in the bleak torture of madness. But at least, as Dr. Catena said, *she's safe now.*

Saved.

My mentor, Marcus Rearden, came to mind. If only I had his help right now. I had never been faced with such an extreme case of psychological trauma. And I, too, found myself pained, like Basil, watching her writhe behind the glass, imagining the unspeakable scenes that lurked in her memory.

"Damn it," Basil muttered.

"What?"

He glanced up at me, noting that I had heard him. "Nothing. I'm just getting warmed up."

"What does that mean?" My voice was laced with worry.

Basil grinned. "Easy now." He reached for a rag and leaned into the standing easel. "Just a value thing—too much blue. Gotta fix it, nothing serious."

Observing him work I saw that his wonted casual manner was hidden. He looked strangely unfamiliar as he painted. Focused eyes, genuine expression and nimble movement combined with his ash green thobe and paint stained top hat gave him the look of some unlikely wizard in a fairy tale. The smell of the oil paints mingled with the stick of incense that smoldered in the far end of the room. I recall Basil telling me how much he loved the combination of the two lingering in the air. Now he smashed his brush into his pallet and stepped back and away from the work, angling his head slightly. He then pointed his brush back into the canvas with long and lyrical sweeps. Moving the brush to the hand that held the pallet, he reached for his cigarette. He stood up straight with a grin and stared thoughtfully at his work, "There, that's better. Very nice."

I'll never forget the final hours of that evening, most of which I spent pacing at the far side of Basil's studio. The memory of *my* portrait—the swirling eyes like glinting flakes of gold, and the dark water of madness—I wondered what sort of hellish fright lay in store for Rentana.

The music stopped.

"I'm done." Basil laid his brush down. His eyes remained rooted in the work.

"Are you okay?"

He didn't answer right away.

"Basil?"

"Let's do this thing," he said.

"Should we let Albion know that we're—"

"Nope," he cut me off. "This one is for you and me to do. Whatever happens, we'll have to own it."

On both sides of the easel were two long boards that pivoted up and away from the painting. He tightened the wing-nuts keeping them taut. A sort of shelter. He then turned and from a drawer produced a shroud of black cloth and spread it over the boards and the painting below, being careful to keep the cloth from touching the wet surface. The shroud dangled over the angled boards like a curtain. He sighed. "I think you should go with her."

"What?"

He rolled the heavy easel toward me. "She may need you in there. Maybe not. But I want to know what happens."

"Basil, I don't think I can—"

"You'll be alright, Loche," he comforted as he moved the easel into position before the glass room, angling it just so. "C-c-come on. I d-d-don't know w-w-what's going to happen here. If s-s-something goes wrong, m-m-maybe you can save it. Just tell me what you see when its all o-o-over."

Rentana was mumbling a string of sobs behind the glass. It had a humming quality, like a powerful machine warming up.

"Get a chair," Basil suggested. "You might want to sit down for this one."

I don't remember moving the chair and placing it before the Center, but I found myself sitting there gripping the seat and slowly rocking my torso back and forth.

With one hand on the shroud, and one hand gently knocking on the glass, Basil called to her, "Rentana? Look up here." And then the break in his speech, "T-t-time to come b-b-b-back." Her eyes lingered on Basil's face and then drifted to the shroud. I heard the cloth pulled from the easel. The sound of a parachute opening, I thought. Somewhere behind her blank expression was a rising gale of horror. Veins along her neck swelled and the pinkish flush of heated blood colored her cheeks. For a split second I thought I saw in her eyes a spark of cognition. Then her eyes widened, pupils dilating like an oozing wound beneath fabric. Her lower jaw sagged open, as she breathed out a single gasp. A fine strand of light lingered out from the Center and gently entered her left eye. *The Silk.*

"Your turn," Basil said quietly.

What if I can't help, can't handle it, or I go in with them? My ears were thrumming as the fear took hold. The rectangular shape of the glass room and its parallel lines were like a line of fence along the ridge of a cliff. "Loche —" Basil's voice was now shrill, "G-g-go with her!"

I snapped my head in the direction of the painting.

Silence.

Flash.

Gone.

The sky was a bruised black and purple stain. It leaked out a flat, oppressive smolder of light, just bright enough to sting the eyes, lurid and dim. A hammer-like heat mingled with the glow and seared down on the powdered dust floor of a wide desert. It was as if the sun was veiled not behind clouds, but beneath the graveled crust under my feet. The landscape was a blinding, dirty yellow. Surrounding me were distant welts of low hills.

Thirst.

Some hundred yards from me was a barbwire fence line. Within its borders squatted several long metal shacks. I quickly scanned in search of Rentana. She was nowhere in sight.

A cry reverberated from the camp, metallic and stifled. I ran toward it.

My stride was heavy, and my feet crunched on the parched waste. A gate caught my attention. It was torn open. I curved my path toward it. The cry intensified.

Just inside the gate I stopped. Squeezing my eyes shut I tried to let my ears discern the direction of my next sprint. There was now more than one voice wailing and each seemed to be coming from different buildings. What's more, they seemed to repeat over and over, much like a scratched record. I fixed my eyes on the nearest building, and lurched toward it, feeling the pressing heat of the desert bear down on me.

I rounded the corner and saw a short three-step stair and a closed sheet metal door. The sound from this shack was louder than the others now. It was a painful moaning mixed with anger—or resistance.

I threw my body against the door and crashed through.

The sharp stench of urine and shit hit me as the door fell from its flimsy hinges. On the floor was Rentana, naked save a torn dirty slip bunched around her middle. Each of her limbs was held tight by four uniformed soldiers, while a fifth, with his pants around his ankles, raped her, pounding into her without mercy. I watched in shock and horror. None of the soldiers heeded my presence.

I hurled my body upon the rapist with an enraged scream, hoping to tear him from his victim, driving my knee into his ribs with killing force. There was no contact. I rolled across the floor and landed on my side against the wall. Beside me, the violence continued. Scrambling to my feet, I pivoted my body, and kicked at the head of the soldier that gripped her left arm. The blow met with nothing but air, and I again found myself on the stained wood floor.

There was a flash. I blinked. Then the same scene replayed before my eyes, like a record had skipped. I waited. Every ten seconds the scene replayed again. A moan from my own lips echoed hers against the metal walls. I turned my eyes away.

—You can't stop it. The voice had an accent. European.

Standing in the broken doorway was Rentana. She looked down without expression at her victimized self on the floor.

—Nothing can stop it now, she said. She looked at me with a hint of a smile. Her eyes were clear and her long brown hair dangled over her shoulders. She wore a delicate white cotton dress.

—You need to come away from here. Here it will stay.

I picked myself up and slowly followed her through the door. The stink of the room evaporated leaving only the crushing heat. She stopped and faced me. Her face was peaceful and glowing.

—Thank you. Thank you for trying.

She raised both of her arms and spread them wide, pointing in both directions along the long barbed fence line.

—Look.

Staring out at the desert was a row of Rentanas, like the Rentana I faced. Each of them stood like an elegant statue, stoic and hopeful. Their faces pointed out to the scorched horizon. And the numbers grew. From each metal shack came a form of Rentana, stepping gingerly out of the crying rooms and finding their way to their place in the row. I felt a hand on my shoulder. Turning I saw Rentana again.

—Thank you, she said. She exchanged a knowing glance with the form before me and moved on, joining the long procession.

—What is happening? I said, or thought.

—We are leaving now. We are leaving it all behind. Come.

I followed my guide through the gate, and she set out into the wasteland. Behind us, the forms of Rentana followed. Once all had cleared the gate, the group assembled behind us. I gazed back at the desolate camp. The mournful cries continued to echo. The gate that was torn down was now intact and locked firmly. I blinked my eyes. I thought I saw a shape move. A blur of a light, like the smear of a body moving behind a fogged window. There was movement. The gate trembled. It rattled as if something was struggling to get out.

—What was that?

—I don't know. Rentana looked back.

Then there were several blurry shapes moving behind the fence. The gate rattled violently now. It was the sound of frustration—imprisonment.

—Come, Rentana beckoned.

Crusted earth and gravel stretched out before us, and the purple wound of the sky glowered down as we walked. The rattle of the gate and the cries faded away.

The heat had become too much for me. My tongue felt cracked and swollen and breathing was difficult. I stumbled and fell.

—We are almost there. Rentana stopped at my side.

—I don't understand. I shouldn't be able to feel *this place.*

She did not answer, but instead stood quietly before me and smiled.

—We are far enough away now, I suppose. It is time.

Rentana turned and motioned for her train to move to her. Each by each the forms of Rentana melted into one. She knelt down.

—Let's go home.

"Here, Loche, take this." It was Basil's voice. "Take this." I could feel his hand gripping my wrist. He was trying to wedge a glass of water into my lifeless hand. The cool moisture on my fingertips startled me. I was back. The room was cool, almost cold.

I gripped the glass of water, raised it to my mouth and poured. The liquid streamed onto my parched tongue, and I guzzled half, the rest drooled down my shirt.

Basil knelt before me. His eyes were concerned. *Brother*, I remember thinking. "More?" he asked.

I shook my head and leaned back in the chair.

"How long was I gone?" I choked.

"A second. Maybe two. You blinked back yelling for water."

I sucked in a deep breath. The water dropped into my stomach and immediately calmed my senses.

"But you wouldn't take the water glass for three or four minutes. You just kept shouting for water. You were out of it for sure. How do you feel now?"

I squeezed my stinging eyes shut and then opened them wide. "I'm good, I think." My clothes still felt hot, as if the desert was trapped inside the fabric. Then, the memory washed over me—the gory sky, the crushing heat, the gun metal buildings—Rentana. Rape.

"How is Rentana?" I cried.

With a slight smile Basil nodded over my shoulder. "See for yourself."

I sat up and slowly turned to the glass room behind me. Rentana was standing with her hand spread out against the glass. Her eyes stared into mine. She was smiling. Her expression was the kind worn by a close friend that you'd not seen for many long years—inquisitive, hopeful and happy to see that you, too, had made it this far.

Without words we knew each other.

Dr. Angelo Catena's excitement was almost comical. He threw his arms around both Basil and me, ranting in quick, jovial Italian phrases, interspersed with English.

"It is good! She is better than expected!"

Nearly a day had passed since Rentana's viewing of Basil's work. My experience inside the painting had left me exhausted, and I had slept long. I was roused in the late afternoon. We sat around a dinner table inside the gothic dining room—Angelo, with his assistant Corey, Albion Ravistelle and the two families from North Idaho.

"Our interviews with her were incredibly positive," Angelo kept on. "It is as if she has come to terms with her past."

"Does she remember any of it?" I asked.

"Absolutely," Angelo nodded. "After you retired early this morning, we brought in a Bosinan interpreter. Our interview lasted until noon. We kept her awake for too long, I think. My assistant here suggested that she get some rest. I was a bit overzealous, I admit. This is an exciting time. But yes, she remembers everything in extreme detail." His smile took on a shadow, "Terrible things, Dr. Newirth. Horrible experiences. It is a wonder she survived any of it." His tone brightened, "But now it is a matter of watching her for some time—and learning from her."

I felt Helen's hand grip mine under the table. She gave a gentle squeeze that said, *You've done it. You've done it.* I glanced at her with a smile in my eyes. *But it wasn't me,* I thought. *It was Basil.*

Basil sat opposite me. He was rolling the stem of his wineglass between his thumb and his index finger. He was deep in thought, his focus trained on the white tablecloth as if imagining his next work.

"I would very much like to speak with her," I stated.

"You will. She will be joining us shortly," Angelo said.

Albion Ravistelle raised his wineglass, "A toast. To Dr. Loche Newirth and Basil Fenn. May this be the beginning of the end for the maladies of the human mind." All, save Basil, raised a glass, and then drank silently.

"However, Dr. Newirth and Mr. Fenn," Ravistelle continued, "I would rather have been present for Rentana's viewing. So too, I believe, would Dr. Catena. I needn't tell you that we've great interest and care for this endeavor. Mind that nothing of the sort happens again, for if anything were to go wrong, we would like to be there to assist."

I looked at Basil. He was still spinning his wineglass, as if he wasn't listening. A moment passed, and it was obviously too much for him to swallow. "Easy there *Al baby,*" Basil quipped. "I'll tell you when you can be a part of it." The air surrounding us grew thick. Ravistelle was unmoved. Basil flipped out a cigarette and lit up.

Angelo broke the ice, "At this time, it is no matter," he said genuinely. "Rentana is exhibiting health, and that is the mission for us all." He nodded to Ravistelle. Ravistelle acknowledged the sentiment and looked at Basil, studying him with the hint of a smile. A smile of either suppressed rage or patient understanding. I wasn't sure which.

"Ah," Catena sighed, "and here she is." A finely dressed man in his mid twenties approached the table, and just behind him was our first patient. "Presenting Rentana Borna of Croatia. This is her translator, Adam."

"Excellent," Albion said, rising to his feet. "Please join us."

She looked beautiful and poised. She wore a long grey-green gown with thin straps over her shoulders. Her smile was glowing, and she looked to me. I returned the smile as she sat down without removing her gaze. She spoke to her translator, and Adam echoed, "She says, Dr. Newirth, that you look better than you did this morning."

I chuckled uneasily, "I suppose I do."

Rentana spoke again. "And your water glass is empty again." I glanced at my glass. It *was* empty.

"I'm still hydrating." Adam repeated my words to her, and she laughed quietly.

The rest of the dinner was spent listening to Adam translate Rentana's experience inside the painting. She recounted the scenes from each metal building; each of which was an entirely different horrifying event that she had endured during the war. She recalled rising out of her body (or bodies), turning and watching the experiences as if she were a member of some surreal audience. My presence she remembered perfectly, and she told of how I struggled to save her from the soldiers. As Adam told the grisly stories, I noticed that the company had stopped eating. I, too, lost my appetite. Helen was captivated by the stories. She was leaning in on the table and waiting upon every translated word from Adam. Howard Fenn noted her interest and, nodding to me as the first tale began, politely rolled his chair toward Edwin and led him out onto the veranda to watch the boats. He returned quickly, not wanting to miss anything, but kept an eye out the window on Edwin playing with another young boy. Helen didn't seem to notice.

Rentana ended her story with what Adam struggled to articulate as *joining together*. The point at which all of her traumatic experiences, her many forms, blended into one. "She blinked and was behind the glass," Adam told us. "Frightened, but safe. Safe when she saw Dr. Newirth."

"And so," Ravistelle said, "you left it all behind you."

Rentana smiled. She whispered softly to Adam. Adam translated, "She feels good. A little confused, but she remembers everything. And it is okay now. It happened, and she must move on. There is no fear anymore. There is no hatred or anger." Rentana spoke and Adam nodded, "It was like a bad dream." The woman's face was resolute and fearless. "And she has left it behind."

Albion Ravistelle placed his palms together and listened intently to Adam's translation. "A bad dream," he whispered to himself. He closed his eyes and tilted his head as if he were savoring every word. A subtle grin crossed his lips. I looked at his hands and thought about the stinging cut that lay there.

But as Adam finished, Albion held his hands up. "It has been left in the dream world, Rentana," he said. My eyes flitted from one palm to the other. There was *no* cut. No gash. No sign of any injury. It had healed. A sharp sting rose from the soft flesh in my fist. *How is that possible?* I thought. Albion didn't notice my captivated look.

"Tomorrow we shall carry on with our labors. Basil, I've another patient I would like you and Loche to meet."

Basil looked lazily at Ravistelle.

"Why, Mr. Fenn, are you not elated with the day's results?" Ravistelle asked, noting Basil's nonchalance.

Basil's eyes flashed to me. "Sure," he said masking his distaste, "I just hope it continues to work."

Dr. Angelo Catena rose from the table. Along with him rose Corey. "I hope that you'll excuse us, but we've much to do to prepare for tomorrow's tests. Congratulations, all."

Corey spoke next, "Mr. Fenn and Dr. Newirth, will you be needing anything else this evening?"

"I may go to my studio and work awhile tonight," Basil said. I could feel Ravistelle smile at the other end of the table.

"That is well," Albion said. "Your hard work is a stepping stone to our goal, Basil."

"If you need anything at all, please feel free to send for me," Corey said.

"Goodnight, everyone," Angelo bowed, "Come, Corey."

I raised my hand to wave goodbye and Corey's eyes shot from my hand to Albion's. He turned and followed Angelo.

A light tapping on the door startled me. I woke with my wife in my arms, her soft breathing warm against my chest. I carefully untangled myself from her and discovered that Edwin was lying close behind me. He was deep in dreams with his mouth wide open. I pushed my body up and over him and got out of bed. As I tied my robe around my waist I could see the moon arcing over the Venetian skyline. The digital clock read, 4:01 a.m. The quiet knock came again. I crossed the room and opened the door.

"You called?" It was Corey Thomas.

I stared at him blankly. *Did I?*

"How can I be of service?" he said a bit louder this time.

He could see that I was confused. He spoke loudly as if the walls had ears, and of course, the walls did. "A *nightcap,* Dr. Newirth? Why certainly. Won't you come with me? Your brother has ordered the same." He raised from his side a bottle of scotch—The Macallan. "Come."

I followed him down the long hall toward the elevator.

Basil was deep in thought as we entered his studio. John Lennon's crackly voice cried from the speakers, *Come together—right now, over me.* "Did you bring the goods?" he asked Corey.

Corey nodded and placed the bottle on a table. Moving to a cabinet he produced three rocks glasses. He poured the scotch.

Basil looked at me. “We’ve got to talk.” I looked at Corey. “Oh, don’t worry about him. We’ve been chatting it up for quite awhile now.”

“What’s going on?” I asked.

“We’re fucked,” Basil said simply.

“What?”

Basil looked at Corey. Corey was silent and took a long sip from his glass. He was eyeing both of us over the rim, amused.

“Can we talk here?” I asked, glancing to the corners of the room.

“Amazingly, yes,” Corey said. “Albion Ravistelle has allowed Basil’s request—*no surveillance equipment in the studio.* Why he allowed it I’m not completely sure. But it doesn’t matter now. He’s got you right where he wants you.”

“And where’s that?” I asked with a tinge of impatience.

Corey reached out with his glass and touched it to mine. “Here.”

“Me and Corey have been sharing some stories, Loche,” Basil said gently. “And he’s on our side.”

“Side?” I said. “What do you mean? We are here helping to cure—”

“Not exactly, Loche.” Basil interrupted.

“Let *this* begin the discourse,” Corey said producing an iPhone. He held it out so the screen was near to my eyes.

“Wait, Corey,” Basil said. “I think he should sit down.”

The man paused, sizing me up. “No,” he said after a second of squinting. “I think he’s getting better at taking shocks.”

The screen lit up. There was Helen. She was being videoed from what looked to be a small surveillance camera from the ceiling. She sat quietly in the back of the gothic dining room looking out the window. Albion Ravistelle stepped into the frame and sat beside her—

close beside her. My stance shifted slightly.

He took her hand, raised it to his lips, and kissed it gently. Helen, with her other hand, stroked his cheek.

"Diana was able to get a message through," she said. "She's *not* sick. Quite clever." The tone of her voice was alien and hard. If I didn't actually see her speaking I would have never believed that the voice belonged to my wife.

"Yes," Albion said still holding her hand. "It is no matter."

"Quite the ruse."

"Quite. A stunning performance," Albion agreed. "However, Miss Goddell's successful attempt will work to our benefit in the end."

"It has Loche thinking," Helen said. "But I believe he is still on track."

"Keep encouraging him, Helen. Now it is just a matter of time."

"Will they rebel?"

"Doubtful," he said threading his fingers through her hair. The silk handkerchief was still wrapped around his hand. "We've an agreement."

"Is that so?"

"Why, yes. A rather ancient *blood brother handshake*, as it were," he said mockingly, showing her his makeshift bandage. "That should hold him for the time being. But as I said, it is no matter. If they rebel, what can they do? I've Basil's catalogue, his closest family, his mother, Loche's child and, of course. . .you. His *dear* wife."

"You wouldn't kill *me*, would you, my love?" Her tone was laced with humor.

He smiled and leaned his body into her. They kissed deeply. I felt the air sucked out of my lungs and the first traces of blinding tears.

As they parted Albion said, "It won't be long now."

Helen nodded. "I can wait. I've always waited. Since the day you found me."

"Tests have begun in the Sun Room. We've treated five patients—shown five works."

"And?" Helen's tone was filled with desire.

Albion didn't answer but instead laid his palms together as if in prayer. With reverence he bowed his head. Helen kissed his fingertips.

"*He* is pleased. Very pleased," Albion said without raising his head.

Helen sat back quickly. "You've shared the news with *him*?"

"*He* will come here soon. *He* is proud of us."

My wife wrapped her arms around herself. The gesture was strange. It was as if she were struggling to master an explosive joy that her body could not contain.

"No more of this now," Albion said. "Go to your *husband*. I will call for you soon."

The screen went black. Corey lowered the device and watched my face. He put his hand on my shoulder and softly offered, "I'm sorry, Loche."

I staggered back a step and lowered myself down onto a chair.

Basil lowered his face to me. "From the first day I met Helen, way back when we dated, I always felt that I couldn't trust her." I saw her sleeping. Her warm body holding my young son. I could smell her skin. "Looks like she's always had another agenda—the bitch. When she couldn't get me she went right to you—"

I jumped back to my feet and shoved him. Basil's riposte was a similar push. "That's right," he said, "get pissed!"

Before I could think, I threw my fist into his ribs sending him to the floor. He folded over and coughed, windless.

Corey stepped between us, holding me back from another blow. "Loche," he said, "please stop."

I lunged again only this time I felt a sharp, cold stab of pain shoot down my spine. "*Brothers*," sighed Corey. His hand pressed on the back of my neck. My body stood motionless. The memory of William Greenhame and his nighttime visit to my office, so far away from here, funneled through my mind—the paralyzing pressure point.

"There is more for you to hear. Please restrain yourself." He let go, and I dropped heavily back on the chair.

Basil was recovering. He held an arm protectively over his stomach. "*Sure*, he's getting better at taking shocks," he managed to breathe out.

I lowered my head into my hands. "This is really happening, isn't it?"

"There is much I could tell you about your wife, Helen. But she is of little importance to us right now. What is important is that you know her betrayal. Albion Ravistelle wants Basil and his work. He's got it. All of it. He also wants you, Loche. He wants your gift to work for him—he'll do anything to get it."

"But I don't know how to do what Basil does."

Corey's eyes sparkled. "Have patience. You will."

"Why are you telling us this?" I asked.

Corey shook his head, continuing to size me up. "Dr. Newirth, let me see your hand."

I raised it. A red blot stained the center of the bandage. "I see you've cut yourself," he said playfully. From the table next to us he lifted a ball point pen. "Watch carefully." He lifted his own hand and without hesitation drove the pen through the soft flesh like a nail. A barely perceptible wince tugged at his eyes. Removing the pen a grisly hole remained, and thick blood slowly oozed from the wound. I looked up at Basil. He was transfixed.

"Wicked," Basil marveled.

"I said, watch carefully," Corey ordered.

I obeyed. Tiny clear bubbles formed on the outer edges of the hole and rapidly turned to a white foam. The bleeding had stopped. Corey watched the process with a blank air, as if bored. Corey wiped the foam away with his other hand. The hole was gone. He turned his hand over and over before my eyes and said, "You see? All better."

"What the fuck was that?" Basil exclaimed.

"That is what happens to an immortal who's been

skewered by a ballpoint pen," he said.

I blinked my eyes.

"Albion has a similar gift—your *blood brother* ceremony?"

"How did you know about that?"

"I have complete security clearance here. I am, after all, Dr. Catena's chief assistant."

Not knowing what to say, I stared at his hand. Corey's next utterance was yet another surprise. "You've the look of a *statue,* Dr. Newirth."

Your statue-like life will crack, and all beneath will melt into motion, came Greenhame's voice from just days before. His words taking shape—the shape of reality. I shivered.

"Yes, William Greenhame, dear fellow. I miss him terribly. I, too, am *Orathom Wis,* a Guardian of the Dream. Though, as of late, I've been trundling around behind Dr. Catena saying things like, '*Oh yes, that's a* grand *idea, Doctor. Yes, I'll get you a coffee. Yes, I'll get you a* sanitary cloth.' Quite funny really."

"And what about Angelo? Does he know about Ravistelle?" I asked.

"Not a bit. In fact, I don't think our inquisitive Doctor is in league with Ravistelle. He is convinced, as you were, that you are here to aid the sick and mentally disabled."

"But isn't *that* why we are here?" I asked.

Corey smiled. "Oh sure. Partly. The two of you have shown great promise. Catena is delighted. So, too, is Ravistelle. You've found a way to end the woes of man's mind. But there is much more to it. Ravistelle plans to share your gifts with more than just the *Saved* mental patients."

Basil's voice was filled with rage, "Who?"

"The leaders of the world, the inmates of every prison, the average person. He'll get your work out there for all to see, but he'll start with those who are powerful."

"I've seen these works, Corey. People won't be able to handle it. It will be damaging beyond recognition. It will likely kill—"

"Yes," Corey agreed. "But I'm not so concerned about that."

Basil and I stared at him in disbelief.

"Oh," he noted our expressions, "don't mistake me. That would be tragic, as death always is, but the death of the innocent, or *not so* innocent, is not *my* chief concern."

"What is your chief concern, then?" I asked.

"The invasion of Heaven." Corey emptied the last of The Macallan into his mouth, let the booze rest there for a moment, and then set his glass down beside the bloody pen.

Julia looks up. Ahead, the high steeple of Coeur d'Alene's Saint Thomas Catholic Church rises from the corner block. The lofty spire shines like a spike of silver in the early evening sky.

"Here?" Julia asks. The car slows and stops. "I think this is a bad idea," she objects. "Don't you think Ravistelle would know how to find Father Whitely?"

"It doesn't matter," Rearden argues. "I want to see him. He might be able to help."

Rearden looks up at the cross twinkling above the quaint neighborhood and thinks for a second. *John Whitely owes Loche a favor to be sure. He saved the priest's skin, so why not collect on it.*

A grey-green stone building stands just yards from the church with an open garage door—it is vacant. He eases the car inside and shuts off the engine. The silence is strangely deafening without the constant drone of the heater fan. Julia looks at Rearden. His hands still hold the wheel, and his face appears uncertain. She hastily opens the door and steps out. For an instant, the notion of fleeing grips her.

"Wait," Rearden says, his hand sliding into his jacket, feeling for the gun. The side door of the garage opens, and a young groundskeeper enters.

"You can't park here," he says, slightly perturbed. "This is reserved for—"

"We're looking for Father Whitely. Is he here?" Julia's tone is more of an order than a question, and it startles the young man.

"Yes," he answers, "but you can't—"

"Will you please let him know he has visitors." Again

her voice is authoritative—too rigid for the youth to dispute.

"What are your names?" he asks.

"Get Father Whitely," she repeats.

Her demand is clear—and the conversation is over. The young man stares at Julia, then quickly turns and walks toward the church.

Rearden's face fills the bathroom mirror. "I hate churches," he growls at himself. "How can these people believe such nonsense? Created sick and expected to be well. Insane."

Who is this person in the mirror? Does he look older? "Yes, you do," he says, rubbing his fingers into the soft patches of tissue sagging below his eyes. "Older by the day," he sighs. The old man is tired. Turning, he lifts his arms over his head, and stretches his sore back. "Long, snowy drive, killing people—"

"It was necessary," he assures himself, "besides, those were no *ordinary* people."

The air smells of sweetened bleach. He stands inside the sanitary white of a 1960s style bathroom that is kept assiduously clean. A small digital clock blinks beside the door. The glowing red numerals flash the wrong time, 2:00 a.m. *Not many of God's people visit this bathroom*, Rearden thinks.

The groundskeeper had led Rearden and Julia down into the undercroft of the church. Rearden's first thought as he descended below the mortared walls of the chancel was—*bunker*.

One long, well-lit hallway links together the furnaces, project rooms and storage areas. At the very end are two windowless living quarters that share a single bathroom. The bedrooms are relatively small, plain and painfully white. But the beds are soft, and after a day like today, Rearden wants nothing more than to fall onto one and sleep.

He turns once more to the mirror and again tries to rub the bags under his eyes away.

"Got to find Loche," he whispers to himself. "Chances are slim. And if you fail, then what, you old fool? You are too old to be running around like some swashbuckler. Look at you—a gun in your coat, your old life abandoned. A couch and a client, that's where you belong. How the hell did you get here?"

His reply is steady and direct, "You know well enough. You wanted *more*. So *more* you've gotten."

"I'll find him," he resolves, pointing a sharp gaze into the eyes in the mirror. "I'll find him for Elanor. And after that, everything will return to normal."

He flinches suddenly, as if a spider has dropped onto his shoulder. There is nothing there, but across the room he sees the red numerals of the digital clock blinking like glowing eyes. He fancies a thin silk line is threading out from them, reaching toward him. The clock squints and Rearden hears it speak, "Soon, Rearden, I'll have both you and Loche. There are always two."

"Leave me be!" the doctor yells at the glowing eyes. "I'll find him before you do! I'll deal with-"

The knock on the door silences him, and the slender web recedes into the eyes of the clock.

"Are you alright, Marcus?" comes Julia's concerned tone on the other side of the door. "Who are you talking to?"

Rearden mashes his eyes shut and stammers, "Uh, Julia?"

"Yes. You okay?

It *is gone, whatever* it *was*, Rearden thinks, and he replies aloud to Julia with confidence, "I'm fine. I'm talking to myself. I'll be out in a moment."

As he reaches for the door latch he does not notice that his hands are shaking.

Julia is sitting at a small oak table beside the door. She looks up as he enters.

"Talking to yourself?"

Rearden does not answer. Instead he starts toward the

door. "I'm going to go and see what's keeping Father Whitely." Julia sits with the book on her knees. She nods and opens it to where she left off.

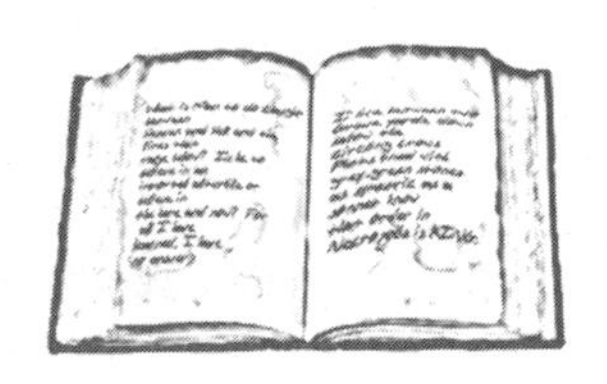

"Invasion of Heaven?" I asked.

The immortal nodded. "Tell me, Loche, when you were transcendent, searching for Rentana within Basil's work, did you happen to see smears in your vision?" Corey squinted as if struggling for the right question, "Like colorful patches of moving fog?"

"Yes," I said. "As the forms of Rentana joined into one I looked back at the fenced camp. Behind the fence were blurry shapes. Difficult to describe."

"Did you hear anything?"

"I noticed that the gate was locked shut when we were out. It was rattling."

Corey nodded again.

"And there were screams, or howls. They were different from Rentana's cries."

Corey turned away. He walked toward the bottle of The Macallan with slow thoughtful steps. The bottleneck plinked on the rim of his glass as he poured another shot.

"You aren't the first to report such things," he muttered.

"What things?" Basil asked.

"Wait," I broke in. "Who else has seen these paintings?"

"I have," Corey said quietly to me. His tone was woeful. "But not without unspeakable regret. I have seen several of your works, Basil. Yes, I have survived—but only because I have a body and mind that can regenerate health and hope. That does not mean that I don't feel what a normal human being can feel, I do, and more profoundly. It took me days to recover each time I entered the Center. But it was necessary for us to learn the dangers that the two of you bring.

"To answer your question," he turned to Basil. "We believe those blurs or smears are the imperfections of mankind left there to contaminate *the Orathom*, the Dream. Sit down, both of you. We haven't much time and what I'm about to tell you is difficult to comprehend."

"Oh, that's a killer surprise," Basil groaned, lowering himself onto a stool.

"Do you believe in the Devil?" Corey whispered.

"If you would have asked me that a few days ago I would have said no," I replied, "but now—"

"Since the dawn of time, from Egypt's evil Seth to Eve's serpent in the grass, since the temptation of Christ, and all the different manifestations in between, *It* has been with us. All the stories, the books, all the human interpretations have been quite accurate in depicting *It*."

"Red with horns and all?" Basil said with sarcasm.

Corey glared at him. "Basil, you would do well to not make light of what I'm telling you. If any image of *It,* in art or words has filled you with dread, or disturbed you in any way, it is of no comparison to *Its* true form. Does *It* have horns? Is *It* red? If you choose. I suppose *It* could appear in that way. But I've experienced something beyond what words can express. Blank and pure hopelessness, without face, without sight. The simplicity of *fear* would be wished for, even welcomed, for fear is a known feeling. What *It* possesses is beyond madness.

"But mortal man's depictions do fall short, as usual. And most importantly, Man's belief of what *It* desires is erroneous and shortsighted. In fact, Man's belief as always, is rather egocentric."

My thoughts drifted back through my college studies of Christian theology. Satan's primary desire is to deceive mankind into rebelling against God. Sin. The old story.

"Man has told himself through the centuries that Satan, Lucifer, Hades, Pluto, whatever you want to call *It*, is the supreme corrupter; *Its* charge is to blind Man through sin. Bar him from everlasting life. *It* wants Man's damnation."

"You are saying that *It* doesn't want this?" I asked.

"No, I'm not saying that," Corey shook his head. "I'm saying that *It* wants it all. The arrogance of Man has always been rather comical to myself and those like me. Your kind has always believed that you were at the center of *It's* desire. *It* has blinded mankind with their own magnificence and self-importance.

"*It*, gentlemen, wants Heaven, or what you might understand as *Heaven*. We call it the *Orathom*—the Dream. *It* wants every deity, every god, every saint, every human soul, and ultimately—*everything*. The real suffering will be if *It* succeeds in the life to come. The invasion has begun."

"And Basil's Center is the breach?" I shuddered.

"The Center is the breach," Corey nodded and took a long pull of whiskey.

"But how can this be?" Basil cried.

"If humans are confronted with Basil's Center, they cross the threshold into the abode of the gods—into the Dream—the *Orathom*. And they take with them their imperfections, their sin, their hate, their fear and their—" Corey broke off and dropped his eyes to the floor.

"Their what?" Basil asked.

"Their disease. Humanity." He drew his gaze back to ours, "Humanity is beautiful, gentlemen, but beyond the Center it—it spreads and fouls what was never meant to be fouled. It suffocates the hope of what lies after this life. The gods visit your paintings, Basil, to feel the human spirit and its passion. A human that sees your work infects the *Orathom* with humanity in all of its glorious and damned manifestations. The blurs you saw, Loche, were Rentana's horrors, which are now forever caught within the *Orathom*—forever gnawing away at the omniscient beings that are present there. The horrors of rape, murder and fear have been unleashed in a place that was never intended to be opened to such atrocities."

Basil's mouth gaped open.

"Rentana left her pain there and returned, unscathed. Unscathed because when she viewed the painting she was but a shadow of a human being. The mentally stable, however, will not be able to survive the experience, here in the *Alya*—the Life. Their minds will be forever scarred by the light of infinity. Ravistelle has begun showing paintings to the patients that you've met. This is only the beginning. He plans to bring Basil's work to those who control government and those who have committed crimes—those whom he can assume possess the darkest and most potent evils."

Basil struggled to respond but was only able to utter, "But, but, I—"

"It is no fault of yours, my friend," Corey consoled. "It is the work of *It* and those who follow *It*. They have waited for you to come. And you, as well, Loche. Though I'm still unsure what part you are to play. I believe that *It* is also unsure of your part."

"Is *It* Ravistelle?" I asked with trepidation.

Corey's laugh was like lurid sunlight cutting through black storm clouds. "No, no. Albion is, like me, immortal. He could have been great, but he is plainly a shortsighted tool. I have plans for him. No, *It* has a name. *It* has taken a human form. *It's* name is Nicholas Cythe. And *It*—he—is coming here soon, and now is the time for you, Loche, to escape."

"Why me and not Basil? Why not all of us?"

Corey nodded with understanding. "I'm afraid we aren't in a position to free all of you. Ravistelle now holds all the cards, and he will surely kill your son, Diana and Howard if both of you were to disappear. Basil will continue to paint regardless of Albion's threats because that is what Basil does. And if I'm not mistaken, Basil, you can't survive if you don't paint."

Basil looked away gloomily.

"What do you mean," I asked, "you can't survive?"

Basil's complexion greyed. "I guess you could say that painting for me is a kind of nutrient—a kind of food.

If I don't paint, I starve. I get really sick. I experimented with it. When I began developing better techniques at rendering the Center, the work started to feel dangerous. I guess, I sensed all of this stuff you're explaining. I stopped. I was scared of it. I went maybe a week without holding a brush. My whole body hurt—it felt as if I was starving. It was awful. When I started up again, I was fine."

"Can we destroy the paintings?" I asked.

Corey shook his head grimly. "We're afraid to do that. The *Orathom Wis* had first believed that incinerating a portrait would be like trying to burn the ocean with a match. We concluded that the renderings had a kind of life of their own. It would be nearer to killing. We fear that the subjects of the paintings, those who Basil has rendered in the portraits, would perish—but so, too, something on the other side would also find its demise. Again, we know too little as to their power and super-nature. *Destroying windows is always a messy affair*, as my mentor, George, says. Much like breaking a mirror is bad luck."

Basil said, "Yeah, after finishing a piece—I felt that it was alive, looking back at me."

My scotch glass was empty. I gazed into it and struggled to make sense of all I was hearing. Thoughts of Helen's betrayal mixed uneasily with Corey's ominous stories. I desired to hear the comforting voice of Marcus Rearden. I imagined his understanding— his empathy. I imagined his help.

"What about our mother, Diana?" I said, still peering into my empty glass. "They know that she's feigning—"

"That has already been arranged," Corey said.

"What?"

"Your father will take care of it."

"My father?" I gasped, looking up.

Corey nodded. He seemed to want to say more but held back. "You will be meeting with your mother again soon, if all goes as planned. The *Orathom Wis* have ordered me to get her to safety by tomorrow. I will say no more. You need only focus on what your muse instructs,

Loche. Write. Bring your *gift* into the light. Let that be your mission."

"I don't know how to—"

"I know. But we must get you away from here so that when your *gift* comes, you may be in a position to use it as opposed to Ravistelle using it, and you. He'll not do any harm to the others until he must. He'll wait for your move. And if that time comes, we'll be ready."

"Where am I to go?"

"Anywhere but here."

"Good evening, I'm Father John Whitely." His cassock is a stark contrast to the surrounding white room.

Julia stands and reaches her hand out, "My name is Julia Iris. We're friends of Basil Fenn and Loche Newirth."

"Yes," he says. "Marcus here has shared that with me. So how can I help you?"

For several awkward seconds the two travelers stare at John without speaking. The priest stares back. There is a knocking on the door. "Ah," Father Whitley says. "I've had some tea brought for us." He opens the door and receives a tray from the groundskeeper. "Thank you," he says to the young man.

Marcus seats himself on the edge of the bed and gladly receives a steaming cup. Each of the trio take silent sips.

"Thank you for meeting with us," Julia says and she explains how she and Loche became acquainted, and that she has fallen in love with him. Slowly she recounts the journey to the Priest's door, leaving out the horrible scene in the snow. She is reluctant to divulge the incredible traits of Basil's work. She wants to hear it from the priest's mouth.

"You introduced Basil to a Bishop Alin?" she asks.

The priest nods. "I did. And I regret the day." He says. "Basil has been my friend since childhood. We took different paths. Mine was God's way. Basil's was Basil's. His was the path of passion, that's the nice way of saying it. Several of my colleagues here might say the path of sin —but Basil has always been too close to my heart for me to view him in terms of black and white. He has a talent not of this world."

Marcus' body shifts on the bed. *True indeed*, he thinks.

"Basil had put together a series of paintings that celebrated the divine, or at least that's what he told me. I felt that by showing his work to Bishop Alin, Basil might find some artistic success."

"Did *you* see the paintings?" Marcus asks.

John shakes his head. "No. And I know that sounds strange, but Basil doesn't show his work very easily."

"Then what prompted you to introduce his art to Bishop Alin?" Julia's tone is confused.

The priest smiles simply. "Faith. I witnessed a miracle with his father, Howard. Basil placed a painting before his father's comatose eyes, and the man revived. I can't explain it in any other way. It was God's hand on the canvas. I'm sure of that." Julia and Marcus nod in unison. "Ever since then I have believed in Basil, even without seeing his work. So when he told me that his latest series dealt with divinity—and, what did he say*? The Godlike, big deep heavy*—something told me I could help him—that *he* may be able to help *all* of us. Sounds silly, I'm sure. But regardless, I followed my heart. It was clear that he was caught up in something that I feared was beyond his scope—and my knowledge. I felt that a man like Bishop Alin could help." Father Whitely shakes his head sadly. "I had no idea that he was corrupt."

"Corrupt?" Marcus repeats. "How so?"

"I don't know directly. I only met the Bishop four or five times, usually at social functions. During that short time we had built a rapport. Most of us at seminary had heard about his influence at the Vatican. Well, I made the introductions, and Basil certainly made an impression. In fact, Bishop Alin made a point to assure Basil and me that he would get in touch with some of his colleagues in Italy —to look into the matter of his art.

"This is all my fault. I'd not heard from Basil since that meeting with Alin—then I got a call from him wanting me to meet his brother—next thing I know I'm standing in Loche's destroyed home—watching a violent raid on Basil's flat—a man was killed right before my eyes. It was because of Loche that I was spared from whatever fate they now face." He puts his head in his hands and bows slightly. "To think that it's my fault. And now he is missing."

Julia forces herself to hold back the expression of sorrow. She recalls Loche's opening passages, *a revolver under Basil's chin exploding upward.*

"Loche has been in the local news, I'm sure you've both been keeping up on the Winship case."

The two nod. Marcus speaks suddenly, "Yes, it is tragic."

The priest studies Marcus. "Marcus," he said contemplatively. "Marcus *Rearden*? *Doctor* and *author*?"

Marcus hesitates, and then says, "That's right."

"I thought you looked familiar. I've seen you on talk shows, and I've read a couple of your books. You're also mentioned in the Bethany Winship case as Loche's mentor. I knew there was something—" The Priest then thinks another moment while Marcus shifts again, uncomfortably. "Elanor Rearden. Elanor Rearden was your wife?"

Silence from the old man answers the priest's question. John reaches out and gently places his hand on Rearden's shoulder. "I'm sorry," he said.

Rearden quickly looks at Julia then back to John and nervously lowers the cup to the saucer on his lap. The sound of the china seems extremely loud. Looking into his teacup he says quietly, "Thank you."

Julia gasps. "Marcus. Marcus? What? What happened?

Your wife—why didn't you say?"

"Julia, it's too complicated. I'm sorry I didn't tell you, but it was so sudden." *It* is *too complicated*, a voice warns in his head. He wonders, *How could Whitely have heard the news*?

"The priesthood always keeps an eye on the obituaries," Whitely replies to Rearden's thought. "And her passing this morning made the evening paper. After all, you are quite well-known."

"What happened, Marcus?" Julia asks.

Rearden raises his head. Avoiding her gaze he says, "Massive heart attack. She died instantly." *The* Center *ripped her heart out of her body*, screams a voice.

The touch of Julia's hand on his seems to break him from a stupor. He smiles. "I'd rather not talk about it now, dear." He is resolute.

"But Marcus," Julia says. "Why didn't you at least tell me? My God. . ."

"I can't talk about it now," he scowls. "You'll know why in time." *All of you will know.* "Right now, we have the chance to save Loche. I'll mourn for Elanor later."

"Doctor, will you be attending Beth Winship's funeral?" The priest asks.

Marcus flinches, and as he does he nearly drops the delicate tea cup. "Funeral? Why, yes. Tomorrow isn't it?"

"Yes," the priest replies.

Julia's eyes flash with a stab of angry light. "Another bit of news that I'm just hearing. Funeral tomorrow?"

Rearden doesn't answer.

"Do you think Loche will be there?" Julia demands.

"Yes," Rearden says. "It would be a good strategy to make an appearance to further his case. If he attends it will show that he cared for her and her family's well-being—and that to him, the legal case is secondary. A move I myself would make."

"You don't believe that he is responsible for her death, do you, Marcus?"

The doctor has rehearsed the answer to this question many times, and he is surprised it took so long for Julia to ask it. "It's not a question of whether he's responsible for it. It's a question of whether he breached our Code of Ethics. Did he do something wrong? Yes, Julia, he did. He failed to follow protocol. But as you and I both know," Rearden glances quickly at Father Whitely then back to Julia, "all of this seems small compared to what Loche is now dealing with." Julia feels the cold leather cover of the journal beneath her fingertips. "He's going to need us."

"Father Whitely," Julia turns, "I'm afraid we're in need of a place to stay. May we spend the night here?"

The priest's body language is hesitant, but in his voice is what both Rearden and Julia long to hear. He says soothingly, "This is a house of God—all are welcome."

Outside the wind has picked up, and a grey evening is drooping in the trees. Rain has begun to fall turning the day's snow to a messy slush. The radio weather report is predicting a warming trend, and as the young groundskeeper finishes shoveling the last of the walks, he adjusts his headphones under his stocking cap and heads toward the garage. As he enters, the evening news broadcast is beginning.

He hangs the snow shovel up by its handle on the wall. Turning, he notes the wrecked and dented side of the visitors' car. Leaning down to take a closer look he can tell that the accident must have been recent because the paint is still flaking in areas. There is no damage on the other side, but above the rear wheel he notices several splattered spots, and a smear of red.

The radio newsman reports—*Two murdered—Doctor Marcus Rearden is a suspect. License plate number—*

A moment later he is running toward the church, pulling his headphones down around his neck.

The sound of Rearden's snoring in the next room is

calming. Perhaps knowing he is asleep allows Julia's nerves to relax. He is a handful. And frightening. And she wonders if she can trust him. But, given all that has transpired, she is not entirely sure she trusts herself.

It feels good to remove her heavy clothes. She slips her bare legs beneath the sheets, lays back and opens the book. She will finish it tonight.

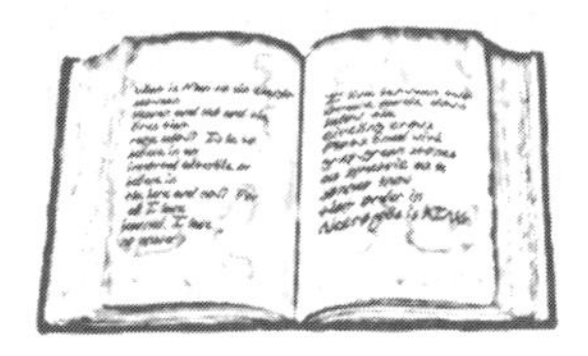

The clock read 5:32 a.m. Helen was sound asleep—*or was she*? Sliding my feet down under the sheets and lying back, I could smell the familiar warmth of her skin—the musk of home. My stomach ached for some answer that my mind could not resolve, and raising my fingertips to my eyes, I wiped away tears. It was the pain of missing. The sweet rising scent of my slumbering wife was, to me, the paragon of intimacy—the silent lines of love that words or pictures could not express. We had exchanged vows, we had made love, we had brought a child into the world, we had shared our lives, memories, hopes and fears together—even in the dim hours of sleep, our communication had always carried on. Home was tangled up in the air around us as we were laced together beneath the blankets of sleep.

Corey's last statement pinched at the nerves of my fragile sanity, "*You must* not *confront Helen with the information you are now privy to. Play along. Play along as if all is well. And remember what I've told you—she is not who you think she is and would kill you if she were ordered to do so. Think of your son. Don't let your emotions get in the way of what you must do.*"

My son. What will this mean for him? Then a shock wave rattled through me. I recalled the image of Albion and his daughter on the dock as we floated out and away. Crystal. Helen embraced that young girl. *"Edwin and Crystal will take to each other like brother and sister,"* He had told us. *Is Helen Crystal's mother?*

How long? How long had they been together?

Helen rolled over and faced me. Her eyes were still closed, and she draped an arm over my chest. On her hand was her diamond wedding ring. It sparked in the dull light of morning. I suddenly felt my own wedding band tightening like a stranglehold. "Good morning," she whispered sleepily. "Where have you been?" I could feel my hands tighten into fists. I released them and sighed as naturally as possible. An exhausted sigh.

"Basil's studio," I answered. "He had some questions about a painting." I reached out to my robe to make sure the contents were still in the pocket—passport, money, given to me by Corey. Comforted I brought my fingertips to the soft skin of her wrist and gently caressed.

"How did you sleep?" I asked.

"Heavenly," she whispered.

"Have you met with Anthony?" Ravistelle asked. We stood at an espresso counter in the main lobby near the lift.

"Yes," I said. Anthony, another of the *Saved,* was currently housed in the glass house in Basil's studio. "Basil is working now."

"Very good," Ravistelle said.

I felt a quick jolt of panic and then mastered it. I was about to take my first step toward escape. *I must sound natural*, I thought.

"I've come to let you know that I'll be visiting the city today."

Albion's polished manner did not falter. "Ah, I see. May I ask why?"

I held his eyes with mine. "I've been writing."

Ravistelle set the tiny cup of espresso down. "That is

well," he said. "And?"

"And I need to walk and think. Simple as that, really. I have some problems to solve for a piece I'm struggling with. Something is different about what I'm producing. I can't say for sure, but I think—I think it's happening."

"Dr. Newirth," he jubilated. "What wonderful news. Your gift is evolving." He reached out with both hands and set them on my shoulders like a proud father to his son. "Yes, please, go. Take your time. Will you be taking Helen with you?"

Helen, I nearly crumbled. "No," I said nonchalantly, looking at the woman behind the espresso stand. I nodded to her, and she began grinding a coffee for me. "I need some alone time," I said, knowing that I wouldn't be alone.

"Yes," he agreed. "That is to be expected."

"I may find a hotel for the night, as well," I ventured, making sure that my tone sounded like a request.

Ravistelle asks, "But what of the work that needs to be done with your brother?"

"I think he will be fine until tomorrow afternoon. I need to find out if what I'm writing is—"

"Yes, yes, of course. This certainly takes priority. Go, Doctor. And may your muse walk beside you."

"Thank you," I said.

In the glass room Anthony slept. Basil was busy with his brush. I closed the studio door and he looked up.

"Did *daddy* say it was okay?" he asked. By my silence he knew that Albion had agreed to my request. He set his brush down, and limped around the easel toward me. "Don't worry, Loche," he said, "I'll take care of Edwin. Corey says he'll make sure that he's safe. And Diana. . ."

"I still think that I should take Edwin with me."

"No," he disagreed, "like Corey says, it'll be too dangerous. Ravistelle won't use him. At least not until he needs to. And hopefully by then you'll have developed your *gift*."

"What if it doesn't happen?"

"It will," Basil said. "Is the plan clear?"

I nodded.

"Don't lose your nerve."

Basil looked over at Anthony. The poor man had stirred in his sleep and was now curled up into a ball.

"There's one more thing," he said.

"What?"

"Ravistelle *thinks* he has all of my work. But he doesn't. I have a single painting stashed away that only one person knows about. She hasn't seen it—I made her promise not to look at it. I felt the painting was important. That feeling was so strong that I separated it from the rest of my work."

"Who has it?" I asked.

A slight smile curved into his expression. "Julia."

Julia's face appeared before my eyes. I shook my head at the thought. "Julia has one of your works?"

"That's right. I trust her. There's something about her I've always liked."

"Does Corey know about this?"

"Nope. But I'm sure he'll find out eventually. You've got to get to that painting. You have to enter it."

"Why?"

"You'll understand when you see it. It's one of my latest pieces. Weird thing about it is that I couldn't finish it. I started it the day I left your office, when the police showed up, remember that?"

I nodded.

"Well, I went right home and started it. It's very weird—different from my other work—like it is still being painted somehow. Like someone, or some *thing* is moving the paint. It blows me away."

"What do you mean?"

A puzzled look crossed his face. "It was finishing itself—or better yet, it was changing by itself. The Center was still there, but its configuration was, well, moving. I mean, the interior of the Center was literally *moving*. I couldn't explain it and thought it was better not to wonder much about it. And every time it changed, it got heavier, and heavier. Like, I could hardly even pick it up."

"So you stashed it at Julia's?"

"Yeah. It freaked me out so much that I wanted it out of my studio. I took it to her that day, before me and John went to your house—and we ended up here."

"What was the image—the subject matter?"

"Someone drowning." He looked away, troubled. "There's something evil in it."

The blue god—pupils of stars swirling—entered my thoughts as if I were again witnessing his struggle in the black waters. I turned toward the door and Basil followed me.

"Take this," he said handing me an envelope. Julia's name was scrawled across the sealed flap.

"What is it?"

"You'll need it to get the painting. I made her promise that she would keep that work a dead secret. Without this letter you'd be talking to a wall."

"Is that all it says, *let Loche see the painting*?" I asked.

"Sure," he grinned. I took the envelope.

"Take care," I said.

"Don't worry about me," Basil smiled. "I'll be right here painting. And don't worry about any of us, bro. As long as I play along we should be fine. Just figure out how to stop this mad shit."

I pulled Basil into a hug. Our embrace was long, and I wondered if we'd ever see each other again.

Basil smiled turning and hobbling back toward his paints and brushes. As I closed the door I could hear the stereo volume rise. Through the door Mick Jagger's possessed cackle crooned—

Pleased to meet you, won't you guess my name?

Stench—boat fuel, raw sewage and other unsavory smells rose from the canal as I moved briskly down the boardwalk. But the odors were soon forgotten as I took in the extraordinary beauty of Venice.

I was out and away.

I relished the brief moments of freedom. But they were replaced by the overwhelming feeling of being watched. Ever since the day in my office when Basil shared his paranoia, I'd not been free of it. Then, Venice. Seeing the gothic architecture that I have long admired, and passing along the countless lanes stained with centuries of age and charm, I was able to smile.

Leaving Helen was surprisingly easy. I told her what I had told Albion, and she responded with his exact sentiment. Perhaps the most difficult aspect of our parting was my sudden desire to confront her—to show her my broken heart. Throughout my career as a psychologist I knew that anger had a role in our lives—and there was a way to use anger despite its wonted negative results. I shook my head at how many times I'd condemned anger as a weakness. *Doctor heal thyself.*

I tried to keep Edwin from sensing my grief at our parting. I laughed with him, held him close and kissed him. But in his face was a shadow of knowing my thoughts, though he couldn't express it in words. He knew I was going away. Our last embrace was enough to nearly change the plan that Corey had laid out for me. But it was when Edwin said, "Bye, Dad. Can I go play?" that I knew I must go—for him, so he *could* play. If I failed, there would be no more *play*—for any of us.

I reached into my coat pocket and produced Corey's hand written map. My walking course from the gondola stop had taken some unexpected turns. The buildings, the colors of the signs blending in like camouflage, and the many possible routes now all washed together. I mused that navigating this city must be like navigating a coral reef. It all looks the same, but intoxicatingly beautiful.

I was lost. I knew the way back to the canal and that

was some comfort. The map was now becoming worn and moist with the sweat from my hands. Scanning the sky I could see that it was evenly divided between a crystal blue and a deepening grey in the West. Cold raindrops began to touch down. It was difficult to determine if the sun would prevail. Either way, it was chilly and I wanted to find my destination. Then, below a weathered clock, LORD BYRON was embossed in the greenish brick of a building. I had found it. I recalled Cory's instructions: *When you see the sign, you'll see a wine bar near. Stop and have a glass—I think by that time, you'll need one.*

I walked a minute or two and came upon the quaint wine bar, complete with a gated patio and the deep wood hue of an old room. I entered and immediately felt the comforting warmth of a fire burning in the hearth near the kitchen. I moved to a seat at the bar. The path behind me looked clear. There was no sign of being followed. I motioned to the woman behind the bar, and she immediately poured me a glass of wine. Within moments I felt its sensual touch, and it eased my anxiety. In the dim glow I surveyed the room. Tucked into the corners there were patrons sipping quietly. One was reading, two lovers were huddled together behind a solitary candle and another man sat at the far end of the bar with his head tilted slightly up. He was listening to the soft voice of Joni Mitchell that drifted through the air like smoky incense.

The last time I saw Richard was Detroit in '68
And he told me
All romantics meet the same fate
Someday—
Cynical and drunk and boring someone
In some dark café.

I knew the song well. It was also the song that Corey told me to listen for when I arrived. "If you hear it, you'll know you're in the right place," he had said.

Was this man at the end of the bar the one I was to meet? Corey didn't say what would happen after the song played. The only comfort that eased my rising panic was the red wine, and after a long pull from my glass I ordered another, keeping one eye on the man to the right of me.

He reached down to his side, and from a bag slung over his shoulder he pulled out a package of cigars. Lifting one to his mouth he noticed me watching him. He held the package out and offered me one.

I shook my head.

"I love Joni Mitchell," he said so that I could hear him. His thick Italian accent ended with, "Amore, amore."

I nodded and watched him place the package of cigars back into his bag. Over his knee hung a closed umbrella.

"Do you know this song?" he asked.

I nodded, nervously.

"Ah," he said, "very good." Lifting his wineglass he drained it and set it back down. The barmaid filled it up a second later, and the man smiled at her. She placed the bottle on the bar and sang along with Joni's refrain.

"I am both cynical *and* drunk now," he said to me. "But I promise not to *bore* you." He then narrowed his focus and rested his eyes on mine. A pained smile shadowed his expression, "Why look, Maria, he's eyes full of moon. Ah, all good dreamers pass this way, you know. Here in this dark café. Just a cocoon before your wings? Yes? Yes."

Love so sweet, the man joined the melody, *When you gonna get yourself back on your feet?*

"Ah, I miss my sweet Leonaie," he said almost in whisper. "Leonaie Eschell, eyes green gold and grey."

A cool midmorning breeze filtered softly into the room. A door behind us had opened. The man set his glass down and tilted his head upward toward the music again and sighed. Before I could turn to the door I heard the shrill sound of metal sliding against metal, and a command, "Dr. Newirth, please step away from the bar and toward the door!"

Turning, I saw a tall figure standing just inside the room. He held a sword at his side. His glaring eyes weren't directed at me, but rather at the man smoking the cigar, his head still tilted to the music.

"Oh, good heavens," the man said through an exhale of smoke, but now with an English accent. "I had hoped it wouldn't come to this." He stood up with a slight stagger and with his glass in one hand and the umbrella in the other he addressed the man in the doorway. "Boun Journo, Felix. Felix Wishfeill," he greeted haughtily, "I am in the middle of boring this young man. Won't you come another time? We don't want to do this, do we?"

"Just protecting what is ours, Samuel" Felix replied.

Samuel turned back to the bar and motioned for his glass to be refilled. "Why not punch a song into the Wurlitzer over there, Felix. Choose a tune that's floaty and sad, and drink with us. Or go and drink at home with all your house lights up bright." He drank again, "Why don't you rush home to that figure skater wife of yours?"

"Dr. Newirth, please step this way," Felix commanded again.

In a flash, the handle of Samuel's umbrella unsheathed a long, thin silver blade. "Let's not, Felix. I'm in no mood. You can turn and call this day a failure and live to see tomorrow—or I'll piece you up and spread you around. I will put your candle out. Simple choice."

Felix weighed the thought. Fear tugged at his eyes. "Dr. Newirth, please come with me," Felix said again. I was paralyzed. The few people in the room backed themselves against the walls. Maria stepped into the shadows.

"Last chance," Samuel said calmly. "You are not thinking clearly. Remember well what they say about our kind, we don't join the *Orathom*. No afterlife for us. If we die here, we are cast into oblivion, to nothing, Felix."

"Some believe that," Felix spat. "Others say that we will rule the *Orathom*."

Samuel emptied his wine and set the glass gently on the bar. "You're an idiot, Felix Wishfeill." With another slight stumble in his balance Samuel raised his sword. "But, very well, you've been warned."

Felix scanned the condition of his enemy and noted

that he had the clear advantage. Samuel was drunk.

Felix lunged across the room with the sword angled for Samuel's throat. Samuel stood firm and waited for him. With a single flip of his wrist he batted the deadly thrust away and stepped to the side letting his opponent pass. Felix crashed into the bar with the flat of Samuel's blade slapping him on the back of the head. He roared in anger and swung his sword at Samuel again. Samuel ducked, staggered and scuttled a bit of distance between them.

"Goodness gracious me," Samuel laughed, "you *are* as boring as I am."

Felix's reply was a series of deadly thrusts and cuts that Samuel either parried or backed away from.

"So be it, Felix," Samuel said, "we shant meet again—I am sorry for you."

Another man entered the room. He, too, carried a sword. Before he could join the fray, Samuel quickly drew a dagger from inside his coat. It shot from his hand like a whirling wheel and embedded itself in the man's throat. His knees banged to the wood floor, and his hands flew to the wound. His choking was joined by a cry from Felix.

Samuel had driven his sword into Felix's right eye. His hands went limp and the sword dropped. "Gracious, Felix," Samuel said to him."Goodbye." With that he twisted the blade ever so slightly in the socket of his eye.

Felix croaked out in agony as the blade scrambled the soft matter in his skull. "I will find you again," he gasped.

Samuel paused, as if weighing what he was about to do—as if there was a finality, a permanence beyond death. Samuel's sword then flashed from the wound and slid through the flesh of the neck, the bony spine and out the other side. Felix's head clopped to the floor. His body slumped down after it.

The sound of the choking man in the doorway got Samuel's attention. The dagger was now in the man's hand and dripping with blood. White foam was beginning to form around the grisly puncture. White foam was splattered on the window along with the deep crimson of blood. "I don't recall your name," Samuel said. The man could not respond. "I've the feeling that you are of like mind with poor Felix over there. Yes?" The man writhed in anger and pain. "Will you yield? I'd hate to turn you to nothing."

As a response, Samuel received a mouthful of the man's spit and blood in his face.

The man's head fell apart into two husks of grey and red.

"Maria, a bag please," Samuel sang, wiping his cheeks with a napkin from a nearby table. The barmaid tossed a black plastic garbage bag to him and he quickly heaped the two severed heads into it. Then he paused a moment. "Um, Maria?"

The barmaid looked at Samuel with a question.

"How about I double bag these? What say you?"

The woman nodded, and tossed Samuel another black garbage bag.

"Sorry to meet on such ugly terms, Dr. Newirth, but I'm afraid it couldn't be helped. My name is Samuel Lifeson. Corey has done his job. Now let me do mine. Come with me, quickly."

He sheathed his sword back into his umbrella, thanked Maria for the nice wine, the Joni Mitchell, and with an apology for the mess, he hurled the heavy bag over his shoulder as he went for the door.

Outside the afternoon sun was bright and the grey was receding. The air still held a deep chill.

"There are more on the way. We were hoping that this wouldn't happen, but I knew that it was inevitable. Certainly Felix called for backup, and Ravistelle knows now that you are with me. They must have recognized me. Ah well, what *does* one do?"

His pace was light and quick. I struggled to keep up with him. "Don't run, Loche," he warned, "We don't want to call attention to ourselves. I *can* call you Loche? Yes?"

I wasn't able to answer.

No one we passed took notice of our pace. The man

walked as if he were late for work. Two elderly women stepped out in front of him, and he halted with polite precision. "Ladies," came his gentlemanly voice. They smiled at him as he gestured that they could pass in front, adjusting the bag of severed heads.

I was speechless. I kept my eyes on the bag that bulged heavily over his shoulder. He noticed. "Oh these? Trophies for my wall at home."

My horror stricken eyes shot to his face. He was smiling, almost laughing. "What? You want them? I jest," he said. The look on my face must have pleaded for reason. "Just making sure that these two won't be visiting us again. You know, *drawn and quartered and sent to the four corners of the Earth*. I'm sure you've heard the saying before. The only way to be sure an immortal can't upset another delightful afternoon glass of wine." He set off again at an incredible pace that looked like a stroll. "Very sad, though. These were men that have lived for many centuries—but they will not live in the hereafter—no heaven for them, no *Orathom*. They are now truly, *gone*."

Passing out into the free air we could see the canal snaking its way through a labyrinth of buildings. A power boat was moored at a small, rickety dock where several gondolas and gondoliers stood at the ready for tourists. One of the brightly dressed boatmen waved to Samuel.

Waving back, Samuel heaped the bag of heads into the boat and climbed aboard. Again, the stench of the canal. "Come, come, Doctor, no time to waste."

I stepped down into the boat with obvious apprehension. My dread of water was noticed by Samuel. "Don't you worry, Loche. I will bring you safely to the shore." He fired the starter, and plumes of exhaust billowed from the revving engine. Slowly, the boat backed out into the canal and turned eastward. "I told you that I wouldn't bore you," Samuel said smiling. "But let's to the open water. I hope you like the ocean." My eyes drifted from the plastic bag to the oncoming sea. A spray of cold seawater misted my cheeks. I felt like I could not breathe.

"This is really happening, isn't it?" I asked.

Samuel eyed me up and down. "I suppose it is."

"You've got to go! And you've got to go now!" John Whitely shouts storming into Julia's room. Her heart booms with adrenaline—

"What is it?" she cries, dropping the journal.

"The police, they're on the way."

"How did they find—"

"The murder is all over the news. Two Sandpoint detectives!" Whitely's face is pale with fear. The last time he had felt this kind of terror was outside of Basil's home where he found himself at gunpoint—before Loche helped him to escape.

Rearden struggles for his balance as he comes into the room. "Those were no detectives," the old man growls. "Come on Julia, let's go."

Throwing the blankets back, Julia reaches for her clothes, "Marcus, I thought those two men were. . ." She snaps her eyes to Father Whitely and then to Rearden.

Rearden is pulling on his coat. "They were not detectives! Come on!"

Julia shoves her feet into her boots and grabs the journal from the bed.

"Take my van, the keys are in it," Father Whitely says.

"Where is it?" Rearden asks.

"It's parked on the street. Hurry!"

In the air is an uncanny humidity. Julia, Rearden and the priest rush toward the garage—and the painting in the trunk.

"How long do we have?" Rearden hisses.

"They are on their way, that's all I know," Father Whitely answers.

The old man's back cracks as he hefts the heavy crate onto his shoulder. *This thing* is *getting heavier,* he thinks. Shuffling quickly toward the priest's van, Julia follows with one arm bracing Rearden's unsteady frame.

A 1971 green Volkswagen van is parked at the curb. John slides the side door open and Rearden sets the crate inside as Julia starts the van.

"Thank you, Father," Julia says.

"I'm doing this for Loche," Whitely says to her while she struggles to get the thing in gear. "I owe him this at least. Be careful." He looks at the old man. "Marcus, may God have mercy on your soul for the wrongs you have done."

Rearden studies the priest's face with a scowl. "God has done more wrong than I," he replies. "And we'll settle that score soon enough."

Julia smashes the gas pedal to the floor, and pops the clutch. The van lurches, then slithers through the slush down the block. Father John Whitely stands in the rain and listens to the low hum of the van fade away. Rearden's parting words make him shiver—the malice in his eyes. Colored strobe lights are suddenly flashing up behind. *I've has let a murderer get away,* he thinks. He feels a sense that it was God's will.

"This is going to make attending the funeral tomorrow a little tricky," Julia shouts. The hollow, can-like interior of the van reverberates with engine noise. "Why didn't you tell me about the funeral? And your wife, Marcus? Why?"

A wall goes up in Rearden's mind. It is a familiar feeling. He dislikes people trying to read him. He had been able to keep his life private even while his career as a psychologist grew beyond the goals that he had set as a young man. Rearden is a well-known figure, and he has achieved a status of importance and renown that has fed his pride. One of his greatest fears is to have it all fall down. He has vowed to protect his achievements and his reputation—at any cost. If Marcus has sinned, no one will know of it. And if the *almighty God* takes note, Marcus will find a way to silence him.

"Tell you what," Rearden replies, "I'll answer those questions when we find Loche. It will mean more to you then. Right now we need to find somewhere to go."

She veers onto the freeway. "We'll head into the woods. I know a few spots where we can spend the night."

A half hour later Julia parks the van beside a stream thirty yards off of the main road. They are surrounded by thick, old growth forest, and when the headlights go out, the darkness is threatening. Julia immediately hops out, circles around and opens the sliding door.

"Let's see what we've got for supplies," she says. There are several cabinets and drawers affixed to the interior walls. Rifling through she finds a propane heater, blankets, candles and water. Everything they will need for the night.

A candle flame pushes the darkness back slightiy. "Marcus, why don't you sleep on the bed back here. I'll sit up front. I want to continue reading."

When Rearden begins to snore, she opens the book again. She tilts the page toward the candlelight while rain taps out a rhythm on the van's roof.

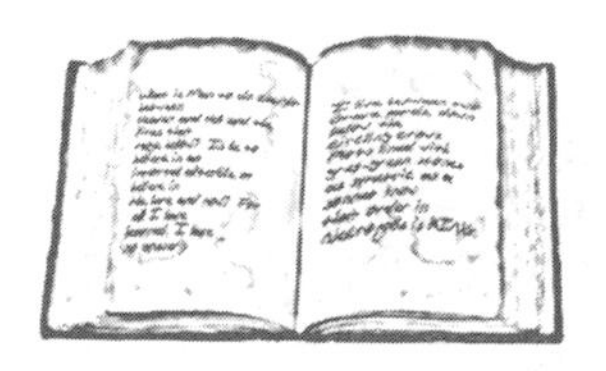

The severed heads were gone. He tossed them overboard as soon as we met the open sea. "*Gallina*," he had said to the lumps in the bag, lugging them up and over. I wondered if they could hear him.

We left the boat on a beach some distance north of Venice. From there Samuel led me to a light grey Audi parked a short walk away from the surf. The car looked rather new though there were several deep scratches in the finish and one nasty dent in the passenger door. Opening that door was a process for him. After pulling on the handle a time or two he eventually threw his body weight against the door, pushed in and pulled up with his hands on the latch. It popped open like a can of soda. "In you go," he said.

An hour later we were speeding toward the city of Padua. The blur of the Italian countryside was framed in the passenger window and it rushed by as swiftly as my thoughts. I had not yet come to terms with my new companion. Smoke from his cigar hung in the air before my eyes, and every now and then he'd curse the traffic on the motorway.

Samuel didn't look to be older than thirty-five. Beneath his long deep grey overcoat he wore a black turtleneck sweater. On his head was a black stocking cap that fit tight against his skull. The cigar he held in his teeth. He had spoken more to the traffic than he had to me. "Move it, you git!" he cried at the driver in front of us. "Long pedal on the right! Bastard!" Strangely, he didn't seem as if he were in a hurry despite his obvious road rage. He was enjoying himself.

"Funny," he finally said to me, "I'm centuries old and

it's still the fuck-head drivers that get to me."

I didn't answer.

With a sidelong glance he asked, "You okay?"

"Difficult question," I replied.

"I'm sure."

The car jerked a left to right lane change. My fingertips were clutching the leather seats.

"We are on our way, Loche. I can call you Loche, can't I? You didn't answer me on that one back at the pub."

"You can call me Loche."

"Very nice. You can call me Samuel. Charmed."

"Where are you taking me?"

"Cinque Terre. The Five Cities—Italian Riviera. Monterosso."

"How far?"

"Other side of the boot. Tonight we'll stay with friends in Padua—catch a plane tomorrow."

"And then?"

"Once we reach Monterosso we'll lay low for a day until I receive orders. Monterosso is a place I like to call home."

Home. What is that? At the mention of the word I felt the images of what home meant crash down like shattering china. The small screen that revealed Helen and Ravistelle—I pressed my fingers into my temples.

"Loche, don't worry about your little son. He'll be taken care of. I've known Corey for years beyond count. And he's got everything under control. You'll see your son soon." With a gentle tap on my shoulder he added, "And Helen? Well, sorry about that, mate. *Frailty thy name is Helen*. I was never a big fan of your wife. Especially when she was going for Basil. Couldn't get to him—too much into his art. You, my dear fellow, though I hate to say it, you were fodder for her."

I looked at him.

"Corey didn't tell you?" He let out a sigh of frustration. "*Damn it, Corey*!" he said to his distant friend. "Helen has been around for at least sixty or so years. Born sometime in the mid to late fifties. Young by our standards. Newly discovered immortals happen every now and again. I guess she was discovered by Ravistelle back in the seventies sometime. He's been grooming her for this task ever since. Hell of an actress that one."

"What task?" I asked.

"You and Basil. When she failed with Basil, you were next."

My focus returned to the blurring landscape. "So none of it was real?"

Samuel took a look at me and breathed an empathetic sigh. "I'm sorry, Loche. Heartbreak, deception—despite all of that, you have a beautiful son. There is something true in that."

"He is *my* son then, right?"

"As far as I know, yes," Samuel said, his eyes on the road. "And besides, who cares? Edwin loves you, and knows you as his father." He took a drag from his cigar. "So, look at the bright side. At least now you know. Ravistelle had hoped that she might be able to bring your muse out of you by loving you, and caring for you—you know, providing that little bit of daily drama. Didn't work. My advice is to let her go, and think of your work and your son."

I looked down at the wedding band on my finger. Samuel noticed. Pulling the ring off I held it in my palm.

"I'm so sorry, Loche," he said, "I wish I could tell you more. You'll get your chance to ask her all of these questions yourself one day. That is, if we're quite careful."

I placed the ring inside my coat pocket.

Arriving at our destination, Samuel had muttered something about not liking the fact that his friend Giovanni lived too far outside the city walls of Padua. "Silly bastard—doesn't have a clue about history. *Stay behind the walls,* I always told him. Hell of a swordsman, but he's young." He turned to me and included, "He's mortal, by the way."

Giovanni's home was, however, surrounded by high stone walls. We were shown into a warmly lit dining room. An elderly woman sat at a table reading. A steaming cup of tea at her right hand.

"Buona notte, Sylvia," Samuel said.

The woman did not notice the greeting.

"Sylvia?" Samuel pursued, "Buona notte."

No response. My companion looked at me and smiled, pointing to his ear. "Smart as a whip, but doesn't hear very well," he told me.

He touched her wrist and Sylvia looked up. Her eyes shone in acknowledgement. "Buona notte, Samuel," and she spoke on in Italian. Though I couldn't understand her, I could discern by Samuel's body language that he was saying things like, *no I'm not hungry, thank you, good to see you, too, yes I've been taking care of myself, my wife is fine, you look well, no I'm not hungry,* and so on.

Finally he introduced me. She looked me up and down and again rapidly chatted out a string of phrases. "Are you hungry?" he asked me.

I politely shook my head and said, "No. Grazie."

She spoke Giovanni's name and pointed toward the stairs.

It was heavy, but not unbearably heavy. I held a swept hilt rapier. *An old sword*, as Samuel had described it, *its seen its share of war.* Before me stood Giovanni, also holding a sword. A blond-haired, solidly built young man of maybe twenty-eight years. He held the blade pointed out at me and took an aggressive stance—his fiery eyes, stout arms and steel sword poised to run me through.

"No, no, no, Loche," Giovanni commanded. "Center body between your feets. Si, better. Now, you stand like I stand, yes?"

I had little desire to take a sword lesson, but Samuel had insisted. He leaned against the far wall and watched Giovanni struggle to communicate with me in broken English. "He wants you to mimic his stance," he offered.

"Si," Giovanni joined, "*mimic*."

I raised the sword and studied Giovanni's pose. It was an en guarde stance. His right foot was forward and the back foot angled slightly left. With his knees bent in readiness he tried to explain, "Body, center. Center. Over your balls," he smiled. I imitated the stance. The point of his sword was aimed at me as the rest of the blade was slightly angled. His left hand was raised up and hovered near his face. "Last defense," Samuel said waving his hand—the offhand. "If all else fails, block with your bare hand instead of your face." I forced my body to hold the pose until Giovanni was satisfied. "Si," he said finally, "Buono."

Samuel insisted, "From that stance you can move and react to nearly anything. *The readiness is all.*"

For two hours Samuel and Giovanni demonstrated graphic and true to life duelist movements and techniques. The three of us went through three bottles of wine during that time, as well. In turn, I was to reproduce their instruction in a series of trials. I was surprised to hear Samuel say, several times, "You are a natural."

Somewhere deep down inside of me I had always been enamored by the sword. Even my castle-like home in Idaho portrayed this sincere interest. And now, in Padua, Italy, I was learning from Master Giovanni Rapasardi. But a weapon in its pure form has always been a cause for distress. A symbol of man's inability to reason. A symbol of might over thought. I lowered my sword and stared at the twisting bars of steel that laced over the hilt. It was beautiful. The thought of man's stylish imprint on a thing made to kill other men stopped the lesson.

"Loche?" Samuel said, noting my distant expression.

"Why are you teaching me this?" I asked, studying the webbed steel bars of the hilt-cage.

"Because guns won't do," he replied simply. "And, *I suppose*, just in case."

"I don't think I have it in me to kill anyone." A statement I never thought I'd hear myself say, and truly mean.

Samuel agreed, "No. And let us hope you won't have

to. But it's always best to be prepared for the weather. Storms will come and it's best to be ready."

I inhaled a deep breath and let it out slowly. Samuel gestured to Giovanni to wait. He approached and took the sword from my hand, "Look, it is time for you to wake up. Even after all you know about your place in this world, your brother's plight and the designs of your enemy, you cannot stand aloof because of some philosophical or moral reason. It is time for action and readiness. Before this is all over I fear that you will be forced to defend not only your life, but the lives of others, as well. I, too, am amazed that the twenty-first century has not brought higher thought to mankind. Humans are still filled with greed, hate, misguided ideologies and are easily brought to war. Funny really. *History will teach us nothing* as one clever songwriter put it. Know that what little you have learned today may aid you, and it may not. After all, the best way to block an adversary's weapon is to stay out of their way. Let's hope we can do that. But for now, consider this," Giovanni handed Samuel a waist high umbrella. Its handle was made of black ebony. "This will be your little insurance policy." Samuel placed it into my hands.

Holding it up, I inspected it closely. It was simple and unadorned. It looked much like the kind of umbrella a bent elderly gentleman might use to make his way to the park on a rainy Sunday afternoon.

"An umbrella?" I said. "For rainy days?"

"That's right," he said taking hold of the black handle. He gave it a quick pull. The bottom of the umbrella separated from the grip and revealed a slender steel blade. He held it up before my face. "For very rainy days."

The plane ride was bumpy.

We landed just outside of Monterosso, midmorning. Giovanni unclamped the headphones from his head and turned in his pilot seat, "Good bye," he said to me. I shook his outstretched hand and followed Samuel out onto the grassy field. We stood and watched the plane turn, roar its engines and hurdle back into the air.

"Good mate that Giovanni," Samuel said as the drone faded. "Young, but a good mate."

Minutes later I was again listening to Samuel exercise his graphic expletives upon Italy's commuters. The car was similar to the one we left behind in Padua, right down to the dent in the passenger door.

"What's with the dented doors?" I asked.

He laughed. "I'm from England. I've never gotten the hang of the steering wheel on the left side." He gave me a sidelong glance. "Hey, I may be immortal, but I never said I was the best driver. You should see me parallel park—now that's a comical sight."

"This is George," said Samuel. "George Eversman."

In the doorway stood a shirtless man that looked to be in his early fifties. He was tall, drawn and awkward looking, especially in the face. Brown pools of color glowed from his deeply set eyes, and his smile was enormous, as if his mouth was too large for the rest of his face. His upper body was covered in light orange-brown hair that spread over his shoulders, down his arms and to his waistline.

He offered bright and cheerful Italian greetings to both of us and stepped aside allowing us to enter. Closing the door he shouted into the flat, "Elainya, Eleni, Eleni."

Around the corner ran little Elainya, his eight-year-old daughter. She rammed her entire body full-speed into Samuel's legs and wrapped her little pale arms around them. He lifted her up and whispered what I assumed to be Italian sweet nothings into her ear.

The air smelled of garlic, hot bread and olive oil. George beckoned us into the small kitchen where he was busy preparing fresh pesto.

We were seated at a small wood table laden with old

framed photographs of family and friends and a dirty dish or two. George poured the wine, gave us each a glass, and proposed a toast.

"Stupid crazy," he said holding his wine up. "All a dis. Here's to it." He tilted his glass and emptied it into his mouth. He then laid his hand on Samuel's shoulder. "You chop garlic, I talk."

"As you wish." Samuel's reply carried a formal tone as if he were responding to an order. He rose quickly, and moving to the cutting board, began to peel the white husks from cloves.

George Eversman stood beside the table and studied me. His fingers thoughtfully lacing through his mesh of chest hair. His long silent appraisal of me, and his weird appearance, caused a sudden flash of claustrophobia.

Finally he spoke, "You Loche, eh?"

"Yes." I could feel the muscles in my neck beginning to tighten. From my seat I held my head angled up to look at him.

"Stupid crazy. Your wife gone, eh?"

Sting. "Yes."

"Hurts, yes?"

I didn't answer.

"You the *Poet?*"

I glanced over at Samuel. He was focused on his task and appeared to be ignoring our conversation.

"Hey!" George called. I snapped my eyes back to him. "You write?"

I felt my shoulders give sort of a shrug when I said, "That's what they say."

His huge mouth spread into a tight grin. "What do *you* say?"

"I'm not like Basil. I can't do what he does."

"Not yet, eh?"

"No," I agreed, "not yet."

"Have you tried, huh?"

"I think so."

"Not yet, eh?" he said again. "No try, no do, yes?"

"I suppose." The pain in my neck, and his odd

manner, was beginning to irritate me.

"Suppose?" he cried. "What suppose?"

"I don't understand."

"Ha! No. No, you don't. Stupid crazy, yes?"

I leveled my eyes and stared at the wall behind him.

"I got you out. Know that, huh?"

"What do you mean?"

The man sighed. Samuel answered. "George Eversman, the leader of *Orathom Wis*, the *High Guard of the Order.*"

I looked up at the oddly posed man. He was still petting his brownish-orange chest hair. There was no smile.

"I got you out," he repeated.

I nodded, not knowing how to respond. *Should I say thank you?*

"You are free now. Free to find your muse."

"How?" I gasped.

"You will know. It will come. You must find the *Elliqui.* The *Elliqui,* my friend."

I shook my head, "What is the *Elliqui?*"

"*Elliqui* is a language. The oldest, most ancient of all languages," Samuel answered.

"I've never heard of such a language before. Where is it from?"

George's smile bent along his face like an archers curving bow. "*They* speak it, Loche," he said, referring to some invisible company above and around us. "*The Watchers*."

Samuel brought the cutting board over to George to show him his progress on the garlic. The shirtless man took one look and snorted, "Thinner. Thinner," waving Samuel back to task.

"What little we know about *Elliqui* is from our ancestors," Samuel continued, turning back to the counter. "Our immortal ancestors, I mean. There are books that we hope still exist, but the *Orathom Wis* have had little fortune in locating them. It is said that over the centuries, most of the tomes were destroyed by war, disaster and the like. It's only been in the last fifty or so years that we've found clues that suggest that at least one tome remains. We fear that it may have already been found by the Enemy.

"*Elliqui* is the language of thought. At one time, man and the gods communed in this purest form of language—a mutual knowing without the misguiding complexities of written or spoken words. A telepathy, if you will. There was an overarching desire for both humankind and the divine to appease and care for the other's needs. Simply, by knowing intention and fully accepting that any outcome is possible, there was little need to fear. Our communication now is filled with hidden agendas, lies, deceit. And truth. But in *Elliqui* there was only empathy and compassion—and ultimately, well-being. Speaking in thought is the real connectivity that we are supposed to have. We like to think that the closest form of *Elliqui* that has survived is music, for music transcends language and elevates our communication beyond this world."

I squinted at Samuel, "You say that *Elliqui* is the language of thought, like telepathy. But you said that there were books? And that it can be a *spoken* language, too?"

"Yes," George replied. "Yes. Long, long ago, *Elliqui* was broken. Some gods rebelled and cut the cords. No more talk with them. And for us, no more talk together."

Samuel cut in, "When the dark powers arose among the gods, it broke the voice. *Elliqui* was destroyed. People had to start from nothing—from ancient cave drawings to Egyptian hieroglyphs to Latin to modern English. It took centuries to get where we are now. Because of the destruction of the true mode of *Elliqui*, man has suffered in ways beyond count.

"But sometime around the eleventh century, members of the *Orathom Wis* began to piece together a bridge to the past. Some of the oldest and wisest of our *Order* managed to create a spoken form of *Elliqui.* And then later, a written form. It was said that they had found a way to commune with one another, and even the gods, through speech. Some said that by reading the written *Elliqui,* one could understand the mind of the one that put the thoughts to paper, or the muse beyond the inked runes. It's our hunch that you and the ancient language were made for one another. We think your gift has something to do with learning how to speak it, and more importantly, how to write it."

"Because I am foretold to write with a power like Basil's painting, you think *Elliqui* is the language I need to learn?"

"Maybe," Samuel said. "Again, we're searching, just as you are. As with most art, sometimes you have to wait for it to come."

A flash of William Greenhame's face appeared in my mind, and the memory of his using many dialects during our sessions. Latin, French, Middle English—he would often scramble the letters of words and phrases. And then I recall hearing him utter a language I couldn't place, and the echo of his words were strangely natural for me to speak. "*Ithic veli agtig,*" I said quietly.

George's eyes widened and he raised his hands to his cheeks in a gesture of surprise and wonder. "*Ithic veli agtig*," he repeated in a whisper.

Samuel's expression was similar, but less dramatic. He stared at me with a half smile and a look of genuine caring, as if I had shared some random, delicate memory of a mutual friend that had passed away.

"*Why does my death delay*?" Samuel translated. "That's what it means in English. And it has an equivalent meaning in *Elliqui,* but there is more to it than that. *Ithic veli agtig* is actually the name of those of us that have been given the gift of immortality on Earth. The phrase is as near to us as our own birth names, for it conjures the ache of memory and the yearnings for the things we cannot have, both youth and death. The phrase is a title as well as a question, but as I've said, *Elliqui* transcends simple subjective definitions. It instead echoes with a kind of super-connotation, resounding the emotion beyond the bounds of its meaning. *Ithic veli agtig* is something that every immortal can feel within as a sorrow and a joy intermingled. Beautiful and terrible."

"You must *feel* the words if you want your gift, Loche —you must *feel* the words," George said. "Stupid crazy, no? And we must do this soon. Maybe *Elliqui* must wait. You must write how you write."

Samuel nodded, adding, "Yes, you must feel the words, but you must start with the language you know. This is your fate. There is only so much that *we* can do, Loche. We can protect you for a time, but not indefinitely. You've got to come to terms with your muse. You must. And whatever it takes to feel the words, we don't know. It could be learning *Elliqui*. It could be facing your greatest fear. It could be a near death experience."

Frustration took hold, and I stood. I paced across the room to the kitchen window. The day was grey and cold. Beyond the rooftops was the Atlantic ocean. I shuddered at the sight. Water, especially large bodies of water, was indeed a terrible fear of mine. I turned away to keep from drowning.

George joined me at the window. "How do we help?"

"I must return home," I said.

"Home?" Samuel joined. "Why?"

"I've got to start from the beginning. Retrace my steps." Julia's face haunted my thoughts, and I was unwilling to mention her or the painting that Basil had told me of. There was a reason it was to be kept secret—I was sure about that. "Going back to my old life and seeing it again is the only plan I have. It feels right."

"You, home?" George said.

My eyes told him yes.

"Then home you go," he cried clapping me on the shoulder. "But you must be quick. Be quick."

Samuel broke in, "*Anfogal*, it will be too dangerous. The Enemy will expect—"

"Home he goes," George said again without turning to Samuel. Instead he forced me to look at his long and lanky smile. "Stupid crazy, no?"

"Stupid crazy," I echoed.

The private jet tore across the Atlantic ocean racing away from the early morning light. Samuel raised his cup of coffee and took a drink. He stared at me over the rim for a moment, then set the cup down. "We are the *Orathom Wis,"* he said. "The Guardians of the Dream. The Dream Guard. Whatever it is that lies beyond this life, we protect its secrets. No one knows why we are blessed (or cursed) with immortality—but we believe we are the creation of the One God. We believe that *It* provided us with long life, and the instinct to seek out and close the doors that might open between this Life (the *Alya)* and the Dream (the *Orathom)*.

"The One God. The One Universe. A thing of such complexity that the only name we can give it is *God.* The Itonalya named It, *Thi. Thi* is the balance. The invisible hand. *It* is unlike the gods or divinities that visit Basil's work. *It* is everything- the Story that writes Itself. *It's* thoughts are the thoughts of all. *It's* very cells are our cells. *It's* blood is the light across the Universe." Samuel took another sip of his coffee. "Heavy. I know."

"When you say you seek out and close the doors," I asked. "What do you mean, exactly?"

"I mean just that. Since we immortals learned our purpose, roughly two millennia ago, we have sought out any kind of supernatural or otherworldly occurrence. History is riddled with ghost stories, hauntings, self-proclaimed deities or messiahs—you name it, we've investigated it."

"And what have you learned?" I asked.

"That mostly, the human race has an incredible imagination," he replied with a laugh, "for there is seldom truth to the many claims of supernatural events. But there have been a few frightful crossings in history, things that have proven our worth. Spirits bridging into *Alya* through individual people, seeking those things that only humans can feel and experience. This causes the worst of human calamity."

"Can you give me an example?" I asked.

Samuel looked out the window. The sky was cloudless and bright blue. He frowned. "You've heard of Adolf Hitler, I expect."

I gasped, "Are you telling me that Hitler was one of these individuals that a spirit used as a bridge?"

Samuel smiled, still looking out the window, "No, Loche. Don't be foolish. Hitler was a relatively good speaker. Once a painter, you know. He was also, unfortunately, very impressionable. No, Adolf had another man in his cabinet, Heinrich Himmler, head of the SS, the one responsible for the killing of six million Jews in the mid-twentieth century. He, my dear Loche, was a chief concern of ours. And an extreme case. It took a war to finally end his influence and destruction." Samuel turned to me. His face was grim. "But he was only one. There were, and are, others, and not all of them are destructive. Sometimes a bridging deity is filled with altruism and joy. But even they must be retired from *Alya*. The *Alya* is not the abode of the gods."

"So Basil and I were thought to be bridged spirits?" I asked. "That's why we were to be assassinated?"

Samuel stared at me as if weighing his answer. "No," he said simply. "You were never thought to be bridges for the gods. You are something far more dangerous. Your coming heralded a new age, for your artistic works, be they paintings or poetry, would open the doors and allow the horrors of humanity to cross into the *Orathom*. A human, Loche, that stares into one of Basil's paintings will have his humanity, his fear, his imperfections—his sin—pulled away from him. And those conditions are like illness in the *Orathom*. Viruses. They become inescapable. You were meant to be assassinated to prevent the invasion of Heaven."

"But we were saved," I said.

"Yes, you were saved. And now the *Orathom Wis* protects you."

"But why? Isn't that against the very purpose of your existence? If you are protectors of the afterlife, why did you save us?"

Samuel again hesitated before he spoke. "I think that story is for another to share with you. You will understand in time. But I will tell you that, in a way, we exist *because* of you. If we had succeeded in your assassination, we wonder what our fate would be? We are unsure if we ourselves would have survived. It is all very difficult to explain."

He shifted his body to face the blue window. "You and your brother were prophesied, long ago. Back when the realm of the *Orathom Wis* was at its height—a place of peace, learning and hope. I've only heard stories about the great realm for it was well before my time. Some of us question that it ever existed. Our own mythology. The city was called *Wyn Avuqua.* It means, The Tears of Heaven. The city where the immortals of Earth sought to understand their curse. Where they once communed with The One through *Elliqui.* And where we learned that our lives are truly here and now, for we have no chance of an afterlife."

Samuel looked at me and sadly smiled. "Ironic, isn't it? We protect Heaven and Earth from suffering—we live to insure that the human spirit has the Dream beyond this life—but we do not get the Dream. We do not get a Heaven. Once an immortal is vanquished, he is no more. He is cast into oblivion. He becomes—nothing." Samuel turned away and whispered, "Nothing. *Ithic veli agtig.*"

I stared at Samuel and struggled to empathize. As mortal men, we labor through our lives pining for more time. We turn our hopes, fears and questions into words and pictures with the vain belief that somehow our souls can find the strength to carry on for another day—and another—until our works survive us. We run out of days. I can see now this is *our* blessing, although, we think it is our curse. At least a mortal man can run out of days. And something waits for us beyond.

But for immortal men like Samuel Lifeson, Corey Thomas, George Eversman—they cannot die, they do not grow old. Physical pain is quick, and quickly gone—but like us, their minds carry the weight of the human condition. For years beyond count, they must endure love, joy, hate and anguish. This surpasses all I've learned about psychological theory—this race of beings and their fortitude for living. Centuries pass, loved ones die, wars change societies, culture shapes and reshapes itself a new vessel—with each secondhand tick of the timepiece, the Immortal watches, remembers and lives on and through. It is impossible for me to comprehend.

"And this mythical realm of the *Orathom Wis*? Where was it?" I asked.

"The city of *Wyn Avuqua* was beside a lake," he answered. "The city has been long decayed and swallowed by time." Samuel stood and moved across the aircraft's cabin to a small bar. He filled two glasses with ice. From the shelves behind the bar he lifted a bottle of scotch. He pulled the cork and poured. "The lake is still there, though it has changed over time. It was once much larger." He returned to his seat and handed me a glass. "It is said that The One can sometimes be seen in the reflection of that lake, like an eye staring into the sky." He plinked his glass into mine and raised it to his lips. Before he took a drink he said, "Your cabin is on that lake."

Julia Iris was smiling at me through the windows of The Floating Hope. She motioned for me to come in out of the cold.

The room was crowded and this was certainly to the liking of my companion, Samuel. His last words to me as I started toward Julia were, "I'll be close by. Don't be long." Then he added, "And order me an egg sandwich."

"Hello, Loche," Julia said. As I stepped closer, her cheerful glow muted slightly, and her eyes were suspended in question. "What? What is it, Loche?"

I realized that my face was not reflecting a simple greeting. With concentrated precision my eyes drank in the sight of her as if she was a far off island, and I was lost at sea. I attempted to lighten the heat of my glance, but it felt awkward—wrong. Often I could wear the gregarious mask of social propriety, but something had changed. It was obvious to me and it seemed obvious to Julia, as well. A slight blush stained her cheeks.

"Hello, Julia," I said quietly.

"Is everything okay? You look *very* serious."

"Do I? I'm sorry. I've quite a bit on my mind."

"If you're here to see Basil, he hasn't been in for days."

"I know," I said.

"Do you know where he is? I've been worried. All of us have."

"I just left him yesterday in Italy," I told her. "He's doing some important paintings over there."

Her eyes widened at the thought. "Italy? Really? How did that happen?"

"That's why I've come to speak with you, Julia. Can we meet today? After you close up? Perhaps a drink?" My anxiety was replaced by a reminiscent flash that I thought I'd never feel again. A feeling I hadn't felt for years. I was as nervous as a schoolboy. I was asking her out.

I watched her long eyelashes flit while she weighed the request. She barely knew me, and I hoped that my invitation didn't seem too terribly ardent. As she considered, I allowed my eyes to study her hoping that she might take longer to answer, for nothing in the past weeks had given me solace until that moment, her face—

"Sure," she said. "I'm done around four."

"Shall I pick you up then?"

"Perfect."

"Get a date?" Samuel teased as I closed the car door. My response was a tightlipped trace of a smile—he knew the answer. "What's the story with Julia? Why is it so important that you see her?"

A number of reasons went through my mind. Basil's painting was certainly important, but there was something else. Something I wasn't sure that I'd completely processed. Was I in love with her? Was she my muse? I'd barely spoken to her. I knew nothing about her. Something inside said that she was mine, and I was hers.

I turned to Samuel, "You'll have to trust me. I think she can help."

Samuel gazed thoughtfully at the road ahead. "Help, you say?"

"Yes."

"Hmmm. Wanna-be poet, beautiful girl—sounds like a recipe for disaster."

"You'll have to give us some space," I said flatly.

"Wait a second," he argued, "that wasn't the deal."

"You can follow us, but you can't ride with us. And you can't join us for a drink."

"Goodness gracious me! Aren't we discourteous? I watch your back, teach you how to use a sword, take you to meet George, get you home, and I don't get to have a drink with you and the pretty Julia. How terribly rude of you, Dr. Newirth."

"Do me this favor."

He pulled out and entered traffic. "As you wish. But keep your eyes open. We aren't alone here in *your* neck of the woods. I'll give you your space, but I'll be closer than you might think. I'm quite good at that sort of thing."

As we drove south, I was feeling the calm of home. The sights along the roadside, the familiar colors and shapes shared both a soothing and haunting emotion. I had spent most of my time in Sandpoint with Helen and

Edwin. And returning alone gave every turn and tree an alien, almost unnatural glow. But it was familiar. That, at least, was a cause to breathe easier.

"Do you know where you're going?"

Samuel scoffed, "Do *I* know where I'm going? What a question for *you* to ask." He then nodded. "Of course. I'm taking you to our safe house."

I remained silent. He drove the exact route to my home. At about a mile from my driveway he turned onto an unpaved road that snaked into the hills. He drove for another five minutes then pulled the car over into a lay-by and got out.

"Come with me."

Twenty yards into the dense trees he stopped, stooped over and began scrambling through the crusted snow and deadwood on the forest floor.

"What are you doing?" I asked.

"A moment, please," came his patient reply. He found what he was looking for—a loop of earthen colored rope. Giving it a tug I heard a grinding squeak beneath us. It was a door. An underground cave entrance. Lifting the door on its hinge he held it open for me. A ladder disappeared down into the darkness, but far below there was a pale, almost indeterminate glow. "Down you go," he said. "Careful on the ladder. It's slippery this time of year."

The shadowed shaft was not inviting, and Samuel sensed my reluctance. I forced myself to the mouth of the hole and lowered my body down. Clutching my umbrella in my right hand I stopped and looked up at Samuel. "Go on," he encouraged. The metal rungs were slick, cold and covered in mud. I placed each foot firmly and made a slow, but steady, descent. As the door closed over us I could see that there was indeed a light down there. Dangerously far down.

Minutes later I stood at the mouth of a long, green-lit passageway. The tunnel looked like an old mine shaft with crude, wooden beam supports at intervals of ten feet.

Along the floor stretched a long plastic tube of green light, much like the glow sticks an outdoorsman would use at night. Although this was one long continuous light source extending down the length of the burrow. The air was stale and thick with moisture.

"Come along," Samuel said, brushing past me he took up a brisk pace. The floor was riddled with puddles and jagged stones jutting up and out. For the first time I felt a need for my umbrella, only now I used it as a cane.

After five or so minutes and several twists and turns in our route, Samuel stopped. He turned and waited for me to catch up.

We stood before a thick metal door.

He smiled a gentle smile, "Ready for another disturbing sight?"

I eyed him carefully. "Not much can surprise me these days," I said truthfully.

"Oh, this might." Samuel pulled the door open and walked through. A comfortable glow of golden white light spilled into the dark passage. "Wipe your feet," he said pointing down to a muddied rug.

A dark hardwood floor led into a wide, gothic, rock-walled chamber the size of a small gymnasium. A living area with pillowed velvet furniture and a kitchen was sectioned off at the far end. Several computer monitors and filing cabinets made up an office-like setting to our right, with tall bookcases serving as partitions. To the left was an armory of swords, axes, shields and other medieval weaponry. Intermingled in the arsenal were modern automatic weapons, pistols and a smorgasbord of ammunition and explosives organized upon shelves and tables. In the center of the room there was a kind of circular boxing ring. In the far corner on a high shelf was a small plant with three luminous leaves.

Wide-eyed, I took the sight in. My companion laughed. "Nice, eh? Bathrooms are down the opposite hall, and the sleeping quarters are through the door at the end there," he pointed out. "We just put in a claw-foot tub. Delightful."

My eyes strayed back to the shelves of weapons, and I scanned the collection quickly. A small snub-nosed pistol caught my eye—it sat on top of a box of ammunition. Samuel noted my curiosity. "Something of interest, Doctor?"

"No," I said turning back to him. "I've just never seen so many weapons before."

"Yes, dreadful things," Samuel nodded. "If only we could get past killing. If things were only that simple."

"So is this what you thought would disturb me? I admit, it does." I said.

He only smiled and motioned for me to follow.

We entered the hallway at the back of the room and began climbing a spiral staircase up into the darkness. At the top was a wall. No landing, no passage, only a wall. He took a step back and said, "Give the wall a little nudge. Not too hard mind you—just a slight push." I obeyed and waited.

"Now what?"

"Half a second," he replied. A tiny green lightbulb lit up before my face and quickly extinguished. The wall silently slid to the side and before me was what looked like clothing hanging on hangers. Women's clothes. It took me a second to realize that they belonged to Helen. I was standing in the interior of my home, in the back of a closet in one of our guest bedrooms.

"This is my—this is—" I stammered.

Samuel nodded sympathetically. I stepped into my home from a door I never knew existed. The scent of the house flooded my mind with pictures and memories.

"Disturbed?" Samuel whispered. The door behind us closed without a sound.

I assumed that he could tell by my silence that *disturbed* wasn't quite the right word.

After scrutinizing my expression he added quietly, "No? Not yet disturbed? That's good, because this is peanuts compared to what *will* be disturbing."

Samuel raised his finger to his lips. "Shhh." He pulled his sword from its sheath and nodded to my umbrella.

"You may need that."

I looked down at the hidden blade and quickly raised my eyes back to his. Before I could question, he stepped nimbly across the floor and into the hallway. I slowly unsheathed my sword and went after him.

We passed Helen's and my bedroom. I glanced into the darkness and breathed in the subtle aroma of her perfume. My heart ached.

Down below there was the faint chatter of television. Samuel pointed to his ears and then motioned to the stairs that descended into the great room. I timidly nodded to him, and he began stepping down the long staircase.

The television screen at the far end of the room silhouetted a man's head. He seemed to be transfixed in what looked to be a History Channel program. The strobe effect of the screen flashed against the various fixtures, sending long shadows against the walls and floor.

Samuel touched my shoulder, gesturing for me to go to the right and he would take the left. I replied with a fearful nod. He stealthily took a position some five or six feet behind the man, and I crept up in tow, staying right. When I came to a breathless stop, several things happened all at once.

The silhouetted figure was now in the air with one hand supporting his weight on the back of the davenport in an elegant somersault. In his other hand was a flashing silver blade. Samuel's reply was a quick and prepared defending back-step, for even before the airborne man's feet hit the floor he had managed to throw at least three deadly strikes with his blade.

I lurched behind the attacker and raised my sword to cut. I felt the tip of my blade batted twice by his. It was so quick and unexpected that I flinched uncontrollably. The third connecting parry left my sword hand empty. My blade flipped behind me and landed point up, leaning against the couch. As I turned to retrieve it, I fell head over feet from a blow to the back of my head—a slap from the flat of his blade. The blow brought a sudden flash into my vision.

I flipped over, reached for the hilt of my sword and stood. Samuel had now been pushed back to the dining room. Their swords glinted in the TV screen light. I sprang back to the fray moving quickly up behind. He was ready for me. As I rushed up, the man reached out with his left hand and grasped a table lamp, shade and all. Shoving his sword against Samuel's blade, he batted my thrust away and smashed the stiff fabric of the lampshade against my right ear. The lightbulb shattered, sending dust-like chards into the air.

I stumbled over and swung blindly. Miss. Two more parries with Samuel and, again, the lamp shade—this time it slammed against my left ear, sending me down again. I felt the wet of blood against my cheek. And then it happened—

Samuel cried out and his sword fell and rattled against the floor. In the flickering light I could see him, his back to the wall with our opponent's blade buried in his chest. His body slowly slumped down.

I sprang again to my feet and rushed the man. Again the lamp swept out of nowhere, and stopped me in my tracks. The warped metal hoop at the top of the shade hammered into my throat. He extended his arm and pushed me against the wall with the lampshade holding me there. Like a falcon with outstretched wings over its prey, he had us both.

The television blinked and chattered at the end of the room.

"Dol en ai," the man said. Over my choking I heard the words. I knew the voice.

"No," Samuel groaned. "Woe is *me*. Easy there, mate. That hurts."

"Well, you shouldn't sneak up on a fellow who's trying to learn a bit about how inaccurate the History Channel is," the man replied, "it makes one rather cross."

"*What*, the *fiction* channel or the sneaking up?" Samuel ventured.

"Both."

I felt the pressure of the lamp on my throat ease off.

"William?" I choked. He lowered the lamp and set it down.

"Hello, Dr. Newirth. I see that you've had a sword lesson from Giovanni. He must have left out how to defend against a table lamp."

"I thought you were—I saw you—you were killed!"

Greenhame gently pulled his sword from Samuel's chest and gave him a brotherly slap on the shoulder. "If I've told you once, I've told you a thousand times, dear Doctor—I'm *immortal*. What part of that confession did you miss?"

Samuel took a deep breath and held his hand over the wound. "Disturbed?" he asked me.

"I don't know if that's the word I'd choose," I replied.

"Good," he said with a slight cough. "That's good, because we've still not gotten to the disturbing part."

❧

In spite of the mess left behind by our skirmish, my house was in better order than the day I was forced to leave. William had done his best to tidy up.

As Greenhame tended to Samuel's *temporary* wound, I walked through the home I had built letting each sight fill me with the ache of missing. From Edwin's toy-filled room where I heard him speak his first word—*Mommy*—to the photograph atop his dresser of Helen and me embracing on the beach at Pend Oreille Lake, the warm blues and greens of summer surrounding us. There was little sense to make of any of it—these memories—lies and truths all tangled up. My past was as unknown as what was to come. I gripped the umbrella handle in my hand, and sunk to my knees at my son's dresser, and wept.

I kept the antique key to the tower on a hook hidden behind the pillar of the spiral stair. It was still there. I climbed the stairs and saw again my office door, smashed and thrown aside. I stared at the empty bookcases and broken cabinets. I wondered if I would ever see my writings again. The key I placed in my pocket.

When I returned to Greenhame and Samuel, they had already picked up the fallout from our brawl. The thought of them being right under my nose for all these years was unnerving. They were in the kitchen opening a bottle of wine as if it were their own home. Greenhame seemed to exude more ownership than Samuel. The two chatted over the events like old friends. William was dressed smartly, as usual, in an ivory waistcoat with brown wooden buttons and an overlarge olive-green bow tie. His long hair was tucked behind his ears. He and Samuel plinked their wineglasses together. It was a reuniting of friends.

I was glad to see William alive. Glad beyond words.

"I won't say *welcome home*, Loche," Greenhame offered as I approached.

"Whose *home* are you speaking of?" I asked.

"It couldn't be helped," William replied simply. "There was no better place to keep watch over you than from right under your feet."

I let my eyes fall to my floor (or their ceiling).

"But I must say this," Samuel inserted, "we never had any audio or video surveillance, save your telephones. If we entered the house there was always cause. That cause being your protection. We merely made sure that if they came, you wouldn't be alone."

"And what about the night Helen and Edwin were taken?"

"Taken?" Greenhame gasped. "Have you figured nothing out, yet? My dear Doctor, she left with Edwin of her own free will. Not without wrecking the house a bit first, setting the computer up for you to meet Ravistelle for the first time and stealing your private volumes of original verse. Of course she did this on the same night that we were a bit busy watching Basil's studio. There isn't an army of us, Loche. There are few of us *Orathom Wis* left. Some of us are still here in Idaho. The rest are keeping watch with George in Italy. We *are* immortal, but we are far from *perfect.*"

"And Helen? Is she included in that number?"

"No," Samuel said. "She is but one of a great many immortals that have turned to darker goals."

Spread out on the counter before him was a newspaper. His index finger gently tapped at it. "Seems there has been a development in the Winship case," he said.

I read the headline at his fingertip, *Beth Winship Suicide or Murder?*

"What is this?" I cried.

"Looks as if Ravistelle is playing his turn. He knows you you are with the *Orathom Wis*, but he knows not whether you have escaped with them or you've been kidnapped by them. He will employ every set of eyes to find you again. The lawyers that represent both the Winship family and you are owned by Ravistelle."

I yanked the paper out from under Greenhame's hand and read it.

Sandpoint, IDAHO. *Investigators have uncovered new evidence involving the death of Bethany Leona Winship. Winship's body was found by hikers along Lake Shore Beach at approximately 2:30 p.m. on October 2nd. Believed at first to be a suicide, investigators say that an autopsy revealed that Winship's blood held traces of a powerful mood enhancement drug. Also discovered were several bruises on her neck and wrists. Investigators suspect foul play. Winship's therapist, Dr. Loche Newirth of Sandpoint is not yet a suspect, but is considered a person of interest. He has been unavailable for comment. During an inquiry yesterday morning, Dr. Newirth's attorney, Alan Chatfield, made this statement, "Dr. Newirth is taking some time away to grieve the loss of his client, Mrs. Winship." Spokesman from the police department said that Dr. Newirth's failure to make contact could lead to a warrant for his arrest. The Winship family has filed a malpractice suit against Dr. Loche Newirth.*

"This is nonsense," I growled. "I was in my office all day seeing clients. They need only check with Carol, my secretary," I said with certainty.

"Ah, sweet Carol," Greehame said. "Carol is owned by Ravistelle."

"What? I don't believe it."

"Believe it. She's making a hell of a lot of money for keeping tabs on you, and she'll say whatever Albion wants her to say. And, by the way, she was not in your office for most of that morning, if you remember."

"What do I do?"

"Lay low and find your gift."

"Was Beth murdered?"

Greenhame's answer was not what I expected.

"We don't know for sure."

"What does that mean?" I yelled.

"Loche, relax and listen. Ravistelle has set you up perfectly. The death of one of your clients serves him in two ways. First, to keep you from escaping—or at least it makes your running more difficult. And two—it causing you emotional pain. He wants nothing more than to hurt you, to bring you to your knees so that in the end, all you can do to release the anguish is to write. He wants the strong, conservative doctor to crack open so he can poke at the delicate, vulnerable poet underneath. Shaking your world to its core is part of his strategy."

"It's working."

"Well," Greenhame said at length, "that can be bad, but it can also be good."

"Why would he want me to be convicted of murder?"

Samuel laid his hand on my shoulder with a laugh. "Many good books have been written in prison. Besides, Albion has connections—he can get to you no matter where you end up—except with us."

I stared at the man and shuddered.

"We won't let that happen, Loche," William consoled.

"What am I going to do?"

"I understand that you are meeting Julia tonight."

"Yes."

"May I ask why?"

"No."

Greenhame shifted slightly in his stance—his long brown hair in his eyes.

"Trust me," I said. "I need to see her, and I need the two of you to watch my back."

Samuel laughed quietly at my words. "And when haven't we been doing that, mate?"

"Very well, Loche," William acquiesced. "But we haven't much time. You said that your coming home would in some way aid you toward developing your writing. It would be a nice gesture to give us old folks an idea of how that might transpire."

"I don't know just yet," I admitted. "You'll have to trust me."

"Be careful not to tell her too much. She might think you are mentally unstable."

"She wouldn't be too far off the mark."

He handed me a cell phone. "Take this."

I took the phone, folded the newspaper article and slipped them both into my jacket.

I was happy to find my car in the garage. Greenhame explained that after the raid on Basil's home, he and his *old cronies* had taken great pains to clean up the mess, making sure that my car was not included in any police report. I pulled out onto the road and began my twenty-minute journey to meet with Julia. Samuel and William stayed close behind in their black sedan—at times, uncomfortably close. I did my best to try to forget that they were there.

Julia Iris was just stepping from the restaurant and into the rain when I pulled up. I hurried out and around the car and opened the door for her with a nervous, "Hi." She smiled. She wore fashionable suede boots with heels and a long dark overcoat.

I caught the light scent of her perfume—citrus and sandalwood oil.

"Great weather," she laughed, "*typical.*"

"Yes," I agreed closing my door. "Typical Idaho."

I looked into the rearview mirror. The black sedan was like a shadow against the black lake.

"So where would you like to go?" she asked.

I turned to her. "I need to tell you something first."

"What's that?" she said absently as she dug for something in her bag.

"I don't think it would be smart for me to be out in public. Have you heard about what's going on with my practice?"

"I know a little. Only what was in the paper."

"You haven't heard the latest?"

"No."

"If I'm seen out and about it could be taken the wrong way."

Julia smiled, "Without your wife you mean?"

I stammered. "No, well yes, there's that, too. But what I have to speak with you about isn't really meant for a public place."

"Sounds mysterious, Loche."

"You have no idea," I said with care.

She looked out the windshield. "Well, where would you like to talk then?"

"Your place?" I hoped I didn't blurt it out too quickly.

"My place?" she replied with a hint of surprise.

"Listen, forgive me if this seems strange. We've only just met, I know, and I would very much like to get to know you, but since the day we met I've been wrapped up in something that is difficult to explain." I paused and leveled my voice. "Really, Julia. Much of what I need to speak with you about is Basil. Something he left with you."

She watched me speak with the glint of the streetlamp crossing her face. By her expression I could tell that she knew I was nervous. She smiled genuinely, "That's fine, Loche. Basil has said nothing but wonderful things about you. I'm not worried about anything. I live just up the hill."

"Well, should you take your car and I'll follow you?"

"No, I walked here this morning."

I glanced down at her slender legs and the high heeled boots, "In those?"

"Hey," she laughed, "I thought we were going out. I keep some emergency girly stuff in my office."

I put the car in gear and placed both hands on the wheel. When I turned to her to ask for directions, she was looking at my hands. "You are *married* aren't you?" she asked.

I saw the empty indent on my ring finger and said, "I thought I was."

Julia owned a craftsman home built on the side of a high hill overlooking Lake Pend Oreille. Mountainous crags, purple in the late afternoon light, loomed up across the wide lake. I was reminded of a train ride I took when I was a child through the majestic bones of rock and mountain heights of the Swiss Alps. It was strange to think that such beauty existed so near to my own home. In her small yard stood an enormous crimson leafed Chinese maple tree. It towered over both her house and the street. She spoke fondly of the neighborhood and how much she liked the quiet nights. Way down below was the two-lane highway. "Being up here the cars sometimes sound like wind," she said. "Or the ocean."

On the way to the front door I glanced back to see my hidden companions parked just down the street. I had to strain my eyes to see the car.

She opened the door and clicked the light on. The living room was humble and delightfully comfortable. Colors of green, gold and red leapt from the walls like light on trees. The furniture all looked to be refurbished garage sale items. Old wood chairs, a sofa from the 1940s, and a collection of worn but decorative accessories crowded shelves and tabletops. In the far corner was an upside-down barstool on newspaper. Beside it was a can of wood stain and a brush.

"I like your work," I said.

"Yeah, I'm into bringing old things back to life. It doesn't take much really—especially with a little creativity. Cheaper, too. I can't see spending hundreds of dollars on new furniture. Seems like a waste."

She removed her coat and hung it on a hook beside the door then turned, holding out her hand for my coat. My eyes quickly scanned her shape. She wore a thick, dark red sweater that clung to her slender form, and deep brown velvet pants flared at the bottoms, giving the impression of a skirt. I handed her my coat and as she turned to hang it, I allowed my eyes to study her again. She was beautiful. Too beautiful. I abruptly stepped into the living room and searched for something to divert my attention.

"What can I get you?" she called as she disappeared into the kitchen, "I've got wine, beer, a little brandy?"

"Wine sounds good."

"Got it," and I could hear her opening a drawer and fumbling for a wine opener.

The framed pictures on the wall of family and friends brought a smile to my face. In each of the photographs Julia looked happy. Sitting on a table beside the sofa was a photo of Julia and her restaurant crew. Tucked in the back row was Basil peering off to the left, dressed in his white dishwashing attire.

"How long have you known Basil?" I asked.

"About three years," she called from the kitchen. "I've wanted to promote him, but he wouldn't let me."

"Why is that?"

"He said he didn't want the responsibility. I'll never forget," she said, entering the living room with two glasses of wine and handing one to me. "He told me, 'Julia, I paint, and if I become a prep cook or a cook, I'll have to spend too much energy learning that stuff—it would take away from my art.' I remember shrugging and saying that it was fine." Seeing my expression, she anticipated my next question. "No, I've never seen anything he's painted. I've never understood why he was so weird about that."

"Yes, *he is* weird about that."

"So tell me what this Italy business is all about," she said cheerfully. She sat down on the couch and crossed her legs. I sat in the chair opposite her.

I weighed my thoughts as I would weigh my footing on a steep and rocky slope. One wrong word and I could trip an avalanche. I didn't want to lie to her but at the same time I couldn't involve her in the dangers that lay ahead.

"Tricky," I said trying to smile. "But I'll do my best. Have you been reading the paper?"

"I try not to," she laughed, "but I've read a bit about your situation."

I reached into my jacket and produced the newspaper article. "I'd like you to read this, and understand that there are some things I can't explain—things I'm not permitted to talk about. Okay?"

"Alright," she said faintly. Her face remained unmoved as she read the article. A moment later her eyes peaked over the top of the paper. "Should I be nervous right now? Are you a fugitive or something?"

"Fugitive, no. But they are looking for me to answer some questions," I stated. "I just want to be as honest as I can with you. As you can see, my world has been a bit complicated as of late."

"I'm sure. So why haven't you made contact with any of these people?"

"I wish it were that simple."

"Do you think this Bethany woman was murdered?"

"I can't say."

"Well, what can you say?"

"That I'm in trouble." I sighed deeply and struggled to form a clear picture for her. "The day Beth died I was in my office all day. Learning of her death was terrible. Terrible. I decided that I needed to get away for a while. Like the article said, *to grieve*. So my wife and I accompanied Basil to Italy. While we were in Venice, I discovered that my wife had a lover. I saw the two together on a security video. It was almost too much for me. I left both her and my son behind. The only place I could think of to go was—" *To you, Julia*, my mind screamed. "Home," I said quietly.

"Loche, I'm so sorry."

"I don't want to burden you with all of this. But for the record, I want you to know. When you asked about Helen and our marriage—I *thought* we were married. But as more time passes, I'm beginning to realize that we never really were. We have been living a lie for years. I've learned that she has been unfaithful for longer than I'd like to say."

"How long?" she asked.

"You wouldn't believe me if I told you."

"Try me."

"Let's just say since the day we met."

Julia let out a quiet gasp. "Oh my god."

I nodded and almost smiled. "Indeed, *oh my god*."

"More wine?"

"Not just yet. Listen Julia, there's more. In spite of the crazy things that have happened in the past couple of weeks, I feel more alive than I ever have. I'm glad that I finally know the truth about Helen. And I'm now prepared to handle the situation with Beth Winship." As I looked into her eyes I felt as if I might topple over and fall into them. They held an aspect of Basil's Center—fathomless and tempting beyond measure. "And I am happy to be here, *with you*." She held my gaze.

There was a long silence. "Well, it looks like *I* need more wine," she said finally.

When she rounded the corner to the kitchen, I stood and began to pace, fidgeting like a smitten teen. The conservative psychologist was eclipsed in her presence. All the dire circumstances of my visit faded. I didn't want anything to do with Basil, Ravistelle, writing, or art. I wanted to take her hand and run.

"Refill?" she asked. She stood behind the sofa with the bottle in hand, and a knowing smile.

"Yes, please," I said, sitting down again.

She circled around the table, topped my glass off and

then set the bottle down.

"May I ask you a question?" I ventured.

"Sure."

"I don't understand why someone like you doesn't have a—" I faltered.

"A boyfriend or husband?"

I nodded, feeling the expression of thankfulness stain my face.

"Who said I didn't?" she fixed me with a serious look.

"Oh, I didn't mean to pry, I just didn't notice that—"

Julia laughed lightly and held up her hand, "I'm only kidding. You aren't the first person to ask me that." She shrugged, and added, "I suppose I haven't been in the right place at the right time. I was in love a couple of times, but it wasn't meant to be."

"It sounds to me like you believe in fate."

"Does it? I guess so. Aren't inexplicable things like love controlled by fate? I mean, I know I'm speaking with a psychologist, and you've probably got an opinion on stuff like that, but—I guess so, yeah. I believe in fate. But I also believe I have a little control, too.

"Lately though," she continued, "I think that fate and choice are both sketchy. Both are a gamble. It's all in thc interior weather," she gestured to her heart. "Sometimes I'm really good at controlling my life, and other times I feel like I'm lost at sea. Luckily, I like both the knowing and the unknown. The gamble is accepting which you're most comfortable with at any given moment. Everyday is like throwing dice. But whether you get something good or something bad, it always leads to growth. Once you stop rolling, you stop growing. Right? You've got to keep taking chances." She laughed, "*Wine*. Don't get me started."

I was intrigued. "As far as a significant other in your life—have you stopped rolling the dice for that?"

She studied my face and grinned. "That sounded awfully *doctor-like*, Loche."

"No, no. I'm sorry. Please—I'm interested, not as a doctor. Believe me, I'm not analyzing you. Sometimes my tone just goes there. It comes with the trade. I mean, is love—the right man—just something that you believe will come along?

"I don't think you can roll the dice for love. At least not a lasting love. You've got to *choose* to make it last," she answered, then added, "and as I said, you can never know what will influence that choosing."

"But you must decide to take the *chance*—the gamble — first, right? Can you roll for fate?"

She set her glass down and reached into a small box on the coffee table. From it she pulled a coin. "Well, I don't know, let's see," she said holding the coin up. "Best two out of three. You call it in the air. If you lose, you leave right now, and call me again when you've sorted out all the things you're up against right now." She pointed to the door with a wide grin. "If you win," she held the quarter up to her eye and pierced me with the other. "You kiss me."

I felt the heat of blood rush to my head, and I knew that she saw it. She waited and watched. I must have looked ridiculous. I couldn't tell if she was toying with me. She said simply, "*Can you roll for fate*? Call it in the air."

The coin glinted as it tumbled upward. "Heads," I called. She snatched it and nimbly slapped it down on her forearm. Playfully, she lowered her head down to peak underneath her palm. Then she showed me and remained silent. It was tails.

Again the coin plinked off of her thumb. "Heads," I called again. When she uncovered the coin, she smiled, "Heads it is. One and one."

She flipped the coin again. I reached out suddenly and grabbed it in the air. "What if you just kissed me," I said, "without flipping a coin?"

With a delicate grin she reached out with her long fingers and gently pried the quarter from my hand, "Fate is a funny thing," she said, "if you aren't willing to roll, you stop growing, right?"

The quarter flipped up and down again. She caught it

and held it against her arm. "Heads," I whispered.

"You were supposed to call it in the air," she whispered back.

I didn't answer. I just stared at her hand over the coin.

Again, she lowered her head down with her focus on me. She tilted her hand playfully back and peered under. A frown came over her face. She then sat up straight again with the coin still hidden. "Fate has it," she muttered.

She lifted her arm up toward my face and revealed the coin. *Tails.*

I stared at the coin, willing it to flip over. My entire being was prepared to reach for her and pull her to me. I sighed quietly and raised my eyes. She sat there staring at me with a thin trace of a smile.

"Fate has it," I said quietly. My hand reached to her arm and pulled the coin away. I laid it on my palm and covered the wound that was now beginning to heal there. I stared at it. Ravistelle's single eye, magnified by the shard of glass that he had held, flashed through my mind —then his words, *But fate, it seems, tends to play tricks on us. Sometimes it has its own plan.*

When I had tried to cheat fate, tried to seize the glass of water, the glass shattered—my world shattered. I closed my fingers around the coin and squeezed. I was resolute. I stood up and started for the door.

But I never made it.

I heard the coin hit the floor and roll away. I had dropped to my knees, my hands gripping Julia's waist pulling her into my body. Her fingers clasped behind my head. She knelt and pressed her lips to mine.

There was no more Center, no Heaven or Hell. And if there were Angels peeking through some inexplicable window beyond, they turned away in torment, and then back again, lamenting their fate, hiding their eyes, and longing for what they could not have—love, with a future unknown.

It wasn't until dawn that we spoke. She was laying in my arms with her back against me beneath a thick blanket in the middle of her living room. We were awake, warm and watching the rain fall through the window.

"How did you know?" I asked quietly.

She responded by cuddling closer into me.

"I had hoped this would happen," I admitted, "but I wouldn't have believed that you felt the same way."

"You had some help, I think," she said.

"What do you mean?"

She craned her neck and looked back at me. "Basil really likes you. Isn't it because of him that you came to see me?"

I kissed her. "Partly. Ever since the first time I saw you, I knew that—"

"I felt it," she said.

"This is really happening, isn't it?"

"You're making it happen. Do you remember the first time we met?" she asked.

"Yes," I said.

"You had a look on your face that I'll never forget. A look like you were fighting something—something that you thought you could control, but couldn't. It's hard to describe really. You were very guarded. After you left, Basil told me all about you." She turned her face away. "He said that you were brothers, and you had just recently found each other. He told me, 'Julia, if there was ever a man I could see you with, it would be Loche.' From that day on I entertained the thought, but you were married. I'm not the type to break up a marriage. So, I waited. And here you are. Fate. The way you looked at me that morning—like I said, I felt it."

"That obvious?"

"Scandalous."

"And I thought I had some control over my expressions."

Julia rolled over and faced me. "But what now?" She asked.

"Well," I replied with a faint grin, "the coin toss was tails, and I have to leave and *sort out all the things I'm up against*. It seems that *then* I can call you."

"What's going on, Loche?" Her tone was serious now.

I hesitated, considering a reply. "I feel that it's better that you only know so much—"

"Well, we've got that nailed. You're in trouble with this case against you concerning Beth Winship. You took a trip with the family to Italy. Your wife is cheating on you. Basil has a big art deal going on. And you are back in Idaho laying naked on the living room floor with *me*. What do I know? Not too much."

I nodded. "Strange isn't it?"

"I like strange, but I like clarity, as well."

"As I'd said before, I don't want to involve you—it could be dangerous, so I—"

"Dangerous?" she asked with wide, excited eyes. "What's dangerous? You need to let me in. Why are you so guarded?"

"Julia, listen to me, and please trust me. I need to clear some things up before I can tell you everything. This deal that Basil has happening overseas is one reason I came to see you."

I sat up and reached over to my jacket that was strewn on the floor amid other articles of clothing. From the pocket I pulled the envelope that Basil had given me.

She tore it open, unfolded the paper and read silently. She smiled once or twice as her eyes traced down the page. Then her focus grew solemn. When she was finished she folded the letter, placed it back into the envelope and sat up gathering the blanket around her. "Come with me," she said.

As I stood and dressed, I glanced up through the window. Samuel's face startled me. He raised his arm and pointed to the watch on his wrist. I shot my eyes toward Julia to insure that she had not seen him. When I looked back he was gone.

In the back of the attic was a rectangular wood box, nailed shut. It was leaning against the wall. "There it is," Julia said.

A wave of anxiety rushed through me at the sight. The

recent events of my life flashed through my mind, and I steadied myself by reaching over to Julia and touching her shoulder.

"I need to see it," I said.

"I know."

Julia handed me a flathead screwdriver and a hammer. Turning toward the stairs she said, "I'll make some coffee."

Getting the box open was not as difficult as moving it. I had heaved it over on its side with great effort thinking that there must be something more inside than just a painting. It weighed at least fifty pounds.

On my knees, I pried the lid off and set it aside. Within was a rectangle of black fabric covered in plastic. I tore the plastic away and struggled to lift the painting up so I could pull the shroud off. The painting had the heft of sheet metal. Once I had it in a position to view it I crouched back and prepared myself. All I needed to do was lift the cloth.

"Here we go again," I muttered. A gentle pull and the shroud slid off.

The terror of it swept over me. Two figures were silhouetted at a long shoreline. The painted sky was a stunning blood red, or was it pale blue, corpse blue? Flitting across the image I could sense the Center in my periphery, and I struggled to keep it there. What I noticed, however, was something different from Basil's other works. The paint was moving as if some invisible hand manipulated the colors and lines before my eyes. I shuddered at the sight. Then it captured me. The Center yanked me into the abyss.

What I saw there I will not write in this journal.

I was hyperventilating. I rolled to the side and felt the cold wood planks of the attic floor. White streaks flashed across my retinas like lightning in a black sky. My lungs begged for air.

Slowly my muscles relaxed, and my chest began rising

and falling in longer, steadier waves. From the floor I grabbed hold of the black fabric and tossed it over the terrible scene.

My ears thrummed with a low rumble—a vibrating hum, like the sound of water pressure squeezing against my ear drums. The sound of a sinking ship through dim waters. I heaved my arms against the floor and sat up. The room was spinning.

Of the few paintings I had seen of Basil's, this was the most powerful. I was alright, I could still breathe, I could still feel, and, I thought, I could still reason. Barely.

Tilting the shrouded painting back into the box I attempted to shake off what I had seen. I tapped the nails back into the lid and closed the painting inside. I now understood its weight.

"Are you okay," Julia said as I entered the kitchen. She moved to me quickly, "You look pale."

"I'm fine. Coffee will help. Must be jet lag."

"Sit down." She pulled a chair away from the table and helped me ease into it.

"The painting must be moved, and it must be moved today. Now."

"Why?" Her voice sounded frightened.

"It's best that it's out of your hands."

She nodded determinedly. "Are you sure you're okay?"

"I've got to go. I need to visit my friend, Marcus Rearden."

"Why do I know that name?" she asked.

"He's a psychologist, writer, pretty well-known—anyway, I think he may be the only one that can help me." I stood and pulled her into my arms. "I've got to go."

"When will I see you again?" she asked.

"I don't know."

Outside the day had turned darker.

"Ah," I said nodding out the window, "just what we

needed."

"Typical," Julia said. "It won't last, though."

"I want you to have something," I said. I reached into my coat pocket. From it I pulled the antique key to my office tower. I laid it into her hand and closed her fingers over it. "This opens my most guarded door."

Julia kissed me.

"It's arranged." Greenhame's voice over the cell phone was breaking up as I navigated the curves south to Sandpoint. "The showing will be in Florence. We must return tonight."

"I need more time—" I protested.

"Loche, you're out of time. Ravistelle has invited some of the most powerful people in the world to this private showing. All of the *Orathom Wis* have been summoned to keep it from happening. You *will* come with us."

I glared at the road ahead and leaned on the accelerator. Their black sedan in the rearview mirror mimicked my speed with mocking dexterity.

"I thought I was here to figure out my place in all of this," I reminded.

"Indeed you are, but there has been a change of plans and we cannot leave you here without protection. A plane is waiting for us." There was a pause, and then he added, "Any poetic revelations last night?" There was a hint of mirth in his voice.

"Julia is a private matter," I growled.

"Ah," Greenhame laughed. "Well, you can be sure that we turned a blind eye when things began to get a bit intimate. Tell me," the humor in his voice faded, "are you in love?"

Samuel's voice in the background, thick with an

Italian accent, "A poet must have a muse."

"Yes," I smiled, "I am."

There was a silence. "Good," William said. "But if this is so, why are you driving away? And so fast?"

"Another errand."

"Negative. Once we arrive at your home we must make preparations to leave—wait a moment," Greenhame's tone shifted.

"What?" I asked.

Samuel had muttered something that I couldn't make out. I looked into the rearview mirror. "What is it?"

"Looks like we've some fellows behind wanting to meet you."

"What?"

"Carry on, Loche. This won't take long. Hold your course."

At the next curve the black sedan swerved off onto a driveway that led down to a lake residence. As they disappeared I focused on the sharp turns ahead. The next time I checked the mirror, there was a different vehicle behind me. And it was coming up fast.

I took a fork that led up toward the mountain.

"Where are you going?" I yelled into the phone. There was static. Quickly glancing at the cell screen I could see the reception bars fading away.

"We'll be right there," Greenahame's voice said, broken by static. "We are getting behind—" The phone went dead.

Sharp bends in the road came one after the other. I had taken the turn that led to Schweitzer Mountain Ski Resort. The rain turned to snow as I climbed. Snow began to accumulate on the roadway. Panic. Thirty miles per hour the speedometer read. Any faster, I thought, and I'm in the ditch. Each turn amplified my anxious need to escape. My mind was racing much faster than the car, and I could not find a balance between the two.

A fork in the road cut up to the right, and I made for it. As I navigated the fork the back of the car pitched to the right and I slid sideways for several seconds. My Idaho driving skills kicked in, and I easily corrected the tack. The car behind remained close, almost pushing me up the winding mountain lane.

Twenty-five miles per hour—twenty. Higher. Colder. My back wheels were skating up and up. I suddenly realized that I may have thrown off Greenhame and Samuel by choosing this path. The mirror showed only one car in pursuit. Again I narrowed my focus at the curves ahead and struggled for more speed atop the ice.

The incline grew sharper, as did the turns, and as I forced my vehicle up the hill my fishtails grew more frequent. My fingers lost feeling gripping the wheel, and they tingled with a thousand pinpricks. In my palm I could feel the cut I shared with Ravistelle begin to burn as if his blood was seeking a way out from beneath the scab.

"What the fuck am I doing here!" I yelled at the road ahead. "I didn't ask for any of this! I don't want to write! I don't want Basil as my brother!" The speed of my thoughts tumbled down over my recent past. I'd lost my wife and son, my home, my career—I was content with my life before I'd met Basil. I had all a man could ever want or need. The walls I'd built to keep my life and family safe were thrown down—and now I was to become some kind of supernatural poet that could save mankind and the angels. Mental illness? What good could I achieve if I couldn't keep my own sanity. *What if I can't help, can't handle it or I go in with them?* I wanted to be free of desire, free of wanting an answer, free of everything. "I don't want this!" I screamed. My eyes began to blur. The big deep heavy.

The car in the mirror was hazy, and when I looked back to the road I was unable to discern the next curve. The small snub-nosed pistol that I had seen in the bunker below my house flashed into my memory. I wished in vain that the firearm was in my possession. My back wheels spun the car out of control and it slid across the lane, lurching its way to a crashing halt against a low snow berm.

I shot my eyes toward the car that followed and caught

only a long, thin middle finger from the driver. They were young skiers on their way to the resort. The car passed by.

I gasped. Saliva sputtered from lips as I panted. My temples pounded and a mist of red anger veiled my vision. I stepped out of the car and screamed at the sky, "I don't want you! I want my life back, do you hear me! I will never be yours!"

Then I recall the sting of cold. I tore off my coat, and then my sweater underneath and finally my pants and shoes. In moments I was naked, running steadily up a tree-lined, cross-country ski path. The sharp crust of the wintry floor quickly numbed my feet. Fifty yards up I entered into a wide clearing that framed a high and distant view of the snow-covered lowlands to the grey lakeshore. The morning sky sprawled colorless and thick. My lungs heaved in the ice-cold air, peering down a cliff face of at least one-hundred feet. Rocks grinned up out of the snow like rotting teeth in a skull.

One step, I remember thinking. *One step and all of this is over. I could stop the Heavens and the Earth with one step. I could stop everything altogether. Stop.* I stood like a statue, frozen with the thought of toppling down, through the Center, to the other side.

Stop.

Beth Winship's face surged into my thoughts. Her word *stop* hung there before me in the fume of my frozen breath. I repeated the word over and over, "Stop. Stop. Stop. Stop."

What could I stop by ending my life? I have no *gift*. I have nothing of what Ravistelle—William Greenhame—Howard—my mother—Basil—said I would have. No poetry to match the anomalous nature of Basil's godlike craft. The *gift* was given to Basil and Basil alone. My death would mean nothing.

I saw my limits, my imperfections, my failed attempts. My craft could not breach the spiritual wall between Heaven and Earth. Basil was the door, not I. If I possessed any *gift* at all, it was my son. And Julia. They are my only

Heaven.

I saw it then.

I was not to be gifted with some powerful art to aid a host of divine watchers. No. *I* am the gift to mankind. My words will save us all. Prevent both the invasion of Heaven, and preserve our gentle, beautiful human condition. The open door will be our doom.

I turned my back to the cliff and fell face first into a soft pile of powdery snow. As I lay there, the numbing chill revealed to me the only way to stop. The door must be closed.

I remember the sound of my voice moaning, "The painting, get the painting," as they pulled me into the backseat of their car. "Basil! Basil! God no, Basil!"

William Greenhame's arms were around me when I awoke. He was assuring me, "We've got the painting. It's in the boot." One arm held tightly around my shoulders while the other briskly rubbed my arms and chest. They had wrapped me in a thick blanket. From the backseat and over Samuel's shoulder I could see the road winding down from my panicked diversion.

In the rearview mirror was framed Greenhame and myself. He cradled me, gently forcing blood back to my limbs while he scanned the oncoming road ahead. He was humming that familiar melody that I'd heard from him so many times.

"What is that song you always whistle?" I asked.

His hazel eyes pierced me. He smiled. "Oh, that's a long story."

"What in the name of Almighty God—" Samuel started, "were you doing running around in the snow with nothing on? You silly man! William, this lad is a sandwich short of a picnic."

"I needed a little waker-upper," I replied as truthfully as I could. Though I shuddered at the reality of temporary insanity.

"You're lucky that you woke up at all, you git," Samuel rebuked. "Don't forget that you're mortal—and running around in this weather bare pickle is not—"

"Believe me," I said, "I know that."

"Well, I think you'll be alright," William comforted. "You weren't exposed long. We were just yards away when you fell on your face. Took us a moment to figure out which way you went. No one said take the right fork in the road."

"I think I needed that terrible panic to get some clarity. I know what I need to do next."

Samuel twisted in his seat and said over his shoulder, "We leave for Italy right away. A plane is waiting for us."

"Your brother will be showing his work day after tomorrow," Greenhame added. "We need to be there to stop it."

In William's eyes was a tinge of worry, and something else I couldn't describe. "What is it, William?" I asked.

"Not a thing, dear Doctor. We just had a moment there where we were worried about you. It's our job to keep you safe." He added, "And you must keep yourself safe as well, Loche. We can protect you from others. I want to know if we can protect you from yourself."

"I wasn't going to jump, I was just—"

"You were just thinking about it," he cut in. "There's no way out by going that direction. Difficult are your days now. There are harder days to come. If you think the walls are coming down now, have patience. *Ithic veli agtig*, indeed. Do, Loche, please delay your death. The Dream is not ready for you yet. You've work to do here."

We were entering Sandpoint. The sights of home cracked my heart, and I longed for the battlements of my house, the love of my wife, and the embrace of my son. But that life was over. Then the imagined soft line of Julia's cheek against mine soothed me. For her I must end what has begun.

"Wait," I said suddenly.

Greenhame turned in answer.

"I must see Dr. Marcus Rearden before we leave."

Samuel shook his head, "No time—"

"Yes, I know," I agreed, "But, it won't take long. Just a few minutes."

Greenhame said. "As you wish."

"Where are my clothes?"

The time read 7:40 a.m. and Dr. Marcus Rearden had not left his house.

I lifted the heavy crate out of the trunk and said to William and Samuel as I moved up the driveway, "Please give us a moment of privacy. Park around the corner."

Greenhame nodded.

"Hello, Marcus," I greeted him. I stood on his doorstep, the crated painting at my feet. The chill of the morning slid under my jacket.

Marcus' eyes traced suspiciously from me to the crate.

"Are you alright?" he asked. "You look terrible." I could see his old criminal psychology wheels turning.

"I don't have much time, and I need to tell you something very important."

"Loche, where have you been? Things have gotten very complex over this case. The police are looking for you."

"Yes, I've read the news," I said. He didn't answer but instead studied me, as he had done so many times. "But that isn't why I'm here to talk with you."

"Well, why don't you come in and we can discuss it," he suggested with a shiver.

"I'm afraid I can't do that. Listen, Marc," I nodded to the crate, "I'm leaving this with you. It's an important painting of Basil's."

His gaunt face squinted at me. "Loche, what are you talking about? This *brother* of yours, did he paint it?" He shook his head, "The police are asking questions. They've come to me for information about you. You need to clear this up for your own sake. Why don't you come inside? This cold is too much for me."

The warmth of his home eased my tension for a brief second. "Go on into my study, and I'll be right there."

"Marcus," I said, the heft of the crate in my arms, "let's put this in a place out of sight."

"Whatever for?" he asked.

"This isn't to be opened. You must leave it encased. Do not, under any circumstances, look at it. Don't look."

Rearden scrutinized my every syllable. Finally he pointed to the opposite side of the house—to the storage room. I carried the crate down the hall and set it inside. I stared at it and backed away. Behind me was Elanor Rearden. "Good morning, Loche," she said. "What a surprise. Would you like some coffee?"

I closed the storage room door quickly and smiled. "No, but thank you, Elanor. I can't stay."

"What do you have there?" she asked, gesturing toward the storage room.

I opened my mouth to answer but no words came. I was suddenly afraid. Afraid to leave the painting behind. Rearden appeared at the end of the hall, listening for my answer.

"It's a painting by a friend," I said, my eyes on Rearden. "And, Elanor," I said focusing on her, "frankly, I'd rather not say, exactly. It has to do with a client of mine. It should not be opened." Her expression told me that she understood completely. I knew, as Rearden's wife, she had experience with matters of confidentiality, but I still squeezed her arm. "Please, do not look," I whispered.

She nodded, took me by the elbow and led me toward Marcus' study. "Of course," she said. "Of course. I am so sorry to hear about your client, Bethany Winship. What a tragic thing."

"Thank you," I said, watching Marcus. His head tilted slightly—still focused down the hall to the storage room.

"Coffee? Are you sure?"

"No, but thank you, Elanor. I can't stay long."

Rearden closed the door and circled around behind his desk. He faced me. Finally, after studying my crumpled appearance he asked a logical question.

"What is going on, Loche?"

"I don't have anyone I can trust but you, Marc. I need your help." The old man nodded slightly, but said nothing. "Basil has run into some trouble overseas—that's all I can really tell you right now. The painting is very," I paused, searching for the right word, "*valuable*. It's been sealed up in a crate and should not be opened under any circumstances. It is dangerous. The painting, Marcus, don't look at it." Another squinting expression from Rearden and a slight shake of his head. I continued, "I will be back as soon as I can to take the painting away. For now it must be hidden."

"Hidden? Hidden from whom?"

I shook my head. "I can't explain it all to you now.""

"What is this? Some sort of mafia-curator conspiracy?"

"Marc, please. After all the years that I've known you—will you please just do this for me? I need your help."

He waved his hand, "Yes. Yes, of course. But Loche, is this more important than being wanted by the authorities? For murder?" He turned away, moved behind his desk, and stared out the window. "I'm afraid for you, Loche."

I sighed deeply. *If only you knew the real fear,* I thought.

"I've been questioned by the prosecuting attorney and the police. They have a case against you. Believe me when I tell you, you're facing some frightening allegations. They'll be difficult to fight."

His voice seemed strange, laced with distrust.

"I've gone over all of your notes in Beth's file, and I was surprised to find—"

"How did you get access to Beth's file?" I snapped.

He turned to me, "Well, since you disappeared, I've been afraid for you. So I've done as much research as I could. Carol gave the file to me."

Carol, I thought, *she's owned by Ravistelle*.

He was looking down his nose at me. "Did she ever mention the name of the person she was having an affair with?"

"No," I said.

He nodded. "Well, that's unfortunate. If there was foul play, that person would be worth questioning. Right now, *you* are the one in question. You must go to the authorities and get things straight."

"I can't do that," I stated firmly. "Not now."

"Loche, there is only so much I can do to help you."

"You can help me by trusting me. Keep that painting hidden until I return. Don't open it. Do you understand?"

"Loche, where are you going? If you run, you'll surely be guilty in their eyes—" I caught a blur of movement out the window. It was William, just out of Rearden's sight. He motioned for me to approach the window. I obeyed.

He smiled at me gently, pointed to his watch, then to the window latch, and then made a gesture that I wasn't quite able to discern. He raised his hand over his head and with one finger he made a series of circles in the air. My confused face made him scowl. He did it again, and seeing my confusion he frowned and mouthed the word, "POLICE."

"The best way for me to help you is to use my connections," Rearden continued.

With my eyes on William, "Did you call the police, Marc?"

Marcus didn't respond. Facing him, I asked, "Marcus, the police?"

He was sitting with his fingers laced in front of his chin. He replied, "I did. Loche, we can only fix this by following the rules."

I spun back to the window, threw open the latch, lifted the pane and quickly maneuvered my body through.

Rearden stood.

Greenhame took hold of my arm.

I paused and stared up through the window at Rearden. He was still standing behind his desk. "Marc, please remember what I've told you. Trust me, please. Don't look inside that crate, *no matter what.*"

No response—only a countenance that said both yes and no.

Greenhame slipped around the corner and pulled me across the back lawn to the adjacent street where Samuel was waiting with the car running.

That was the last time I saw Dr. Marcus Rearden.

I leaned against the dark wood of my office wall above what I used to call home. Still disheveled, furniture broken, cabinets overturned—the room seemed to reflect my thousand attempts at writing something of worth—broken and chaotic. Helen had left none of my work behind for me to thumb through—but it didn't matter. It was all rubbish. It was all bullshit. Behind my desk, splintered on the floor was another smashed picture of my family, posed in domestic bliss. The perfect portrait of what life was supposed to be. Lying beside the picture was an empty leather bound journal that Helen had given me as a gift, long ago. I picked it up and flipped through its pages. All blank. On the inside cover was her inscription—

To my husband, Loche—for your words.
I love you,
Helen

I stared at her name, reading it over and over. I didn't recognize it. It had no meaning.

From underneath my top desk drawer I tore away a taped envelope of cash that I had placed there in case of an emergency. Some four-thousand dollars. I never thought I would actually retrieve it.

I was tired. I lowered myself onto the floor. With my back to the wall I looked up to the ceiling—the memory of Greenhame's visit here, and his quiet disappearance—his feet pattering away on the roof. As if mimicking my recall, I heard the gentle tap of footsteps on the stairs. Greenhame appeared in the doorway. "Living the life, and the dream, I see." He said with a smile.

I didn't answer.

"Loche, are you quite alright?"

"Quite," I responded sarcastically, but with a slight smile.

William strode to the center of my office and took up the pose of a graceful ballet dancer, frozen. Eyeing me from this memorable position he whispered, "Dol en ai."

I smiled and repeated, "Woe is me."

"Six-hundred and thirty or so years and counting—and still, why does my death delay?"

"Do you really want to die?"

He began to dance, whirling and floating in graceful ballet steps. And while his slow and beautiful movement captivated me, I recalled all of the times he'd struck that frozen position. Statue-like. And now, here in my office tower he delicately hovered over the floor like a feather in the breeze.

He answered, "Sometimes, yes. Sometimes, no. I cannot say it has not been wanted, even needed. Death, that is. There are two things that have kept me from truly wanting that path. You are one of them. Your brother is the other. There will be a time for me to go. Until then, I will keep a watch over you both. That is why I am here, and truly, my only reason for being. After we bring you and Basil together again with your mother, there will be much to discuss—and to hope for. But now, we've an enemy to face."

He spun one last time and then reached out his hand to mine, and offered his best Polonius, "*Aboard, aboard, for shame!The wind sits in the shoulder of your sail, and you are stay'd for. There, my blessing with thee. Come.*" I took his hand, and he pulled me to my feet, then gave me a sort of slap on my back. "*Tehefil Dratehem*," he offered grinning.

"What, more *Elliqui*?"

"Not exactly," he said, "*Tehefil Dratehem*."

"Ah," I sighed, shaking my head, "another word scramble? I don't think I'm quite in the mood for this, William."

He repeated it again. Seeing that I wasn't in a playful mood he offered a hint, "*Alya, Orathom.*" I smiled.

"The Life, the Dream," I said.

He nodded like a proud teacher. We both turned toward the stairs and began descending the spiral tower to the car waiting outside. The leather bound journal I placed in my coat pocket.

At the landing William stopped. He held out an object wrapped in black cloth. "It is my hope that you will never need to use it, but one never knows. It will ease my heart to know that you've some added protection. I think it is well chosen, though your umbrella holds greater charm." Placing it into my hand I could feel the hard chill through the fabric. It was the small pistol I had seen in the armory.

"I know how to stop the showing of Basil's work," I said quietly.

Greenhame halted. Staring forward he asked, "How?"

I looked down at the wrapped firearm, "With words."

"You've found your gift?"

"I believe so. But first I must win back the trust of Ravistelle. If I can do that, we may have a chance."

"And what will that achieve?" William asked.

"It is up to Basil and me to stop things. I need to see him before the showing."

Greenhame was unmoved. He stood staring ahead weighing my words. "It will be dangerous," he said finally.

"Yes," I agreed, "but it is the only way. I'll go to Ravistelle when we arrive in Venice, but you must be ready to intercept the paintings if we fail."

"Plans for that have already been made," he said.

"Then I will take care of the rest."

I could see a shadow of concern. "What will you do?"

"I will use my *gift*."

My brother, Basil Pirrip Fenn, sat cross-legged on the floor in his studio with his back to the door. A pounding drum kit thumped from the speakers. He didn't notice my entry. Nearly every inch of wall space was crowded and covered with pencil sketches and half rendered pieces. At the far end of the room there were four shrouded easels. The glass room was empty.

I reached for the volume knob and turned it down. He immediately looked in my direction. He asked, "Want a drink?"

I explained meeting Samuel and George, my journey to Sandpoint, and my reuniting with the supposed-to-be-dead, William Greenhame. When I described the subterranean quarters below my house, Basil's face lit up, and he quipped, "And I thought *I* was being watched. That place sounds killer. After this is all over, can I rent it from you? I'll live in your basement."

It was easier to return to Ravistelle than I had feared. From what Basil and Corey shared with me, Ravistelle had been informed that I was taken by force, and during the abduction two of his associates were killed. I hoped that he thought I was still holding true to our blood oath. Albion Ravistelle's first words to me as I strode up the long staircase to the compound were, "I knew you'd return. Come, there is much to discuss."

The refined and articulate Albion Ravistelle spent an hour with me discussing the event that was to take place in Florence at the Uffizi on the following day. He assured me that the paintings to be shown were Basil's earliest works, the ones that only *hinted* at the Center. "Enough of a Center to quake their souls, but not harm them," he said. It was his belief that the paintings would place Basil in front of the influential and powerful. "This will, of course, allow us to gain the support of the world community. With their blessing we can pursue our end—the cure to the dark maladies of the human condition." I thought of Howard in his wheelchair, and how he had stumbled upon a painting Basil had done in his teens. One of Basil's *early* works. *Ravistelle is full of shit*, I thought.

"How can we be certain that there won't be an accident?" I asked Albion.

"We've been testing different forms of the Center in the Sun Room. We're convinced that we have the right renderings for a memorable effect," he replied.

"Well," I said, "we'll need all the support we can get. But we should have a plan if something goes wrong. I would hate for—"

"Never fear, good Doctor," he said smiling. "We will have everything ready."

We shook hands. "What an exciting time," I said.

"Indeed," he agreed. The cut in my hand burned.

I was then taken to Helen and Edwin.

The two rushed across the room and embraced me, Helen around my shoulders, Edwin around my knees.

"Thank God you are alright," she cried, "when we heard that you were taken—" She broke off and began to cry.

"I'm fine," I said. "And I'm so happy to be back."

"How did you escape?" Through her tears I could see her studying my expression.

"I got lucky," I said. "There are still some loyal to Ravistelle within the *Orathom Wis*." She nodded. A subtle crease appeared between her eyebrows. "There was one that helped me to escape." Helen nodded.

"Who was it?" she asked.

"He told me that names were dangerous." I sighed and

pulled her closer, "And now we're moving forward with Basil's work."

"Yes," she said. "I'm so glad you're back."

"I am glad you're safe."

As for Edwin, he chatted about the black boats and the men with round hats. He had apparently been on several gondola rides with Crystal. He wrapped his little arms and legs around me. My entire body quaked with anger and fear, but hearing his little voice describe Venice, I felt hope.

"Edwin has been having a blast with Crystal," Basil said. "They've been free to run amuck at the *Ravistelle Memorial of Freakishness*." He swirled the scotch in his glass. "She's cool, by the way—Crystal. We've had a chance to hang out. She loves Zeppelin. She seems very different from Ravistelle."

"Really? How?"

"I dunno. I trust her. Not sure why." He sipped. "Zeppelin, probably."

I shook my head. "How is Howard?" I asked.

"Fine—but getting crotchety. He's been reading quite a lot. And was he pissed off when he heard about Helen! Holy shit!I thought the guy was gonna get up out of his chair, grab the bitch and chuck her into the canal. In front of us at dinner one night she did this whole crying thing, right in front of all of us—it was fucking pathetic."

"What does he think of Ravistelle's plan?"

Basil thought a moment and then answered, "You know, I don't think he gives a shit. Pop has spent a good chunk of his life reading about all of this stuff—and has *faith* that it's all in the hands of fate—or some higher power. Last night he told me that no matter what happens, he's along for the ride, and will see it through to the end here in Italy, or wherever my art is—he'll be nearby. For him, this is the stuff he's dreamed about since the accident. He wants nothing more than to stand by and learn. It seems like Albion has taken to him. Pop's been grilling the poor bastard with a million questions. Of course, Pop can't stand the dough-head, but the overly curious part of him can't resist his knowledge."

"And he's not afraid? What about Cythe—and the real reason Ravistelle wants us here?"

"Well, Pop doesn't think this *showing* is a good idea." He fell silent. "Neither do I. But what am I gonna to do, get a gun?" I felt a chill rake across my shoulders.

"What's going to happen when the paintings are shown, Basil?" my voice shook.

"I think you already know." We shared a defeated stare. "He claims that he's chosen works of mine with Centers that are less potent. I told him he was fucking crazy. It'll be a massacre."

"He doesn't care," I said. "The people that come to the event will be sacrificed for his real purpose. In a way, they are his weapons. He'll use them to damage your *real* audience."

"I have a title for the show," Basil said. "I'm going to call it: *A Collection of Answers*."

I heard myself laugh softly. I felt more like crying.

He turned away. "Diana is safe."

"What?"

"Corey got her out yesterday."

"Where is she?" I asked excitedly.

"No clue," he shrugged. "Corey said, she's safe. That's all I know."

I wondered why William hadn't told me the good news.

"Has Albion said anything about it?" I asked.

"Not a word," he said. "I think he doesn't want to interfere with my work or the upcoming event."

I carried on with my story and Basil listened without interruption. I told him that I had retrieved the painting from Julia and moved it somewhere safe. At the mention of Julia he could see in my face a spark of light. He smiled. "Yes, and?" he encouraged.

I nodded slightly. He mimicked.

"Magical," I said. His response was another smile, only this time it was laced with sadness.

He stood and went for The Macallan. "So tomorrow, it'll be quite the party," he chuckled gloomily. "*Toss me a cigarette, I think there's one in my raincoat.*"

I smiled at the Paul Simon lyric. "*We smoked the last one an hour ago,*" I replied, completing the line.

Basil didn't look up from his pouring—but I saw his grin. "They got me a turntable, finally," he gestured with his glass.

The turntable in the corner of the room was spinning a record. An album cover with a red star in its center was tilted against the wall beside it—*Rush 2112* was printed in bold type across it. The vocalist sang quietly, *The sleep is still in my eyes. The dream is still in my head. . .*

"Ravistelle has the site nearly finished. It's at the Uffizi in Florence." I pulled out a fresh pack of Marlboros and flipped it over to him. He caught it and tore off the top.

"Yeah, I know. Corey filled me in on the plans," Basil said.

"Then you know that Corey, Greenhame and the others *won't* let it happen, or at least, they will try not to let it happen."

"Yeah," he said, returning with a full glass of whiskey and a lit smoke. "So I'm told. But eventually it will all come around again—and again. Someone will always be meddling."

Outside the sun was letting go of the day to make way for the night's turn. Slender bleak shadows spread like long fingers across the canals and narrow streets, and the empty vineyards and harvested farmlands in the distance. It would soon be dark. Autumn is the night's victory, for the possession of its prize lengthens. Its cold and gloom reap the last blooms, the last fruits, and the last leaves. A stranglehold that has always been.

"I know a way to stop all of this." I reached over to him and took his hand. "But it's something that we can't return from."

He looked at our joined hands uncomfortably.

"Basil my words are for humanity. They don't open the Center like your work. There's been some mistake. I have a *gift*, but it's not like yours."

"Loche, wait a sec, it'll come—it is just a matter of —"

"Time?" I interjected. "We're out of time. Tomorrow night your work will be shown to leaders, powerful people, the rich and influential. And they won't survive it. But their sins, their humanity and their souls will take on a shape and be pulled away by *the Silk* to contaminate the afterlife. The door will be thrown wide. What can *I* do? Destroying the paintings is not an option because we don't know the consequences. It was Greenhame's hope that I would stumble upon an answer to this horrible reality. I have. I want to live for my son. For Julia. For the world that we know. Think of Howard—and our mother. What will all of us do once the paintings are unveiled? The destruction begins? What will you do? Will you paint on?" I squeezed his hand tightly, "You are a gift, Brother. But your *gift* is not for man, it is for the forces that rage for what we have, our questions. You are *their* gift—*their* possession. You belong to the gods. Can't you see? You are the door." I pulled my hand away. "And you must *close* the door."

"I paint for myself," he said. "I won't allow myself to care about anything else. It's why I live."

"Do you really live, Basil? Cloistered in your studio, isolated from everyone around you? You're being controlled by not only Heaven, but also by those here who will use you, exploit you. You have become a slave to your existence, to the gods, to powers like Ravistelle. You must *stop*. Stop everything. You will never be free—while you live."

Basil's eyes widened and his head tilted slightly at my last words. "While I live?" he repeated.

My hand slowly dropped to my jacket pocket. I could feel the cloth—the cold metal inside—the weight of the weapon. Grasping it tightly I lifted the black shrouded gun out and set it on the table beside my brother.

I held his eyes in mine.

His gaze did not stray. There was an acknowledgement—a knowing. Without looking, he knew the answer was there and it was sitting upon the table beside him. For a moment longer we searched each other's eyes.

My brother stood up, went to the door and opened it. Stepping to the side he held the handle and said, "I'll see you tomorrow at the Uffizi." He did not show me his face.

Slowly, the door shut behind me and latched.

From out of the hallway window I could see the moon gently rising up from under the distant fields. I felt as if I had just returned from those fields—from a terrible errand. My legs sore from tilling the sod, my heart heavy that the harvest yielded little, and my hands stained with blood.

Another door was now before me. My fingertips traced the thin veins of wood grain as if searching for a pulse. Beyond the door my wife waited.

She wore a sheer, grey-violet caftan that spilled over her body like a thin layer of evening-lit water. Her dark hair draped over her shoulders and over one breast. The other shone through the transparent silk. Between her fingers she pinched the stem of a wineglass, and its base rested on her thigh as she lay on the divan near the window.

"Edwin is with Albion's daughter, Crystal," she said playfully when I closed the door behind me. "He's spending the night."

A wave of nausea came on as I pictured Albion babysitting my son—I lowered myself into the chair opposite her and attempted to appear impassive.

I looked at her. My wife was beautiful. Like a lightning storm.

"Would you like some wine?" She asked.

I didn't answer.

"Cat got your tongue, husband?" she mocked, knowing the full effect of her appearance. She reached down to the floor, lifted a full glass of wine and extended it to me.

I took the wine with trepidation. Supporting herself on one arm, she arched her body and rolled the rim of her glass along her lips, waiting for me to speak.

"You look lovely, Helen," I said finally, forcing back my fear—my fury.

She lowered herself to the floor, set her wine aside, and on all fours crawled toward me, all the while keeping the sensual slope of her body arched. "I was so worried about you," she said, crouching at my knees. Her hands slid up my thighs. "What would I have done if you hadn't come back?" Dropping her eyes down toward my waist, her fingers followed.

I caught her hands in mine. "Helen," I said slowly. "I can't."

She looked up at me—her lips softly tracing the lines of our joined hands.

"Tell me," her warm breath against my skin, "have you been writing?" I could feel her teeth now. Biting gently.

"Helen, I—"

"Loche," the heat of her mouth, hushed and wet, "don't push me away. I need you tonight. We don't know what tomorrow will bring."

There was a storm coming. Tomorrow night was the unveiling of *Answers*. So many answers. The changes I had experienced in my recent past could in no way compare to what would transpire at the Uffizi.

I heard my voice suddenly, "Cythe."

The air from her lips sent a chill up my arm, ice cold. Her body froze.

"Excuse me?" she replied. "Who is that?" She was moving faster now, biting a little harder at my fingertips.

"You didn't read anything about *Cythe* in your research? It's all right there."

Rolling her cheek along my hand she looked to the box. “I didn’t read anything in there with that name.”

“He’s apparently Ravistelle’s superior. He’ll be at the event tomorrow night.”

“No more talk,” she whispered, or hissed. She slid her tongue between my fingers. “Don’t you want me?”

“I think it would be better to celebrate after tomorrow, Helen,” I said, forcing her hands from my lap and kissing them. “I’m in a terrible state. You understand, don’t you?”

A flash of lightning blinked across her face when she looked up at me. “Loche, please,” she lured. “You’re killing me here.”

I heard Corey’s warning, *she is not who you think she is and would kill you if she were ordered to do so.*

I reached with one hand over to my wineglass and brought it to my lips. Helen immediately dropped her head down between my legs. I let the glass fall and it shattered on the hardwood floor. “Damn it!” I said. “Let me get that.”

“No,” she pushed me back. “I’ll clean it up. Why don’t you get ready for bed?” Her hands began to carefully gather the shards. As I rose, I intentionally stumbled, crushing her fingers against a jagged splinter between my foot and the floor. She let out a quick cry of pain.

I crouched down, “Are you okay? I’m sorry.” Taking hold of her hand I inspected the cut. She pulled it away. Tiny drops of blood tapped onto the floor, mixing with the wine.

“I’m fine,” she cried, placing the cut in her mouth. She stood quickly, turned away and walked to the bathroom. “Get ready for bed,” she said over her shoulder.

It is difficult to say if I slept. Helen tangled her arms and legs with mine as the night passed. I do recall brief dreams—pieces only—visions of Helen *watching* me sleep—her eyes unblinking, with slashed, catlike pupils.

We rose in silence and didn’t speak until we were ready to join the company below for breakfast. In the elevator, watching the numbered lights flash our descent, Helen said, “I’m sorry about last night. I hoped you might have missed me, too.” Her tone was humble, and sad.

I didn’t answer right away. Instead I forced myself to turn to her and smile. “I’ve missed a lot of things with us, Helen. After tonight I’ll show you how much all of this has changed me.” Edwin reached up and held his mother’s hand. She wore a bandage around her ring finger.

Howard was seated in the dining room. He told me that Basil had worked all night and was still at it. He added, “He wasn’t very hungry.” Edwin ran to the table and started in on the juice and strawberries.

Albion Ravistelle and Corey Thomas approached the table. Ravistelle’s smile shined with its usual practiced sincerity. “Good morning,” he said scanning the table. “All has been arranged. Your short flight to Florence leaves in an hour.” Ravistelle’s eyes stopped on me. “I’ve tightened security for your safety. Again, Loche, I am so sorry about our security failure. I assure you, it will not be repeated. I also want to give surety that my increased security measures will in no way affect your ability to move about freely. You are no one’s prisoner, and I am anxious to finally see your gift come to its glorious fruition.”

“Thank you, Mr. Ravistelle,” I replied. “I am happy to be back with my family.”

My sentiment pleased him. “You and your wife will have a limousine to take you from your hotel to the Uffizi. Howard, you shall travel with Corey, Crystal and myself. Basil will be traveling with his paintings, accompanied by Catena and the Sun Room staff. We should be going now.”

“Very well,” I said. “Edwin, do you want to take a plane ride?”

He nodded and pointed toward the canal where two gondolas were gliding by. “Black boats on the water. Black boats!”

THE UFFIZI

The sky was grey and ragged. As the sun settled on the mountains in the West, it shot its rays of gold below the cloud cover. It was the kind of sky that was too dramatic to be believable, gory and light. I shook my head at it through the passenger window.

Our limousine driver cursed at the Italian traffic. We were brought to a halt with no way out and a long wait ahead. I noticed that we were just three city blocks from our destination so I motioned to the chauffeur that Helen and I would walk the rest of the way. We stepped out into a sunlit mist of rain, but I kept my umbrella closed.

"No, no," the driver protested as I opened the door. "I have orders to deliver you to the venue myself—please Dr. Newirth, I must insist that you wait—"

Helen lagged a little behind as I got out—I could picture her face as she comforted the driver—*we'll be fine.*

Arm in arm we strode to the Uffizi. Before us we could see lines of photographers, celebrities giving interviews and the replica of the statue of David beyond. We joined several other finely dressed invitees and proceeded down the entrance route. Helen's posed and gaudy performance matched the ostentatious atmosphere. Several times during our walk I took a step to the side and observed. She was a complete stranger to me. Her gown of silver-grey flashed like lightning behind a cloud, and around her neck she wore a tight necklace of tiny red rubies. I had noted the jewels as we were leaving Edwin with Crystal back at the hotel, and I asked her where they came from. She replied truthfully, "Albion let me borrow them," and she pawed at them against her throat. "Aren't they splendid?" Noting my lack of response, she smiled, "Loche, you're not *jealous* are you?"

"*Of course not*, darling," I told her. "Why would I be jealous? They look lovely."

And now she stood in the Uffizi piazza, in the center of a sea of faces, dark evening gowns, and black and white tuxedos, barely able to conceal her euphoria. Soon she and her lover would be one step closer to their goal—one step closer to being together. I half expected to see the feigned bandage upon her finger from the night before, but when I inquired she explained that the cut was tiny. She held up her hand. "See," she said, "it's already healed."

"Isn't that remarkable?" I had said.

The narrow *U* shaped Uffizi piazza could be accessed from two directions. The statue of David stood at its entrance and at the other end was a stage that had been erected for this occasion. Behind the stage were the stone arched passages to the canals. I studied my surroundings and made mental notes of the possible routes in and out. The door to the interior of the four story museum was open to the left of us, as was the exit on the opposite side of the *U*.

Above was a canopy of bright white silk, gently breathing with the evening breeze, and a web of black cables, woven with intricate care. Each thin cable hung down and was connected to its own black shrouded painting below. These ebony cloths that draped over Basil's work were the only barriers between us and infinity. Monolithic and ominous, they loomed like a host of sleeping Grim Reapers waiting for the command to awaken, gather us all and marshal us to hell.

"The artist Basil Fenn is endorsed by Albion Ravistelle," I overheard a woman saying to a small group. "This is Mr. Fenn's first showing."

"Stunning," another woman commented. "And all of this international attention—all by private invitation."

The sudden interest in Basil Fenn was certainly a worthy subject, and it was expressed in varying ways. The collected audience of rich and famous figures only added to his mysterious public image. I mused on the old saying, *people will like what you tell them to like*. His work had never been seen, yet these people wanted to be seen *near* it.

Howard Fenn sat in his wheelchair twenty feet from us. He was backed against a pillar. Standing beside him was Corey. They both noticed Helen and me. Perhaps it was Corey's expression that made me look to the right, or maybe I felt eyes on me. I turned my head. Standing directly beside me was a thin-faced, orange haired man. It was George Eversman. His suit was akin to those that surrounded us, but it looked odd clinging to his lanky frame. His bare wrists jutted too far out of the cuffs and the pants rode a tad high over his shoes. George flashed me a wide, thin-lipped grin and held out his hand, "Stupid crazy," he said. "You the *Poet?*" His smile disappeared.

Behind I could hear Helen chatting with someone. Oblivious.

"George," I whispered, "I—"

"You the *Poet?*" he asked again. His brown eyes wide as mud puddles lit by sunshine. "You better be. . ." He growled. "Hello, Helen," he said lifting his eyes over my shoulder.

Helen beamed. "I don't think we've met," she said charmingly, "Helen Newirth, and you are?"

He reached out with his long thin arm and took her hand in his. He brought it to his lips and held it there for a long moment, eyeing her. Helen's discomfort was barely muted.

"I am George," he said.

The Duomo bells rang through the assembly.

My wife trembled. Her expression shadowed. It was apparent that she knew the name. A voice sounded over the public address system near the raised stage at the end of the gallery, *"Good evening ladies and gentlemen. Welcome to the Uffizi, my name is Albion Ravistelle."*

George let Helen's hand free and stretched his weird smile across his face again. "Ah," he said finally. "Time to pay attention, yes?"

"Thank you all for joining us here in Florence. This will be a night to remember—"

As George sauntered off into the crowd. Helen hissed

into my ear, "George Eversman, that's the leader of the *Orathom Wis*. We need to tell security."

I shook my head. "There's nothing he can do here," I said. "He's only trying to get under my skin. Wait until the unveiling." She was shaking. "Helen, we're safe here. Just wait."

Ravistelle was charming from the podium. The ease and craft of his magnetism infected even me. For an instant, what he truly had in mind for us all fell away.

"Before unveiling these answers, I would like to turn the stage over to this evening's honored guest. . ."

George's words repeated in my head. *"You better be. . ."* It was a threat. I shook it off. I had played my role. Like my brother Basil, I would no longer be controlled.

"Please welcome Mr. Basil Pirrip Fenn. Basil?"

Basil limped up the stairs to the podium. My mind again filled with the reality of my proposed *answer*—the opposite of all I believed and desired. I blinked at the truth, a psychologist suggesting the unspeakable. And at the sight of him, there was relief. He had not gone through with it. But what now? I felt a tear welling. My eyes widened with fear. *Breathe*, I told myself. The impending horror of the Center being opened caused my hands to shake.

". . . No one has ever seen my w-w-work," Basil was saying from the stage. The stutter in his voice made my skin crawl. His manner was frustrated and quite removed from the pomp that hung on his every word. Perhaps he thought it time to teach the world what art *really* was—to show them how art had been misused by those with fortunes—treated cheaply for personal gain—that society celebrated mediocrity, and by so doing found comfort in mediocre truths—that art was *not* a thing, but a way. Maybe what he was about to reveal wasn't his fear, but ours—that gods do live among us, though we only see them when we are told to. We had forgotten how to seek them out for ourselves—we had forgotten how to question. Perhaps we had never known how.

He turned his back to the audience and pulled a long

cord attached to the red curtain behind the stage. As the cloth split across the back of the gallery it revealed a blank, snow white canvas as high as the pavilion ceiling. Basil scanned the crowd. His pause was long this time and I could feel an unsettled air rise from the assembly. His eyes stopped on me, and he smiled warmly. His expression said simply, *the big deep heavy*.

"What is a man to do caught amidst Heaven, Earth and the fires that rage below? Is he to believe in a creator or himself? In the wonders of an immortal afterlife or the drama and passion of the here and now? The answer isn't what you are about to see, but the answer lies in what I am about to do. I am protecting the q-q-questions. The questions are worth living. Goodbye."

The questions.

Worth living.

Worth living.

Basil.

I raised my hand and whispered, "*Stop.* Don't. Please God no, Basil. My brother. No."

He smiled at me.

He placed the small, snub-nosed pistol below his chin. With his eyes on me Basil pulled the trigger, and the back of his skull exploded upon the canvas behind him. His body crashed back and down. A light haze hung over the podium, and for a fraction of a second the assembly was silent—then panic and chaos—then the Center opened for all to see.

Silence.

Flash.

Gone.

"Loche!" The sharp sting of a hand cracking across my face pulled my eyes from the Center. I fell away from the blow, my eyes aching and flitting across the gallery.

"Loche!"

Basil's body was on the stage—the smell of blood in the air.

"Loche!"

I've killed my brother.

"Loche!"

Not five seconds had passed since the gun's report. What had I seen? It had all replayed—my first meeting with Basil to now. So quick. So vivid. I had experienced it all again in the time span of a blink.

Surrounding me was the entire assembly frozen in time like statues. Their eyes trapped within Basil's last canvas. I reeled around searching for the hand that had struck me.

"Loche!"

A man—middle-aged—stood in front of Helen, studying her as she stood mouth agape, entranced by the Center. He gently traced his finger along the blood colored rubies around her throat. His hair matched the shadow of his tuxedo. When he turned his eyes to me, a chilling fascination stopped my breath. Green and gold flecks of light spilled from the sockets. *It* was beautiful.

"Pleased to meet you," he said, "I am Cythe. Nicholas Cythe." I marveled at him and took a step backward. "You are the *Wordsmith*—the *Poet.* How I've wanted to meet you." I felt my hand extend to shake his.

There was a terrible, mournful cry from the stage, "*Awe mines shoene chindes lip! O min chind!*" Then silence. There was a clashing of metal behind me and cries of injury. The sound of feet shuffling and running. Then silence. In my periphery a shrouded painting was being carried away. I gripped my umbrella and couldn't help but study the beautiful creature before me. The face of Cythe.

"You are—you're—"

"I've many names," he nodded. "Many I'm sure you've heard." Attracted and repelled simultaneously, I couldn't speak. "What have you done?" he asked gently, stepping closer to me, his eyes flashing from green-gold to fire red. "Listen, your brother cries out." Then my body crashed down on the white canvased floor—an unbearable pain searing from my ribs. He had struck me with unfathomable quickness. Unmoving, pillar-like sets of legs were all around me, frozen, save one pair that shuffled up to me—one pair with pant legs a tad high over the shoe. A sword blade hung beside.

"Stupid crazy, *Poet*." I looked up and George's face was crimped in anger, "Run, you silly man! Away!" Getting me to my feet and shoving me through the pillared bodies he quickly dashed to the side, evading Cythe's lightning quick punch.

Oxygen was returning to my lungs, but the pain forced me to hunch over. George's orange head was now darting in between the crowd, bobbing up and down as Cythe pursued him. For the time being, I had been saved. The Devil was occupied. I turned back toward the entrance of the gallery and maneuvered through as quickly as I could.

Weaving in between statues of onlookers, more figures in black moved in, funneling toward the shrouded paintings. Three passed me with barely a glance. Several of the works had already been pulled down and were being carried toward the Arno River behind the stage where boats waited to transport. George's plan looked as if it would work. Now, it was my turn to finish my plan. The door was closed, and I had to escape. My hand rifled through my jacket pocket and I felt for the money and my passport. It was there. A fantastic pain throbbed in my chest. I lurched forward and floundered around the standing obstacles. The statue of David stood twenty yards away. I drew my sword.

More paintings were being yanked down and moved, and I could hear the shrill sounds of clanging steel all around me. Albion must've had his own guards prepared for this. The two paintings at the opening of the piazza were still standing. Passing them, and then the David, would allow my escape. As I rounded the final static body and shrouded painting, I saw Ravistelle. And along with him was a group of finely dressed men in suits and ties—

each holding long, flashing rapiers at their sides.

I froze and backed into a tall, blanketed easel.

"Leaving so soon, Dr. Newirth?" He hissed. "Come gentlemen," he said to his entourage, "let us finish this. Please take Dr. Newirth to the car. The rest of you, inside!"

Two men lunged toward me with swords outstretched. When they were within distance I hurled my sword counter clockwise and knocked both blades away as I shifted to the right of the painting. They recovered quickly and before I could lift my blade again I felt two razor sharp sword tips at my throat.

"Let go the weapon, Doctor," one of them ordered. I recognized the man—Basil's and my escort on the plane—the one that had smashed his pistol into the back of my head. "I'm happy to say that this time I can do *more* than just knock you senseless." I stood firm.

"Senseless?" I replied, my fingers clasping the woven shroud behind me. "You don't know the meaning of the word."

"Let go the weapon," he repeated, pressing his sword-tip into my throat—hard enough to draw blood.

"Senseless," I said again, and with all of my force I pivoted back and yanked the fabric shroud down and away. Instantly, their rapiers fell to the canvased stone floor—their eyes widened and fixed to the gaping Center.

Were these men immortal? I couldn't take the chance. With both hands gripping the hilt of my blade, I swung it like a baseball bat at the first man's neck. It slid through his flesh and nearly snapped his spine. His head dropped onto his shoulder as he fell. Still attached by cartilage I deemed it good enough. I raised my sword again to swipe at the other man, but was only able to thrust. I missed. Instead of his throat I had skewered through the soft flesh of his gaping cheek and out the other side. He fell away—my blade slid out of his face, ringing from the slide across teeth. On his knees he had only a moment to spit out a mouthful of white tiny bubbles and look up at me before I struck again. The foam was a clear sign. I swung. This time his head dropped to the floor and rolled to a stop at some woman's high heels.

A blow to my left shoulder knocked me to the floor. It felt as if a bowling ball had struck me—followed by a burning sting. I'd been stabbed. Looming over me was Albion Ravistelle, sword in hand. His other hand fumbled with the shroud, placing it back over the painting.

"Gentlemen," he said again, "please, take Dr. Newirth to the car."

At the sound of a familiar voice, Ravistelle jerked around, "Goodness gracious me, Albion, you silly fuck. You've stabbed a poet."

It was Samuel Lifeson. He held a thin cigar in his teeth. As he smashed his fist into Albion's acknowledging expression, I struggled to stand.

"Get up! You've been going the wrong direction." Samuel sang as Albion reeled back from the punch. He reached down to help. I stood, barely.

Ravistelle remained with his back turned to us. Four of his men remained at his side. The rest had entered the Gallery.

"You can't stop this, my brother," Albion said. "Heaven shall fall."

"Don't call me *brother*. Brothers stick together," Samuel scoffed.

Albion said nodding to me, "Your *George Eversman* ordered them to be killed. William and I saved the boys—it was he and I that rebelled. Imagine if they had died in that crash. Would you and I be enemies?"

Samuel didn't answer.

"In the end it is really because of Greenhame that Heaven will fall. He and I convinced even George that if the boys lived they would play a role in the eternal plan. And the entire Guard went along with us, believing that fate can be changed. I have come to agree, fate can indeed alter. I have seen the path to greatness—survival. And so have many others of the *Orathom Wis*. They have joined me."

"You are such a douche bag, Albion," Samuel said,

raising his sword.

"You are brash, Samuel, but I have a certain respect for you—and William Greenhame, as well. Though he and I have become estranged, I still admire him. But he has always been shortsighted and content with being a slave to the gods. I will no longer live under their dominion."

"You will bring another calamity to all of us," Samuel said. "It was this kind of yearning that destroyed *Wyn Avuqua*."

"*Wyn Avuqua*," Albion sneered, "fell because they struck before they had the right weapons." He motioned to the frozen figures surrounding them. "Only now we have the right kind of weapons. I look forward to talking with George about all of this, for he will always be a slave."

"Yes," Samuel replied, "I know George would love to have a little chat with you, too. It will happen yet."

Albion raised his sword. "Oh, I doubt it. You see, he's having a bit of a chat with someone else right now. Unfortunately I don't think he'll have the *head* to speak after they are done."

Samuel stepped back slightly and turned to me, "Time for you to go. You know what to do."

I was well aware of where I was supposed to be—on the boats with the paintings. I had my own plan.

"Oh, so soon?" Albion mocked. "He shall be coming with us. No matter how worthless his *gift* seems to be now, we will help him develop it." He pointed his sword at me, "I'm sorry, Doctor, that I couldn't have been more honest with you—but I believe you were fated to be with me. And that is a fate that I will not be deprived of."

I raised my sword. Samuel's arm thrust out and halted me. "Go now," he said, "I'll see you shortly."

"Does he know why his life was saved? Why the assassination failed?" Albion pursued.

"Loche, go!" Samuel snarled.

"Oh dear," Ravistelle mused, "he's doesn't know. Surely, Samuel, he knows the feeling well enough. A father would risk everything when his children are in danger. Greenhame was willing to risk *man's existence* itself."

Samuel lunged toward Albion with eyes like a snake. I ran into the still frozen audience behind us, back toward the stage. The sounds of Samuel's parrying blade quickly mixed with the din of other skirmishes. Ravistelle's men followed after me.

Gaining the chest high stage I heaved my body up and rolled onto it. Painfully gathering my balance I looked down and saw streams of blood leading to a body heaped on the floor. It was my brother. Crouched beside him was Greenhame, one hand on Basil's chest, and the other pressed to his own heart.

Behind me Ravistelle's men stopped at the edge of the stage and beckoned to me, "Doctor, running is pointless."

I backed away with my sword held out and peered over the piazza. There were four paintings still standing, and around each there were melees and flashing lines of steel.

Suddenly, Corey was at my side, along with two others dressed all in black. One stood at an intimidating 6'5". The size of a mountain. Beside him stood a woman with eyes like slivers of moon. Her sword was drawn.

"I don't think the Doctor is taking patients today," she hissed.

As quickly as they had come, Albion's men retreated back into the crowd. The mountain and the moon lurched into pursuit.

I lowered myself onto the stage with Corey's help and laid my bloody sword down. Greenhame still crouched over Basil.

Barely audible was the sound of William humming a tune through sobs and tears, and that once bewildering melody was now known to me. A lullaby of his own making. A melody that I knew by heart, and heart only, from a time when memory was only a feeling. He was singing it to Basil.

"There you are," he said without looking at me. His

ageless face was torn by anguish. The childhood scar below his right eye was deeper, heated red. For a brief flash I saw him as an elderly man, pained, sorrowful and hopeless. Yet in his voice was the sinew of authority. "You should be on the boat."

Basil's face had been covered by Greenhame's vest. Blood pooled around it.

"He was my son." William said. "And so are you."

I stared at the man and believed. My body had no feeling save the tingling wave of vertigo crashing through my heart.

"How could this happen?" William cried. "Why did he do this? A son I have watched from afar—always have I wanted to aid him, show him the way, give him guidance. But it was too dangerous. Never did I think he would take his own life. *O gas nugost thialya on falio! On falio!*"

Corey knelt beside Greenhame and laid a comforting hand upon his shoulder. His face burned with anger and confusion. "William," he said gently, "we must depart. There is a time to grieve, but it is not now." He fixed me with an expression I could not identify, "Answers to your questions will come, but not now. Come away, we will bear the body."

My soul shook with dread. Both men looked up to see my unconscious movement, a quavering moan. "Was this your plan, Loche?" William asked, "Is this your *gift*?" The gun laid heavy on the stage floor. I cowered and crawled backwards. I had killed my father's son. I then stood and backed away, crying, loathing the sight of these men huddled on the stage—blood stained swords upon the planks, a man cradling his dead son, his friend weeping beside him—all beneath a glaring spotlight. I hid my eyes.

"Loche," my father called to me, "where are you going. It's not safe. Stay with us—"

I retreated, bolting through the arches and across the back landing of the Uffizi. Without a thought I hurled myself off of the ten-foot ledge and rolled onto the pavement below, my wound burning at the impact. I didn't look back when I gained my footing, but I could feel that Corey stood at the edge of the landing watching me run. He was letting me go.

Get to Edwin! Get to Julia! my mind screamed. *And go home. Home.*

Hours later, I looked down at my sleeping son, caught in a dream, somewhere distant. The train was threading through the narrow passes of the Swiss Alps to Zurich. The high peaks tipped with caps of ice scratched the steel colored sky. They passed across the fogging window like ancient palaces—like the homes of gods. I imagined Julia's little craftsman home cut into a tiny dale—a candle shining from the window.

It was Crystal that brought my little boy to me. She met me at the back gate of the hotel. "Basil said you would be here tonight. He said you'd be here to take Edwin home, but you wouldn't come in through the front door. He just knew."

Edwin had clasped his arms around my knees.

"Thank you, Crystal. Thank you." I knelt down—his tiny dark eyes sparkled in the streetlight. He grinned at me. "Heavy, Dad," he said.

I grinned back, "Where did you learn to talk like that?"

"Uncle Basil," he said.

Tears stung my eyes. Basil, as usual, was steps ahead of me.

Crystal asked, "Is Basil coming back here? I was going to play him this new song."

I stared at her, unsure of what to say.

"Probably not 'til late? Yeah? Well, I gotta go. They'll wonder where I am. See ya'." She hurried back inside.

"Goodbye, Crystal. I hope we see each other again."

At each train stop I held Edwin a little tighter. The chances of us being picked up and hauled back to either

Ravistelle or to Greenhame were very real, and more or less accepted by me at this point. I was traveling with the papers that had been given to me by Corey the night before I escaped Ravistelle—and with a simple phone call I could be detained at any border. But it was all I could do. Part of me wanted to be found—the other part of me hoped that they would let me go. Either way, I was prepared.

Thankfully, Corey had chosen a rather forgettable traveling name for me, and he told me to memorize it and learn to answer to it. The name, Bill Hagenemer, was printed on each of my official documents along with my picture. It was one of my father's *many* names. I recalled reading the name in the documents that Ravistelle had provided for me when we arrived in Venice. At least there was some comfort that if I was wanted by the police for my absence in the Winship case, my true identity would be hidden, for the time being anyway. I read the name over and over again on the passport—*Bill Hagenemer.* Then a sad smile crossed my lips as I scrawled the anagram on a piece of paper—

BILL haGENEmeR
WILLIAM GREENhame

He'd been my client for years and had never once lied. He just didn't tell me the secrets before my very eyes.

I laid my head back and tried to sleep.

In closing,

I've written it all down. It is my *version. I'm sure that there will be others. From the many perspectives will come interpretations and ultimately the truth will be twisted to suit the teller. But as it is now, so shall it be—for me.*

My actions were human. At least that is what I tell myself. Some men might have risked their lives for "the answer" as my father called it. I have risked mine.

Am I a coward for running? Could I have made a difference? Were my actions wrong? Perhaps. I planted in my brother the seed of suicide so that humanity might survive. It allowed the rest of us the chance to live on in the world that we know. The Life- The Alya. *The skies will not fall. Not yet, anyway.*

But in that sacrifice, I am nothing. My desire to cure mental illness has left me clinging to my own sanity, for every moment of every day while I wrote this chronicle, I saw Basil's final canvas. His blood has stained my will to search for the cure.

Marcus. The game is on. The pawns, the knights, the bishops and the kings are calling us. You have always been too smart for me to beat. Your past has captured you. Make your move, but beware. Searching for the hands that move us will bring your kingdom to its knees. Like me, you crave to defeat the disease, and like me you will find written across your heart a forgery. Something that will lose you the game. You will become what you've struggled to cure. Words and pictures, Marcus. There are always two.

October 31st is Beth Winship's funeral. I will be there.

Julia closes the book and looks over at Rearden sleeping. The old man's chest rises and falls in uneven, gentle waves. A quiet rasp flutters in his breathing. Outside a grey glow slowly nudges the shadows back. The landscape is a flat and colorless wash. Julia leans her head back against the seat and closes her eyes. "I will find you today," she whispers.

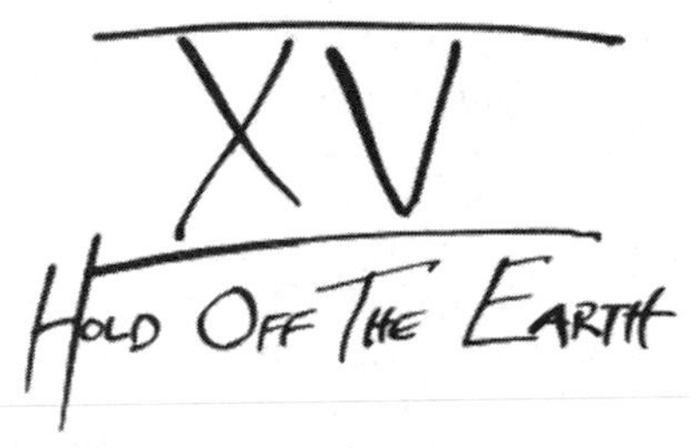

Loche Newirth stands in the rain outside the cemetery. He looks down at his black suit, tie and deep grey overcoat. Water has leaked into his leather shoes. An open umbrella is spread out over his head. The heavy sky mirrors his mood and he is reluctant to step into the view of the gathered mourners. His shoulder burns. As he moves through the gate and down the slushy path he sees them look his way, one by one.

Bethany Winship's voice drifts into his memory. She had shared her family history during several of their sessions. The city of Coeur d'Alene, Idaho, knows the Winships. Three generations have grown up in this lakeside town, and in that time they have built themselves a reputation as a hardworking, conservative family—good kids, good parents, reliable people.

Loche marches steadily toward the huddled group, mindful that every step is more difficult than the last.

He sees Roger Winship, Bethany's husband, striding out to meet him. His pace is rigid and determined, arms tight to his sides, hands clenched into fists.

"Really?" Roger says approaching Loche, his voice hushed, quavering with fury. "You son of a bitch. You decide to reappear now, at her funeral? You're not wanted here. The police, however, would very much like to have a word—" Roger raises his cell phone and points his finger to dial.

"Wait," Loche says. "Please, Roger. Please listen. I'm sorry that I haven't been available to comment—"

"Comment?" Roger cries. "Comment? You're wanted as a suspect in this."

Loche raises his hands. In one hand is the red envelope. “Please, give me one moment to explain.”

“Your disappearance has explained plenty.” Roger turns away, dialing.

“Roger,” Loche says, pulling on his arm. Roger shrugs it off. “Read this letter. My absence has been spent trying to discover the truth and I think I have. Though I’m afraid it won’t comfort you. Please, just read this letter.”

Roger turns back to Loche and stares at him. He grabs the envelope angrily, tears it open and reads. Loche watches his face. When Roger reaches the end of the letter he lowers his arms. “How can this be?’

“There’s one last confirmation to make,” Loche says quietly.

“So there you are!” a voice shouts from within the marquee. “There you are, Dr. Loche Newirth!”

Both Loche and Roger look back at the gathering and see Marcus Rearden beneath the funeral tent. He is on his tiptoes with his head high and his gaze pointed toward his old friend. Under his arm is Loche’s book. Behind him looms a large black rectangle of fabric, leaning against the coffin.

Loche places his hand upon Roger’s arm and says quietly, “Let me deal with this, Roger, won’t you?” Roger does not answer. The two men walk back toward the tent.

“Marcus,” Loche acknowledges, moving through the group and positioning himself before the old man.

“My wife is dead,” Marcus says, smiling. “Elanor is gone.”

“I know,” Loche replies. “I’m sorry.”

There is a pause. Marcus’ smile vanishes. “*You* killed her.”

Loche does not respond, but the gathering shifts uncomfortably.

“Do you know what it is like to lose the one you love? Do you know the madness that settles upon the mind when there were still words to share? Confessions? Confessions to make?”

"Like Bethany?" Roger's voice cries from beside Loche. "I have here a letter written to Bethany—by you! A love letter, much like the ones you gave the authorities. Only this one is *signed* by you. The only one with a signature!" The old doctor does not seem to hear him. "You son of a bitch. You told Beth to never use your name in her letters to you, and you never signed your name! That made it easy to frame Loche. When she wanted out, you wouldn't let her go, so she threatened to tell your wife. You killed her. You murdering son of a bitch!"

Roger raises the typed letter up for every witness to see. Rearden's bold signature is scratched below the words, *All of my love*.

In Marcus' face is a trace of pity for the man.

A deafening pop jolts through the assembly. Roger's left shoulder explodes, and he drops heavily to the ground. The sickening report of the firearm in Marcus' hand sends a surge of panic through the group.

But Marcus speaks before there is time for anyone to scream. "She never loved you, Roger," he hisses at the groaning man.

Loche steps forward, his umbrella in his grip. "Marcus, put the gun down."

"I'd hoped it didn't have to come to this," the old man says mournfully. "I didn't come here today to hurt Roger. I feel sorry for the poor bastard. He had no idea how to love Beth. I knew how to love her. I discovered a new passion in my life, and it was her. I decided that I wanted to begin living my life again. And sweet Bethany was the doorway that led away from the darkness. She made me a new man. She was the answer I'd been looking for. And Roger—Roger is partly correct, I couldn't let my wife know about our love, but I also couldn't allow my career to be scandalized. Only I know the truth of what we shared, and I can't let my peers, the public or my clients twist our love story to pieces. Passion, I've learned, has no bounds."

"Marc," Loche speaks calmly, "put the gun down. There's no way you can keep from scandal now. Put it down before you hurt anyone else."

"How rational of you Dr. Newirth, but you must forgive me. We aren't through just yet." He scans the terrorized faces. "Please don't move, any of you. There's more to see."

The weapon traces across the crowd slowly. Every frightened set of eyes follows the barrel. The eerie, playful movement sways to the right and then to the left until it finally stops, aiming into the center of the congregation. "Julia, my dear, will you please join me."

A woman steps forward with slow, focused steps. Loche studies her briefly and then looks back to Marcus. She pauses beside Loche and grabs hold of his hand, squeezing desperately. Loche looks down at their hands and then to her face. "Loche?" she says. He flinches, catching his balance—his body recalling the fall, the icy water, the black pupil below.

"Ah, how touching," Marcus says. "Julia, step away from him. Now."

Loche squints at the name *Julia*.

Marcus grabs the woman's shoulder, pulls her to him and then wrenches her around so that she is facing Loche. The cold steel barrel is pressed to the back of her head. "Feel that?" Marcus growls at Loche, "Feel the pain of want? You want to hold her, but you are separated by the fear of death. Loche, I've struggled to find you for one reason, and one reason only. So you, too, can feel what it is like to lose the one you love and not be allowed to tell her *everything*. As I was robbed of words for Elanor, your words will never reach Julia. Your love will never be fulfilled."

Julia's face is pleading to Loche.

"Marcus, let her go," Loche says finally.

"In the end, it was you that took my wife from me."

"I don't know what you are talking about, Marc," Loche says carefully.

"Elanor! The painting, you fool." Marcus raises his opposite hand and holds up the leather bound journal. "I read your book, and I know what Basil's paintings can do.

Elanor broke into that crate of Basil's because she suspected something. You, good Doctor, knew of my affair. Bethany was your client for God's sake! You planted that painting with me to get my wife thinking! To expose our affair!"

Loche remains silent.

"Today, I will be at peace. The only peace I can provide myself is your punishment."

Marcus clicks the steel hammer back. Julia's eyes squeeze shut.

"Wait," Loche says. "What does this woman have to do with it? Let her go."

"This woman?" Rearden sneers. "Really, Loche? Are you going to pretend that you don't know who she is? Seriously?"

"I *don't* know who she is," Loche says. "Just let her go."

Julia's eyes open. Her expression is confused.

"Ah," he says to Julia, "do you hear that, my dear? The love of your life doesn't know you." He then hisses at Loche, "You can play whatever game you like, Dr. Newirth, but don't take me for a fool. I am well aware of how you feel about this woman." He holds the book up again. "You've shared your heart quite amply within these pages. We'll see just how well you know her when I put a bullet through her brain."

"Loche," Julia whispers.

Loche's eyes shift to hers. He lingers there. She is struggling to say more—something only the eyes can convey—as if he should understand—he should know.

"And her death," Rearden says, "will almost pay for what you've done to my wife."

"Marc," Loche pleads, "your wife had a heart attack. Nothing more. We can be done now. It's over."

"Far from it, Loche. You see," he says with ease, "the best part about this situation is that I'll walk from here without fear or regret. When I pull the shroud away, everyone present will forget what they've seen. They will forget my name—hell, their own names for that matter.

Your spilled blood will be wiped clean by the Center."

Loche sighs nervously. "Okay. I see that my writing has truly made an impression. I hoped that it would. Then why take the chance?" he offers. "Why not blind them now and be sure that you have no witnesses?"

The question crosses the old doctor's face. He considers Loche's tone. Loche seizes on the momentary pause.

"Basil said that there was something special about it," Loche continues, "and I've seen it myself. It is ever changing. Do you want to take the chance?"

Marcus drops the book onto the muddy grass and grabs a corner of the black fabric. "I'm sorry, ladies and gentlemen," he says to the congregation. "I'm afraid we can't have you witness a killing. You'll be glad you didn't. Enjoy the journey, and again, my apologies."

His hand yanks the fabric away as he pulls Julia to the side so that every set of eyes can view Basil's harrowing work.

The group takes the work in. There is a subtle victory in Rearden's eyes as horror spreads across their faces. An elderly woman faints, dropping to her knees and then to the ground. He sees several expressions shadow—mouths agape. Loche wonders if Rearden is waiting *The Silk* to appear in his periphery—a thread of light for each set of eyes.

Then their faces, one by one drift from the painting to Rearden in visages of disgust and malice. Marcus takes a sudden step back, the force of their collective glare like a frigid wind. With the gun still pressing against Julia's head he casts a hesitant look at the painting.

There he sees his own countenance, twisting in hues of red and black—a monstrous, lurid smile, lips of thin blood like scars mingled with gargantuan, murderous eyes bearing down upon another face, a pale, sleeping form. Bethany Winship. Around her throat are gripping, claw-like fingers. A wounded, bleeding sunset fills the background glowering down and mirroring itself upon a still body of water. Reflecting in the water are the two figures, but instead of the foreground's strangling embrace, the figures are intertwined and intimate—delicate and pure. The right corner of the work holds a signature—*L. Newirth*. And below that, the title— *Marcus Rearden Murderer.*

Marcus freezes. Color fades from his face.

Julia drops to her knees and kicks backward, knocking Rearden's right leg out from under him. He tumbles against the casket and the gun fires. Loche thrusts the tip of his umbrella into the hand that holds the gun. It drops into the mud. Three men rush the old man and tackle him. They all crash into the casket and then to the ground. Beth Winship's body arches halfway out of the coffin as it thuds to the wet grass.

Rearden twists free. He reaches out and pulls the weapon back into his grip, gets his feet beneath him and springs up. He bashes his way through the circle of onlookers and reels across the muddy patches of grass and snow.

Rearden's shot had hit its target. Loche stares helplessly at Julia. She is gasping for breath, lying on her back. Her hands are bearing down on her stomach. The blood is bright red and welling up between her fingers. A woman cradles Julia's head. Loche kneels down and presses his hands upon the wound. He feels the heat of her blood.

"Loche," Julia whispers. Her face is whitening. Her eyes are wide and frightened.

"Someone help us," Loche calls to the gathering. Two more people join him on the grass.

"Help is on the way," one of them says.

"I love you," she says to Loche. "I love you." She then winces. "Say something, Loche. Please say something." He stares at her face. Her eyes are amber brown. There is something missing. Waves roll behind his forehead. He feels his hands numbing—the fall—he watches the surface of the lake flicker to an iris, the center abyss opening through the Earth—it widens and churns—he sees the tip of his pen and ink pooling, draining into the white paper. His thought begs, *Do I know this woman?*

"I am sorry," he whispers. Tears pour from his eyes. She is fading. "I am sorry."

She grips his arm. Her other hand clutches at her chest —at something beneath her coat. "Loche, don't let Marcus get away. Don't let him get away." Julia's hands stop moving and fall.

He turns his head, straining to see where Rearden has gone. He looks back down at Julia. "I am sorry," he says again. He climbs to his feet and pursues Rearden into the graveyard.

Marcus Rearden makes anxious, random ninety degree turns, steadily dropping down the hill into the older section of the cemetery. The high tombstones hide his escape. His knees ache. He cranes his neck, looking back. He can no longer see the funeral tent. Distant sirens quicken his pace.

Thick bursts of dread quake through his frame at each nervous footfall. He continues farther down the slope where the grey and aged monuments grow in size. *Better cover*, comes his inner voice, and from out of that shadow within his mind he sees a slight flicker of hope. A hope that he may escape. But as he descends, a wet chill cuts at his ankles, and then his feet. Cold grains of ice fall into his boots. The snow is getting deeper the lower he goes, and he can sense the zigzag trail he is leaving behind.

When he reaches the bottom his feet slide to an unsteady stop. Between wheezing gasps for air he strains to listen. The sirens are closer now. Surrounding all above are countless crucifixes and headstones rising up out of the snow like decaying teeth. He stands in the lowest point of the basin as if the burial ground is pulling him down into its mouth.

"Marcus." Loche's voice stabs at his ears. He spins around toward the call with the firearm pointed. His eyes flit, scanning for movement within the monolithic landscape—movement in the city of the dead.

"Now you've killed two people, Marcus,"

"So she's dead, eh? And only two? Try four. Soon to be five, Loche." Marcus hisses, searching the landscape.

The old man whirls around again as Loche's voice echoes from the stones. The gun trembles in his grip. Panic rises to his throat and a slow, maddening moan issues from his chest. His frantic thoughts flash desperately, *Where is this voice coming from*? *Is it Loche or is it my* other *voice?* Tormenting seconds pass, and Rearden can feel that he is teetering on the edge of a fathomless pit. *Is it Loche or is it my* other *voice?* Chatter, laughter, madness in his head.

"So you've read my book?" the voice comes again.

His lips are numb, but he hears himself respond, "Yes, you are *The Poet. The Wordsmith*."

"Well, I suppose so." The voice is now directly behind him, close enough to feel the heat of his breath. He swings around with the gun outstretched and stops with the barrel aiming directly between Loche's eyes.

Loche Newirth stands calmly. One hand is in his pocket and the other rests upon his planted umbrella. Rearden senses several police officers taking positions on the edge above. "Please, put the gun down, Marcus," Loche says.

The old man risks a quick glance to the surrounding rim. He sees several rifles spiking out from the stones. "How fitting," he says, raising his other hand to support the outstretched weapon, "here we stand at the Center. At the end."

"This is the end," Loche agrees.

"There is more to come," he says, slowly snapping the firing pin back. "I'm so glad that you followed me here. We'll soon both be joining the surrounding dead, and maybe, just maybe we'll see Heaven before it becomes Hell. The *Orathom*."

"The *Orathom.* That's right. The Dream."

"We'll make our own Center, our own departure. I'm afraid, dear friend, that you'll have to go first. After that,

I'll place this gun below my chin and follow you."

"Like Basil?" Loche asks carefully. "Like it says in my book?"

"Yes, like the brother you've slain."

Loche slowly raises his right hand with his palm out. He exhales a deep breath that mists between them. His face is pleading. "Marcus," he says, "there is no Basil. There is no Center." Rearden glares. A shadow crosses his thought. "What you have read," Loche continued, "is not real. My book, is not what you think it is."

Rearden's eyes dart up the hill again, then return to Loche's. He squints.

"Marcus, the writing is fiction. It is a story. I wrote it to trap you."

Rearden shakes his head and spits in disbelief. "Don't be a fool—"

"I am telling you the truth. What you've read—some of it truly happened—most of it I made up."

Rearden stares. His breathing is irregular. "No. No. Julia, Julia knows."

"Julia? I don't know who you are talking about. Marcus, I made Julia up. I made Basil up."

"Don't try to make a fool of me," he yells. "You just *saw* Julia. I just *shot* Julia."

"I don't know the woman that you've killed, Marcus."

Rearden lets out a qualmish laugh. "You expect me to believe that you don't know Julia?"

"I made up a character named Julia. I made up an entire story—and I see now that my plan worked beyond my hopes. How else could I bring you to justice, Marcus?" Loche says. He holds his hands out. "How could I beat you if I just turned you in? You who have every advantage when it comes to politicians, judges—even your friends and connections in law enforcement. It would be impossible to get a conviction. As we both know, you're the best. *You could* get away with murder. I had to come up with another way. I had to figure a way for you to incriminate yourself. I wrote the book for *you*. I wanted you to think that I had a mental break. I wanted you to believe."

"Nonsense!" he shouts. "What about Helen?"

"*What about* Helen?"

"Where is she?" Rearden watches Loche's face. He sees Loche struggling with something. "I would think she is still at our home," Loche replies. "I told her that I needed some time to figure out what to do, that I would be away for a few days."

Rearden blinks. He feels tears. "Basil's painting killed my wife. You delivered it. You put it in our house!"

Loche does not reply. Rearden's eyes are now racing between his prey and the police moving slowly inward.

"That is true," Loche says. "But I painted it. I painted it. It was not my intention for that to happen—to hurt Elanor. There is no such thing as a Center, Marcus. There is no supernatural element to the painting. It is just a piece on the chess board."

Rearden sees the painting in his memory, the gargantuan, murderous eyes bearing down upon another face—Bethany's face. *It is a picture of the murder itself,* a hated voice cackles in his head. He shakes it off.

"But. . ." Marcus cries, his quivering lips arching into a smile of disbelief.

"Marcus, you were trying to frame me. I'm afraid that you've fallen into the trap that I have laid for you." Loche bows his head. A tear trails along his cheek. "The painting was a *warning* to your wife—I regret that the shock of it —" He then glares at Marcus, "You murdered Bethany Winship. You didn't want your weakness to be discovered. You did not want the truth to be discovered. And because of that you allowed my fiction to feed your delusions. You've placed faith in a myth, Marcus. Myths won't save you."

Rearden's spittle drops onto his shirt, and he begins to cry openly. "And my signed letter?" he manages in sobs.

"She mailed it the day you drowned her. It was Bethany's final *word*. The *picture* was clear to me. Words and pictures, Marcus. There are always two. They were only words and pictures."

"Turn around, Loche," the old man hisses.

Loche freezes.

"Please. Like the old days." Rearden watches as Loche slowly understands the request. Rearden always sat behind, listening. He hears the faint echoes of Loche's idealistic ramblings—his desire to end mental illness.

"Marc," Loche starts.

"Turn your back," Rearden orders.

Slowly, Loche turns away and stares up the hill. Rearden struggles to see through Loche's eyes—to sense his fear. Will this rim of gravestones be Loche's final sight?

The gun is now heavy. Rearden can feel the police rifles trained on his every move. "Say something," Rearden demands.

Loche does not respond, and the silence is maddening. He hears breathing. It is his own. Unsteady—a panting, fearful sound like a wild animal caged.

"Speak!" Rearden demands again, taking a step forward and pushing the weapon against Loche's scalp, pushing his head downward. "Say something."

Loche says quietly, "The big deep heavy."

Rearden lets out a slight chuckle. "Perfect," he says. He pulls the barrel away from Loche's head. Marcus crimps his eyes shut, points the gun into his own temple and tears at the trigger. *Click, click, click.* The pistol's empty cylinder circles around as the hammer snaps against hollow chambers. He had failed to reload the weapon since his journey began, and now, dropping to his knees, he continues to pull the trigger with the vain hope that one bullet remains—the one that will kill at least one side of him.

Loche steps backward as the police rush in and force Rearden face down in the snow.

"A little waker-upper!" his menacing cry echoes. "A little waker-upper! It can all be true! It can all be true!"

Loche walks up and out of the headstones and he can see the strobing lights of several police cars. Two ambulances are parked just outside of the fence line, yards from the funeral marquee. The area has been partitioned by yellow police tape. Several officers are taking statements. Roger Winship is lying on a gurney. A paramedic is rolling him toward an ambulance. Loche steps over the yellow tape as two men notice him.

"Dr. Newirth." one of them says. "I am Detective Stiddam."

"Yes?" Loche answers.

"We would like you to accompany us to the station. We have some questions for you."

Loche nods. "I will help in any way I can."

"Good," Stiddam says.

Loche searches the confusion surrounding them. "Where is the woman that was shot? Is she okay?"

Stiddam does not answer, but instead points to another gurney that is being rolled away. The figure's face is covered with a blanket. "I'm sorry," Stiddam says.

Loche watches the paramedics wheel the woman to the ambulance. They lift her body into the back. The doors shut and the vehicle speeds away.

"She managed to tell the woman that was with her at the end to make sure you got this. It was around her neck." Stiddam reaches into his coat and pulls out an antique key. The broken chain is dangling from his fingers. He puts it in Loche's palm.

Loche stares at it. It is the key to his tower office.

"What was her name?" Loche asks.

"The name was Julia. Julia Iris. She's from up north, Hope, Idaho."

Loche's eyes rise to the detective. Stiddam returns the stare, but his face quickly turns to concern. He braces Loche's shoulders, steadying him, "You okay, Dr. Newirth? You don't look so good."

Loche Newirth drops to his knees and loses consciousness.

Art is a lie that reveals the truth.
PABLO PICASO

Now to 'scape the serpents tongue,
We will make amends ere long;
Else the Puck a liar call:
WILLIAM SHAKESPEARE

Life, he thought, is a blatant act of imagination.
JESS WALTER

The black ink spreads open like a pupil in the dark. Loche Newirth wakes up.

He can see red slashes hemmed in black. He struggles to focus. The blurring marks tighten into the shape of an eye—slathered in paint on the cedar ceiling. He shifts slightly and knows that he is at his lake cabin. Turning his head he sees the picture window is filled with a pale blue sky. He sits up with difficulty.

Beside him, beneath the blankets is a sleeping form. She is turned away.

"Helen?" Loche says. His side aches—hands are cold. "Helen, what time is it?" The digital clock on the bedside table is blinking 12:00. White sunlight is streaming through the window. "Helen?" he says again leaning over her. He pulls the covers back. The woman lying beside him is not his wife. The sheets are stained with blood and the woman's hands are resting upon her midsection.

Loche's body lurches away in shock.

"I am glad to see that your confrontation with Marcus Rearden has ended with you still alive." William Greenhame sits in the corner of the room with the leather bound book upon his knee. Behind him in the kitchen are two other men. One is seated at the table, the other is standing at the sink sipping from a coffee cup.

Loche struggles to stand and falls against the cedar log walls. He holds his hands up in front of him. "Please, help me," he cries, "please, help me—I don't—I can't—"

William stands and says gently, "Take it easy, son. Take it easy."

"He's reached his limit," one of the men in the kitchen says.

Loche scowls and shakes his head, "William, what are you doing here? How did—I'm scared—"

"I know, Loche. I know. Please, you are safe here. You are safe. And I think I know why you are scared. Please. . ." He motions for Loche to sit.

Loche's tears fall in long lines. "How did I get here?"

"Do not fear, Loche. You passed out. The police released you to us. We then brought you here."

"Where is Helen? Edwin?"

"Edwin is at a Halloween party with friends from his preschool, you dropped him off this morning before Bethany's funeral, remember? I do not know where your wife is, exactly."

Loche's raised hands slowly drop and ball into fists at his side. He looks down at Julia. "She was shot."

"Yes. Still is shot."

"Why is she here?" Loche cries.

"You will know in time." William sighs deeply and moves to the foot of the bed and kneels. "Loche, please sit down." Loche remains standing.

"It seems that you have a *gift* after all, or I should say, *before* all." Greenhame laughs gently. He sets the book upon the bed. "I suppose it is to be expected that you should not understand anything just yet. Your *gift*? Your writing? Your power that you thought dormant? Well, reading your latest work has revealed much," Greenhame pats the book's cover. "And what a magnificent work it is. Perplexing, diabolical and truly divine. It is inspired. Let me test my theory, yes?" William asks. Loche nods. "Very good. Do you know who I am?"

Again, Loche nods.

"I have been your client for quite some time?"

Loche's eyes appear to agree.

"I am not really, *immortal*, right?"

"No."

"Am I your father?"

Loche shakes his head slowly. "No. I *wrote* that you were my father."

"Yes, I read that. I'm flattered." William says. "Do you know these men in your kitchen?"

Loche studies the two men. "No," he says, "I've never seen them before."

The two men look at each other—a hint of surprise in their faces.

Greenhame grins. "The man on the right is Samuel Lifeson. Seated at the table is Corey Thomas."

Loche knows the names. "How can this be?" he says suddenly. "Samuel and Corey are made up. They are characters that I created—"

"And this woman beside you?" Greenhame asked.

Loche turns to Julia. There is a dim, blinking star in his periphery, like a familiar dream. "I was told her name was Julia Iris," Loche points to the book, his gaze searching Julia's face.

"You have never met?"

"No!"

"Interesting," Greenhame says. "Do you recall the last time you and I spoke?"

"I do. It was in my office. The day you stood on my desk like a statue."

"I see. So it was not at the Uffizi in Florence," William's voice quavers, "beside your fallen brother, Basil?"

"No," Loche says shaking his head. "Basil does not exist. Julia, Samuel, Corey—they are not real. Why are you doing this? Who are you people?"

William rises and stands in front of the picture window. A red haze of paint is still smeared into the corners.

"It could be a mental break," Samuel offers. "A kind of amnesia."

"I think not," William replies.

"He believes what he is saying," Samuels says. "There is no doubt in his eyes."

"Yes," William agrees. "But I believe this to be

providence. The Invisible Hand, The One, that which we call *Thi*, revealing itself through its own story. A story within a story. Creating life within its creation."

"The chicken or the egg?" Corey says. "You're not suggesting that Loche has *created us*, are you, William? As if we suddenly winked to life out of his imagination."

William says over his shoulder, "*You* may have winked to life—I was already alive. I was his client, remember? I would guess that my existence was augmented. But you, Samuel and poor Julia—"

Corey's tone is skeptical, "But this is all too incredible. How can this be?"

"Incredible, yes," Greenhame agrees, "though, no more incredible than the Judeo-Christian creation story. The whole of creation in seven days? Adam from clay. Eve from his rib. Come now. We've seen how entire cultures have fought and died to preserve that belief. Or what of the Egyptian creator god Atum—created himself and then sneezed out humans?"

"This is preposterous," Samuel says. "Loche has merely written down what he has experienced in the last fortnight."

"I agree," Corey adds. "What you are suggesting cannot be, William. It would mean that Loche has not only created us from his imagination, but he is also the architect of the *Alya* and the *Orathom*—that his writing created Basil, Basil's paintings, The Center, the divinities, the immortals—shall I go on? I have memories and a life of my own. Centuries of memories, William. He may be your son, but the story he has written here is nothing but an account of what is, and what has been, well before his time."

"And I have memories too, Corey," William says. "But that does not mean that Loche should know of them. Nor should he know of all of your experiences. He has brought you into the story by conceiving your shadow. But by doing so he has opened up the *Alya* for you to create your own destiny. You were a seed in his imagination—you have flourished on your own."

Loche feels lightheaded again. His vision skips from the three men to the volumes of books stacked upon the kitchen counters and the piles of square Post-it notes—notes that outline the book before him. William is still framed in the picture window. Loche presses his knuckles into his eyes and lowers his head. "I wrote the story to capture the smartest man I know. To bring him to justice. I fed his already delusional perspective by giving him something fantastic. It was the only way to beat him. Something he would never expect. I lied to reveal the truth."

"And beat him you did," William agrees, still facing the blue sky. "At least for now. Myths have a way of causing men to act out of belief from the very beginning. Marcus Rearden is a dangerous man, Loche."

Loche says, "You only know of Marcus Rearden because of what is readily known about him—"

"I know of Marcus Rearden because of what he knows of *you*," William interrupts. "I have watched him for years, since the two of you met. And Marcus Rearden knows your mind better than any that live. Perhaps better than you know yourself. He has been your mentor, your confidant and your supposed friend since you began your practice. It is well that you have won this victory, but I feel that Marcus is still a threat. I believe that providence is again playing its part. How else does a drama continue without treachery? Without betrayal? Without death? What more could the gods want? A master betraying an apprentice. The apprentice outwitting the master. Chicken or the egg? Who made whom?"

"William?" Samuel asks. "You don't truly believe what you are saying, do you?"

William turns slowly. "I suppose it doesn't matter, does it? What is, is. Whether or not Loche created us, we have work still before us. But I do, Samuel, believe that Basil's brother here, Loche Newirth, is the one prophesied. He has made us what we are by writing that book, and he has made a way for the divinities to peer into the *Alya*. A way that none of us could have expected."

"William," Samuel says, "you're saying that Loche prophesied himself—as the *Poet*—the one to open the doors to the *Orathom.*"

"That is exactly what I am saying," William agrees. "Perfectly paradoxical."

Loche looks through the window, through the layers of sunlit blue. A cold and clear October sky. The sight brings no relief. His thoughts reel and break against each possible scenario. William sits down at the desk and lifts the pen from its surface. He inspects it, holds it gingerly like it is made of delicate glass.

"Have you ever heard the tale of The Tears of Heaven, *Wyn Avuqua*?" Greenhame asks Loche quietly. He turns slightly and points through the window, down the treed slope to the ice blue water. "Just across the lake and slightly north there was once a city called *Wyn Avuqua*. Many, many centuries ago. It was there our distant brothers and sisters communed with The One, mighty *Thi*—on these very shores."

"I made that up," Loche says sharply. "It's not real."

William's eyes narrow at Loche's words and he smiles slightly, "It was said that an Eye would sometimes appear on the surface of the lake. The water's Eye would fill with sky." In his face is a solemn question, "Loche, did *It* look upon you? Was there an Eye in the water?"

Loche's legs weaken suddenly. He braces himself against the wall. His side can feel the smack of the water, the sting of cold in his bones. "I fell. Five days ago now. I fell into the water. I thought I saw an Eye there, but I can't be sure."

Corey stands and asks, "Did you or did you not see an Eye?"

"As I said, I think I saw something. It's difficult for me to describe, especially after the ordeal of getting lost—the hallucinations brought on by the incident."

"And after you fell—after this *incident*, as you call it, you returned here and wrote?" Samuel asked.

"I did," Loche answers. "I was in a kind of trance, I

guess. I emerged three days later. I was staring at the page. There was a spot of ink—" Loche breaks off pointing at the book. He shivers at the stabbing chill of the memory. "I was near to death."

Both Samuel and Corey look at William. "Loche," William says, "I believe that you have arrived. Your writing is now an open door. I believe that your muse arrived when you faced your deepest fear—standing upon the threshold of this world and the next, here in this enchanted place." William thinks a moment. "It matters not how you've brought existence and reality to *our* story —what matters now is how we handle the terrors you've created. And how to prepare ourselves for the next time you commune with the water's Eye. The next time you write."

Loche's face whitens and he quickly glances at the door. "I must go," he says. "None of this can be true. I must go." He takes a nervous step toward an escape. William moves and blocks the way. Loche freezes.

"Where will you go?" William asks. "You are better off staying with us. Safer." Loche stares at William's chest. "Have patience and you will soon understand."

With all of his strength Loche throws his weight into William, shoving him back. William pivots slightly and crosses his ankle into Loche's stride. Loche tumbles to the floor. Corey and Samuel move to help Loche back to his feet. Loche slaps at their hands. As he does this he sees his umbrella leaning against the wall. Stretching his arm out he takes hold of the handle, climbs to his feet and swings the tip around catching William's cheek. Samuel and Corey quickly restrain Loche and pull him back toward the door.

William touches the cut on his face and then looks at the blood on his fingertips. "Loche," he says, "did you learn nothing from your sword teacher, Giovanni, in Padua? Twist and pull at the handle of your umbrella. I think you'll find it much more affective." Corey and Samuel release Loche's arms. Loche looks down at the grip and rotates the silver latch. The umbrella falls away revealing a gleaming blade. Loche stares at it.

"Weren't expecting that, eh?" Samuel says.

From behind William, "Loche?" It is a woman's voice. "Loche?"

William steps aside and turns. Loche sees Julia sitting up in the bed, her hands still covering her stomach. Suddenly there is something familiar about her face, as if from a dream. From a wish.

Her hands pull slightly away from the bullet wound and move down to the bottom of her blood soaked shirt. She pulls the fabric up exposing her bare stomach. There, just below her rib cage is a fading pink blot. Surrounding the mark is a halo of white foam. The wound is gone.

"Loche, this is really happening, isn't it?" Julia asks.

Here ends Part One of The Newirth Mythology

Acknowledgments

The character of Basil Fenn appeared in my journal one afternoon while I was on a concert tour through the Mediterranean in 1998. Basil died before dusk that same day at the Uffizi (see *Chapter 2, To Marcus Rearden*). The time between then and now has been spent trying to figure out why—and thus, more and more questions came (and confusion), as is the case with such pursuits. *The Invasion of Heaven* is a kind of answer to those questions, or an attempt, at least.

So for better or worse, I wrote the book you're holding. But not without a substantial amount of support and love from nearly every person I know. Many of which may not be aware they were in any way lending a helping hand, but they did. Many were kind enough to read some of the early drafts, some were kind in giving thought to the project, and some humored me, kindly. Getting to spend time and learn from them was the best part of writing this book. And so, too, the giants whose shoulders I teeter upon—their influence started this whole writing affair in the first place. I'm fairly certain they aren't aware of their involvement either.

If only I had the kind of time that William Greenhame has—for if I did I would most certainly ramble on for pages providing a thorough record of each and every influential encounter and contributing relationship—then I would end with a pantheon of writers, musicians, film makers and painters that dinted the hard shell that is my head. But that kind of time isn't available to me, nor would such a list be worth your time perusing—and Greenhame, I've been told, talks too much and for too long. I happen to love it when he does that, but never mind.

So I'll try to be brief.

I have dedicated this book to my mother Diana who has battled depression for most of her life. Though this first installment may not provide the kind of *cure* that Doctor Loche Newirth is after, it is a son's attempt to fight the malady.

Mom, Dad and brother Bob (Bobbi and Bean) put space wizards, music and books in front of me. I haven't enough gratitude for these things. My uncle Stan Koep served as my first editor when I was twelve and to this day he inspires me and is always ready to discuss *Elliqui* lore and the prospects of the *Orathom*. Professor Michael Herzog has guided me, encouraged me, enlightened me and fed me countless ass-kicking breakfasts. Scott and Dani Clarkson (Prudence and Jude), have been unwavering listeners, offered thoughtful suggestions and continue to be fanatic about the project. Many thanks to Scott Clarkson (*caw minle*) and Mark Rakes (my band mates, *KITE*) as well as Cary Beare (*teavoy Belzaare*) and Cristopher Lucas (my band mates, *The RUB*). My dear friend, Psychologist Michael Roberts, has been vital in helping me to imagine Loche Newirth. Andreas John at Will Dreamly Arts, my editors Allison McCready (*Luminaare ~ dech fo ag shivcy fafe fogal*) and Marlene Adelstein. Eric and Laurie Wilson for steadfast vision and support (and scotch, song, joy, autumn breakfasts and sweet pipe smoke in the study).

To *The Core*, Mark Lax, Greg and Sara White, and Lisa Koep—thank you for mingling the *Alya* and the *Ora*, holding me up and clearing the way.

And more thanks for the delightfully long-winded conversations, imaginings and in-depth mischief: Monte Thompson, Jeff Hagman, Joe Lynch, Bob Kelley, Tom Brunner, Jolynn Koep, Mel Koep, Calvin and Majorie Langley, Jason Williamson, Rich Chatfield, Dave and Heather Dupree, Bob Burdett, Doug Smith, Jane Mauser, Andrea Brockmeyer, Margaret Hurlocker, Greg and Jillian Rowley, Randy (Vlad)

Palmer, Dan Spaulding, Darin Schaffer, Aman Nothere, Geri and Walter Perkins, Tyler Davis, The Cd'A Arts and Culture Alliance, Anthony Nelson, and The Heren Sindaril.

And of course, my dear wife, Lisa, and son, Michael.

thia alyoth thave ni tunefore

the story continues...
Part Two of the Newirth Mythology,

Leaves of Fire

AVAILABLE NOW WHERE BOOKS ARE SOLD

In the spring of 1338, young William of Leaves knows only of remedies, herbs and his mother's kindness. When he is forced to watch as she is dragged to a witch's pyre by a mob led by the Bishop of London, the mysterious immortal apothecary, Albion Ravistelle, promises the boy a chance at vengeance.

In the summer of 1972, Helen Storm is a stoned groupie on the sunset strip with a very special condition: she is immortal. When her life intersects with a famous guitar player, she is introduced to her future as a deadly and remorseless assassin.

In present day, psychologist Loche Newirth and Julia Iris must come to terms with Loche's prophetic writings that have changed the course of history and shaped the lives of William, Helen, and countless others. As a war breaks out between the immortals on earth and Albion Ravistelle, Loche must accept the realities he has authored and cross over into death—he must enter again into Basil Fenn's paintings to find a way to end the conflict.

In *Part Two of The Newirth Mythology, Leaves of Fire,* Koep entwines these lives and lifetimes as he explores myth, memory, revenge and the hope of forgiveness.

Michael B. Koep is the author of *The Newirth Mythology Trilogy,* He has been called a "Renaissance Man." An avid world traveler, educator, accomplished visual artist, swordsman, award winning poet and professional musician, Michael's spirit is imbued in the arts. He lives in Coeur d'Alene, Idaho with his wife and son.